To The Whipkey'

Thanks for your interest in the Book. I hope you enjoy reading About the people in Ridge Valley.

With appreciation

Bill Menarchuk

July 21, 2008

RIDGE VALLEY

Living Life in a Coal Mining Town

by

Bob Menarcheck

AuthorHouse™
1663 Liberty Drive, Suite 200
Bloomington, IN 47403
www.authorhouse.com
Phone: 1-800-839-8640

This book is a work of fiction. People, places, events, and situations are the product of the author's imagination. Any resemblance to actual persons, living or dead, or historical events, is purely coincidental.

© 2008 Bob Menarcheck. All rights reserved.

No part of this book may be reproduced, stored in a retrieval system, or transmitted by any means without the written permission of the author.

First published by AuthorHouse   6/2/2008

ISBN: 978-1-4343-7578-0 (sc)
ISBN: 978-1-4343-7577-3 (hc)

Printed in the United States of America
Bloomington, Indiana

This book is printed on acid-free paper.

Map used by permission from the Penn State Fayette/Coal and Coke Heritage Center.

Dedicated to

I. J.   Julia

and

All

who lived in a patch

or

rode the cage

Power tends to corrupt, and absolute power
Corrupts absolutely
Lord Acton

A fondness for power is implanted in most men,
And it is natural to abuse it.
Alexander Hamilton

ACKNOWLEDGEMENTS

I would like to thank the following for their support during the writing of Ridge Valley:

Two individuals who encouraged and prodded me to complete my work were Anna Saracina and Peg Terembes. I am forever grateful for their suggestions and extensive time spent in editing the manuscript.

Connie, a wife who was generous with her comments and allowed me the time and space to work.

Members of the greater Canton Writer's Guild for providing insight that assisted with my writing.

My family who endured my many inequities and to all those friends and acquaintances who supported my efforts.

I am indebted to Donovan Ackley and Linda Blankenship for their suggestions, recommendations and editing.

A special thank you to Pamela K. Seighman and Elaine Hunchuck DeFrank

Director's of the Coal and Coke Heritage Center, Penn State Fayette, Uniontown, Pennsylvania.

Finally many thanks to the people of the "Patch", who I recall and continue to think about to this day. You provided me with the inspiration to write this story.

I am indebted to a number of publications that provided me with the inspiration to pursue Ridge Valley. These include: <u>Cloud by Day</u>, Muriel Early Sheppard; <u>Common Lives of Common Strength</u>, Evelyn A. Hovanec; <u>Patches of History</u>, Regis M Maher; <u>Patchwork Voices</u>, Dennis Brestensky; Evelyn Hovanec and Albert Skomra, and <u>A Coal Mine in our Veins</u>, Ralph Rosendale and Tim Hroblak.

This is a work of Historical Fiction. A number of noted historical events written about in the book are factual as far as my research indicates.

The main characters and some of the secondary players are fictional. Any reference to real-life people from this group is purely coincidental.

Any reference to historical figures, places, localities and events are intended to provide a realistic and objective understanding of the story.

There are instances where the author's interpretation of a person's character and personality was brought into play in order to provide a continual flow to the novel.

PROLOGUE

THE EARTH, IN her infinite wisdom, millions of years ago, decided to take the ugly rotting decomposed forests and decayed vegetation and create something of value. The earth's resolve was to enlarge and develop swamps, add dead trees and brush, provide constant pressure to the contents through millions of years and produce a usable product and call it coal. The process repeated itself, time after time, over and over, pushing deeper and deeper into the earth. Thickening, the minerals developed from a sliver to a ribbon, and with patience plus time the black vein matured into a nine-foot height. The earth was now satisfied with her completed work.

The earth was determined to find a way to protect her treasure She decided to cover it with rock, limestone and shale; to bury it deep by adding more stone and dirt and cover it with grass, flowers and trees to disguise its presence below. Like an animal fiercely protecting her young from predators, the earth protected the coal by locking it far under the surface. Also, like a cornered animal, the earth will react furiously to protect her resources. She did not give up her prized possession easily.

She'll give the earth's inhabitants who live on the surface all they need to survive, including good air to breath. Below the surface, especially in the confines of the seams of coal, she'll protect her cherished mineral by adding a gas, a gas that will escape when the coal seam is penetrated. She will disguise it by making the gaseous fumes odorless, colorless, tasteless and volatile. These gasses will take the place of good air in the tunnels. Not knowing of its presence, the vapor will confuse, disorient and eventually consume any who venture within. Furthermore, the earth will develop one last protective devise by making volatile gasses seep from open fissures and with a spark release a devastating explosion as a final act to rebuff the intruders.

After millions of years, at this precise moment in time, in this specific place, the earth in protecting her prized possession from intruders reacted with a vengeance. The lack of air, the release of methane gas, and a spark will produce an event that will change the lives of Ridge Valley residents forever.

BEGINNINGS

CLUSTERED ALONG THE base of the Chestnut Ridge of the Allegheny Mountains is the Connellsville Coal and Coke region that contained the nine-foot Pittsburgh seam of coal. This seam of bituminous coal was famous for its high quality and excellent for producing coke. Geographically the coal region was a strip of land measuring one hundred miles long and forty miles wide running from Latrobe, Pennsylvania south through Connellsville to the West Virginia border. In just about every valley within this region, coalmine owners built autonomous communities, and concentrated them in small isolated valleys solely for coal mining operations.

Jonas H. Filbert, a mining engineer, was responsible for selecting sites for sinking mine shafts for the H. C. Grant Coal and Coke Company. His exploration for a new location in 1909 took him to the southern section of the Grant district where he found a beautiful narrow valley, with towering steep hills on each side. This beautiful valley was a place where laurel grew in abundance, along with mountain flowers and spreading old maple, walnut and oak trees. Flooding the scene were wild berries that attracted birds and butterflies of all colors and descriptions. A creek spread its waters into the lower section of the valley creating a marsh that housed muskrat, groundhogs, possum and crickets that chirped at dusk. The creek gathered its waters for a short distance run which soon drained into a small pond. White tailed deer migrated to the pond everyday for fresh grass and a refreshing drink.

Jonas finally decided that a flat section on the western edge of the valley would be the best location for the sinking of the mineshaft.

Jonas and his wife were both outdoor enthusiasts. He often shared the sightings he found in his exploration with her when he returned home. She, along with Jonas enjoyed the scenery, bird watching, and hiking and fresh air away from their home in Pittsburgh. To experience the natural beauty of the mountains they often visited and camped in the remote sections of the Alleghenies.

Jonas, after describing the valley in detail and seeing the delight it brought to his wife, decided to take her to this beautiful place before it was transfigured into a coal mining community. He decided to wait until the fall of the year when the full effect of the colors changing in the leaves of trees reached their zenith.

"There is no other section in the Connellsville district as beautiful as this ridge and valley," Jonas announced to his wife.

"The colorful ridge, this gorgeous valley, the deer will all be gone when building the mine complex begins. What name will you give this location?" asked Jonas's wife who quickly suggested, "Why not use your name…Filbert," she stated.

"Within a year a mineshaft, tipple and outbuildings will be built. Roads, train and streetcar tracks, a slate dump, and houses on the hills will change this view forever," said Jonas.

A name he pondered?

Jonas looked around the area, surveying its beauty. He looked at his wife, turned away to again scan the scene, hand on chin he thought for a moment, faced his wife and announced, " I appreciate your thought, dear, but I want to remember this charming location as it appears now, not what it will look like when it becomes a mining complex. I'll name this gorgeous site as I see it now, Ridge Valley, yes Ridge Valley."

The Connellsville Coke Region

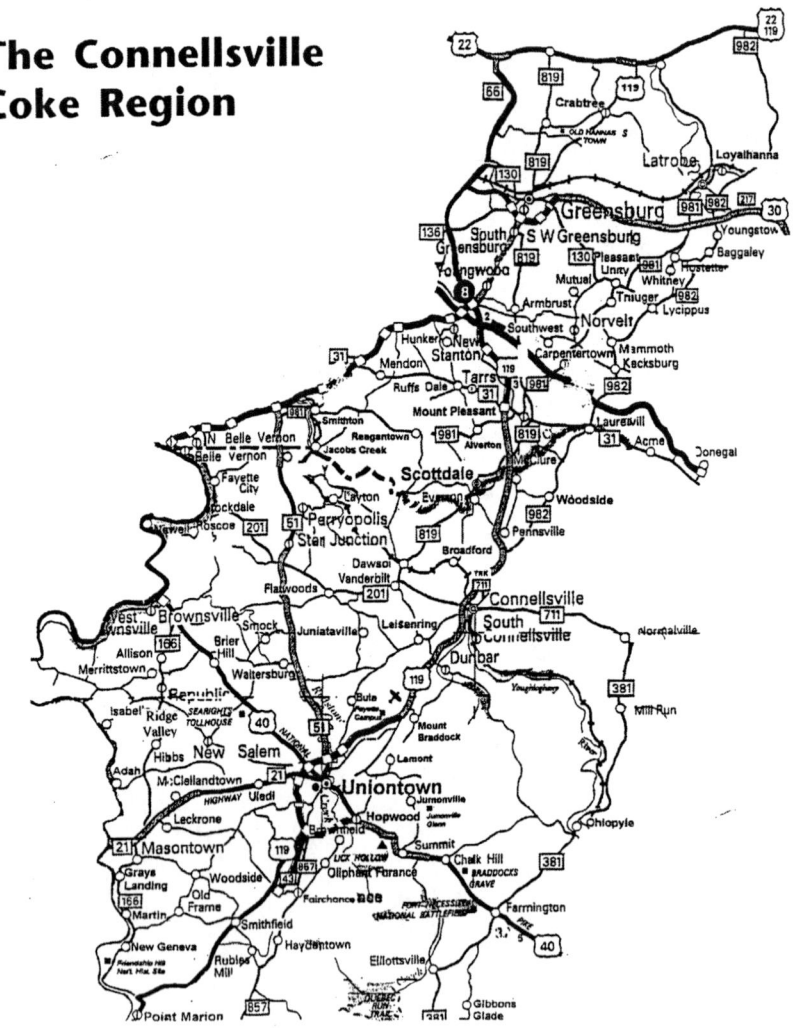

CHAPTER I

IT WAS HOT. A muggy, sultry, oppressive kind of hot. Any movement brought perspiration, and as John turned from side to side, rivulets of salty sweat seeped from his body into his pillow and soaked the sheet. Sleep was intermittent as John flopped to his back, and then rolled to his stomach. He continually searched for that one position that would allow him to rest.

John, like all others in the coal patch town, was growing tired and weary from the stifling heat. The one window at the east end of the bedroom was fully open with the hope of providing a breeze. There was none. The incessant stuffy atmosphere remained.

The heat and humidity began to build early in the summer, welcomed initially because of the winter spent inside cramped quarters. Rain, heavy early in the spring, dissipated as the season wore on. There were occasional sprinkles at the start of summer, then no precipitation for months. So day after day the sultry weather pattern continued through June and July into the dog days of August. The heat sapped a person's energy, and it was no different for John as he tried to sleep in the muggy atmosphere.

John slept in a room that contained two double beds, one used by his mom and dad, the other bed he shared with his younger brother Mike. His two sisters occupied the other upstairs bedroom. The Mullins family, their neighbors, lived in the attached four-room house next door. Rows of identical four room double attached houses were terraced on the side of the hills rising from the valley. The adult male occupants of the patch houses were there for one reason, to work in the Ridge Valley mine. Three rows of hillside houses, numbering sixty-five on the north incline was known as the number one side. Another seventy houses were located on the south incline known as the number two side. The hillside double attached dwellings were connected in the valley by the Union Supply Company Store on the east and the mineshaft located in the far western section of the valley. The place existed for one reason, and that was for the workers to service and extract as much coal as possible from the mine. The coal was needed to feed the coke ovens that in turn fed the steel furnaces in Pittsburgh and the Allegheny valley.

John awoke with a jolt from one of his short naps and found himself twisted in damp sheets his brother somehow willed to him. He struggled to untangle himself, and the exertion added more perspiration to an already sweaty body.

" OH NO," he muttered to himself. " I'll get you," he promised an invisible mosquito that buzzed in his ear. The pest already succeeded in enjoying a meal from the back of John's neck. It left a welt that both stung and itched at the same time. John felt slimy, the back of his neck stung, and now he felt an itch from around his ankle. He thought about getting up but, "hey its still dark outside." He tried to sleep, and did doze off for a few minutes, only to jump up into a sitting position slapping his ear in an attempt to kill another buzzing mosquito. Laying down on the bed and placing his head on the damp pillow he tried to sleep but this time the whirling, chugging sound of the air fan running at the mine sang in his ears. He turned from side to side trying to ignore the humming of the fan that by now began to play a tune on his brain. "Funny thing," he thought, "that fan is always there, always present in our lives, accepted without thinking about its presence, just there working incessantly providing fresh air to those working in the mine. The steady purr of the whirling blades was in a way soothing and peaceful and always an acceptable part of life in the patch. Why? Why now at this moment does the music released by this windy monster continue to vibrate in my brain?"

Ridge Valley

The fan, the irksome mosquito, twisted damp sheets and the unrelenting sweat convinced John it was time to get up and out of bed. It was still dark outside. "What's a fourteen year old have to do at this time of the day?" he wondered. He glanced over to the opposite bed and saw that it was empty. "Must be time for Dad to go to work," he thought. Unable to sleep, he finally exited the bed and walked over to the open window. He was disappointed at the lack of a breeze. He saw the sky in the east was beginning to lighten and now could see his father join the other men from various parts of the patch walking together down the dirt road leading to a railroad bridge then to the mine tipple.

A new day, a Monday, dawned in the Ridge Valley patch. John was ready for outside air so he dressed in a tee shirt, jeans and clodhoppers and left the room. He walked down a narrow flight of stairs. Arriving in the kitchen he walked briskly to the sink that contained one cold running faucet. The running water had been installed in the house only a year ago. The water was brought in through exposed pipes, climbing the outside back wall behind the kitchen, then through a small opening in the wall to the sink. The exposed pipes had a tendency to freeze in the winter. The only way to avoid disaster from exploding pipes was to allow water to drip constantly when temperatures reached the freezing mark. The water was discarded from the sink through a drain that exited the house through the back wall. The drainage flowed into a cement ditch that ran along the entire first row of houses. The wastewater, following gravity, flowed down the ditch into a gully beyond the last house in the row. Due to the distance, poor construction and failure to slope the ditch properly, the contents collected and remained in the cracks or low levels of the cement. Festering over time a green slime formed over the sitting water and smelled like rotten grass. The hot days of August provided a good opportunity for the slime to grow in abundance in the cement ditch.

John found his mom scrubbing clothes over a washboard that was sitting inside a metal circular tub. The tub, sitting in the center of the kitchen floor was half-full with sudsy water. He could see she was perspiring profusely as she vigorously rubbed each item over the washboard. She then proceeded to the sink where she rinsed each item by hand. John wanted a drink in the worst way but did not want to interrupt his mom's quest to finish the laundry before the heat of the day.

John felt the additional warmth of the kitchen because the stove directly across from the sink was in full blast emitting heat. The coal-fed stove was not only used for the main source of heat in the winter, but was always operating throughout the year. It was used for baking, cooking and heating hot water to wash clothes and to heat water for Saturday baths. He saw a bowl of dough on the table waiting to be placed in pans and baked between washings. On the opposite wall from the table stood a cabinet that housed cups, dishes some canned goods and a funnel-shaped flour bin. Above the sink a small shelf was crowded with laundry supplies and a glass used for drinking. A large calendar, with a picture of the Last Supper, and the inscription Saint Procopius Church showing the month of August 1919 was tacked to the wall above the shelf. An electric bulb hung on a cord with a pull chain from the center of the ceiling.

"Morning Mamma, sure is a hot day for washing clothes; if you need me to help…"

"Thanks for your offering, John," she interrupted, "but I'll be done soon, just wanted to get an early start to beat the heat. What are you doing up so early?" asked John's Mom.

"Just couldn't sleep, too hot and the mosquitoes, well I just couldn't sleep so I decided to get up, and I'm mighty thirsty, mind if I get a drink?" asked John

"Let me rinse this last load first. I sure would like to get things on the line as soon as I can."

"I'll help you hang em. That'll give you the time to get started with your baking. Anyway, all I need is a good drink and a quick wash and I'll get started."

"Okay John, the sink is all yours."

"Thanks Mom."

John approached the sink, turned on the faucet and let the water run to allow it to become as cool as possible. Satisfied, he cupped both hands together under the faucet and slurping the liquid like a horse at the trough, got his drink. He then splashed the cool water on his face and the back of his neck. He could feel the welt left by the mosquito. Because of the cool water he felt the itch leave only briefly. The nuisance soon returned.

He picked up the basket near the door and began to walk out and began hanging clothes. His mother joined him and together they completed the chore as the sun climbed in the sky signaling the beginning of another sunny hot day.

Finished, John made his way up the hill in the rear of the house to the outhouse. Attached to the double wood frame privies were coal sheds on each side for use by families who occupied the houses below. John entered and sat on the first of four stalls. He left the door ajar, hoping to capture any flow of air into the close heavy atmosphere. The stagnant air in the small space left a person's body sticky and clammy. Two huge horseflies, relentless in their pursuit for a hearty meal, attacked. John rolled up an old newspaper to use as a weapon to fight off the flies. John always checked an ever- present spider web in the corner of the smelly room each time he visited, and could never recall a spider being in the web; today was no different. A daddy longlegs skirted around the far corner and disappeared into a small crack in the wood. The beam of light entering through the door opening unfurled a host of golden dust specks, dancing in the glow.

Looking down the hill through the slightly open door, John spotted Mrs. Mullin making her way up the steps leading to her side of the outhouse. John hurried to finish so he could leave before his neighbor entered the other side. He met his neighbor about half way down the yard.

"Morning' Mrs. Mullin, looks like the garden is just about finished for the season."

"Oh John, yes, that's true but we did put up beans, beets, pickles and such. Had to work extra hard carrying water up the hill almost every day. Looks like you folks did all right yourself."

"Yep, and like you we had to water a lot and did a lot of canning, except for the piccalilli."

"You like that John, the piccalilli I mean?" Mrs. Mullin asked.

"Matter of fact it's my favorite. My mom makes a special effort to put up small jars so I can have my treat all to myself during the winter."

"Listen, tell your mom she's welcome to anything we have left for your treat."

"Thanks Mrs. Mullin, I will."

John's neighbor turned and headed up the hill to the outhouse. She glanced back and paused briefly at the top step, then entered and closed the door. John returned to the kitchen sink for another drink. He cupped his hands under the faucet and drank until he ran out of breath. He finished, breathing heavily, finally wiping his mouth with the back of his hand.

"Don't drink so fast or you'll get sick," cautioned his mother.

"I can't get enough Mom," said John, "no matter how much water I drink I'm still thirsty. Think I'll go outside for a bit, if you need anything I'll be out front.

John exited the house through the back door, and turned the corner walking toward the front porch steps. The heat of the early morning sun brought beads of perspiration to his forehead, "Wow, going to be another hot one today, feel it already." He stopped short of his journey, looked toward the Company Store a short distance away, smiled and said to himself, "Yep that's it, a cold bottle of pop at the store, yeah, that's it, and I got the money. I'll get a cold Root Beer as soon as it opens," John said to himself, licking his lips at the thought.

He sat in his favorite spot, the front porch steps that faced east giving him a good view of the store. He'd keep an eye on the front entrance, and the minute they opened the doors off he would go to get his refreshment. He sat on the top step with his legs stretching over the second step allowing his feet to rest on the ground. A large maple tree shaded the area where John was sitting as well as the front yard and the dirt path that passed in front of the house. Most days a breeze flowed down from the hill, but not today. Nothing, no air, just stillness, not even one leaf on the maple moved. He watched his Mom fluff and shake the clothes hanging on the line, a routine carried out by every mother in the patch this morning. It was Monday, a day reserved for washing clothes in the patch. Time passed slowly as the sun's rays baked the valley.

"The birds don't sing in the morning like they used to. I don't even see any. I guess they're hiding in the shade like me," John said

Ridge Valley

to himself. A grasshopper landed in a puff of dust at his feet, stayed briefly then jumped for cover in the dead grass nearby. He leaned back, stretched his legs, cupped his hands behind his head and found a resting spot at the edge of the porch. John gazed into the tree, mesmerized, thinking about a cold drink, he closed his eyes and lapsed into sleep. He dozed about ten minutes, awoke slowly, remembering, looking, he was disappointed to find that the store was still closed.

His long lanky frame was stretched out as far as possible to relieve his muscles that became stiff from the constant sitting position. With the spurt of growth experienced this past year, John was growing tall "like a bad weed" his Mom would say. He enjoyed physical activity, willing to work spading gardens for his Dad and neighbors if they asked. He spent hours picking coal at the slate dump and hauling it home in sacks. All the work added muscle to his frame to a point where he could be mistaken for a young man instead of a boy. He had piercing blue eyes, along with high cheekbones that melded into a strong protruding chin, His long nose was overlooked by all who were attracted directly to those eyes, "the deepest blue I've ever seen," he heard often. His dark brown hair became lighter when exposed for a long time in the summer sun. He possessed a low-key easygoing personality and was willing to help anyone at anytime.

John was not one to look for problems and avoided physical confrontations by finding ways to discuss issues and solve a problem by talking about them. He never shied away from the physical part, which was the norm in a coal-mining patch, where strength of a person was admired and fighting was the way to settle disputes. John gained a reputation among his peers as a person who someone could go to for advice. John would listen intently to all who came and in most cases said little during the conversation. He let others talk, rarely offered counsel or suggestions, just listened. In due time the issue would be solved and John thanked enthusiastically for helping to solve the problem in a peaceful manner.

John's Mom recognized her son's intelligence and held him in high esteem. Now that he is fourteen, actually close to fifteen she would quickly change the subject when talk started about him going to work. Lately she became more adamant and direct in her statements that her son will continue in school, and become the first in the family to graduate from High School. She bristled at any mention of work in the mine. When that was mentioned she would place her hands on her hips, take a wide-legged stance and give that no-nonsense look that made others know it was time to back off. John felt uncomfortable when the conversation about him occurred and he felt bad for his younger brother who lacked the mental ability to succeed in his schooling.

John sat on the front porch steps observing the only happening at the moment, women scurrying about hanging clothes on clothes lines in their yards. None had time to talk to their neighbor and simply nodded to each other on occasion. Besides the difficulties in communicating due to the many different nationalities and languages, there was no time to dally since baking, cooking and canning chores awaited.

"Watcha doin?" questioned Jerry, who approached John from up the path that ran in front of the first row of houses.

"Nut tin', just sitting, waiting for the store to open," said John

"What do yeah need from the store?" questioned Jerry

"Going to get me a nice cold root beer, that's what."

"You got the money?" interrupted Jerry.

"Yep, I got the money, Jer,"

"Where did you get it, I haven't had any money for a long time?"

"Been saving from cashing in bottles."

"Wow, it's been a good while back when we collected bottles John. I done spent mine, and you saved yours all that time."

John looked at Jerry without answering, but smiling. Jerry sat down on the bottom step, hands on chin, elbows on knees, thinking. After a short time Jerry turned to John and in a serious tone of voice said, " You know I spent mine and I do recall that I shared, yes sir John, I remember clear, I shared," said Jerry hoping to get an offer of at least a swig.

"I'll share," said John.

Jerry smiled a big toothy grin, "Let's go then, I can taste it already, c'mon let's go John," said Jerry as he stood up from the step smacking his lips.

"Can't"

"Why not?"

"Isn't open yet. Be open in a little while, sit down and take it easy, Jer."

"I can hardly wait," said Jerry elated at his lucky break. He sat on the lower step and played with the dirt at his feet, keeping a watchful eye on the store. He became anxious and edgy and had a hard time containing himself at the thought of sharing a cold drink. They sat and waited, four eyes watching the front entrance of the store for any activity. Mr. Mullin who worked the night shift as a watchman came walking up the path from O'Malley's tavern, a stopping off place for most men after completing their shift. A shot of whiskey and a glass of beer was a must for washing down the "dust from your throat" and O'Malley's was the place of choice for two reasons. He served the biggest mug of beer for the money, and regardless of your financial status you were assured a drink. If you were out of cash all one had to do was to get into the book at the bar, and a lot of men had their name in the book.

"Good morning," grunted Mr. Mullin as he passed. Both boys nodded.

"Hey, that's Mr. Steiner opening the doors, look," said Jerry in an excited banter while pointing a finger in the direction of the store. "C'mon let's go, it's open, c'mon."

"In a little bit," replied John looking straight ahead.

"What do yeah mean wait? C'mon, let's go, store's open!"

"There's Bull and Corky down at the entrance and Jer, I just don't want to get into it with them today. So let's wait a bit until they leave, okay?" asked John.

"John," Jerry said with emphasis. "John listen, I'm not afraid of them and I know you're not afraid either. Listen John, listen, they just walk around like they own the place and think they're real big stuff, but they're not. Anyway, I told you I'm not afraid of 'em, and they don't own me either, John, they don't and furthermore I don't care if they say or do something. I'll tell them what for and that's that," said Jerry slobbering his words as he talked.

John just sat and listened without reply to Jerry's outburst and continued to watch Bull and Corky.

"They went into the store Jer, as soon as they come out and leave, we'll go down."

"Who do they think they are anyway, and look John, I'm tired of staying away from them, so c'mon John, lets go. I'm getting more and more thirsty for a swig so c'mon John, what do yeah say, c'mon lets go," pleaded Jerry.

"Jerry take it easy will yeah. You're getting yourself all in a tizzy and I know what'll happen if we meet up with them, so hold on for a little bit, then we'll go."

"Aw John its just not right, that's all," said a despondent Jerry.

"Settle down Jer, we'll be going in a bit."

"Listen John, remember when we used to play buckety-buck and Bull would jump on my back on purpose, and as big as he is I never buckled, never, never, caved in John, never," said Jerry.

John just listened. Jerry finally sat down on the bottom step, elbows on knees, hands cupped under his chin, sulking, making faces that John could feel but not see. John's Mom came out to check her clothes then returned to the kitchen. John sat silently watching, as Jerry sat muttering "isn't fair" in a voice loud enough for John to hear. John ignored him for a time, but began to get irritated as Jerry began mumbling things like," I ain't afraid, and we should go, they're nobody."

Finally, Bull and Corky exited the store and walked across the streetcar tracks, moving out of sight.

"Hey look they're leaving, going up the road, c'mon let's go," said Jerry.

"Let's wait a bit longer, looks like"…

Before John could finish what he wanted to say Jerry interrupted. He stood up, faced John and said emphatically, "Listen John, listen, we can go up through the back yard and…."

Before Jerry could finish, John interrupted and said quizzically, "Do what, go where?"

"We can go up through the yard, it's higher on the hill, and go down the alley and if we spot 'em we could duck behind a coal shed."

"Don't want to do that Jer, honey dippers are working their way up the alley."

" C'mon John, lets go, be no problem, besides being up above 'em we can spot 'em if they come our way so c'mon, lets go huh?"

Jerry was unrelenting when he made up his mind about doing something, for when he wanted to do something; he wanted to do it now. No waiting, no messing around. Frustrated he kicked at the dirt, and then paced back and forth in front of the steps. John for now ignored the antics. Jerry never quit as he started to pout, began grinding his teeth and continually starred at John.

"You look like a cat ready to pounce, Jer"

"Look John," Jerry interrupted, "you promised a swig, and those guys are stopping us, and once more I ain't scared of em."

John wasn't afraid of Bull or any one else for that matter. He knew that someday he would have to confront Bull but he was not in the mood for that today. Jerry continued his bandy rooster antics without let up, scowling, mumbling and pacing his antics finally got to John.

"All right, lets go."

Jerry's attitude changed in an instant, a smile crossed his face, and with a quick peppy step he started to walk down the path toward the store.

"Jer, this way," said John, pointing toward the alley.

Jerry turned, smiling, and joined John as they walked toward the back of the house. Quickly up the hill, around the garden in the back yard they walked past the combination outhouse and coal shed, through the gate into the alley. The two turned right and walked down the narrow dirt road, scattering dust with each step. Grasshoppers and other nameless bugs skittered out of the way as John and Jerry tramped along. Flies, the huge horse kind with their purplish glow, attacked sweaty bodies searching for a meal. The odor aroused by the honey dippers became more and more pungent as they approached the workers. The men were dipping buckets attached to a long pole into the bottom of the outhouse. They worked in the alley, dipping through a door leading into a cement pit in the back of the buildings where they extracted the contents. Then they hoisted the full bucket from the outhouse, and deposited the matter into a large tub resting on the back of a truck

"How they do that, gads?" choked Jerry.

"It sure is something," replied John.

As they walked down the alley toward the dippers, they began to plan their route around the truck that sat in the middle of the road. They had to be careful not to get to close and get the waste on them as they passed the truck. They knew that the honey dippers had a reputation of depositing the contents on anyone venturing close to their kingdom. They also had to be certain not to touch the truck in fear of getting the sticky stuff on their hands or clothes. The truck sat in the middle of the alley allowing the workers to remove the waste from outhouses on both sides.

"I think it best to wait until they scoop the goop into the tub, then when they place the bucket into the bottom of the outhouse we move."

"See yeah on the other side," said Jerry.

"Aw damn, I just stepped into a big glob of shit, Jer. Look, it's all over my shoe," John yelled in disgust as he emerged from the other side of the truck

Normally Jerry would be howling with laughter at John's unlucky step into disaster, but he hesitated for fear of losing a good slug of pop. Another misstep and John planted the other shoe into another glob. Jerry seeing this could not contain himself any longer. He laughed so hard he began to choke, bending over, laughing, coughing, and holding his stomach because it began to ache from all the exertion. Sweat in streaks poured down his face. He knew he might be jeopardizing a cool drink but he simply could not control himself. Lord knows had this happened to Jerry he would have shouted loud enough for the entire patch to know what happened.

Jerry was a good six inches shorter than John, and much thinner, "Not much meat on them bones," his dad said often. They had been friends since they found each other in first grade. John's easygoing demeanor and Jerry's hyperactivity were as totally opposite in personality as one could get. Jerry, through his antics, could disrupt things around him as was done often in Sister Ann Marie's first grade class at Saint Procopius.

She scolded Jerry constantly, isolated him from the other students as best she could, but teaching two grades with thirty in each grade, she had difficulty in segregating this fidgety boy. She tried detention, whacks with the switch, notes home, but nothing worked.

One of Sister's customs after a few weeks was to rearrange the seats of students in the room. It so happened by chance that Jerry's seat ended up next to John. John was a serious student who enjoyed the challenge of learning and wanted to succeed in his studies. He was conscientious in his work and did not like being interrupted when studying.

One day Jerry's tantrums reached the limits beyond what John could tolerate. John ignored the Jerryisms previously, but not this time. He turned to face Jerry. John did not say a word but gave Jerry a look, a scowl, so pronounced it struck Jerry into silence. Sister ever vigilant, noticed Jerry's reaction, smiled to herself, looked up to the ceiling, and one student thought he saw her bless herself, saying, "Thank you Lord, thank you." She would team up these two in every project she could think of, spelling partners, checking each other's homework and even the dusting of erasers at the end of the day.

Jerry for whatever reason, fear, the want of a friend looked up to John like a brother who he could talk to better than anyone else in his life. Jerry settled down in school and John was the reason. He helped him with homework, for example, and in games when John selected him as part of a team. John helped settle a major problem for Sister, and for that matter, fifty-nine others in class.

Jerry was a red-haired boy who had matching red eyebrows the color of carrots. Some said his green eyes danced with mischief and on his pure white cheeks were freckles; tiny brown specks that dominated his entire face. If one had the opportunity they would see them all over his body. As he grew he became conscious of everyone looking at him, and thought there was something wrong with him. People simply stopped and looked, often pointing and chuckling. He did not know how to react to all the attention until one day a girl his age told him he had the best looking hair, and wished she had hair like that. This helped Jerry accept his appearance, but did little to dampen his hyperactivity.

John ignored Jerry's comments and actions and began to walk along the alley stepping carefully in order to avoid any further encounters with excrement. He searched for some high grass to clean his shoes.

Bob Menarcheck

Jerry, who kept his distance ahead of John, came back and began to apologize for his actions with a sympathetic, "Gee I'm sorry about your shoes John. Maybe I can get some water somewhere to clean 'em and get the smell out. You know, once you get something like that in your shoes it's really hard to get out."

John looked down at Jerry without saying a word; he just looked at him for a moment and went back to shoe cleaning. The lack of sleep, along with sneaking around to avoid Bull, getting shit all over his shoes, and Jerry's continued agitation was starting to get to John. Hot and sweaty, he needed a cool drink now more than ever, and once he cleaned his shoes, he decided to go directly to the store for that root beer.

"I'll look up ahead John, maybe I can find something to clean your shoes," Jerry said then added" I'll find something."

Jerry hurried ahead. He advanced a short distance up the alley when he spotted Mrs. Casserly washing clothes outside in a half-full tub of sudsy water. "Maybe she'll give me some of that water and an old rag for cleaning," he thought.

"Hey John," he shouted up the alley, "I'm going to get a bucket of sudsy water and a rag from Mrs. Casserly, I'll be back in a minute."

Jerry, running, turned the corner around the Casserly's outhouse.

"Gotcha you little squirt," grumbled Bull, spitting out his words. His huge hand grabbed and held tight to Jerry's shirt collar, squeezing hard and shaking Jerry to the degree that his head bobbled back and forth.

"Heard yeah and saw yeah coming so now what do yeah got to say, squirt. Yeah always got something to say so let's hear it now big mouth," said Bull spurting spit into Jerry's face.

Jerry grabbed Bull's wrist with both hands, trying to relieve the choking pressure of the grip. The shock of meeting up with Bull and the tightness of his grip had Jerry coughing and wheezing, trying to catch his breath. "Let me go, you big fat pig, let me go," said Jerry coughing out the words. "I don't have nut...tin' of y...yours and never did nut tin' to you so let go," Jerry sputtered.

"He owes you, Bull and I bet he's got some money on him," said Corky, who stood at the side, "C'mon, get it out, squirt. Bull, I think he was heading down to the store, sneaking around with John like we didn't see you, but we did, squirt. Anyway, where is your buddy John? Probably left yeah couldn't stand yeah either, right, just left yeah. C'mon fess up; you know you owe us, right, Bull? Get it out of him, Bull," snickered Corky.

"Like I said, I ain't got nut tin' of yours, and I don't have any money either, even if I did I wouldn't give it to you," slobbered Jerry. Now taking a deep breath he yelled as loud as he could, "Let me go, you big fat pig, I'm not afraid of you, let me go and I'll show you." He was hoping that John who was out of sight up the alley could hear him.

Bull, as his name implied, was big everywhere with arms the size of Jerry's legs. Tree trunk legs supported a broad chest connected to a stomach that hung over his belt line. Well over six feet tall he had a pudgy face that matched his body along with size twelve shoes to act as his foundation. He was large by any standard and his size was used to play the ruling game. The only negative about Bull's size was that he had more fat than muscle.

Corky, a constant companion to Bull was at his side to encourage him to take what he wanted when he wanted. He would then partake in the rewards.

Holding Jerry with his left hand, Bull formed a fist with his right and shoved it in front of Jerry's face, "So what do yeah have to say, big mouth? If yeah got anything to say, say it now before I pop yeah one."

"Quit playing with him, Bull," said Corky, "it's hot, c'mon whack him one and let's go."

Bull held Jerry, tightening his hold even though Jerry was in constant movement. Now grabbing Bull's arm with both hands trying to get some leverage, he twisted and turned struggling to get loose.

"Let me go you goof; you're hurting me." It was hard to tell if there were tears welling in Jerry's eyes or rivers of sweat rolling down his face. Bull's answer was to add more pressure to Jerry's neck. Panic began to build as Jerry had difficulty breathing and began to choke. He reacted by removing both hands from Bull's arm, making fists, then beginning to swing wildly in an attempt to land a punch. Bull held on and avoided any damage by extending his arm

"Go ahead, gunner, hit me if you can," Bull said laughing then added "go ahead hit me, you know you're just a runt and couldn't hurt anybody anyway, right, Corky?"

"Yeah he's a runt, c'mon whack him one and let's go, he's nothing!"

Jerry's windmill arms continued flailing at the target but failed to connect. Bull held him at arm's length, laughing, and while holding tight to Jerry's shirt, stuck out his chin just beyond reach of Jerry's fists. Jerry continued flailing, sweating, tears flowing, and not giving up, cursed under his breath and kept on swinging.

"Leave him alone, let him go, you're bigger than him, Bull, and you're hurting him so let him go," said John from behind Bull, who turned to face him. "Like I said he didn't do nothing to you so let him go…now," said John in a serious tone. A grunting laugh was the answer as Bull tightened his grip on Jerry's shirt, tearing it in the process. Jerry continued his flailing without letup. John could see that Jerry was getting weaker by the second.

"What say, Bull? Like I said before, whack him a good one and let's go, you…you made your point, " said Corky. Bull turned to answer facing away from John, ignoring him for a moment. John acted quickly. With a short run and jump he landed on Bull's back. He clamped his arms as tightly as he could around Bull's neck and wrapped his legs around Bull's midsection digging his heels into a huge flabby stomach.

The move shocked both Bull and Corky, with Bull lurching forward, stumbling, but he stayed on his feet.

The smell of shit on John's shoes was so pungent that the odor puzzled Bull as the remnants from the outhouse were being deposited on the front of his shirt. Concentrating on John, he momentarily forgot about Jerry, who continued his swinging, and it cost Bull a blow to the face. John held on, face buried into Bull's back, arms tight around his neck, heels digging into the stomach.

Suddenly the windmill struck again, finding Bull's pudgy nose with a cracking sound. A trickle of blood began to ooze from Bull's left nostril. He held tight to Jerry with one hand and tried to grab John with the other. The pressure from John's chokehold started to cut the air from Bull's lungs. This resulted in Bull staggering forward when the windmill struck again with a good one to the mouth, drawing blood that the receiver tasted.

"Goddamn," he grunted, "you little asshole." He tossed Jerry to the ground and followed with a swift kick to his side. Turning, shaking, jumping, Bull could not dislodge John from his back. Sweating profusely, Bull now tasted the salty liquid and blood as he tried to shake John loose. Through it all John held on with both arms squeezing Bull's neck, closing the air passageway to the lungs. Gasping for air and weakening, Bull bent over, hands on knees, finally going down to one knee. He relaxed for a brief moment then with one rapid jerk flipped John over his shoulder. Bull, momentarily spent, tried feebly to reach for John who scrambled away. John rolled to his feet; glared at Corky, then grabbed Jerry by the arm helping him as they stumbled up to the alley. They took a right turn down the dusty road to an intersection. Instead of going in the direction of the store they moved beyond the last row of houses, and climbed to the top of a steep hill. They looked back to check on Bull and Corky, and saw Bull waving his fist in the air. Bull then turned toward Corky and hit him on both shoulders with both hands, knocking him backwards.

"Whatcha do that for?"

"You just stood and watched and didn't do nut tin'."

"Thought you could handle em, and besides that John had shit all over his shoes. Look Bull you got it all over your shirt, and your arms."

"I have a notion to rap you one, Cork"

"Jeez, your nose and mouth are bleeding a bit, let me see."

"Get away from me, Cork, I'm going to get that little squirt and John too, and get em good, you'll see. Damn you anyway, Cork."

"I'm glad you're going to get 'em, Bull, and I swear I'll help the next time; you can count on that. We'll whack 'em good and I'm glad you're going to do it because you should have seen the look on John's face when they left, scary I tell you. Look at them running up the hill, I think you put some fear in em for sure 'cause look at 'em go." Said Corky.

Bull, looking up the hill, wiped his mouth on the sleeve portion of his tee shirt and searched for other clean parts to wipe his nose. He was having a difficult time because of the remnants from John's shoes and soaked sweat along with a few drops of blood. He finally removed his shirt exposing reddened marks around the neck and abdomen. Instead of Jerry, it will be Corky going down to see Mrs. Casserly for some sudsy water.

John and Jerry reached the zenith of the hill, panting from the climb. They sat down in tall dry grass; John began again the work of cleaning his shoes while Jerry checked his side.

"Thanks for saving me, John, sorry I didn't get the stuff to clean your shoes."

"Thanks your trying."

From the top of the ridge, well above the third and final row of houses, the boys had a panoramic view of the entire valley below. John could see houses on both sides of the patch where in every back yard clothes were hanging on lines. Women were seen scurrying about hanging, checking and fluffing. The honey dippers were dredging another outhouse further up the alley. John saw two young girls exit the company store located on the east end of the valley. Streetcar tracks ran in front of the store with a spur of railroad tracks behind. Rail cars on a siding next to a dirt road sat waiting. In the very bottom of the valley a creek with clear mountain water tumbled along, filtering through a marsh then under a one-lane plank bridge. Just past the bridge the flow of water made a sharp right turn. The abrupt change of the flow hit a carved-out bank, adding mud to the water, turning it a light brown. The creek continued for a short distance, now under a railroad bridge that connected the rail tracks to the mine. The brown water met another bank, forcing an immediate left turn, marching the flow west past the side entrance of the mine. There it met a small ditch that contained a bright incandescent red and orange liquid that flowed from the mine to be discarded into the creek. The brown and bright colored waters swirled, curling in a circular motion, each fighting for dominance. The ugly purplish brown solution that resulted continued its flow between a set of railroad tracks and the slate and mine waste dump. The creek and railroad tracks continued their journey to the Orient mine where the creek gathered more of the sulfur liquid. The rocks along the creek bank glow from deposits made by the solution from the mine.

Ridge Valley

Up close the fumes from the rocks gave off a suffocating odor that burned the throat with each breath.

"Hey look, Bull is taking off his shirt and holding it out, you sure cleaned your shoes pretty good on him," said Jerry.

John smiled without answering. He then looked beyond the valley to the opposite ridge, known to locals as the number two side of Ridge Valley. The hill contained rows of company houses. Further up the ridge a dirt road led to an airshaft that assisted the flow of air in the mine. Two company houses and a farm owned by the Glover family rested on these heights. Further beyond the heights were dense woods where blackberries, elderberries and black walnuts were picked in season.

A brilliant light that flashed in the sky awakened John from his thoughts.

"Wow, what was that?" asked John. He looked up searching the sky for an answer.

"Can't be lightning, no clouds, a little hazy, probably from the heat," John thought. He looked at Jerry asking, "Did you see that?"

"Yeah I saw something bright and felt it too, my hair tingled, did yours?"

John didn't answer; he was watching the women who were out tending their clothes looking skyward. The honey dippers ceased their methodical movements of dipping and dumping to take a look at the sky.

"Did you see that, was it lightning?" asked Corky

"Can't be, Cork, You need clouds to have lightning and besides I didn't hear any thunder," answered Bull as he washed his shirt in Mrs. Casserly's sudsy water.

Another flash, more pronounced than the last one, struck again.

"Boy, I felt that one real good. What about you, John?" asked Jerry

"Yeah, sure did and I felt a tingling on my skin this time, and look it made my hair stand up."

As before, all who happened to be outside searched the sky for an answer. There was none. Bull went back to his washing. He finished by twisting his shirt as tightly as possible. Wringing out the excess liquid he watched it fall to the ground. He noticed something shiny in the grass.

"Well look here Cork," Bull said, holding the treasure for him to see.

Up on the hill Jerry noticed Bull and Corky jumping up and down laughing and pointing to the ground, then pointing to his hand, "Look John. Bull is holding something in his hand and pointing to the ground, sure acting funny."

John knew what it was, but to be sure he patted his front pocket. "I lost my money, Jer."

Jerry sat down hard, pouting, and so frustrated he didn't know what to do or say. He didn't sit long, got up looked at John and muttered, "It just ain't fair, it ain't right."

"This hasn't been a good day for me so far, Jerry. I'm hot, sweaty and thirsty, my shoes smell like manure and now I lost my money, and a cold root beer."

Jerry's demeanor changed immediately as he noticed John's dejected attitude. Trying to pick up his friends spirits Jerry said, "Yeah, I know you lost the money, but listen John, we stood up to 'em, we did, and to me it was worth more than anything in the world."

John sat down and Jerry did the same. They just sat in silence thinking about the happenings of the day. John continued his shoe cleaning. Finally giving up he lay down on his back scanning the sky, thinking he might find an answer to the bright flashes.

"Look over yonder Jer, over beyond Republic, all the way toward Brownsville."

" What. Where?"

"Over this way," John said pointing. "Doesn't that look like a dark cloud formation straight across the sky, from one end to the other, and I saw some lightning flashes in those clouds. It's moving this way do you see it?"

Before John finished, and as sudden as a heartbeat, a flash, the brightest and longest yet, caused both boys to duck their head and bend close to the ground.

"Wow, that was close, and I heard something, like a cracking sound, did you hear it Jer?"

" No, covered my ears that time."

John surveyed the patch below where clothes hung limply and women who were out checking the line looked skyward for an answer. There was not a wisp of a breeze, just an eerie silence so quiet even the birds are hushed. The men cleaning the outhouses are spreading lime on the ground over the area they finished, closed the back doors and began moving up the alley. Down in the patch back yards women who seldom took time to speak to each other were talking and gesturing across fences. They all looked skyward, some folding hands like praying and a few were striking their breast, probably uttering mea culpa.

"You know John, I never in my life saw or felt anything like this," said Jerry with a look of anguish on his face, "I mean it's so quiet and still, I don't even hear the fan running at the mine."

Turning with a jerk, John asked, "What did you say?"

Jerry did not have to answer. They looked at each other, fright showing on their faces. John stood up shouting, " Can't be, my God, it can't be!" A sudden rush of blood to the brain created a crimson flush to his face. A queasy feeling crept into Jerry's stomach. Looking at each other they turned in unison bellowing, "The fan stopped, the fan stopped."

The sudden stoppage of the fan created a deafening silence that took a few moments to sink into the brain. Once it became reality it was so pronounced it hit like being struck by a thunderbolt. The air fan at the mine that forever sent lifesaving air to the workers was silent. The lung of the mine was no longer providing ventilation to its chambers.

The women of the patch, who knew mining, realized immediately what happened. For others, it took a moment to understand but once reality struck the brain a sudden shock hit and hit hard. Without the fan methane gasses will build up rapidly. The fact is that without the fan providing air to the mine could mean death to the inhabitants inside.

The men who worked in the mines talked after a few drinks, about their exploits most often at weddings and funerals. They understood the dangers and accepted all of them without fear. All except one and that one was the lack of air in the shaft. They knew that without the fan operating methane gasses could accumulate quickly in the vast interior of the shaft. Released from fissures, cracks and crevasses, the gasses replace the good air with afterdamp that slowly sucks the life from its victims. Getting out quickly was essential, for if the damp doesn't get you, an explosion from a spark is a high probability. The rats will sense the lack of air first and begin to scurry about searching for better air. The men hopefully notice the frenzy, questioning their moves at first, and then they begin to feel the change. The flow of air is stopped and the men now join the rats in a hurried procession to the cage. They must reach the cage quickly for a lift out of the bowels of the earth.

John and Jerry, realizing what happened, stood frozen. They quickly turned, wide-eyed, facing each other. Without a word both abruptly turned and began to run down the hill, through high grass, passing third row houses, around backyard gardens, finally reaching the alley. Turning west up the alley, as they ran Jerry noticed the line of clouds now looked closer. John thought he felt a breeze but discarded the thought because he was running as fast as he could up the alley. Sweating profusely, he wiped the salty liquid from his eyes with the back of his hand. He bristled from the stinging and burning this produced. Eyes blurred, he did not realize the honey dippers' truck was in his path.

"Watch out, John, the truck!" Jerry shouted.

John stopped a few feet from disaster. He followed Jerry around the truck. Up the road he cut across a neighbor's back yard. He saw his mother exiting the back door with his two sisters, one in each hand, his brother trudging behind. He saw Jerry running down a back yard a few houses up the row, waving to him until he disappeared around the corner of a house. A few paces from his mom and sisters, John stopped dead in his tracks. The siren, the dreaded siren sounded and reverberated throughout the valley, it echoed off the hills and houses…so loud and terrifying it stopped everyone in their tracks. The deafening blare was coming from the mine and the signal meant a major problem at the tipple. The wailing high-pitched voice initially entered deep in the soul, causing an immediate uncertainty as to what to do first. Reality soon followed as all in the patch dropped everything they were doing and prepared to answer the call. The

Ridge Valley inhabitants are now following ancient mining lore by rushing to the mine and rally to loved ones working there.

Because of the oppressive heat upstairs in the bedroom, Mr. Mullin decided to sleep on the front porch. The siren woke him with a jolt.

"What's the siren for?" he yelled to his wife.

"Mrs. Ignatius said the fan stopped earlier, might have something to do with the siren starting up."

"Oh my God! The fan is down, that sure could be the reason for the siren," he thought. He walked from the porch around the side of the house, up the back steps to the back yard. He wanted to move to higher ground to get a better view of the mine.

Dolly Dorek, recently married to her husband Joseph, had just moved into the house in the second row across the alley directly above the Mullins. She, like all others today, was washing clothes when she heard the siren blast. Exiting her door to investigate she saw Mr. Mullin crossing the alley and entering her yard. Dolly left her house and approached Mr. Mullin. She moved next to him and shouted, "What's happening? Tell me please, my husband is working today so can you tell me, please?" she yelled as loud as she could into Mr. Mullin's ear.

"The fan, air fan," he shouted cupping hands around his mouth so Dolly could hear and continued, "the fan is down, not running, they got to have the fan to survive."

"Is that dangerous?"

"Well, without the fan, there is no air circulating, you need the fan running to get fresh air into the sections where work is being done," said Mr. Mullin to the mine, not Dolly. After a brief time he continued, "Listen, without air circulating, methane gas will accumulate quickly, and this is a gassy mine so things can build up fast and then all that is needed is a spark then an explosion...."

"Oh my God," Dolly choked, hands to an open mouth, "can they get out?"

"They have to move fast, real fast, because again, gasses can build up in a hurry and even without an explosion the damp can get you."

"What's damp, what do you mean? Joseph never mentioned any of these things to me when he decided to go into the shaft."

"I guess what I mean is that damp leaves no air to breath, like, well like stale air, I don't know how to explain it but they call it some kind of monoxide, when the good air changes to bad air and guys in the bad air get mixed up like, confused."

Mr. Mullin paused and faced Dolly who returned a look of concern and worry. Her look made him realize that he should not have said all the things that could happen when the fan goes down.

"Look, your husband is young and with good people, he'll be fine."

Dolly saw women and children leaving houses and forming a procession towards the mine. The siren continued to wail as Dolly thanked Mr. Mullin. She started walking down the hill towards Mrs. Mullin who exited her back door. They would join the others on the march. A slight breeze, the first felt in days rustled the leaves on trees, and should anyone look up and to the west they would see a dark line of clouds slowly approaching Ridge Valley.

Mr. Mullin went into the house to change into work clothes, knowing he would be needed. "Very probably," he thought, "a lot of men would be needed."

CHAPTER II

THE HIGH-PITCHED CALL came from a shrieking siren and they all answered the call. Everything else paled at this moment in Ridge Valley. The only thought now was to get to the mine as quickly as possible. The scenario began for those who felt uneasy because of the silence of the mine fan. The uneasiness turned to terrifying shock at the sound of the alarm, and without hesitation the people of the patch rushed to its source.

Extending along the entire bottom row of houses was a path, and beyond a dirt road then a steep bank. The road, cut from the side of a precipitous slope, created an embankment so severe that it was practically impossible to negotiate. The shortest distance to the mine was over this steep terrace. The first dash of people who were not aware of the steep descent of the bank and eager to get to their destination, arrived at this location. Throwing caution to the wind, two women dashed over the edge. The consequence was an immediate loss of footing and tumbling they went, uncontrolled, to the bottom.

Mrs. Simkovich ended up scratched and bruised. Mrs. Stromski, her traveling partner, fell hard striking her head at the bottom.

"Don't come this way, too steep, go down to the cutoff by the Company Store," Mrs. Simkovich yelled to the crown gathered at the top."

The squadron of mostly women and children heeded the advice and began their trek as one. They moved down the road and when reaching the cutoff turned right, crossing a set of streetcar tracks, finally reaching the dirt road that passed in front of the store then on to the mine.

The siren continued to wail. The noise that initially sent a shock to the population was now beginning to be an irritation, clawing at the nerves. The sound seemed more intense as it reverberated in the valley. The wind, which began earlier as a whisper, now emitted brief shouts adding to the shrill. Once the group reached the cutoff and turned west toward the mine they saw a line of dark clouds stretching across the sky. The shouting wind picked up occasional gusts that scattered dust and dirt into eyes.

"Mamma I can't see."

"Walk backwards and don't rub your eyes, that only makes it worse."

The women took babushkas from their head and held the colorful scarves over their faces to protect themselves from the swirling dust. They passed clerks who came out of the front door of the store to investigate the high-pitched alarm. Some migrated back into the store while a few others, who had husbands working in the mine, joined the march.

John and Jerry braved the embankment. Descending the precipice was a challenge both accepted as a cliff to be conquered. Sliding down, they worked their way about half way when both lost their footing, tumbling to the bottom. Scrambling to his feet unhurt, John ran over to Jerry, helping him up.

"Jer, there is Mrs. Simkovich over there with Mrs. Stromski. Lets go over and see what's wrong.

"Are you two all right?"

"I'm fine, couple bruises, that's all, but my neighbor hit pretty hard…kind of stunned from hitting her head. Please help me get her to her feet. I'll get her home to rest, I can always bring the news back to her later."

The boys helped get the women on their way, and then walked to the road.

"Look John there's Bull and Corky are coming." John. Look."

"Where?"

" There in front, and look they're coming this way," shouted Jerry excitedly.

Both Bull and Corky edged ahead of the group, challenging the wind and dust by walking sideways into the fury. They made much better progress than the mother's who had small children slowing their progress. Seeing John and Jerry by the side of the road, Bull followed by Corky came over.

"Your Pa working?" questioned Bull.

"Yeah " said John.

"Mine and Cork's too, we're going down to see what's happening."

"Us too," said John.

Corky, who was standing behind Bull, moved up beside him to hear what was being said. The conversation ended by the time he moved to Bull's side. The four stood looking at each other, not blinking from the wind and dust, just staring into each other's eyes. Normally, when these four met, dirt would be kicked, heads turned sideways eying the other as an enemy, mumbling derogatory remarks, looking past the person and not at them. Things were different now and they looked at each other silently, somehow understanding the thoughts and feelings the other one felt. A short time ago they played kids games, doing silly kid things, fighting dumb kid fights. That was yesterday, actually this morning, and now they stood beside the dirt road their fathers trudged over early this day on their way to work. Would they soon be doing the same, in the early morning hour marching to the call of work at the mine? They were the oldest males in the family, and knew the rules of the H. C. Grant Coal and Coke Company. They also understood what the silence of the fan meant, and more so the finality of the siren. They were on the way to learn the fate of their fathers, hoping beyond hope that the news would be positive.

"We're a' going," announced Bull, hands cupped around his mouth.

"Us too," countered John who continued, " Hope the siren is a mistake, happened before, but with the fan down, well, let's go and find out."

Bull and Corky walked away leaving John and Jerry standing next to the road. John scanned the sky to see black rolling clouds inching closer and closer to the valley. They appeared to hover for a moment over Orient, another coal-mining patch a short distance to the west. A faint sound of thunder rumbled.

"What was that Jer?" asked John.

Jerry did not answer.

The gusting winds when blowing at its maximum were difficult to knife through. Progress slowed to a crawl for those with children at their side. The mass of humanity fighting the wind finally approached the railroad bridge. Traversing the planks placed there to allow passage again slowed the crowd. The boys, making better progress, moved to the front of the pack.

THUNDER BOOMED

"Wow, that was a big one," yelled Jerry as a drop of rain fell on his arm soon followed by another, and another.

The black clouds, low in the valley looked like a rolling mountain with their rotation revolving over and over. They appeared to be just overhead, close enough for a giraffe to reach up and touch with his head.

"Look John, over the other way, the sun is still shining," said Jerry.

"Not for long," yelled John.

The dark as midnight clouds descended into the valley, churning, rolling; they billowed higher and higher until they reached a pinnacle in the sky. They paused for a split second then topsy-turvy the mountainous thunderheads tumbled over and over plummeting downward. The blustery wind and rain joined the rolling cloud mountain as it stretched across the heavens covering the sun.

"It's dark, why is it dark?" stammered a little one trying to keep pace.

Within the clouds a burst of thunder from the low murky mountains attacked with deafening explosions that reverberated from the sides of the steep hills and caused ringing in many ears.

Continuous lightning, thunder…lightning…thunder…siren…rain…lightning…thunder lightning…thunder…siren…lightning…thunder…it shook the soul.

The only way, to make progress against the wind and rain was to walk backwards. Turning around, John spotted his mom and sisters a short distance in the rear of a group that made it just beyond the railroad bridge.

"I'm going back to help my mom, Jer, looks like she's struggling with the girls."

"O.K. John, meet you at the shaft."

John turned and, pushed by the wind, retreated to the bridge. The thunder, lightning and rain continued without letup. The shriek of the siren and booming thunder created a noise overload rattling the brain. The driving rain soaked those in the open heading to the shaft.

"It stings bad, ouch, it stings bad, like bees stinging," said Hanna to Mamma.

Mrs. Ignatius bent down and with her back to the wind and rain like a duck protecting her young with its wings, snuggled the girls with both arms as close to her as possible.

"I'm wet and cold, its dark. I'm scared momma."

"You'll be fine 'cause God will care for you and your sister," consoled Mrs. Ignatius. Her sister remained silent as she continued to cower close to mom.

The crowd descending from the patch houses on both sides of the valley were either approaching or passing the railroad bridge. The points of the group were at the slate-covered field one that was used as an outdoor storage area. The acreage housed various sizes of timber and logs for shoring up roofs in the mine, iron rails, extra steel girders for tipple repair, red bricks, cement blocks and corrugated sheeting. At the greatest distance from the shaft, beyond the storage field, a junk graveyard of damaged rusted coal cars, old wooden coal wagons without wheels and an inoperable steam engine were left to rust.

The entourage, because of the conditions, made slow progress against the storm.

"Let's make a go of it, others are moving forward and maybe we can find something to protect us from this wind and rain. We can't stay here so lets go, Hanna, Joanna, now."

Without speaking the girls obeyed. They moved a few feet forward. When a gust of wind dominated it shoved them back a few steps, after recovering they tried again. The wind was relentless; giving up some ground, then like a mad growling bear, stood up and by massing extra energy slammed the strong concentrated blast of fury into its victim. Back and forth they went. Moving with the wind John half ran, half stumbled back to his mom's location.

"Come with me, over here, this way," he yelled as he gently grabbed his mom's arm and directed her across the field in the direction of an abandoned coal car resting on its side in the junk graveyard. John leading the way tripped and fell to the ground, tearing a hole in the left knee of his jeans. A sharp piece of slate pierced the lower part of the knee, creating a cut deep enough to draw blood. John grabbed his knee while looking back to see what caused the fall. He saw a piece of dirty canvas entangled and half buried in the slate. The canvas was the kind used to set up a brattice for adjusting air flow in the haulages and must have been discarded with the slate. Grabbing a corner he pulled to unearth a piece of canvas, blanket size, he could use as a covering for his family. Reaching the mine car, mom and the girls huddled inside and John covered them with the canvas. The girls covered their ears, trying to block out the loud thunder and roaring wind. They also snuggled their face as close as they could to mom.

"How are your legs, do they still sting?"

"No, they're all right."

"How about you, Joanna?"

"I'm fine," she answered.

"Oh my, look, look, it's sleeting," shouted Mrs. Ignatius.

The sleet was pure white, about the size of a pea, bouncing as it hit the slate field. The sleet initially melted because of the warm surface, but it came so fast that it began to accumulate. The melting caused an eerie fog to form close to the ground, only to be blown away by the wind. John would swear later that he heard a sizzling sound like bacon frying in a skillet.

"Mom, look over there."

"Where?"

"By the bridge, isn't that Mrs. Mullin with that new girl that lives above them?"

"Yes John, you're right and they're out in the open, we got room, John, think you could fetch them and bring them over here? We'll make room." John left the shelter and hurried to the bridge. The sleet abated as John reached the two women. He pointed to the shelter where Mrs. Ignatius waved and motioned for them to come over. They accepted the invitation.

"This way Mrs. Mullin, you too," gesturing to Dolly, "you can sit next to the girls."

"Thank you, Bless you, bless you," said Mrs. Mullin.

"Yes, thank you, thank you," repeated Dolly.

"Here, get in closer, we got room," said Mrs. Ignatius who added, "get in front of me and wrap this canvas around yourself, Misses?"

"Dorek" They adjusted positions, each holding a corner of the canvas. John helped, ignoring the sleet and hail falling from the sky. He then left to join his brother behind a stack of logs. Dolly sat between the girls.

"Look, you can sled ride in August, sure sounds like fun to me, how about you?" Dolly said to the girls.

"Think we can?"

"Sure we can, be nice and slippery. I bet you could go faster than in snow."

" Would you go with us?" asked Joanna.

"Sure, I'd be happy to go."

Dolly exchanged names with the young one's, talked girl talk and bantered to each other like long lost friends. The girls forgot for a moment about the storm and the reason they were all hiding. Their shaking and trembling from the elements slowed and then stopped. Dolly too appreciated the girls; for in talking to them her attention was momentarily diverted away from thinking about her husband. The girls enjoyed having Dolly there for now they had someone to talk with, like a big sister.

Hanna tugged at Dolly's dress, "What is your name again."

"Dolly. Dolly Dorek," she answered.

"You sure, I never heard anyone named Dolly, that your real name…for sure?"

"Yep, my real name is Dolly, that's my name, what's yours?"

"I'm Hanna."

"I'm Joanna."

"She doesn't talk much, my sister," said Hanna.

"Cause Hanna is always talking that's why," answered Joanna.

"I sure appreciate your brother coming for us, I enjoy your company."

"Me too," countered the girls in unison.

"I wonder what's happening at the mine? I'm really worried 'cause they don't blow the siren unless something is wrong, bad wrong, and the siren sounded before the storm hit. Just can't figure it out" said Mrs. Ignatius who asked. "Is your man working?"

"No, he works at night," said Mrs. Mullin.

"Oh yes, I forgot, what about Mrs. Dorek?"

"Yes, she is so young, just moved into the house right above us on the hill. Nice girl and scared to death because her husband is working and she doesn't know much about his job. They've been married only a few months and she told me she grew up on a farm up by a place called Whitney where she met him. She said that word was they needed men here and a house was available, so they decided to come. Like I said, a farm girl who has no idea about mining." Mrs. Ignatius nodded each time a point was made and expressed her thanks for Dolly talking to the girls.

As fast as it began, the sleet stopped, only to be replaced by large drops of intermittent rain. The shower abated then stopped. The wind, losing much of its velocity slowed considerably. The sky turned from dark to dusk. People left their impromptu shelters and searched the sky to find the storm moving rapidly eastward, out of the area. The siren stopped, a welcome relief for all. Quiet returned to the valley.

The storm left behind a white landscape that soon disappeared as the sleet melted into the warm ground. Small branches, leaves, and countless numbers of twigs littered the area. The torrent of rain clouds moved in rapid fashion to the east. The storm front now moving to the east in the vicinity of Fairbanks, then on to New Salem, would pass Uniontown and attempt to leap the Summit Ridge. The patch people, relieved by the end of the storm, gathered themselves and started to complete their journey.

"Looks like the rain is over, but it could return, seen it happen before. You know once it gets in this valley it doesn't want to leave. C'mon girls, let's hurry," said Mrs. Ignatius.

"They're with me, I'll take em," said Dolly, holding on to each girl's hand.

Women and children now approaching the mine were wet from the rain and stinging from the sleet. The rain broke the oppressive heat spell providing moderation to the temperature and clean fresh air. Now, as much as the rain was welcomed under the present circumstances, they were happy to see it leave. They now could move without delay to the mine. The people did just that, walking fast. The crowd went a short distance. Feeling the earth shake they stopped in their tracks.

The earth quivered then convulsed; it told of a concussion resulting from a blast below ground.

"What was that?" Dolly asked herself.

The answer came from the pit mouth with a loud *WHOOM* followed by an enormous plume of purple and red smoke. The force of the blast was muted as the purple and red cloud turned to suffocating smoldering black fumes. The black cloud rolled along the ground, obscuring happenings near the shaft. Bull, Corky and Jerry, who had arrived at the pit, dropped to the ground and covered their heads to protect themselves from falling debris. Those further out near the junk graveyard, or moving across the bridge stopped in their tracks, shocked at the sight at the pit mouth.

The men working in the mine first saw the rats scurry about the section, soon understanding why. The flow of air to the section turned stale and heavy. The miners ignored the lack of airflow; initially thinking a simple change of brattice to adjust the flow was all that was needed. Everything would soon return to normal. It didn't. The air got worse, the rats, sensing the difference, now began running up the haulage. The men in the crew finally decided to walk out.

Workers closer to the cage smelled the bad air immediately and moved quickly to exit the mine. Riding the cage to the surface they

Bob Menarcheck

noticed immediately that the fan was down. They quickly returned the cage to the bottom to pick up their buddies.

The walk became a run. Men working at the face were thousands of feet from the cage. The cumbersome clothes and heavy boots slowed the trek but persistent and determined they moved forward. Above ground, families were also on the move and just as persistent in their quest to reach the mine.

The initial point of the explosion was deep in a section off the main haulage. Gathering more and more force from the escaping methane gas, the direction of the blast took the same route as the men from the face. Just as the worker's began their final rush the force hit, engulfing its prey. Continuing its journey the blast finally released its energy up the shaft. The cage starting its climb was caught. The heat generating force blew the cage like a projectile fired from a cannon about twenty feet from the opening.

The rain returned to Ridge Valley. Dolly and the girls arrived at the pit followed by Mrs. Ignatius and Mrs. Mullin. Joined by most of the residents in the patch they faced the black acid smoke that hovered over the area. It was difficult to see the damage caused by the blast at first, not only because of the dense smoke, but also because of burning watery eyes. The dark smog filtering the air was replaced quickly by more black smoke coming from the mouth. The blast that originated deep in the bowels of the mine sucked out the air as it flashed up and out of the tunnels. Because of the lack of oxygen, no further fires existed. The result was that the smoke rising from the pit lessened considerably throughout the day and stopped entirely by late evening. Members of the crowd who had loved ones not accounted for stood vigilantly in the rain and remained in position throughout the night. The rosary, along with prayers would be said often and the families would stay until a final answer was rendered.

Throughout the afternoon and into the evening the mine complex became a beehive of activity. District Managers, Supervisors and miners descended on Ridge Valley to prepare for initiating a rescue.

Those that made it out and were close to the mouth ducked for cover from coal chunks, splintered timber and a combination of shrapnel shapes that fell from the sky. Choking from the thick smoke engulfing the pit mouth, men stumbled into buildings while others hugged the ground.

Tim Johnson, the mine foreman, once he could see through the smog ran outside from his office, observed the happenings. He saw men trapped in the cage and ran over to help. He found that all aboard were severely injured.

"She blew and blew hard," a miner yelled to Tim.

Tim, seeing the injured men getting the help they needed, retreated back to the entrance of the doorway that led to his office. Andy Stisczco, an assistant foreman, was standing at the door when Tim arrived. He grabbed Andy's arm and motioned for him to come to the office. Julius, a combination office clerk, accountant, and general company overseer, was there waiting. He was a sixty-year-old fussbudget who reported everything happening at Ridge Valley to district manager Joseph P. Waters, who then answered to the head of the H.C. Grant Coal and Coke Company.

"Julius, please post a message on the board saying that all men available to help with rescue work are to report to the meeting room immediately. A wave of the hand sent him on his way. Andy, locate Frank Petoskey, I saw him here a minute ago, tell him to see me and then get someone to get the room ready. I need you and Pete here."

Julius made his way to the message board in front of the Lamp House. Announcements of importance were posted at this location where a place for urgent or special messages were reserved at the top right corner of the board. Julius posted the announcement in this special area of the board.

"What's it say?" asked a worker standing close.

"Calling a meeting."

John was standing with his mom and sisters, observing, like everyone else, the men moving about the area. He saw a group move quickly to the cage and noticed the activity at the message board; the happenings there aroused his curiosity.

"I'm going over to the message board, see what's being posted. I'll be right back."

John's mom nodded her approval while keeping a watchful eye out for her husband. John started to walk toward the message board when he heard his name being shouted from behind. He turned to see Bull and Corky who ran toward him.

"John, I'm looking for my dad, did you see him?" questioned Bull.

"Naw, I just got here, haven't seen my dad either, Have you?"

"No."

"What about Cork and Jerry?"

"Cork's dad made it out, hurt bad though, I don't think Jerry's dad is working this shift," said Bull now hurrying away.

The pit area was jammed with humanity. Workers who made it out of the pit, boys looking for fathers, and men from other shifts, returning to help all needed direction that was provided by the message board. The word spread of the gathering in the meeting room. John decided to follow the surge of men heading to the meeting. Once there he found the benches filled, forcing an overflow to line the walls around the room. John was fortunate to find a space in the back corner. More arrived, jamming the doorway and as additional men came they had to remain in the hallway. The crowd of workers extended out the door. Messages were passed through various ethnic dialects causing some confusion from speaker to the end of the line.

"The smoke from the shaft lessoned considerably, we know that without oxygen the fire can't continue. This situation may permit us to start the fan as soon as it is repaired," announced Tim Johnson.

"What about the men down there?" asked a worker pointing to the shaft, "How long can they survive under these conditions? Can the fire start again? With air?"

" I'll let Frank Petoskey answer that, he's the fire boss and the best I know when it comes to air flow and such, Frank can you help with that?" asked Tim.

"If they brattice themselves in real good, yes they can survive, of course it depends on their location, hopefully they moved near the air intake shaft."

"If we start the fan, will that revive the fire?" asked another in the room.

"This is doubtful in my mind. You must remember that the exact mixture of methane and oxygen must be precise in order for an explosion to occur. Once the blast starts it immediately seeks more oxygen to sustain itself. The monster, after sucking up the available air, must continue to look for more good air to survive. Now as it seeks more air, and more methane, it is moving faster and faster in a confined space. The sequence follows a pattern producing a rapid violent series of explosions, becoming hotter and hotter…in the process developing a brute force, literally a wall of flame, destroying all in its path. This tremendous force is gathering energy, seeking a release and that release is finally up the shaft, blowing the cage."

"What if the men were in its path?" asked some one who should have known better.

"Let's move on and get organized but before we do, remember NOT to say anything, especially to the families of those not accounted for. We must stay positive."

"Just tell us what you want, Tim,"

"All right. As I see it, three things need to be accomplished for us to start our rescue mission. I'll list them on the blackboard, and the name of the person in charge. You can come up and write your name under the one area where you feel best qualified. Report to your leader and keep things within your group. Better yet…all information will be reported to me and I will handle all announcements from this office. Are there any questions?"

Hearing none Tim listed three items near the top of the blackboard, allowing for names below. The three items were, CABLE-CAGE…FAN…TIPPLE. He stepped aside as the men moved forward to place their name on the board.

John listened to the presentation, emotions running back and forth depending on what was being said. He wanted to believe the part about the brattice wall, yet was confused about what was said about the lack of air. If the lack of good air snubs out a fire, could it also snub out a person's breathing.

"Wait," he shouted loud enough for the person standing next to him to hear.

The meeting was finished; men proceeded to register their names in the appropriate spot as John dashed from the room to the lamp house nearby. His heart was beating fast and his breathing became labored as he wiped sweat from his forehead. Breathing hard from the quick dash he came to a sliding stop in front of the lamp house window.

"My dad's check number, is my dad's check number up? Is it on the board, is it there?"

Mr. O'Ronney, in charge of the lamp house, moved ever so slowly, using crutches to navigate. His left leg had been severed when run over by the wheel of a mine car. He had to leave the pits and was later hired for his present job.

"My father is his number on the board?"

"You are."

"Ignatius, John, yes, I'm his boy."

Known to all as Mr. Shaun, Mr. O'Rooney limped to the board. He quickly returned.

"What's his number, I need his number?'

"Number's 1427."

A circular metal tag, about the size of a one-half dollar with a small hole for hanging, had check numbers stamped on both sides. The tags were always given to Mr. Shaun when the men collected their lamps before entering the shaft. This procedure indicated that the lamp was picked up and it also meant that the person was in the mine working. When the men completed the shift, they returned the lamp and collected the tag. This was one way of knowing who was working.

"No, sorry, he never punched out, his number is on the board, and he must be inside."

John silently turned and walked away. He walked slowly to where his mom, brother and the girls were standing. A deputy was extending a rope in front of them and others in order to keep people back from the activity near the pit. Noticing a bench beside the blacksmith shop he picked it up and carried it over for his mom. Soon others followed with benches from various parts of the complex.

"Mom, Dad's check number is on the board"

They looked deeply into each other's eyes. "John. You must keep up hope for the girls' sake, and your brother, say no more, we must, and we must trust the Lord."

John sat down at his mother's side, looking but not seeing the rescue activity happening in front of him. His mind was elsewhere.

"That elsewhere was what Mr. Johnson and others said about setting up a brattice. Then again, he wondered, "if this is successful, what about the blast sucking out the air. Isn't that the same air a person needs to breath? Thoughts swirled in his brain until he accepted the positive, for the men knew how to survive, how to protect themselves…he looked at his mom…she believes, so must he believe. He bowed his head and began to pray.

By dusk the repair teams were organized, the materials needed listed and workers dispatched to secure the necessary supplies. A plan of action was started but it would take until midnight before activity directed toward actual repairs would begin. Lighting in the area had to be installed and this took hours. Tools for unwinding the cable were needed because none were located in the tool shed. Some items would have to be fabricated in the welding shop and this would take time. A new cage was located at a site under construction about twelve miles away. The new cage would arrive by morning.

"Should all go well, we expect to go down the shaft sometime tomorrow," said Tim Johnson to reporters on the scene and added, "That's all for now."

"Wait, we want to know the numbers of men still in the shaft! How did this happen? Is there any hope for those trapped?"

"Look, we are in the process of a rescue mission, we have work to do. Please understand that any information about causalities will be provided to the families first, then you. That's all for now, so please stay out of the pit area so the men can work."

The reporters left and filed stories for the morning papers. The soaked families ignored the elements and continued standing in the rain, waiting. They refused to budge from a front location close to the rescue action. Neighbors and friends, who understood their concern left only to return with umbrellas, jackets and blankets to protect the grieving families.

The welders began climbing the girders, making their way up the tipple to first remove damaged parts then replace and weld new sections. The wet beams, slick from the rain, caused the welders to slip frequently. The crowd gasped in unison when the slippage occurred. Once in place the climbers used ropes to secure their position. The brave simply held on with one hand and worked with the other.

Bob Menarcheck

The food supplied by the Red Cross was running low and more supplies for their canteen would arrive in the morning. The Salvation Army personnel and tents would also arrive in the morning. Food for the men working was the first priority so coffee had to do for families who stayed at the site.

The curious onlookers that came began to disperse in the early evening, voicing their willingness to return if needed. Father William Pzarpotozcski from Saint Procopius church in New Salem rendered blessings on the rescue crew and melted into the crowd of families to give comfort and blessings to the families waiting. Reverend James Richmond, a minister from Republic Methodist, was present also comforting the flock.

The rescue teams worked throughout the night in short shifts. They exchanged places frequently in order to have fresh workers available at all times. Their goal of getting a team down the shaft as quickly as possible was paramount. They would rest once this was accomplished.

Early morning arrived damp from the previous day's rains. Fog that formed throughout the night settled in the valley like a guardian cloud protecting those waiting outside the mine. Tiny bright crystals danced with delight around light bulbs strung between buildings. They dashed for cover with the arrival of the sun, but for the moment they maneuvered about happily.

The Red Cross workers struggled with wet canvas they placed on the moist ground. With added manpower the tent was erected. Men in Red Cross uniforms along with volunteers put up chairs and tables along with cots in the rear. The tent was located where the families could see the activity around the tipple and watch the rescue operation in progress. Red Cross ladies set up a cooking station at one end of the tent and began making a large pot of vegetable soup and a pot of coffee. The tent chairs and cots were welcome sights for those who had stood their vigil in the rain and fog throughout the night. The people moved into the tent, always keeping a watchful eye on happenings at the shaft.

A cage was transported into the pit site during the night and placed near the pit opening. A crew of men loosened the cable from around the collecting drums. The drums were damaged beyond

Ridge Valley

repair. Bull wheels replaced the drums at the top of the tipple. The cable was connected to the cage, and once the girders are stabilized the cable was attached to the wheel. Then the cage was lifted over the pit mouth. A new motor and belt were installed on the fan housing, electricity connected and the fan motor started. The fan wobbled off center and had to be stopped. Tim Johnson was seen everywhere checking the progress and all was going well except for the fan problem. Everything involving the fan was checked and double-checked yet the fan continued its weird ways. A new belt was installed and the motor ran freely and with power. One problem solved, two more to go.

"You should get something to eat," said Mrs. Mullin to Dolly. "You look a bit peeked and you must keep up your strength.

"I just don't feel good, my stomach won't handle any food, can't seem to hold it down, nerves I guess," answered Dolly who continued, "I'm really worried 'cause it's been a good while since the blast and we haven't heard a thing." Dolly sat wringing her hands.

"There is always hope until you see one way or the other," said Mrs. Ignatius.

"But it's been so long."

"There have been men recovered after four or five days, and it looks like they're making good progress. They should be going down soon. Keep hoping and praying for the best. Listen, Mrs. Mullin is right; you must keep up your strength and eat something. Would you like for John to get you something at the canteen?"

"No thanks, not right now, just not hungry."

"How about you, mom, you look tired with Hanna and Joanna hanging on yeah?" said John. "Hey, let me take the girls over to the cots to lie down. Give yeah some rest."

"It's okay, I'll be good John."

"Oh hello, Father," said Mrs. Ignatius to Father William as he approached and made the sign of the cross. The congregation called him Father William because Pzarpotozcksi created a challenge, especially for the children.

"God bless you," he said as he sat with the ladies and prayed, " God Bless the miners, God have mercy on them. Please protect them in their hour of need and may we never give up hope for their return." He blessed the group and left to pray with others.

John returned from getting the girls settled and sat down next to his mom. She suggested he go over to the Salvation Army Canteen to get something to eat. He accepted her suggestion. He greeted neighbors and friends as he walked past tables on his way. He left the tent, finding the sun casting a glow into the valley. It felt good as John walked to the Canteen and ordered a cup of coffee.

"Here you are, good and fresh, just made," said a smiling lassie.

"What's your name?" he blurted without thinking.

"Oh, Ann, Annie they call me," she answered without giving a last name. Her green eyes and dark brown hair was enhanced with rosy cheeks and a lovely smile. She glanced back at John as she moved away to serve another.

"Thank you," said John raising his cup to her as she left.

John walked to the edge of the tent, wrapped both hands around the container, felt its warmth, and smelled the vapor rising from the cup then took a long sip. The brew was hot and tasty. He drank while watching Annie go about serving others. He couldn't keep his eyes off her. I wonder if she is my age. Can't be more than fourteen he thought. Now observing the activity around the pit, he became curious about the number of men roaming the site that are obviously not miners. The fedora hats, high collar shirts, black low cut shoes they must be Pittsburgh people he thought.

"Whatcha doing John? Been looking for yeah. I saw your mom and she said you were over here. Hey, where did yeah get the coffee? I sure could use some," sputtered Jerry

"Over there," pointed John.

"Look, there's Bull and Corky at the counter getting food. You hungry John? I am. Maybe I'll join 'em and get a bite too. How about it John?"

"No thanks Jer, plan on taking some coffee back to my mom, maybe I'll sit with her for a while. Go ahead, see yeah later."

Jerry left and John returned to the canteen to refill his cup with coffee and get one for his mom. He was hoping that Annie would be the one doing the chore. He was disappointed to see her serving another customer at the far end of the counter.

Ridge Valley

He returned to the tent, finding his mom holding a Rosary, head down, praying Hail Marys and Our Fathers. You didn't disturb mom when she's praying the Rosary. John sat for a while watching the events taking place at the pit. There was a reporter talking to the mine foreman and a rescue team member checking equipment. He decided to walk over and see if any new messages were posted. None were listed but he saw a person one could not miss. Tony Baritone had been a fixture in the neighborhood for years. The miners accepted him as the "banker" in the coal-mining patch. He was a needed commodity the miners used when desperate for cash. He loaned money at a price, charging a fee to be collected at the next payday. The cycle once started never seemed to end. The men needed cash to buy their beer and liquor at O'Malley's tavern. Sure you can get in "the book" at the bar to charge your drinks but O'Malley had to be paid on time. When he called for the tab to be paid or no more drinks, "The Banker," Tony Baritone, was the person to see. Following a shift in the pits, a miner needed to wash down the coal dust with a shot of whiskey and a beer, and to do this one needed cash.

The Union Supply Company Store, a subsidiary of the H.C. Grant Coal and Coke Company that owned the mines where the men worked, deducted the money owed for purchases at the Store, for rent, and blacksmith fees. Any money left went to the worker. Forced to buy and charge items at the Company Store to feed families, the amount spent often left little or no cash for the worker. This created a desperate situation for a guy who needed a drink. Tony was the person called upon to solve that problem.

There was Tony, standing in the doorway of the lamp house. The Italian Banker, thin in stature, dressed in a white shirt and black-cuffed trousers heightened with a sharp crease that looked like one could cut their finger if it was run over the edge. Black polished leather low cut shoes completed the outfit that was topped with a waistcoat that moved from side to side when he swaggered as he walked. He had a dark complexion, winter or summer. His sharp facial features were topped with midnight hair, slicked straight back over his head. Tony was a person who stood out like a whale in a fishpond. It was puzzling how anyone could ignore him as men passed by without acknowledging his presence, but they did.

There was one thing you counted on when dealing with Tony and that was that all transactions were between him and the loaner. He never divulged information on loans to others. He knew the men, understood they were honest to a fault and that he would be paid. His losses were few.

Tony found it necessary to bribe Mr. Shaun into giving him names of miners that had check numbers hanging on the board. Shaun did not verbally answer, but simply shook his head up and down, or back and forth after a check number was read from his little black book. Shaun nodded up and down twenty-nine times. Tony quickly totaled the amount owed and once done felt an immediate pounding in his head. Should the check numbers indicated as yes by Shaun meet their fate in the mine, his losses would reach an amount that would take a year to recover.

"John, John," repeated Dolly while punching John on the shoulder, "John, isn't that man posting something on the message board over there?"

"You're right, that's Mr. Julius and he is posting something in the upper right corner."

"Will you go over there with me to see the message?" asked Dolly.

"Sure"

The men moved to the front of the crowd of miners dressed in work clothes. They were crowding Julius so close that only a few people in front could see the message. Those in front shouted back the message to those in the rear.

"ALL AVAILABLE RESCUE TEAM MEMBERS ARE TO REPORT TO THE MEETING ROOM IMMEDIATELY."

"John, does that mean they're going down?"

"I think so at least I think they are getting close."

"How many are going?"

"Cage holds about fifteen, but with the equipment they need the first group will probably be twelve I'd say."

"How long, John before we will we get any news?"

"Soon after they get to the bottom. Listen, my mom is probably wondering about the message also. I think I'll go back and give her the news…how about you, do you want to go back to the tent, maybe sit with my mom?"

"Thanks, but I think I'll wait here a bit. Maybe after the meeting they'll post more news about the rescue and I don't want to miss any."

"Well, okay," said John as he walked away, leaving Dolly standing close to the board. The rescue teams and other men had vacated the space and dispersed to the meeting room and elsewhere in the pit area. She decided to read the message once more, just wanted to be sure the man in front was right.

Satisfied, Dolly felt better since something was being done, except for her stomach that has been "acting up" since she arrived at the pit. "Maybe I will try something at the canteen, the coffee smelled good earlier when it was brewing, yes a coffee." She glanced at the message board once more, turned and left for the canteen.

Tony, waiting inside the doorway to the lamp house, checked and double-checked his figures. He came to the conclusion that they were correct and that his losses will be substantial.

"This rescue has got to work," he mumbled, "They all can't be missing."

He pocketed his little black book, twisted the cap over the working part of his pen, and clipped it to the inside pocket. He walked out the lamp house door, looked in the direction where Dolly was walking, "Yeah for sure," he said to himself.

Tony watched for a second then began following Dolly to the canteen counter. He maneuvered himself to a position slightly to the left and behind her. He was gambling that she would turn this way after getting her drink.

" Excuse me, I'm sorry," said Dolly as she began to wipe spilled coffee from Tony's waistcoat with her handkerchief. "I'm so sorry, I didn't see you."

"That's okay, no damage, no problem."

"Oh my, let me get this spot here and there, that's the best I can do for now except maybe to wash the coat. I live above the Mullins and…"

"That's fine what you did, and haven't I seen you around? I believe at the store, yes I noticed you there with your man."

"My husband Joseph, I don't believe I've ever seen you there, what's your name?"

"Tony, Tony Baritone, and yours?"

"Dolly Dorek, live in the house, number forty-one, above the Mullins."

"You lived there long?"

"No, me and my husband been here 'bout two months. Joseph was looking for work and there was a house available so we decided to come." She was talking while looking at the coffee in the cup. "And"…Dolly stopped talking, sipped a little coffee, and then looked down into the cup again. Tony thought he saw a tear well up in her eyes.

"He's working," she blurted out.

"Is he in the mine, now?" asked Tony, who already knew the answer from information he received from Mr. Shaun.

"Went in yesterday morning."

"He'll be fine, real fine, he's a good strong man. I know your husband, I remember him, and he's a big strong man." Tony struggled, trying to find the right words to say for the first time in his life, "Don't worry, he'll be back soon and things will be back to normal."

Tony stopped talking and took a sip of coffee, already knowing what the outcome will be, after all he was a gambler and he knew the odds and decided long ago that the percentages were not good. He continued talking as Dolly sipped coffee. Suddenly without warning tears began flowing from her eyes. The tears became a steady stream, a flow that gained momentum as they rolled down her cheeks, ending on the top part of her dress. She stood as if in a stupor, looking straight ahead transfixed.

"Are you all right?"

She did not answer. Tony reached into his inner pocket and retrieved a clean white linen handkerchief. He lifted it to Dolly's face and began dabbing the salty liquid from her cheeks and from the corner of her mouth.

She jerked back, "What are you doing?"

"I just thought I, you're getting the dress wet and wanted to help, sorry here take this," he gave her the cloth.

She took it wiped her face and dress, "I'm sorry, I'm not myself I guess, I only hope they get to the men soon, that's all…I think I better go back to the tent."

Tony watched as Dolly turned to leave; she walked a few steps when Tony shouted her name. She stopped, looked at the caller who said, "He'll be fine, you'll see." They both departed in silence.

John returned to the tent and told his mom the news. He sat with her for a few minutes then decided to go to the meeting room. He arrived in time to hear Mike Christian, the man assigned to head the first rescue team, speaking to the group. He started by reviewing procedures and specific duties assigned to each rescue team member.

"First we gear the fan into the reverse position." The word REVERSE was written on the black board. "There is a good amount of damp rising up the shaft. We feel the best way to start is to blow the fresh air through the haulages and out the airshaft at the heights. We will run reverse for fifteen minutes, then return to the forward position to pull air from the airshaft. The team will proceed down the shaft five minutes after the forward fan starts. Gentleman, please bow your heads and say a prayer for a positive recovery."

John prayed for the rescue team, and his dad as well.

"Amen, let's go, " said Mike Christian.

Mike led the rescue team across the compound under the watchful eyes of every person in or near the tent. They passed through groups of men who wished them well, while others stood in silence. Tim Johnson was there at the cage to see them off. He shook hands with Paul Baxter, the second in charge, acknowledged as a quiet determined capable leader. He greeted Tom Lekowski, an air specialist and Pete Solcheck, an emergency expert. The remainder of the team contained the most experienced miners available.

"Tom, what about the ventilation, is there a good draft?"

"Reports from the heights where the air shaft is located indicate that the draft is pulling hard, funneling a flow of about forty per cent. This shows some blockage, but not total since air is getting through it appears that a small amount of toxic fumes are present but nothing to hold us back. Anyway, got my little angel here; she'll let us know if there is any serious problem with gasses or fumes," said Tom as he held up a lively canary. The men entered the cage with a thousand eyes watching, hearts pounding and lips praying in the tents.

THE CAGE STARTED ITS DECENT   THE RESCUE IS ON

The cable lowered the cage slowly into the depths. The men in the cage stood holding ropes suspended from the ceiling to steady themselves as the car continued its descent. Tom, who now relied more on the reaction of the canary, continually checked the quality and flow of air. After dropping a short distance, they were aware of an odor, a stench that grew stronger as they descended. Moving from daylight to dark now, illumination from carbide lamps worn on hard hats lighted the way. Some lingering smoke along with the telling smell of carbide burning was imminent as it lingered for a brief moment in the nostrils before rising up the shaft with the breeze. The canary jumped from rung to rung in its own cage. The pace of the descent, slow and deliberate, seemed like a snail's pace in comparison to normal operations.

THE CABLE UNWOUND, THE CAGE DROPPED DEEPER AND DEEPER

The news of the pending rescue operation spread throughout the region. People that charged the area yesterday at the sound of the siren left when it became apparent that nothing would be done until repairs were made The word was out that the rescue was starting, so swarms of humanity descended on the Ridge Valley mine. They joined the immediate families that stayed and continued their vigil in the Red Cross tent. The masses crowded around the roped off sections near the pit, some spilling beyond to the very edge of the tipple. Boys climbed on the roof of the blacksmith shop, where they sat to view the proceedings. The company doctor and extra sheriff deputies were summoned to assist.

THE BULL WHEELS TURNED SLOWLY-RELEASING MORE CABLE

The population near the mine increased rapidly, particularly from patches adjourning the valley. Entire communities emptied of people now, clogging the roads, thus delaying ambulances and additional local deputies from reaching the mine. The workers who repaired the fan and attached the cable to the cage remained on the scene to help if needed. They milled around talking to fellow miners and would not leave until an outcome was evident. Like all with a view of the tipple, they watched intently the turning of the wheels releasing the cable, hearing the whirl, waiting for it to stop, telling all that the cage has landed at the bottom.

THE HUMMING OF THE FAN, THE UNWINDING WHIRL OF THE CABLE

Officials from the State Department of Mines, along with the Vice-President of the Grant southern district, M.L. Blanchard, arrived overnight. They all reported to the superintendent's office where they stayed in touch with the rescue operation. Other state officials and a state congressman arrived and were directed to that office. Pinkerton security forces were hired to guard this office. Some guards roamed the grounds acting as the eyes and ears of the officials. To accommodate the needs of this expanding group, the district superintendent J.P. Whittaker requested a railroad dining car to be sent from Pittsburgh to a spur behind the Union Supply Company Store. Once this car arrived the officials could transfer their "office" from the cramped, stuffy room to the larger more elaborate and comfortable accommodations.

THE CAGE CONTINUED IT'S SLOW DESCENT

The morning sunrise gave way to a partly cloudy morning, accompanied now with a warm breeze to help move the hanging clouds along. An isolated dark cloud hovered directly over Ridge Valley where it released a smattering of sprinkles. The families in the tents centered their total attention on the cable, checking every inch as it departed the wheel, allowing the cage to fall.

The rescue team accepted the fact that they were riding the cage down to save trapped fellow miners, anxious with a confidant excitement to get there, retrieve the trapped men and bring them out alive. The workers who fixed the tipple, cage and fan continually checked their repairs, ready to act should a problem occur. The hoist man maintained the constant pace of the cable.

LOWER AND LOWER, ALMOST THERE

A hush came over the crowd as they anticipated the cage soon reaching the bottom. The fan hummed on, helped with twelve pairs of eyes glued to a troublesome belt running from the motor to the fan axle. For now the fan was moving in a smooth and effortless manner. They dropped, continuing lower and lower, soon to cover the six hundred twenty-six feet to the bottom.

"Mom, looks like she's slowing down, means it should hit bottom soon," said John.

"Thank God," she murmured, and then added, " maybe you better look to Hanna and Joanna and if they're awake bring them here. If not, let them rest."

John left his mom and walked to the back of the tent where cots housed the girls. Seeing them asleep, he arranged blankets and started to return to his mom.

"John."

"Oh, hi Bull"

"John. Looks like we'll hear something soon. Listen, I saw Corky a while ago and he told me that Jerry's dad was working and in the mine yesterday. He said Jerry thought his dad was helping with the rescue since he had not seen him, but word is he was in the mine working yesterday morning. Have you seen Jerry lately?" asked Bull

John listened intently, not knowing what to say. He had his own things to think about. He looked around the tent to find Jerry. He noticed Jerry's family at the far end of the tent but no Jerry in sight.

"No, I haven't seen him for a while I'll look for him later, got to get back to my mom for now, for Jerry's sake I hope it isn't so."

As John walked back to his mom's location, some in the crowd pointed up toward the top of the tipple.

"The cable stopped," one person shouted and others soon joined in by pointing and shouting in unison. "The wheel stopped, the wheel stopped!"

John hearing this looked up and seeing the cable stopped, silently prayed for his dad, the rescue team and another he added to the list, Jerry's dad.

THE RESCUE TEAM ARRIVED AT THE BOTTOM

The last few yards of the trip down crawled along to a stop. The men noticed a drastic change in the odor coming from the haulage. A putrid stench like the smell of rotting fish caused a gagging sensation from some in the crew.

"Let's tie up," said Mike Christian.

The crew obeyed by grabbing a section of a long rope and tying it to their belt. This move connected all of the rescue crew together. They now moved as one in the darkened shaft.

"Air tastes sour, bad, real bad, how's the canary?" asked Mike.

" Doing fine, not as lively as before, but doing okay. Air smells bad, but it's not toxic and we have a blockage somewhere, but not a total one," said Tom.

Mike heaved up the gate and stepped off the cage. He started walking to the main haulage with the crew. The haulage following the coal seam made a slight curve about forty yards from the cage. Three members of the rescue team joined Mike at the front, carbide lamps burning, lighting the way as they moved slowly forward. Tom watched the canary closely for any indication of a change in its activity. Mike took the lead in "sounding the roof" as they moved along. He tapped the ceiling with a long stick listening for a solid sound, then moving forward repeating the process. Smoke from carbide lamps sizzled, the fishy odor became stronger, the taste of the mine bitter

Thump, thump, thump. Mike pounded the roof, and the men moved on. There were no support timber and the walls' ribs were as smooth as glass to the touch.

Approaching the curve they all noticed something was amiss ahead; getting closer it became obvious there was some type of blockage and the odor became more abusive and their euphoria of a positive rescue began to fade. The free passage into the depths of the mine would certainly be delayed. Mike reached the curve with Tom and two others first. A lattice-like wall met the group. There were tiny openings to allow air to pass through but nothing large enough for a man to get past.

"Let's give it a good look," said Mike.

The lattice-like structure started when the force of the explosion picked up the car rails and drove them deep into the ribs and roof of the haulage at the curve. More and more rails collected at that spot, adding strength to the structure. Along had come pit cars, cement blocks, timber and more rails, gathered in the maze like insects caught in a spider web. Anything or anyone caught in the fury of the moving wall of fire was vulnerable to the forces. The power, strength and energy of the blast gathered all in its path. What it did not blow up the shaft it deposited in the web.

Tolerating the stench, the crew searched the structure for openings large enough for a man to get through. They worked in teams of three and together concentrated the lamps in one spot at a time for better lighting.

"Air tastes awful, really bad."

"Yeah, sure does, not letting up either."

The teams moved along the lattice wall as the air whistled through bringing with it the ever-present foul smell. Some began to choke and cough from constant exposure to the stink. Others complained of watery eyes, but Tom assured all the air was breathable.

"Any large openings?" asked Mike.

"None found here."

"No not here."

"Mike, Mike, come here and hurry," yelled one of the rescuers.

"Mike over here, over here Mike," shouted a voice from a different location.

Mike hurried to the first call.

"Look Mike, over here and there, look"

Men were bending over while others knelt straining to see through the small openings. The answer to the putrid odor they encountered came in a sudden frightful shock. Even the veterans of rescue work, coughing and choking stared in disbelief. Others were frozen in place unbelieving. The toxic carbide taste, along with the stench of rotting flesh, the fried guts spilling from blown bloated human stomachs caused some men to turn away from the sight. Those who could stand the scene viewed a smattering of brains seeping from a split skull and entrails oozing from a bowel A head here, an arm there, a leg, human parts scattered about, many burnt as black as midnight.

"That looks like a mask, dark as Halloween, a skull with hollow eyes. My God, was that a living walking man yesterday?" said one of the crew.

"Looks like they were dropped into a searing oven."

The men gazed with dismay at the sight, mumbling to themselves, unbelieving, a sight so gruesome it would be etched into their brain for an eternity. Mangled bodies were wedged in with the pile of debris. There were black bloated bodies, slivers of wood imbedded into an abdomen, a hat welded to a skull, eye sockets gouged out and faces blown away.

"Could anyone have survived this inferno?" asked Mike.

"Appears impossible to me," answered a crewmember. "How are we to know who they are? Just no way, only God knows."

"Do you think they knew what hit them, could they feel what was coming?"

"Yes, I think they knew they were in trouble, seems they got away from the work stations, probably trying to get to the cage, and didn't have a chance."

The rescue team had more questions than answers as to what to do next. No openings were found but the big question now was how to handle the blockage with its human parts.

"Have any of you ever seen anything like this?" asked Mike

"No never, me neither," a shake of the head from side to side, came the answers.

"Listen, based on this, this sight, and what you see, do any of you believe that this represents the total number missing, or could there be some elsewhere in the mine?"

"Doesn't appear that survival is possible and I have never, never seen anything like this, yet it may be possible. The heat that built up, along with the tremendous force generated with that heat had to develop way, way back in the mine and build in intensity as it traveled up the haulage. It started in a flash and ended in a flash," said Tom.

"We know that the fan went down, I wonder how long it was between the fan stopping and the explosion?" asked Mike who continued, "Would a group anticipate they were in trouble and brattice themselves in somewhere? Could the force of the blast pass them by and are they waiting for us?"

"The only hope I see is if they moved toward the air shaft instead of to the cage, and if the direction of the blast traveled this way, like a path of least resistance. Then and only then would anyone have a chance? They could survive on air from the intake shaft even though the fan was down. That's the only thing I can think of," stated Paul.

"We can talk and surmise about things, but we've got to attack this obstruction and go beyond to check out the rest of the mine. How do we handle the body parts? Should we ask a priest or minister on that, and what about bodies, how do we identify them?" asked Mike.

"We got to make a decision and move on this," said Tom.

They all looked at Mike for the answer and he responded. "Okay here is what I see. Regardless of the human remains, we must assume that there are others alive back in the mine waiting to be rescued. We must clear an opening and proceed into the mine as quickly as possible. First, we need an experienced welder to cut the rails. Look, we have thirty-eight unaccounted for, and in my mind I don't believe they are all here in this pile. There has to be more beyond this stoppage, alive or dead we attack this pile, now. You boys see what you can do with this blockage, find a place to start, I need to go top side."

"We'll do what we can, Mike."

"All right, I'll go up and report our findings to Tom Johnson and get welders down here and prepare for other teams to relieve this crew. Get a system going; get fresh people down as often as possible. I was hoping to have better news for the people up there," said Mike.

Ridge Valley

"Mike, maybe the good news lies ahead," said Tom

With that Mike moved toward the cage. Those remaining crewmembers would attack the pile, as it was now called, to begin the task of rescue or recovery. Mike reached the cage and belled for the hoist man to bring him up to the surface. The bull wheels began to collect the cable. An ominous quiet settled over the huge crowd. The whirl of the motor collecting the cable was loud and captured the attention of the families. They all watched and waited. The cage arrived, finding the emotions of the tent people at the bursting point. A man emerged and began walking to the office.

"His name is Mike Christian; he is the leader of the rescue crew. He came up awful fast, wasn't down there very long," said John.

"Wonder what he found, John?" asked his mom.

John shrugged his shoulders in a "don't know" gesture as he watched Mike Christian move across the compound.

"What's the situation Mike?" asked the hoist man.

"Some blockage, need a couple hours work to get through."

Others along the path to the superintendent's office asked similar questions of Mike who moved along, only stopping to tell rescue members he recognized to report to the meeting room. After completing his report to Tim he reported directly to the meeting room.

"There is an obstruction across the haulage, substantial enough so that a man cannot pass through. The team is clearing as much debris from the pile as they can. Then, to get through we will need welders to cut the rails that are imbedded in the roof and ribs. It looks clear beyond the curve where the snag is located." Said Mike Christian.

"How long you think, Mike?"

"Find anyone?"

"No, but, he paused to collect his thoughts, "Well we found some miners who got caught in the blast." He went on to describe the devastation and about finding human remains in the pile. "There is always hope that others may have survived and are alive. We decided to be as careful as possible in clearing the pile but move ahead. We must do all we can to get through. I want to warn all of you that it will be tough down there, and I want crews relieved every hour. Lastly, we don't want any unfounded rumors, and until we know the fate of all, lets keep things to ourselves. That's it, let's move, be careful and God Bless."

John was now a fixture at the meetings with no one challenging his presence. He was stunned at what he heard; he sat by himself in a corner seat in the room, thinking what he should say to his mom who was waiting for his return back at the tent.

"They have some blockage to clear away, about two three hours work. They also think that if the men barricaded themselves near an air shaft they could survive," John told his mom with Dolly and others listening.

"How can they do this, I mean block themselves?" asked Dolly.

A retired miner who listened to the question said, "They can do it."

"How?" asked Dolly

The old man came to volunteer his service to the rescue. He was politely turned away so he decided to stay around just in case they change their minds. He coughed and wheezed as he began talking to the group gathered around him.

"I've got to tell you that miners know the place where they work, and how to handle any problem that comes their way," said the old miner. He talked as he hacked phlegm into a dirty rag. He was toothpick thin and the clothes he wore were two sizes too large. His voice was raspy and just above a whisper; probably from all the coal dust and carbide fumes he ate in the years spent digging coal.

"They got cement blocks, brattice board and canvas to use to close themselves in. They can stay there, conserve energy, and wait. The important thing is to have patience and trust in the rescue workers. I don't know all the facts, but I do know miners do not give up on fellow diggers." The talking loosened phlegm he coughed up; now hacking hard the old miner retreated to the back of the tent.

The old miner gave John's mom and Dolly new hope. John decided to leave the tent since he knew about the burnt and dismembered bodies. He did not tell his mom about what he knew. He did not want to give any indication of the real problems facing the rescue teams. He did not want to take any hope of recovery away from his mom. He decided to find Jerry.

He walked around the mine complex, inside the lamp house, blacksmith shop, the canteen, but did not locate him. Checking behind the tipple he saw him, sitting halfway up the slate dump.

"Hi John."

"Hi Jerry," John answered breathing heavy from the climb.

"You heard didn't you?"

"Yes Jer I did, and I'm sorry. Glad I found you, I wanted to get away from down there myself, and thought about seeing you, so here I am."

"John, I found my dad's check number was still up, and talked to my mom. She said he was working an extra shift to help a buddy." Jerry sobbed.

"Jerry, listen, I decided to take my mom's attitude, and that is to think positive thoughts until facts tell you otherwise. You've got to believe he will make it. There is no other way, and think of your family; you have to keep up their spirit. They need you more than ever now, listen, they will make it, and they WILL make it."

Jerry sat speechless so John sat with him, halfway up the slate dump, away from the crowd below. They sat for ten, fifteen minutes in silence, John waiting, biding his time until Jerry was ready to talk. Finally Jerry opened up and the two talked about everything related to family and friends. They both reminisced about the past, helping each other to accept as much of the present situation as possible and promised to always be friends. They finally felt that it was time to return to the tent.

They returned to the mineshaft to find the rescue operation settled down to an organized activity, replacing the frenzied bustle earlier in the day. The newspaper reporters, sheriff deputies, security personnel, rescuers, people in tents and volunteers from the Red Cross and Salvation Army continued as part of the scene.

The word came by late afternoon that a breakthrough was made. Members of the rescue team made their way, beyond the pile further into the mine where they found more burnt bodies. The inspection of the entire mine was completed and the findings reported to Tim Johnson.

"Found a total of twenty-seven complete bodies, some missing body parts. Many disfigured and burned black beyond description.

Bob Menarcheck

None were found alive, all lost," said Mike Christian who ended the report with his face buried in his hands.

"Mike, you're certain that the entire mine was inspected, all the way to the air shaft, every section and every coal facing? You said no one alive, what about damage?

"We scoured the entire mine, Tim. No one survived. This explosion was devastating. The force of the blast was so great it took down every timber support, every roof support and blew four-ton coal cars along the entire haulage and imbedded them into the pile. Tim, the incredible, unbelievable sight of rails picked up like tooth picks and deposited into the roof, ribs and floor is hard to fathom. The searing heat smoothed out the sides, roof and floor to feel like polished glass. The ribs have a shine to them when a light is cast on it. Amazingly, there were no roof falls."

"Julius, for the time being we will post on the message board that a breakthrough was made and we are now proceeding to thoroughly inspect all sections. Once we are certain of our findings the families will be notified. Mike, I know how thorough you are and I hope you understand that I want the mine canvassed one more time. This will also give us time to plan on how to notify the families."

"I understand," said Mike.

John and Jerry checked the message board where a buzz about the breakthrough was posted. They joined their families in the tent where all were ecstatic with excitement about the news, save one, John's mom.

"Finally God's answer will be known and his decision will be accepted…he has always provided, and I trust will again," she said in a calm soothing voice as she went back to saying the rosary.

"Where are the girls? They aren't in the back of the tent," John interrupted.

"Mrs. Dorek had to go home so I asked her to take the girls and your brother to the Fitzmorris house to stay until we get home. I thought it best for them to be with friends and have a place to rest.

"Don't worry, the girls are delivered and your brother is fine," said Dolly, who had just returned.

"Going over to the message board, just to check it, be back," said John

Ridge Valley

Dolly's emotions were spent as she waited for news the last two days, and now that an answer was near she accepted the attitude of Mrs. Ignatius who became a calming presence. She felt at ease talking to John's mom who comforted her with a reassuring positive attitude. They had talked often the last two days. Dolly spoke about farming, her family, her fears and her husband. Mrs. Ignatius talked about her God, and her family. Once again Mrs. Ignatius was talking and it centered on John.

"He is a good person, John I mean, actually you have a young man who seems to be helpful and considerate…one you can trust and depend on," said Dolly.

"We have four children to spend our life with. My husband is a good man he works hard. He thinks that John is close to the age when he should begin working; well I never disagree with my husband, except for this. He wants John to work; I say he goes to school. John is a smart boy, and God willing he will get his chance." She stopped talking, a tear came to her eyes; she looked straight down to the floor, lifted up the bottom of her dress, turned it inside out and lifted the cloth to her face, and wiped wet cheeks. Now it was Dolly consoling her new friend.

'You told me many times to have faith, and I do. They'll get out and I believe that and my husband will get out too. We must trust in God, and have faith like you always said."

"My dear, you are right but you know death and injuries are both a constant companion with every family in the patch. I never expected it to be me. You think it always happens to someone else, now it's me, and I only fear for my family. If you don't mind, I'd like to get back to my rosary."

"Yes, please go ahead. Excuse me, I see someone who may have some information, I'll be back." Dolly left Mrs. Ignatius to go speak to Tony who was at the canteen.

"Mr. Baritone, we heard there was a breakthrough and have heard nothing more. Have you any information you could tell me?" asked Dolly.

"Sorry to say this but the rescue teams don't show that they have good news. I can tell by the way they look and they don't look like they have good news," said a man standing near who heard the question. Dolly turned in shock.

"Don't listen to him. Listen, Mister, you don't know nothing," said Tony.

"Does he know what he is saying, Tony?" asked Dolly.

"I think he's been drinking, it's the booze talking, forget what he said."

"I'm going back to the tent, Tony. Please let me know if you hear anything."

"Did you get any news?" asked Mrs. Ignatius on Dolly's return.

"Nothing worth talking about, no real news, just hearsay is all," Dolly said.

Another hour would pass as the two sat and talked. John brought some soup, bread and coffee they accepted. The evening turned to dusk as the afternoon shadows stretched to the east. The mine superintendent sent Julius to the message board to post a notice stating that all medical personnel were to report to the meeting room immediately. John sat in the back corner, a place he had occupied at previous meetings.

Mr. Johnson did not delay but went straight to the news.

"The mine was thoroughly inspected twice and all thirty-eight in the mine at the time of the blast are lost. You all are to prepare for a recovery of bodies and body parts. You are required and must record exact locations of where and what is found. Please bring all bodies or body parts to the back shop area for family identification."

John could not move from the spot; he sat silently pondering. He felt sure that his mom knew the outcome and he should go to the tent and be with her. He would tell her and confirm the loss.

"Mom, at the meeting, medical people were called in and they confirmed that all are lost." Tears ran down her cheeks as son and mother embraced.

Dolly sat, stunned, speechless, and looked into space, bending over, seemingly in pain. Holding her stomach with both hands she sobbed, shaking, saying over and over, "God no, God, no."

Everyone in the tent joined her in expressing their grief by crying, wailing the names of the men shouting things like, "He was a good man, why, why?"

"Mom, I may as well tell you now, the explosion was so fierce and hot it burned the men bad, real bad." John could not go on, he choked back tears and embraced his mom holding on for a long time.

She released him from their embrace; she understood the need now to help him relieve the awesome pressure he faced as the man of the family. Her full attention would now be on John and his siblings. She took him by the shoulders with both hands, looked him in the face and said in a comforting voice, "John for better or worse, I will take your father regardless of his condition. I will remember him as a strong man who was good to us, for we must remember the good, always. Your father would want you to be strong, and we must for the sake of the girls and your brother."

She hugged him and he hugged back, "I'll try hard, mom I'll try."

They sat for a time in silence thinking, remembering the good times with dad and silently praying.

Darkness was at hand when Tim Johnson the superintendent walked into the tent. He first expressed his sorrow then announced that later in the evening the remains of all family members would be placed in the back shop area. Once that was done they would be permitted to enter and identify family members. He then proceeded to read the names of the few they identified and continued with names of those who had checks remaining on the board in the lamp house.

"John, I must attend to Mrs. Dorek. As much as we are hurting I'm certain it is worse for her and she is alone. No one should be alone at a time like this." She moved over to comfort Dolly. John would later join his mom along with all the families who must identify the burnt black bodies and then prepare them for burial.

"Once we find him I'll be sitting with him a spell, I need to talk to him. You are welcome to remain for a while. I believe you know I need to be alone with him."

"I'll stay for a short time," John said.

Mrs. Mullin got word about the recovery of bodies while at home and decided to return to the tent at the mine. She wanted to be with Dolly, knowing her plight, and accompany her to the makeshift morgue. She heard the news about the number of missing from her husband and the names of those lost or unaccounted for. Until Mrs.

Mullin arrived at the tent the only person Dolly knew besides the Ignatius family was Tony. She needed someone to grieve to, and Tony was that person. He was at the site for other reasons, but soon found himself comforting the young pretty widow he vowed to see in the future. He did his best to sooth her loss but lacked the fortitude to view bodies in the morgue. For this, he turned her over to Mrs. Mullin.

The presentation of the dead mortal souls was like opening up the gates of hell. Burnt, disfigured bodies looked like a poorly done partial cremation. It was a scene of dead mangled dismembered bodies that would haunt forever those who entered the room. John prepared himself by asking God for strength, not only for himself but also for his mom, and Dolly. He vowed to be at his mom's side and support her until she gave the word to be alone with her husband. The families initially rushed the morgue area. They soon stopped in dismay and shock. They began walking among the holocaust, many in a daze. John and his mom looked and looked. She then abruptly stopped. She had found her man. John stood for a moment in shock and amazement at the sight. He secured a chair for her, knelt at her side for a period of time, hearing the wailing and screaming of the women. He was sick, devastated, breathing fast with a heart running wild. He would vomit if he had something in his stomach. He was lightheaded, feeling he was going to pass out. He held on, and suddenly, as if his mom knew his state of mind, she gave him the word that she now wanted to be alone with her man and he could leave. He kissed her on the forehead, looked one last time at the burnt body, gave her another kiss, and left the room.

The fresh early evening breeze was a welcome relief to John. He walked with no destination in mind. Rescue workers, newspapermen, and security personnel lingered, along with miners waiting to assist the widows of their downed fellow diggers. He wanted to get out of sight of the pit so he walked alone in the direction of the junk graveyard. Thoughts swirled like a whirlpool in his brain as he tried to understand the happenings of the past two days. He tried to put things in order as he stopped to view the tipple, lamp house and tent where he spent many hours the past two days. He wandered about until he found himself at the railroad bridge and decided to sit down on the rails directly above the creek. He looked into the running water, tears welling in his eyes.

"I can't remember what he looks like, my God, please help me. Why did he have to end up burned? Black as the coal he mined, why this way?"

"Whatcha doing, John? " asked Jerry.

John did not answer, for he was in such a state of concentration on his father that it blocked everything else from his mind. He was so within himself he did not hear Jerry.

"John," said Jerry again. Not getting an answer, he placed his hand on John's shoulder, shook it and asked again, " Whatcha doin, John?"

John, startled, jumped up from his sitting position, tripping backwards. He reached for Jerry, getting a grip on his arm, a move that prevented him from falling. The quick action surprised Jerry who apologized immediately. It took John a few seconds to compose himself from the deep focus on his father. John looked wide-eyed at Jerry, hesitated for a moment then acknowledged him with, "Oh Jer, sorry I just didn't see you."

"What you doing here Jer? I had to get away and do some thinking about things, so what brings you over here?" asked John, who recovered from the shock.

"I was a' going home, my ma is staying with my dad, she would not leave his side. People are trying to get her away, but she refuses to move. She's a' going to stay, she keeps saying she wants to be sure, told me to go home for a spell and to come back later, so here I am."

"What things does she want to be sure of?" asked John.

"Well," Jerry hesitated, "she wants to make sure he is who he is, says the body in front of her is hers and no one is going to say otherwise, so she's staying to protect what is hers."

"You sound like you're not sure that the person your mom is with is your father, and others are saying it is someone else, is that right?" quizzed John.

"Yeah, I guess that's what I'm saying. I want to believe it is him, it looks like him, but he's all busted up and burnt," cried Jerry who added, "I only hope he died quick."

"It happened so fast that I doubt they felt anything," said John as he sat again on the track. Jerry joined him. They both sat in silence, both friends thinking about the uncertainty of the body identification.

"Seems like my mind is in some one else's body, Jer. I mean, can you believe that in this short time, like two days," gesturing and pointing back to the mine, "all this happening to us? I mean the storm, an explosion, and people from everywhere, rescue workers helping, for nothing. All lost, all gone, the mourning will go on forever because families don't really know if the dead person is theirs, they will never forget this day. I know I won't."

"John," said Jerry in a low voice, "John can I ask yeah something?"

"Sure, what is it?"

"John, there is something else I mean how are you sure the one your mom is sitting with was your dad? John, how did you know?"

John hesitated and looked at Jerry who in turn looked away, allowing John to gaze down into the flowing creek. Talking to the creek not Jerry, he answered," It's his hands, I recognize his hands without doubt, for one was only partially burned and that helped, so no doubt it is him."

The water made a gurgling sound as it passed under the bridge and over rocks, around boulders, then to the sharp muddy turn. For some reason John wondered where the water came from. The water always flowed in a steady pace all day and night; he'd never known it to stop. *"We humans live and eventually die but not this creek, it goes on forever."*

"John, when we used to talk in catechism class I remember it being said that when your time is up it's up. Does that mean God has a plan for us and no matter what happens the plan is set for us to follow? Does that plan have choices like going down the shaft, even though I don't want to? I mean I don't want no part of going down into the pit, I'm scared to death of that, but if the plan is made, then do I have a choice or not?"

"Have to put some deep thought into that one, Jer. I just don't know."

John found solace watching the water flow by as Jerry fidgeted. "God's plan or not," John thought, "not many choices available. We got our family, the house, the patch, the company store and the mine. Is it God's will, or is it fate, or just pure happenstance to be in this place, at this time? Regardless of the circumstances, the real choices are limited to only one, and that one is spelled out for me now…the mine."

Jerry broke into John's thoughts by saying, "I've got to go back, John, to sit with my mom, and, well, if she is sure then I'm sure."

John got up from the tracks and took a step to leave.

"John, one more thing before you go."

"Yeah, what Jer?"

"How many bodies did you see?"

"I don't know the exact number," answered John not wanting to recall the gruesome task again. "I remember the priest coming over to take my mom into the area and the shocked look on her face. I'll never get out of my mind the women and children, yes children, Jer, walking the rows of dead bloated burnt corpses. They all were looking for some type of identification, no, too small, over there, families not knowing, running from here to there looking, no, then off to look at another."

"I think about Mrs. Kolinsky, never forget her, Jerry, as long as I live, because, well here she is, trampling along with four, imagine four little girls, holding two, one in each arm and one on each side of her hanging on to her dress She kept saying, while trudging along with these girls, "He will come back to her, he is not here," then, then, Jer out of the blue one of the girls holding on to the dress, let go and pointed to a body and said,"Daddy, there's daddy." "No!" she shouted, "no," as she dropped to her knees, and with all watching she tried to lift the body, and, couldn't because when she grabbed him, the black skin peeled from his back to his belly."

John stopped talking, he swallowed hard, Jerry wide-eyed speechless; finally John asked, "How's she going to survive with all girls? Finally some ladies from her church came over to help her and the girls leave the area. Other women wailed and cried as they circled the bodies, children sobbing, running after their mothers, not sure what was happening. Wives of husbands lost in the explosion searching and when finding what they know is theirs, claim the corpse and stay refusing to move."

"John, one reason I asked about bodies is, well it seems to me there is more people looking than bodies available," said Jerry

"You're right, you know I attended a lot of meetings and heard a lot of things. One was what you are saying, that many will not be identified and that, and that some may not have anything to recover."

"I'm positive, definitely positive it is him, no doubt in my mind," Jerry said.

"I know I'm sure also, and that's good you're sure. You know that not finding yours among the dead causes a person to get a bit crazed wondering if they're still alive somewhere. There will be a lot of dismal days ahead for these finding their loved ones body, but no doubt that many days will by truly dark and fretful, a nightmare for those not recovering anything."

Jerry got up from the rail, brushed the back of his pants and said, " I'm going back. I have to go back. I'm sure but I have to go back," Jerry turned with a jerk and started to walk back to the shaft and the makeshift morgue.

John stood and watched Jerry walk toward the mine. Jerry was well on his way when John turned in the opposite direction and walked across the bridge, then up the railroad tracks a short distance to the dirt road that lead to the company store. Before entering the hill on the dirt road, John paused and turned with a bowed head said, "I hope you're sure Jerry, I really do."

John continued walking up the hill, following the road to the Company Store where he would take the cutoff then proceed to his home. He advanced a short way, when he saw two railroad cars parked below on a spur of tracks below the Company Store. He never saw railroad cars like these before, "Real fancy," he thought. As he moved further up the road he could see through the windows of the cars. "Wow!" he said out loud.

Well- dressed men were sitting at tables, being served food and drinks by white clad servers in tall white hats. He recognized the men, he saw them at the pit, dressed in suits but without their fedora hats; standing in the back of the car, arms folded, observing the group. The men being served must be big shots from Pittsburgh he guessed. "They come, they observe, then they leave. What kind of feelings do they have to just leave death and destruction behind, leave the poor souls to their misery, not even offering an ounce of sympathy? Here they are within our midst, without offering any assistance, amazing they could help immensely, but don't and won't." A locomotive came rolling down the track, stopped and began to back into the spur.

"Looks like they'll be leaving soon," thought John.

John arrived home for the first time in two days. Clothes that were hanging on the lines on Monday were torn and shattered, but still there. They were damaged severely from the sleet and hail. Clothes props either fell or were knocked away from the line by the storm. The damaged clothes, hung limply, straining the rope. He walked inside the house, splashed water on his face, and moved to the stove to start a fire. He saw loaves of bread, still in the pan, sitting on the table. He would take care of removing the loaves from the pans and wrapping them in towels. Feeling the urge, he climbed the back steps, got half way to the outhouse where he stopped in his tracks. Leaves of plants shredded, vegetables pitted from hail, nothing in the garden appeared salvageable to make his favorite winter snack. That was the final blow for he now felt very, very tired. His legs felt heavy as he shuffled up the path, entered the outhouse, relieved himself, left and refused to look at the garden on his way back to the house.

John, entered the house checked the upstairs rooms, returned to the kitchen where he stoked the stove, folded the good clothes he found as best he could, then washed himself at the sink. The washing refreshed him. He decided to boil some water for coffee and to enjoy a slice of homemade bread with butter. His mouth watered at the thought.

Dusk was turning into evening as John felt alone and lonely. He was by himself and all of a sudden felt uncomfortable He did not like the feeling. Surely his mom felt the same, probably worse.

"I've got to go back, no one should be alone at a time like this." He checked the fire in the stove, wiped the table, covered the bread and exited the door.

CHAPTER III

HENRY CLAY GRANT, became a millionaire by first taking control of the Connellsville Coal Fields, and established the H. C. Grant Coal and Coke Company, in the early eighteen seventy's. The coal mined was ideal for producing the finest metallurgical coke that was vital to the steel making industry. In a large beehive style oven, the bituminous coal was "baked" for two or three days at about two thousand degrees. This produced a yield of two-thirds ton of coke from one ton of coal. The resulting product was nearly pure carbon and in great demand. Grant through many shrewd moves eventually owned 41,000 acres of land, 43 mines and 10,148 coke ovens.

Needless to say that the coal mining and coke production was labor intensive requiring thousands of workers. Because coal mining, coke production and steel making were closely linked, it led to an intimate association between Grant and Andrew Carnegie, owner of large steel making facilities in Pittsburgh. Their association became a partnership with Grant emerging in 1881 as the director in charge of Carnegie steel operations. Grant's ruthless anti-union stand against the Amalgamated Association of Iron and Steel workers resulted in a clash of wills in 1892 at a steel making plant called Homestead.

Grant's resolve to break the steel worker's union began when, after failed negotiations he "locked out" workers. A strike was called and thus began one of the most serious labor disputes in United States History. Grant hired private security guards and planned on getting them past strikers and on to plant property. The strikers resisted and violence erupted resulting in men being killed on both sides. To break the strike "scabs" were hired to work and live on plant grounds. An incident that brought national attention to the Homestead situation occurred when a man entered Grant's office, shot him twice, and stabbed him twice. Grant survived. The strike slowly evaporated, the union became disorganized and finally disintegrated as workers on a wholesale basis crossed the picket lines. Grant succeeded in busting the union.

Around nineteen hundred Grant was prominent in negotiating with the Barons of industry to form the United States Steel Company, America's first billion-dollar conglomerate. This merger included the Grant coal and coke works as a subsidiary to the U.S. Steel and netted him a profit that rose into the sixty million dollar bracket. The Company name, remained as he continued to serve as the Director of U.S. Steel until 1905 when he began shifting his social life between Pittsburgh and New York.

Finally in nineteen twelve, he left to live permanently in New York City. There H. C. and his wife pursued a life of luxury, capped off by travels to Europe and Asia to seek and purchase expensive art, sculpture and jewels. When in New York his time was spent attending opera, lounging at high-class restaurants and always in the pursuit of art, especially by the masters. His travels led to purchasing some of the most distinguished, priceless collections. He possessed masterpieces by Rembrandt, El Greco, Bellini and Whistler and housed them in his mansion.

He continued to live in opulence in New York but never quenched his thirst for having to know about occurrences in the U. S. Steel conglomerate. Mr. Grant could not fully let go of following events in the mills, mines and ovens. He was confident in and relaxed his vigilance when Thomas Lynch became the director of the H. C. Grant Coke Company in 1912. Mr. Lynch worked his way up from a common laborer to the top position. He understood all facets of mining, and was recognized for emphasizing a safety first campaign during his tenor. Mr. Lynch died unexpectantly in December 1914.

W. H. Clingerman followed Thomas Lynch in the leadership role at a time when World War I was heating up in Europe. The war developed a strong need for steel to build ships, tanks, armament, munitions and artillery weapons. Here at home unfilled orders for steel to make rails, railroad cars and locomotives were pressing the need for more coal and coke. With orders pouring in, and to meet the demand, more coke ovens and mine openings were essential. The need for workers to operate the added operations was imminent. The problem facing the Connellsville coke region was that the source for supplying workers to the field was curtailed because of happenings in Europe. To solve the dilemma young boys were permitted to enter and work in the pits. This arrangement lasted until the United States became totally involved in the war, and the call to enter the army was made. The many foreigners, along with American workers who worked the pits and coke ovens, joined the armed forces. Many recent Immigrants working the mines returned to Europe to fight for their motherland. The laborers were not replaced and this loss cut heavily into the Grant workforce at a time when they were needed the most.

H. C. failed to accept this for in his time someone was always available to take the place of the injured or fallen. To add to this dilemma, the coal and coke operations lost their recruiting territory since Europe was now closed to labor agents. Mr. Grant was never informed of this problem, and became highly perplexed and frustrated at the failure of his subordinates to solve the labor situation. After all, prices were skyrocketing and with the exceptional profit in every ton of steel sold, the need for more and more production was growing. The labor situation continued in disarray, not only during, but also after the war ended. This lack of manpower lowered the production and cut into the profits for the H. C. Grant Company and the U. S. Steel Corporation.

H. C. Grant became one of the industrial barons of his time. He was adamant, when running his company to have dictatorial control and to make money, more and more money on the backs of workers. He did just that, and then retired to New York, but he never let go.

Finally in the fall of 1919 he telegraphed the Head of U.S. Steel stating that he was highly concerned with the severe negative direction the coal and coke production was taking after the war. He felt that the man now running the mining and coke operations, namely a Mr. J.P.Hayes, was not succeeding in producing the coal and coke products they needed to meet demands. Something had to be done. This on going problem cut deeply into profit. The " King of Coal" as Mr. Grant was called, instructed the Director of U. S. Steel that the time had come to seek a solution to the problems in the Connellsville Coke region.

He demanded that the Director assign an official to find out what is causing the lack of production. We've added new coke ovens, and mineshafts but are not producing enough coke to keep up with demand. "They keep saying the problem lies in the fact that there is a shortage of workers. I don't understand nor do I accept those excuses. The war is over so men should be available for work. I suggest that you check on the entire operation, and take the steps needed, particularly personnel adjustments."

And so it was that at sixty-nine years old H. C. Grant secretly made the demand of the Director of United States Steel to take the step and solve the manpower numbers. "There is an answer, there always is, so take the next step and find that answer."

"TAKE THE STEP, take the next step," played on Mr. Grant's mind. He heard these words before, many years ago. He reminisced about days in Pittsburgh when he recalled often looking down from his fifth floor office window to observe the traffic moving along Fifth Avenue. In his mind, although blurred from his advanced years, he followed the movement of cars making their way up the street until they came to the intersection of Fifth and Avondale. He smiled vaguely remembering Avondale Lane, a unique street with its ornate streetlights and brick lined roadway leading up Knob Hill to the Overholt mansion that sat on the very top of the heights.

"Yes, I do believe, wait its been so many years, hard to remember. Yes, I believe it was at the Overholt's home, there standing in its magnificence," he said to himself.

"Take the step," he mumbled, recalling the time and place where he heard these words. He smiled as his mind drifted from the review of accounting forms and manpower reports to the evening that was the beginning of his empire. He grinned and shook his head, "having a hard time remembering," he mumbled, as he reflected on the one special evening at the mansion. Then recalling the many positions he held as he rose quickly in various stages of production at his uncle Overholt's Whiskey Distillery. Always a precise individual, so precise and exacting, for example, he knew to the second what should be happening at all times during the distilling process. His intense demands for perfection from the employees angered the workers who resented a young nineteen-year-old nephew of the owner telling them what to do and when to do it.

Eventually the word about the intrusions into processing procedures this young buck changed reached his Mr. Overholt. The workers who were involved with the whiskey making process for years, threatened to quit if this young nephew continued his interference into their domain. The owner was forced to investigate the complaints by the men and discovered that the exact measurements suggested by this young manager, instead of the "doing by feel or what we think method" resulted in a consistently better tasting product. He moved the foreman of the distilling department to another job and, to the chagrin of workers in the distillery, placed H. C. in charge. Henry Clay immediately instituted the, "do as I say or I will get another who will" attitude. A young, cocky, brash dictator was now in charge of a department of men who despised his presence. H. C. would not be in that department long. He pressed himself to gain more and more understanding about the overall operation of the plant. This young man continually made suggestions and offered ideas for improvement everywhere he went. His uncle, ever mindful of the many proposals that improved the distillery, decided to place H. C. in the chief accounting position, a job that gave this young man a supervisory role. As head of the accounting department, he had total control of production, distribution, purchasing and manpower. His word was law, and he used the profit and loss statements as leverage in important company decisions. He left no stone unturned to distill a consistently good drinking whiskey that reaped profit. He gained power and once in charge ruled with an iron hand, then demanded and got more production from his managers through intimidation. Those under him remained on the job by working more hours, for the same pay, more and more, always seeking more. The managers in turn passed the added labor requirements on to the labor force. H. C. reaped the benefits. He was rewarded handsomely for his efforts with bonus money. The added financial incentives added to his tyrannical methods, and the want for more.

The greed for more was initiated as a plan was devised to pay the employees in script. He then made a deal with a storeowner to have the script used only at that store, and the owner would kick back a certain percentage of sales to the distillery. They both profited from the deal. The workers were held captive in their work and where their script would be accepted. Money, a lot of money was made by both the storeowner and Overholt. A revenue agent from the Federal Government finally put an end to the scheme. H. C. learned a lesson from this venture that would prove to be highly profitable for him in the future. If you control the entire income of a worker: where he lives, works, and spends money for necessities, you reap returned assets over and over.

To reward his young accountant, Mr. Overholt invited his nephew to an evening at his home on Knob Hill. The evening would be one of elegance and would be attended by businessmen, entrepreneurs and bankers, "And I want to have you there, my boy."

The invitation caught H. C. off guard, surprised at the unexpected invitation to such a grandiose party. He said at the time, "Are you certain, sir?" displaying the ornate card.

"Yes indeed young man, you have done well for me, and I appreciate it immensely. This is the least I can do to show my appreciation."

"Well thank you, sir, I look forward to the evening.

He was still mulling over why he should be invited to such a prestigious affair. "After all, Carnegie, Mellon, and the Governor, probably the Mayor of Pittsburgh, and congressmen from Washington and Harrisburg would be in attendance. There would be other notables I'm sure, so why did my uncle feel the need to invite me, his accountant, to his outing?" he wondered.

After a short time pondering H.C. Changed his mind. "I do believe I deserve to be there, yes absolutely, without question, Furthermore, I'll be the youngest in attendance by far. I personally saved the Overholt Distillery thousands of dollars by improving the company from ordering the grain, to a new work process in distilling the whiskey to delivery. The workers know precisely the ingredients and new procedures. They will perform or be released immediately. Anyone can be replaced, and new workers brought in will be trained to our standards. Naturally, the new men receive a lower rate of pay, saving even more. I not only saved money by improving the product, but also organized the distribution beyond the local area to other counties and I'm in the process of extending the territory. Yes, he recognized what I did, and now I believe I deserve a higher pay and I will ask for that raise soon; and get it."

Visualizing the carriage that picked him up at his residence, now turning from Fifth Street on to Avondale Avenue up Knob Hill. The area earned its name from the elegant homes that lined the street. The edifices, built by entrepreneurs, became more expensive and ornate as you proceeded up the grade. It appeared that each new dwelling was intended to dwarf the previous one with expansive grounds, adorned with foliation and surrounded with decorated iron fences. All possessed an adorned, resplendent, florid gate; some so big and covered with decorations they went beyond the beautiful to the gaudy. The lengthy drive from gate to door was lined with brick. Shrubs and overhanging limbs of trees obscured the view from the street, an intended desire of the inhabitants. They wanted their privacy and only those invited to the premises would enter their domain.

He recalled the excitement as the carriage made its way up the hill, taking him to the holiday party that was considered the event of the year hosted by the Overholt's.

The cabbie stopped in front of a decorated closed gate that had a vine-like feature, which started at the bottom and wound its way to a grape and leaf design at the top. Two guards opened the gate and motioned the cabbie through. They checked the invitation and tipped caps as the carriage passed and entered the grounds.

"Certainly didn't expect this."

"I know a lot of movers and shakers will be in this house this evening, and opportunities may be available. I really plan on listening and learning all I can from the best.

The horses clomped around the circle and pulled the carriage behind four others waiting to drop passengers. He finally arrived at the departure point.

He entered an elegant mansion and was stunned by the European furnishings. Tiffany chandeliers and a tile floor cast a shinning brilliance like moonlight on ice. A short distance down the hallway on the right a doorway led to a large dining room. Large circular banquet tables with linen covers, silverware, plates and glasses filled the entire area. Straight ahead, just beyond the dining room door was an extra wide staircase. Two men in their elegance were descending the gold and purple-carpeted stairs.

The reception room is down the hall to your right, please be careful as you descend the stairs."

H. C. moved to the entrance of the reception room. From that position he viewed people mingling, talking, sipping drinks and eating hors d'oeuvres. Waiters, some carrying trays of finger foods, others drinks, were circulating among the guests. Reaching the bottom of the stairs where he was welcomed, a card was handed to a servant, who announced, " Presenting Henry Clay Grant." He walked slowly to the back of the room, slightly bowing his head as a greeting to those he passed. He gazed at the velvet-lined walls, and inlaid ceiling of gold, red and green squares. Velvet drapes matched the gold and maroon carpet. In the east section sat a grand piano on a marble floor. A waiter approached, offering a drink he accepted. While sipping H. C. looked about. He recognized only one person in the room. The man was Jim Stevenson, a retired manager from the distillery. He helped H. C. immensely with his upward transition from one department to another.

Jim, seeing H.C., raised his glass to him. He motioned for him to come over and join them. Henry Clay moved to the Stevenson's location. After pleasantries, the men began discussing distillery business.

"Who is that gentleman over there. The one near the stairs."

Ridge Valley

"Why, that's Henry Clay Grant, who is the controller of my distillery. He performed well beyond expectations. Made me a fair profit in a short period of time, with more to come."

"You sound pleased Sir, tell me more."

"He set up a new accounting system, a new inventory process, cut out a lot of inefficiency. Now wait a minute Andrew, this lad belongs to me," said Mr. Overholt, who realized he had made a huge mistake in bragging about this young man.

" I must ask a favor from you, my good man."

There is an unwritten protocol at gatherings like this to grant a favor to a guest should it be requested. A nod of the head indicated a yes as his answer.

"Would you please arrange for Mr. Grant and his gentleman friend to be seated at my table? A simple request wouldn't you say," smiled Mr. Carnegie.

Mr. Overholt took a puff from his cigar and blew the smoke out slowly. He looked at his guest, knowing he could not deny the request to someone visiting his home. He searched the room to find the master waiter, and when located motioned for him.

"Would you please rearrange the seating order and place the Grant and Stevenson party at table two," said Mr. Overholt. A wry smile of conquest came over the guest's face. "Why did I mention anything about H. C. to him, for without question he will certainly ply for his services," he said to himself. He took another draw on his cigar, and then raised the drink to his lips, and with a quick jerk of the head, downed the remains of the glass.

"Always looking for the good ones," he mumbled as he reached for another drink.

Andrew Carnegie satisfied said to himself, "We'll find out how good a controller this young man is."

Grant and Stevenson accepted their seats without question, thinking that this is the way things are done at dinners like this. They were unaware of the pecking order, while others seated around the room were curious about those seated at the number two table. The meal moved along as Mr. Carnegie asked and H. C. answered. The information garnered by Mr. Carnegie would be registered in his memory for later use. He was impressed, but felt the young man needed some seasoning and experience. H. C. glowed at being the center of attention. This was much better than he dreamed and now he was even more certain than ever before that he deserved to be here.

Mr. Grant walked back to his desk, with the intention of reviewing the stack of information resting there. He instead let his mind drift, thinking, trying to recall the moment back in time, long ago and the billiard room where the men retreated for brandy and cigars after dinner. He would endure the smoke, and to be sociable, carried his drink, never at that point bringing the glass to his lips. Flowing freely, the alcoholic drinks were consumed quickly. The waiters moved in a hurry around the room, collecting empty glasses, and then offering full ones from the trays they carried. Gentlemen gathered in groups and following introductions, began discussing happenings of the day. After consuming a few more drinks the conversation changed. The guests began bragging enthusiastically about their success in not only making money but their roll in making the firm they own prosperous.

H. C. stood to the side of the room near a billiard table. He was alone, observing and listening. He meandered about listening to one group, and then walking over to another, eavesdropping, never offering to join in on the discussions that grew in intensity and loudness as more drink was consumed.

"I appreciate your invitation, sir, the meal was exquisite and the drink, cigars outstanding. Tell me, Sir, how are things at the distillery, and this champagne, is it yours?" asked Mr. Carnegie

"No, my dear man, the wine is from France, where I'm told the finest grapes in the world are grown. I only wish I could duplicate this. You know I deal in hard liquor, Old Overholt it's called and, I may add, the preference of our locals."

"How is that, sir?"

"The drink of choice is a shot of whiskey, followed by a glass of beer. I provide the shot of whiskey. Thousands of men are working in the mills and mines where work is physical, very physical. Following a shift to relieve the stress after work a real man has a good strong drink; mine. Sir, we are thinking men, and thinking men drink champagne, and you are always thinking of ways to best another, or steal a good prospect in order to improve your company."

"Do you think I would take advantage of your hospitality, sir?" Andrew chuckled.

"I know you're eying my young accountant, and I know I will lose him someday, but I am reluctant to let him go now. I still need his services."

"I do appreciate your rearranging the seating order to give me the opportunity to sound him out. Made an excellent dinner more interesting, and elegant," said Andrew who raised his glass in thanks.

"Glad you enjoyed it."

"I am impressed with him, but not now, yet tell me what made him so good."

"He is intelligent, well organized, knows business and he is shrewd, uses people to his advantage," a puff and drink before continuing, "he can manipulate to get the best price for grain, for transportation and for labor. He works fourteen-hour days, six days a week. He is most frugal in time and money, personally and in my business."

"I judged him to be too young, good possibilities of course, and what you are telling me is almost to good to be true. Surely there are some concerns?"

"I must admit the labor situation became a concern to me. He changed managers frequently. However I thought since he's making great profits, I should stay away. Actually, since he was so adept at taking care of business, I found time to catch up on some vacation with the family. Andrew, we all want to profit handsomely don't we? You and I will do what it takes to accomplish this, and so will this young man."

The drinks flowed and the gentleman consumed their fill. The liquor raised the volume in the room as well as a bragging atmosphere from the speakers. What started out as a formal gathering changed as the evening wore on. The alcohol induced men left their conservative demeanor to one of a bragging free willing give and take exchange.

"If you will excuse me sir, I hope you understand that I must attend to my other guests."

"I understand, and thank you for an enjoyable and informative evening."

"Land is abundant, and cheap, buy the land and make money, gentleman. This is a good farming area, a bit hilly of course, but with excellent soil, deep and rich, virgin land that produces crops in abundance," pronounced a boisterous gentleman who held court in the center of the room.

"I'm not interested in farming, Mr. Penderghast," came a reply from a gentleman.

"Aha, then what do you have interest in my man, pray tell me?" Mr. Penderghast countered in a loud deep voice that drew the attention of all in the room.

He got their attention and the guests surrounded him, wanting to hear more. H.C. decided that he too wanted more. Many knew or at least heard of this Penderghast fellow. His reputation as one of the top entrepreneurs in Pittsburgh certainly required one to listen and to take him seriously He stood six feet five inches tall and simply demanded attention just by his stature. With a huge physical frame that carried in excess of three hundred pounds, he ruled a domain of railroads, steel-making facilities and building firms that landed the large lucrative government contracts. A friend of high government officials as well as local politicians, he maintained that relationship by donating large sums to election campaigns regardless of party. Obviously one to eat and drink plenty, he could consume liquor at a tremendous rate without feeling its effects, but when it happened it happened quickly. His facial complexion changed to crimson red. His short forehead, puffy cheeks and large round nose now glowed bright red from the large amount of alcohol downed this evening. Heavy eyebrows hid deep brown eyes that now appeared forceful when he emphasized a point as his brow widened with each remark. His demeanor, along with a rosy face, changed quickly from one of quiet sober conversation to that of a loud boisterous bragging moneymaking Robber Baron.

The gentleman who asked the first question was hesitant in stating his remark a second time, so another standing near him answered instead.

Ridge Valley

"Farming is hard work, there is no money in farming, a farmer works long hours, from dawn to dusk everyday, no sir, not for me… no."

"Obviously you don't understand sir, so let me explain to you how it is," announced Mr. Penderghast while puffing heavily on his cigar. He then paused to take a long draw of his drink, finishing the glass, pausing now calling for another. He waited for the waiter to deliver, savoring every moment of silence; he grabbed his drink from the tray, cleared his throat and began again.

"First of all the gentleman, you, you sir, yes you, you are totally correct. Farming is indeed hard work, except for those that love and thrive on its merits. Farmer's work maybe fourteen hours a day, yet earnings are poor. That being the case, tell me gentleman, how do farmers acquire land to farm if they lack the finances to purchase and banks are reluctant to assist?"

"That is true sir," interrupted a man from the crowd," please get to your point sir, we are all waiting, we know you are heading somewhere and, where sir, are you going? Will you please inform us of that direction?"

"Yes get to the point sir," countered another raising his drink in anticipation.

" Well, here it is gentleman, you actually make money two ways, yes two ways I tell you," he paused to let his words sink in then continued, "Gentleman, as I have said, farming is not a money making process, yet there are those who love to do this for a living, but lack the money to buy the land to farm," a sip and a puff, "you out there, you out there," he repeated, " buy the land yourself at a good price, a lot of land, then you lease the land to be farmed, yes a return on your investment, buy more, lease, yes buy and lease and this is vital, buy as much as you can, and on it goes."

"That is one way, but you mentioned two ways sir."

"The second," rolling the cigar between finger and thumb, hesitating for maximum effect, "The second, and I tell you most important, and potentially the most lucrative is to retain ownership of mineral deposits below the surface." He glanced around the room as a young man moved from the back to the front of the circle. "Just east of where you now stand is the world's yes, Gentleman I said the *WORLD"S* richest vein of soft coal, the type used to convert into coke for making steel. Many of you may not have the finances individually to buy the land, but one of you may be able to take the step to acquire the money needed, as I said this is the first step to making money."

"Tell me sir, how much land do you own in that area."

"I own very little, and what I have I use mainly as a retreat up in the Blue Ridge Mountains. Look sir, you must reside there, near your land, to have complete control and oversee the progress, you have to be committed to take the step to ownership. Look, I know my business, and I'm kept as busy as I want to be by expanding mills here in Pittsburgh. I have all I can handle, but listen, a lot of coke made from coal will be in demand. The need is there gentlemen, and opportunity knocks for the one that takes the step."

H. C. could swear he was talking to him personally and urging him alone to take the step.

"Take the step, take the step," echoed through his brain, "so why not do it?" he thought to himself. "I know the area better than anyone else in the room. I've saved the money and I know the bankers, the Mellons and my uncle will vouch for me. The land is inexpensive, the time is right. I live in Mount Pleasant, which is right in the middle of the mining territory he speaks about. I know I can build the ovens. Connellsville is the key to everything affiliated with coal, railroads like the Pennsylvania and Baltimore and Ohio (B & O) have lines that run from there directly to Pittsburgh. This location is in the center of the coal seam. Build the coke ovens close to the rail junction, and buy land up to fifty miles both north and south of this town and forty miles east and west. Take the step, do it now while the land is cheap, lease and buy more."

The speech ended and the guests began to leave the room. A small number remained to converse with the speaker. H. C. sat by himself, thinking.

"I will need maps, locations, and will purchase the land where coal is located and reserve the mineral rights. Where is that information? Does he know?" He sat and waited; he had the patience and bided his time, get the information, then act, take the step. Where do you get workers for the mining operations? How does one gain control of the labor force? He must have total and complete control of the operation for experience with labor at the distillery taught him a lesson. The men who worked making whiskey were good and reliable when at work. The distillery work force was made up of mostly farmers and the major interest of these men was the land. In the spring planting, summer cutting hay, or tending stock and in the fall they bring in the crops. Their absence during these times created havoc in meeting production schedules at the plant. You can't depend on the local population to man the mines; one needs a captive group of workers where they are under complete and total control of the company.

First establish a mining complex, build simple houses in close proximity to the shaft and boarding houses for unmarried workers, and establish a company store; control, have total control.

H. C. returned to the papers on his desk. He would spend time reviewing reports and organizing his thoughts regarding the manpower problem. After all, he did it once before. He recruited in Europe and controlled the coal-mining patch by owning the company houses, streets, the Union Supply Company Store, the local government officials and local deputies. He smiled when he recalled his demand for the "Grant Hump" which required that a pit car be loaded with a hump high enough for a hard hat to roll from top to bottom or the loader would be docked. This one decision added money to each and every car without the worker getting credit or paid for the extra amount of coal. He regarded this as his best decision ever. From this Mr. Grant went on to be a part of the largest industrial complex in the world. Now the realization is for another to take the step to advance the profit-making conglomerate.

Henry Clay Grant pondered the fate of United States Steel Corporation without the needed coke to make steel. Other smaller firms could take their business away, meaning less profit. The "King of Coal," fretted feeling that things back in Pittsburgh are not good and his beloved Grant Coke Company is responsible.

"There is an answer, there always is, why can't those in charge find that answer?" Over and over the question played on his mind. Over and over he questioned "Why?" He began to pace, back and forth he walked until the pace became a quickstep. The faster he walked the more questions came to his brain. He stopped. "Good God, they haven't done anything for a good while, they don't know the problem so how are they going to take the step in solving it. I'm the only one who knows coal mining and coke making better than any other living human. I must take the step myself and return to Pittsburgh he concluded.

I'll notify the Director of U.S. Steel of my willingness to return for a brief time to investigate the situation in the mining district, and take the steps necessary to resolve the problem. I'll ask him to contact a Mr. Schaeffer, my former secretary to see if he is available?

CHAPTER IV

BLACK CREPE CIRCLED around doorframes of houses in Ridge Valley indicated that a deceased person was laid out in the living room. In addition, the Ridge Valley community also used a black wreath placed in the center of the front door as a symbol to show that the "Death Angel" visited. Thirty-eight doors had black crepe and a wreath hanging on the front door of their house. Miners from other patches, even though they did not know the dead, searched for these houses with wreaths and black crepe. They felt the need to pay respect to their fellow diggers. Throughout the next few days men would approach the front of a black draped door, doff their cap and bow in reverence to the fallen. The melting pot of Slavs, Poles, Czechs and others would file by the house. The one true fact facing each of the ethnic groups, living in the same type of patch houses, digging the same coal, and facing the same obstacles; was that all wanted to work for their families. They realized the inherent danger each faced every day and although different in nationality, they were as one in the pit. They came, they prayed bareheaded, then left.

People in the Ridge Valley patch were exhausted from being at the mine hoping and praying the past three days. They came home after the ordeal to face more exhausting and overwhelming life changing events.

"Families that have a son old enough to work can make it, but those poor families without sons, how they going to survive?" was the talk heard at wakes.

"That young Mrs. Dorek, she's all alone, young women like her, lost her husband so soon, they certainly will have a tough time of it for sure. I called on her and all she does is sit at the coffin," said Mrs. Mullin to a group of women at the store where they were buying food to prepare for friends of deceased miners.

"Yes, and a pretty girl she is. One thing on her side is her age, and did you notice that Tony fellow hanging around? I certainly hope he's there to help, but I wonder," stated a neighbor lady waiting to purchase groceries.

"Saw him at the mine with her a lot, I did, and I don't know about his intentions. I hope they're honorable for she is so vulnerable right now. I'll be trying to watch out for her and help when I can," said Mrs. Mullin.

"Got some cooking on the stove so."

"Yeah, me to," came a chorus of voices in the group, as some women left with their packages for home. A few stayed to talk.

"Thank God my husband wasn't working, poor souls, some who lost their man have big families to feed, at least they have family, but the Dorek girl, I think I'll take her something and sit a spell with her," said Mrs. Mullin as she left the store.

"That is nice of you," replied a neighbor.

Bodies throughout the patch were laid out in the parlor, some covered with white linen and placed on a bier, while others were placed in simple closed caskets. Tradition at John's home called for a paschal candle, about six feet long and two inches in circumference to be placed at the head of the deceased to burn for the entire three days of mourning. The tradition of three days time for a wake came from years of burial services for the Ignatius family. The tradition was carried on to be certain the person buried was truly dead. There was no doubt in this case, but tradition dictated three days and from the mouth of John's mom, three days it is.

"You see John, people in the past thought to be dead were buried in a hurry, many the next day. Years later it was found that a mistake was made, the person was not dead and was buried alive."

"How did they know that?" asked John.

"They found scratch marks on the inside of a casket lid when one was opened. Others were checked and scratches were found in some of them, so the three days, John. A lot of callers will be coming and we must honor your father's life, and show respect for the living that honor his memory."

John's father's remains were placed in a closed casket. Windows in the room remained open regardless of the weather to allow evil spirits to leave the premises. All mirrors were covered to avoid any reflection. A large crucifix was placed directly behind the kneeler in front of the casket. The deceased was never alone. Someone must be present in the room the entire time to accompany the deceased and to greet mourners.

Callers stayed for a time to talk with the family and friends. The many who came consumed food and drink brought to the residence by neighbors. The conversation usually centered on the deceased. Fellow miners who ventured into the parlor accepted a shot of whiskey to show respect by having a final drink to honor their fallen comrade.

They came, the miners who understood the vigor of the trade and what it took to go down every day to dig and load coal. Tough men who admired the physical exploits of fellow "diggers" and their accomplishments. They drank alcohol with the same vitality as they approached work.

The atmosphere became more and more boisterous as the evening wore on as more fellow miners appeared. They stayed to talk about the physical feats and offer shared memories of the deceased. The more they drank the more exaggerated the stories became regarding the strength and endurance of their fallen comrade. They then turned to laughter and joking as they celebrated life, not death. Through merry and loud epitaphs they recounted the good things; the fun of laughing at themselves, their dancing at weddings and drunken forays home to the missus.

The women mourned and wailed in the room containing the corpse as the men immortalized the fallen. The drink and camaraderie provided a respite from thinking about work in knee-deep water, coal dust and unstable roofs.

"Tomorrow, it's into the pits for us, you and me, but not for him. He no longer has to worry about bad air, or the roof falling as his time has come. The Lord called him and let's hope he will save a place for us," said Patty a close family friend as he raised his glass to the group in attendance. This signaled the end of the gathering as miners departed to the outside, some staying to talk while others ventured to other homes with black crepe and a black wreath gracing the front door.

John never left the side of his father from the moment the undertaker brought him in and placed the casket on the bier. Being the man of the house, it was his duty to remain in the parlor to greet callers. He endured, actually gained strength somehow, never tiring from the vigil as the wake continued late into the evening.

The flow of callers came and went in a steady procession until midnight. All left except one man sitting in a corner of the room, hat on knees, staring straight ahead. His hands, hidden under the hat, a hat that moved slightly every few seconds because of Patty saying the Rosary on beads that dangled below the hat. John took this moment, knowing that Mr. Driscall, who was his dad's close friend, would remain in the room for a time, encouraged his mother and sisters to go to bed. He made arrangements for his younger brother to spend the night with the neighbor. John assured his mom that he intended to stay the night with his dad. John returned to the parlor where he sat in silence and began thinking about the events of the evening.

"You know dad," he said to the coffin speaking softly in order not to disturb Patty, " to a man, every one of them welcomed me to the mine. They said not to worry and offered their help. You need not worry, I'll do my best to take care of the family, work hard, and make you proud."

"You remember me don't you," interrupted Patty.

"Oh yes Mr. Driscall," said a surprised John.

"Had many a drink with that man, your father, and I will say without a doubt and with due respect that he was one of the best at work and at O'Malley's."

"Thank you, sir."

"He was a good person, started to work with him the first day, been together since."

"Mentioned you often, Sir, enjoyed your company, liked working with you."

"Went for tools at the time of the blast, not my time I guess, and wish it wasn't his."

John stood in silence, first looking at Mr. Driscall, then the casket.

"One thing John, if you please well I would deem it an honor to walk along to the cemetery, next to the casket. I been with him all my working life and, well one last time if you please, for I wasn't there when." Patty stopped talking displaying glassy eyes.

"Mr. Driscall, my dad would want you there, and sir, would you honor my family and accept being the head pallbearer? And if you would get five others to assist, I'd be most grateful."

"John my boy, consider it done," said Patty as he approached John and as he placed his hand on John's shoulder continued, "I will take care of that for you."

"Thank you, thank you, Sir."

"Be certain to get your mom's approval, John, and one more thing before I leave. " After things are settled, take time to help your mom your sisters and brother, then look me up. You know I don't have a son, always wanted one, Lord thought otherwise. Your father and me, we agreed to take care of each other's family should one of us not be around. When you are ready to go down, I want you to go with me."

"I'll probably be looking you up, sir."

They hugged, a long and hard hug, and then Patty turned and left.

Families in the patch not adhering to the three-day ritual completed the wake and buried their loved ones. The funeral wagons moved throughout the patch to the houses with black wreaths. Meanwhile the Ignatius family greeted the callers as relatives arrived from the northern section of the district during the second day of mourning. As more wagons made the trek in the valley on the third day, a prayer vigil would conclude the wake service at the Ignatius family home.

The family will take the casket and depart for the church the next day.

Bob Menarcheck

The priest reminded the family that the Easter Liturgy would be used at Mass to signify the joy of the departed meeting the Lord in Heaven. He explained the reason for the paschal candle burning at the head of the casket. "The candle is also used at Easter to remind us of the risen Christ. Now the servant before us, like his God, will await our presence with him in heaven."

John sat in the church pew exhausted and emotionally spent. The lack of sleep and the continuous greeting of friends at the wake finally took its toll on mind and body. Tears rolled down his cheeks. He shook uncontrollably until his mom embraced and cuddled him. The statement that kept him going was the remarks of the Priest, especially the statement about his dad meeting God, and that we should be happy, even joyous for the dead for they are resting in heaven awaiting our arrival. The priest speaks for God, he represents God, then it is so. The priest continued the service in Latin.

In Nomini Patris Et Spiritu Sanctus Amen
Dominus Vobiscum
Et Cum Spiri Tu Tuo

The liturgy began, eulogies given, a tribute to life made, The Eucharist distributed and the final blessing rendered as follows:
May the Angels bring you to paradise
And may all the martyrs come forth to welcome you home
And may they lead you into heaven
Like the forgotten and poor, you shall have everlasting rest

The priest invited the congregation to the service at the cemetery. Prayers committing the soul were rendered and the wooden casket lowered into the grave. Patty picked up a new number four shovel and handed it to John, who deposited the first shovel of dirt on the casket. The family retreated as Patty and the pallbearers followed with additional shovels of dirt. The ceremony was completed. One worker's life was over, another working life soon to begin. John would have no choice, for in order to support the family; he would soon enter the pits at the Ridge Valley Mine.

CHAPTER V

"LEROY," HE SHOUTED, Leroy come here, now."
In his rush to answer the call, Leroy Johnson reached for the door handle, but missed. He pushed his hand through the rusted screen. He pulled it back out, found the handle and yanked the door open. His father, who called him, met Leroy two steps inside the door. Pointing his finger in the direction of the road he said in a stern voice, go on and get Mrs. Washington and run as fast as you can. Your Grandma is ailing again and looks like she's worse off than ever before. Tell her to come now and to bring the reverend with her.

Rufus Johnson, a tall burly Negro, looked down at his fourteen-year-old son with tired watery eyes. He placed his hand on Leroy's shoulder and in a soft voice said, "Its real bad this time and she's been worsening the last few days. She's mighty sick this time. Go and fetch the Washington's as fast as you can." Leroy felt the sadness emulate from his dad more so than ever before.

" I'll hurry as fast as I can, I'll fetch em sure."

The strain of caring for Grandma over the years, as bad as it was for Rufus and Leroy, was many times worse for Mrs. Johnson who provided constant care for her mother. She rarely took time for herself except for her church activities. The ebb and flow from good to bad and back again worked the Johnson family's emotions like a seesaw.

Now it was bad and another call was made to her preacher and his wife to seek the miracle of their healing prayers. The Washingtons and the parishioners who were able to be present upended the illness each time Grandma turned for the worse. They prayed and chanted their healing prayers, sang to the Lord for forgiveness, then asked for his help to heal this beloved lady. Grandma rallied each time the group prayed over her. She recovered and maintained her health for a short time, but whatever ailed her returned as it did this time, so prayers by the preacher and Mrs. Washington were needed once again.

Leroy turned from his father, and in his haste to please pushed again on an already torn screen. He pulled back, placed his open palm on the wood part of the screen door, shoved the door open and jumped the porch steps charged across the dry dusty yard and turned down a narrow sandy road.

" There goes that boy running again," shouted Mrs. Jones to her husband. " What you in a hurry for boy?" she yelled out to Leroy.

" Got to go and fetch Mrs. Washington and the reverend," he stopped to answer. " It's Grandma again and Pa says it's a lot worse this time, so I got to hurry."

" Be gone with yeah then, and the Lord be with you," shouted Mrs. Jones as she sat up in her rocker to get a better view of the Negro boy in bare feet kick up the red dust as he ran down the road. Once Leroy disappeared around the bend she arose from the rocker, walked to her front door and announced to her husband, "Mrs. Smith is having another spell. I'm going over there to see if I can help."

Leroy continued his journey down the narrow sandy road, passing the tin roofed houses that lined its southern edge. He turned around a bend to a widened road that ended in Carbon Hill, Alabama. A short sprint brought him to a Y. He took the left spur where he dashed onto a narrow road that tapered off into wide path to the Holy Gospel Baptist Church that sat at the end of the trail. Perspiring heavily from the run he slowed to a jog as he neared the church. He saw the front door of the building was open and he headed in that direction. Entering he found Mrs. Washington placing bibles on front pews and the reverend at the podium arranging some papers.

Ridge Valley

" Leroy, what in the world are you doing here?" asked Mrs. Washington.

" My Grandma, she's real sick again," he said breathing hard.

" Mrs. Washington, holding a bible, walked closer to Leroy and stopped in front of him and asked, " You say your Grandma is ailing, how bad is she Leroy?"

" Dad said she's real sick this time, real bad, and asked if you and Reverend Washington would come as quick as you can."

The reverend dressed in his preacher clothes of white shirt and black pants and black shoes, walked from the front of the church to where his wife and Leroy were talking.

" Hello Leroy, what brings you here?"

" It's his Grandma again," answered Mrs. Washington.

" Yes sir, she's feeling poorly, very bad my Pa says. Wants you and Mrs. Washington to come to the house right away. Please, can you come now?"

Mrs. Washington dressed in a plain brown cotton dress along with flat worn black shoes, had a red bandana tied around her head. " I've got to get my calling clothes."

"You're dressed fine ma'am. Please come now, don't matter how you is dressed. I promised to fetch you and the reverend and have you come as fast as you can. I know they will be waiting."

"Okay Leroy lets go."

Reverend Washington, who insisted on dressing always as a preacher, grabbed a black waistcoat from the front bench and put it on. Then gesturing with open palms like someone chasing chickens from a coup said, "C'mon, let us hurry."

Rivulets of perspiration formed on their foreheads as the reverend and Mrs. Washington followed Leroy out the door, down the steps and up the trail heading for the Johnson's. They began to move close together at first but the pace was too slow for Leroy who started to inch ahead. Soon the distance between them lengthened with Leroy leading followed by Mrs. Washington, then the reverend. Leroy became impatient with the pace and began to move faster and faster up the road. The Washington's lagged behind Leroy. They could not maintain his pace. The shade provided by the tree limbs hanging over the trail protected the three from the noon Alabama sun. This was a momentary relief from the direct rays as the trio continued their journey. The reverend's robust body allowed only a trot. He found himself losing more and more ground to his wife and Leroy. He tried to put a jaunt to his step, but as he left the shade of the trail and approached the Y, he faced the direct rays of the sun. The heat was unrelenting causing him to stop often and wipe perspiration from his face.

They all passed the Y with Leroy hurrying far ahead of the preacher and his wife. She decided to wait for the reverend and walk together with him to the house. Leroy approached Rufus who was sitting on the porch steps, his long legs extending to the ground with his elbows on knees and his hands covering his face.

A neighbor of the Johnson's saw the pastor and his wife walking fast up the road.

" Is it Grandma Smith again?" asked the neighbor.

" Yes it is," answered the reverend.

" Be right over after I get Mrs. Jefferson."

Leroy arrived at the base of the front porch steps facing his father. "I done got Mrs. Washington and the reverend like you asked, and they're a coming right behind." Rufus heard but it didn't register until the boy placed his hand on Rufus shoulder, shook it and said again, " I brought the Washington's and they is here."

" Thanks Leroy, but I'm afraid it may be too late. I judge the Lord's a thinking your Grandma done suffered enough and decided it's time for her to be with him."

" I went as fast as I could, and they are here, can they still help? Look, look, the reverend is coming across the yard right now."

" You done good son, real good, did all you could."

Reverend Washington, hearing the crying and wailing inside, passed by Rufus and Leroy and entered the house.

" She was a good women who believed, and this day she is with the Lord in paradise. She is reaping the glory of God and the fruits of heaven. God bless her soul, God bless her soul," intoned the preacher.

Leroy listened at what was said and with both hands stuffed in his pockets, head down, he slowly walked away feeling sad, depressed that he failed to get the Washington's to Grandma before she passed.

Ridge Valley

He walked to the back of the house, and sitting on a bench he gazed beyond the one-person outhouse and the cornfield just beyond. He got up and began walking through the cornfield to a hideout he established in a cluster of trees and sat to ponder the passing of Grandma.

Mrs. Washington joined other ladies inside the small bedroom with Grandma Smith. She embraced the daughter of the deceased, expressed her sorrow and apologized for not getting there in time. Mrs. Johnson feeling and seeing the dampness in the brown dress returned the hug and said, " You tried, and I know you did your best to get here."

" Bella, there is no doubt. Your mom is with the Lord."

The reverend returned to consol Rufus then proceeded to the small bedroom where he began to say prayers loud and true. The women present ended each prayer with a wailing, Amen, Praise the Lord."

More neighbors crowded into the house, some pushing their way into the bedroom hoping to assist with the prayer service. "She never missed a preaching no matter what," said one woman to whomever listened then added, "she livened up the singing loud and true with a voice no one could match."

The sound of people wailing, praying and the reverend preaching echoed in Leroy's brain as he reached his place of refuge in the trees behind the cornfield. He sat down in the shade of the trees thinking about Grandma when a thought brought a smile to his face.

" Yes Grandma, y'all is at a better place, one where all of your ailments are gone and you are with the Lord," he said looking to the sky. He smiled, and then chuckled to himself as he recalled the many Sundays he spent with her, and all the stories she told. He thought about how Grandma acted out parts of her stories by rolling her eyes and screwing up her mouth in the most dramatic way in order to emphasize her tales about her life. She was especially anxious for the children to know their roots and preached to the high heavens to reach deep into their souls. Leroy leaned back supporting his head with his arms. He enjoyed the coolness of the ground moss on his back as he watched a hawk fly circles above the trees. He smiled again as he recalled how Grandma waved her arms, raised and lowered her voice, and gestured with her entire body to liven up the story. Yes she went on and on.

"You all must remember my message so that y'all will tell your children and they tell their children. Promise my stories will last forever," and we promised Grandma, we sure did.

At first he recalled how he resented having to sit and listen to Grandma every Sunday after church. He often allowed his mind to wonder during her long talks, until one day when she told stories about living through the War between the States. She was a child then, yet she recalled being set free and told how happy she was when that happened. She told of how her husband bought the very house where Leroy lived. She preached to the children every Sunday, a ritual that never changed and Grandma insisted the time for her took precedence over all else, and it did. Leroy remembered Grandma telling of the past with so much vigor and drama that she totally exhausted herself in the process. The remainder of her afternoon and part of the evening was spent resting. Lately it took more and more time for her to recover.

"Funny, that I understand her now as never before. I'll miss her and without Grandma Sunday's will never be the same. She was a wise old lady," he told the hawk.

The afternoon wore on with more neighbors and friends stopping by the Johnson's house to express their condolences. Everyone who came knew and respected Grandma. With the departing of this lovely soul all understood that an era has passed. As dusk approached Leroy left the shelter of the trees and started to walk back to his house. He felt relieved and in a way happy he came to his hideout and now leaving with good thoughts and pleasant memories of Grandma.

Rufus, while comforting his wife, was remembering also. He recalled the strength and determination displayed by Grandma Smith and her insistence to stay in her home. She closed out any talk of leaving this spot. The four-room house she called home was considered just a bit better than a shack by most but not Grandma Smith. She talked about living under the rule of others and despised every second. This place was her kingdom, all four tiny rooms, the tin roof, and no indoor electricity or plumbing. A pump in the back door provided water, and a short walk up the path from the back door led to a one-person outhouse.

No one knew Grandma's age, " because they never made a record of them things back then."

Bella Johnson due to the many health setbacks by her mother had asked Rufus to move in with momma. They did, and from day one Grandma Smith informed them that one thing was as certain as death itself; she would never leave her home. She was forced out of other places against her will before, never again.

The Johnson's honored her wishes and stayed with Grandma and accepted all the difficulties living together presented. Rufus religiously worked every day at the Carbon Hill coal mine. He did his best to support his family. Working hard did not result in earning a good pay. All of his effort simply provided a meager subsistence. He wanted more for them in money and space to live but he never strayed from the promise, until now.

For a long time Rufus received letters from his uncle and cousin who left the area and headed north about four years ago. They told of working in a mine that has nine-foot seams of coal where they made good money working there. They lived in two-story houses that had inside running water and electricity. They could buy everything they needed at this Union Supply Company Store and could charge it on an account you could pay later from money earned working for the company.

" They always need workers and if you want to come your sure to find a job."

Since Rufus never learned to read, Reverend Washington read the letters to him in private. Rufus did not mention the correspondence to Bella. He thought about the messages from up north often and just as often dismissed its contents because of his promise to Bella and Grandma.

The day following the death of Grandma, Rufus thought heavily about the letters. He decided then and there that after a proper burial and giving it some time, he would talk to Bella. He was no longer anchored to this house. Grandma was gone and he honored her wishes without wavering. He constantly thought about the letters now and the good money he could make. Yes he would talk to Bella, in due time, yes he would talk to her, about two-story houses.

CHAPTER VI

THE EARLY OCTOBER morning was cool and damp. A low hanging fog engulfed the city as Schaeffer exited the streetcar at the corner of Fifth and Carnegie. A breeze, strong enough to arouse the leaves on the maple trees lining the street, shook drops of moisture collected overnight onto the people walking below. Leaves of trees across the street, protected from the wind, hung limply from the branches.

Schaeffer turned up his coat collar as he hurried down the sidewalk. He crossed in the middle of the street to the Grant office building. The early morning dew that collected on the median grass moistened his shoes as he proceeded to the entrance. Dawn was an hour away as Schaeffer opened the front door and entered the lobby. He removed his greatcoat to reveal a thin body and a face with a sharp chin, sunken cheeks and a small pointed nose. His dark eyes were topped with a mixture of gray and black eyebrows, and a head covered with white hair. Schaeffer returned back to work reluctantly, but relented at the request of Mr. Grant who promised, "to work no longer than a month. I want to review some records and get back to the Big City as soon as possible. Please it is imperative that you not inform anyone of my presence."

"We have been together a long time, and you could help a great deal since you know my routine and the business. I will pay you the regular rate for your service," said Mr. Grant.

Schaeffer agreed to return. He could use the extra money, plus the old secretary was curious. "What reason does he have to leave New York and return after being away all these years?" he wondered.

"He's coming back, I'm guessing to replace someone high up," Schaeffer said to his wife who disagreed with his decision to return.

"You served him for thirty years and worked beyond the call of the job. You did more than anyone to help him get through the hard times. He never recognized your input. The money you saved him for example, and he never offered a token of appreciation. Never gave you an honest wage. One would think you were his servant, not his secretary, for what he paid. Then off he goes with his money and his wife. Now he wants you back, and at the same wage. Yes, we could use the money, and I know you will do it. But, you'd think he'd reward you handsomely for your returning to work, but not him," said Mary Schaeffer.

"I don't believe it will be long, and if he is looking for a replacement, as I believe, then perhaps I can be of service," said Schaeffer in return hiding a toothy smile.

"You're a good and loyal person and I thought he would at least offer you more in wages after all these years. How long has it been?"

"Excuse me, sir, may I pass?" The request interrupted Schaeffer's thoughts as he stood in the lobby of the Grant building.

"Certainly, sir," Schaeffer stepped aside and let the man pass. He then took the stairs to the mailroom in the basement where a number of overnight messages awaited. He climbed the six floors of stairs to the Grant office. His morning routine of dusting, arranging the desk and organizing the office was finished when Mr. Grant entered the room. He assisted him with his coat and welcomed his boss with a good morning.

"Yes it is."

"I prepared the mail, got fresh water, are you in need of anything else, sir?"

Ridge Valley

"One thing, Schaeffer. I spent the evening going over the reports for this year. Would you retrieve the production and manpower reports for the last five years?"

"That will take little time, sir."

"Soon as you can."

"Very good, sir. I'll get on it right away," said Schaeffer as he hurried out.

Mr. Grant sat at his desk. He reviewed his mail and saw only one reply was needed and that one could wait until later. He retrieved the reports he had on hand, reports he reviewed at home. He looked them over another time, just to be sure of his conclusions.

A soft knock at the door interrupted his routine.

"Yes"

"Your reports, sir. All five years, organized and ready."

"Thank You."

"Sir, if you please, I must run a personal errand, and that will take only a short time, with your permission." A wave of the hand indicated a yes. "I will inform you of my return and deduct the time gone from my pay."

"Please lock the door on your way out, I do not want to be disturbed."

Schaeffer was gone exactly thirty-eight minutes and noted the time. This amount would be deducted on his next pay. He hung up his coat and placed his hat on the shelf. He notified Mr. Grant of his return.

W. H. Clingerman served as Director of the H. C. Grant Coke Company until 1917. The position was passed on to Mr. J.P Hayes who presently holds the post in 1919 when Mr. Grant requested the Director of United States Steel intervene. A change of mind brought the "King of Coal" back to sound out this Mr. Hayes regarding his understanding of issues facing the company.

"Did you notify Mr. Hayes of my request for a meeting?"

"Yes, sir, he will be here promptly at eleven."

"Do not show him in on time, have him wait, I will call for him when I am ready."

"Yes, sir."

Schaeffer took his leave, convinced that the present director was the man in trouble. After all, being with this man for thirty-plus years is enough time to know what a person is thinking. He stopped short of the door and turned to ask, "What about the meeting you planned on having with some of your managers?"

"Oh yes, hold off on that for now. I have a few things to settle first."

"Very good," with that Schaeffer exited the room.

The reports on this man's leadership were initially very good, but now indicate a slow but sure downward trend the past few years. What happened and why wasn't this problem caught earlier? Mr. Grant had to know.

He placed a glass of water on the back shelf behind his desk. Next, H. C. moved a chair directly in front and center of his desk. Returning to his chair behind the desk, he removed all reports. The penholder and pen, along with clean writing paper, were the only items on the desktop. Satisfied, he called for Schaeffer. The time on the clock read eleven twenty-nine.

"Have the gentleman come in."

"Have a seat," said H.C., pointing to the chair.

"Thank you, sir."

After introductory greetings ended Mr. Grant motioned for Mr. Hayes to be seated and entered the chair behind his desk. " I want to get directly to the point. I received reports in New York that the profit along with production in the coal and coke division was declining to dangerous levels. I reviewed the accounts personally and concluded that I must investigate why this is happening. I come to you for the answer. Hopefully we can find the problem and correct it. Then I will be on my way and inform our Director's that any problems or immediate concerns in the coal and coke division have been cleared up. What do you say?"

"Well, sir, at the beginning of the war when factories were booming, we supplied huge quantities of coke to meet the needs of the mills. We had miners working seven days a week to keep up with the orders. We expanded our operations by opening new shafts. Because of the war we lost our recruiting source for new men to replace our losses. Early on we transferred workers from one shaft to another

Ridge Valley

and replaced those who left with young inexperienced workers. We kept up the pace for years, but slowly, primarily due to accidents, we began to lose our numbers. The miners worked overtime hours every day, seven days a week. They worked hard, maybe too hard, got tired, I suggest. Exhaustion can lead to carelessness and then a price is paid when more accidents take their toll. Replacements were nonexistent, so the cycle of demanding more from fewer began to falter. Now, adding to this scenario, immigrant men began leaving to join the army of their mother country to help with the war. As the war dragged on a number of the younger workers enlisted in the U.S. Army, adding to the loss of manpower. The latest blow was the explosion at Ridge Valley where we lost thirty-eight, but everyday accidents add to lost time. Things have changed since your time here with the labor situation. With accidents men are out of work a short time, but return. When workers are killed, their widows have no place to go and since we don't have replacements, as long as they pay the rent they stay in the houses until."

"Until what, until what? Until we have the entire patch full of families living in houses without a worker in any one of them. I thought you understood that if a house does not have a man working in the mine, the family is evicted, period. Besides, this is a good excuse for not finding replacements. New workers have to be somewhere. There is no such problem in the steel making sector, why yours.

"We have exhausted all efforts, sir. I have come to believe that we should be patient because the miners give all they have. They work a double shift when asked to meet the demand for additional coal. They worked to help win a war. They go home, rest maybe six hours, and then return to the pits, never complaining. They work in bad places, poor conditions and never complain. I'm convinced that we take all of the working conditions into consideration and have to change our outlook toward these people, we have to give them time."

"Change, give them time you say," said Henry Clay emphatically. He asked, "What change, how much time?"

"Mr. Grant, I took to traveling extensively around the entire district. I wanted to see the mining operations first hand. I went from Hostetter in the North to the Leckrone Strip in the southern area.

Stopped at a number of mining shafts in between. Each and every mining patch contains various ethnic groups, representing varying cultures, speaking different languages. They are all intertwined, living side by side. For the present they stay with their own kind and restrict their association to those who speak the language and observe the same social customs. The men do communicate with each other in the mine for it's their livelihood. The wives generally stay to themselves, tending to a large family, work at chores all day. Rarely do they have time to speak to the neighbors. Even those with the same religion show their differences by attending specific ethnic churches. Most of the inhabitants are Catholic, they follow the same religion, but in different churches, using their own dialects. They are the same, yet different from each other."

"Divide and conquer, keep them separate, no problem there," interrupted Mr. Grant.

"For now, sir, for now." Henry Clay got up from his chair and walked to the window. Once there he waved his hand motioning for his invitee to continue.

"I began to ask myself, particularly over the last few years how long can the status quo continue? What would happen if the people got together? Sooner or later, under the present conditions, the odds of their doing just that are good. For example, for years the wages have been frozen because of the war. The war is over, but the President has not signed the armistice, so the wage freeze continues. Because of shortages, the prices of staple food items have risen. This leaves less money for the workers."

"Just a minute," interrupted Mr. Grant holding up his hand. He walked to his desk and scribbled a note to contact Congressman Stewart for an invitation to dinner, "Got to keep them happy," he mumbled as he wrote. He motioned with a wave of his hand for his guest to continue.

"You can drive people only so far until they realize they must break from individual traditions and begin to think about working together for everyone's benefit."

"Been there, Sir, you remember the strike at Homestead and Morewood? The union men tried to take over then and failed, should they try again, they will fail again. We have the government and the local law enforcement officials on our side. We can hire Pinkertons to police the situation if necessary. Hundreds marched on Morewood where we met the revolt head on, I recall seven or eight marchers shot and killed, don't recall the number injured, but it all ended with good results for us. They went back to work, and we had no more trouble since," Mr. Grant said emphatically then added, "They must understand that any work stoppage will be challenged and it could be worse for them, much worse than what you describe."

"Sir, with all due respect that was then and yes, I do remember, but sir, we cannot continue our old self-serving ways. We must consider changing our attitude of running the mines through fear and intimidation to one of respect and understanding. The miner's work close to death every minute on the job, they fight the fear of roof-falls and the methane gases, the damp fumes, and explosions like at Ridge Valley. They are a hardy people who want to only take care of their families. They work hard, are rarely absent, they're honest, religious and enjoy the simple things of life. A garden, for example, is their pride and joy. They are prideful people; show much patience, kind in many ways and generous to a fault. The men extend their pride to their work, brag about their exploits in the mine, and certainly do not want any kind of confrontation, but if we continue to take away their pride..."

"That's nothing new, Sir," interrupted Henry Clay once again. "Labor is simply a factor of production, always has been, like any material cost, you know that. The good businessman takes advantage of these kinds of prideful workers. For example, we all want to gain excellent profits, and I am included in that, like Carnegie, Phipps and others. Look, my man, when we can maximize workers output, while reducing the price paid for wages, then that is an excellent business decision. We need to continue to look for ways to gain profit, be it on the backs of labor, cheaper materials or better pricing. That's what we need."

"Sir, Please understand that, well, what I'm trying to say is that the men, and yes, the women in the patch endure a lot without complaint. For example, they have accepted the wage freeze because of the war; the war is over, yet the freeze continues. Prices are rising, wages remain stagnant and money is hard to come by, but they continue on constantly in debt to the Company Store. A wage adjustment should be considered, and soon."

"The war isn't over until an armistice is signed; hasn't happened yet so the wage freeze stays. Anyway it's in our favor, and that's good business. Besides, they have houses, and a place to buy food and supplies, so as long as we have control, I don't see any problems."

"Mr. Grant, Sir, please understand. I am saying that a change, even a slight adjustment in wages will go a long way to help your employees. I believe that it will help immensely in the long run and guarantee profit far into the future."

"No, we are protected by law, no wage considerations, and that's the way it will stay."

"Sir, the way things are progressing, our President Wilson and the Congress may take months to agree on terms for an armistice. I suggest that a wage adjustment be made as soon as possible. The men will work to show their appreciation beyond what they are doing now. Sir, you have been away for a number of years and I need to present you with a set of numbers to consider, so if you will."

"Go ahead," but please understand my patience is waning."

The Director reached into and retrieved a paper from his briefcase. "Thank, you, sir. I have the wages and expenditures for a miner for one week of work using a ten-hour day. This assumes he loads clean coal with no slate in the wagon to cause a deduction. A car is considered four ton, and must be "humped" or a deduction occurs. This demand you made years ago continues to this day."

"Good businesses decision, a very good one," said Mr. Grant.

"Sir, at thirty-eight cents a ton a weekly wage comes to twenty-two dollars and eighty cents for a six day week. Again it must be clean coal or the weight master makes a deduction resulting in less money made. He pays rent for the house and a weekly fee for the company doctor. He buys his own carbide, dynamite and tools. He purchases food for the family at the Company Store. The deductions I mention often are more than what he earns. The Company Store is carried over to the next pay. If a man runs into a bad seam, more slate than coal for example, he earns less of course. I forgot to mention the setting of timber and laying of track that eats up his time."

"Part of the job and the way to do business, providing a house, company store, all profit. But one thing you have not addressed and that is the replacement of workers lost to the war and accidents. There is always someone to take the place of another."

"I agree we need men, but experienced men. Until that occurs we use what is available. But sir, I feel there is a transition in the air, I can feel it, and I sense it particularly among the younger workers. The older experienced miners are stalling the younger workers' frustration over wages and the decisions of the weight master. However, should the older group balk, all the Pinkerton police, and all the local deputies will be hard pressed to control them"

"You present a bleak picture. I must say I totally disagree with your analysis. You were placed in your present position to carry on based on proven company philosophy, but you have changed, changed drastically, you and the change you speak about may be part of the problem, or the problem itself."

" Mr. Grant If I may," the invitee interrupted to the chagrin of H.C. who bristled at the intrusion.

"Mr. Grant, I tell you sir, things are calm; people are working, accepting for now. I assure you this condition will not continue. Please act for their benefit, and in turn your company will also benefit. Do this before it's too late."

"You continue to amaze me."

"I am serious and appreciate your being here and listening. We must accept the worker as a person who works to help us grow. We can't continue to treat them as a disposable object like some rusty wheel. Unless we do something we will face a more serious confrontation than at Homestead," said Mr. Hayes as he slid to the back of his chair, now feeling very tired from the discussion.

"We took care of the rioters then and will again. Now do not interrupt me and listen carefully. I judge from what you are saying that you lost the direction and understanding of how this company operates. You lost your way. First, we do not, I repeat, do not acquiesce to anyone; we have the power, the backing and control of our own destiny. You have lost that understanding, totally and completely. I must admit that I am perplexed at your attitude. I am very uncomfortable with your philosophy. I judge now that I should have paid more attention to company business these past few years. Things have gone in a downward spiral for too long and unless something is done, and soon, that downward spiral will continue. Sir, I have been patient in hearing you out. I have heard all I want to hear from you. I have but one choice in this matter and that choice is to dismiss you immediately from your position. You will proceed to your office and remove any and all personal belongings from your desk and leave the building."

While talking H.C. walked over to the door to beckon Schaeffer into the office. "Mr. Schaeffer will accompany you to your office, and assist you in your departure. Before you leave, you are to proceed to the payroll office and instruct them to draw your pay up to one o'clock today. You may now consider your services to me as terminated."

H. C. Grant turned in his chair away from the door, refusing to hear any more. He faced the wall, as the two men left the room.

He sat in his overstuffed swivel chair, ascertaining his next move. He just finished a scenario that ended with the firing of his Director of Operations. He still had the production problems and the manpower concerns to solve. He wanted to return to New York but now added the hiring of a new director to his list. "That man diverted his thinking completely in favor of the workers, and that kind of thinking is foreign to our philosophy," Mr. Grant verbally punished himself for overlooking the obvious change in the present Director. His emotions ran from anger to frustration for taking so long to recognize the problem and for being blinded by the Director's actions. He got up from his chair and began to stroll around the room, talking to himself.

"I gave my whole life to maintain control over my company. I was attacked for lowering wages, not raising them like he wants, I was shot, almost killed. I deserve all the money I make, have the right to dictate conditions and wages to stop unionization. Now this man wants to change it all, give in to, no, he is gone, now I must concentrate on his replacement. Who? Where can I go for advice? Been away from this for years. I must find a person who believes as I do. After all I am a Christian, and own this Company. I have the God-given inalienable right to gain as much money as possible, be it from labor or any other means. Lord, I need some direction now."

The only person of rank in U. S. Steel knowing of his return to Pittsburgh was the President of the Company. He had stated many times to his acquaintances in New York that he would never again get involved in every day business transactions. His intentions were to stay only a few days, make necessary adjustments and return to New York. He had already stayed beyond the planned time and unless he named a replacement quickly, he would be stuck here for a month or more. His wife had been pressing him via telegram to establish a date for his return. He searched the right side of his desk for the latest message. He read it once more.

"The fall season for theatre and opera opens in a few weeks. You are expected to be here. You promised to attend the art auction at Mobley's that will present the Renoir piece. Please forward a date of return so plans can be confirmed, Adelaide."

"She is correct in being concerned. I must make a decision soon, yet I can't be hasty, I must be certain, not take chances. Who is available? Well, there is Anderson; maybe Baldwin or Walters, all possibilities, all have experience. Looks like they did a good job, wait, they are part of the last regime and may have adopted his philosophy, can't take a chance, I have to look elsewhere, but where? The President of the steel division is of no help. He knows about making steel at the mills but nothing about coal mining and coke making. Wait; maybe he can help after all. I have to find someone completely divorced from my company who will accept my philosophy and have no association with the previous Director."

H. C. got up from his chair and walked to the window. The sun had reached its noon zenith and had started its descent in the west. He returned to his desk and began scribbling names of men he considered for the director's job; methodically he crossed each one off the list. He considered calling on friends, but dropped the idea. They were probably away from the working scene, and true to his nature, he could not swallow his pride enough to admit to a failed decision. His only recourse is to call upon the President of U. S. Steel for suggestions.

A soft knock interrupted his thought process.

"Yes?"

"Sorry for the interruption, sir. I wanted to report that the gentleman cleared his desk, garnered his final pay, and left the building. If you please, I took the liberty to get you a sandwich, I know it is well past your lunch time, just thought you would like a bite, sir."

"Did he say anything?"

"No sir, nothing."

"Well, you say you have something for me, a sandwich?"

"Yes sir, your favorite as I remember, shall I bring it in? And how about a cup of hot tea with your lunch, sir?"

"That would be fine, thank you."

Schaeffer left the door open and was gone only a few minutes. He returned with a tray carrying a sandwich, a carafe of hot water and a cup and saucer, along with condiments. He placed the tray in front of Mr. Grant; dumped tea leaves on the bottom of the cup and poured in the hot water.

"Enjoy your lunch, sir," said Schaeffer, arousing H.C. from a thought. The secretary turned to leave,

"Have you eaten your lunch as yet?" asked Mr. Grant.

"All except for desert, sir, plan on eating it at my desk."

"Join me here, will you? Bring your desert and have a seat. I have been taken back a bit and still wonder how the man lost his direction"

H. C. picked up the spoon and began to stir the hot water in the cup in order to rustle the tealeaves into rendering a strong brew. He observed the clear water darkening. He continued mixing the liquid as he talked, focusing on the ever-changing hue.

"I spent all my waking hours since coming from New York reviewing reports and checking profit and loss statements. I conclude that the major reason for the downward spiral in profits coincides directly with the lack of manpower. There are some other factors of course, but not of this magnitude." He took a sip of the hot tea, sat the cup in the saucer, and then began stirring vigorously.

"I fought the Ford and Chrysler companies who wanted to build factories here in Pittsburgh, yes here, to build cars. They wanted to be near the steel production facilities, to save on steel transportation costs," he paused to take another sip of tea.

Schaeffer took advantage, giving him time to speak.

"Yes, I remember that sir, and you were correct denying them…"

"Stopped them cold. And do you know why? Because it would cut into our labor supply, that's why. They wanted our cheap labor, and I couldn't let them have their way, had to protect our interest." He reached for his sandwich, lifting it only a few inches; he placed it back on the plate.

"I must forget about the past for the decision was made, now I must take the next step," He lifted the cup and emptied it with a long gulp.

Schaeffer immediately got up, added new leaves, poured in a new supply of hot water, and returned to his chair. He had yet to taste the pie.

"I must move on, take the next step and replace that man with someone outside his influence. I must eliminate everyone under his jurisdiction. So, Schaeffer, the question is, who do I trust?" He paused to stir and sip.

"May I speak, sir?"

H. C. in a slow and deliberate manner replaced the cup on the saucer. He took a napkin, eyed his gray haired secretary then waved an okay for Schaeffer to speak as he dabbed his mustache and wiped a drop of tea from his beard.

"May I suggest that you seek out the Pinkertons, sir?"

"What is that you say, the Pinkertons? How can they assist me, they are primarily involved in security?"

"The firm expanded their influence beyond being policeman. They have begun to recommend people to fill specific jobs. I understand that since they are involved in policing factories and mines they see the best directors in action and began recommending replacements. They may have excellent recommendations, wouldn't hurt to ask."

"What kind of information would they require?"

"I'm only guessing, but I think you tell them what you want and they find the exact person to fit your needs. I neglected to say that a fee is attached."

H. C. sat, silent, thinking, sipping, and stirring.

"You are telling me that if I give them a summary of my requirements they will provide someone for me to consider?"

"Yes sir. I must confess that Mr. King, the man in charge, contacted me a time back and offered a position. I had to refuse because the job was in Cleveland and my wife was insistent on staying here. You remember Mr. Pratt from U. S. Steel; he was with you at Homestead and remembered my working for you. He is now with Republic Steel. He asked for Mr. King to contact me; that is how I became acquainted with this operation."

"Sounds possible, where is their office?"

"Over on Seventh Avenue."

Mr. Grant sat in silence, taping the desk with fingers, stirring the tea, a sip, a wipe, looking about the room, pondering, asking himself, " Is this the answer?" He exited the chair, head down, hands deep in pockets he walked to the window, still thinking hard. "How sure is Schaeffer?" The Pinkertons have been around for years, been involved keeping labor in check, know their work, do excellent work in providing a police force to quell riots, not afraid to use their force. The question is, can they transfer these efforts to personnel placement as Schaeffer describes?" He looked to Knob Hill. "I was young, brash, and confident and took steps then, dare I do it now? Come to think of it my secretary has always been reliable. Is he now? Yes, and I can get input from the U.S. Steel Director to verify any decision. Why not take the step?

He turned to Schaeffer, pointing a finger at his secretary he said sternly, "Go there and request that this Mr. King see me in my office as soon as possible. I want to sound him out, find out about his operation, see if he'll help, then I can get back to New York"

"What shall I say is your availability, sir?"

"I am available immediately, today…this afternoon would be fine."

"I judged the urgency of your request and because I'll be away from the office next week, I thought it best to come over immediately. If you give me the goals you have in mind, I will have my staff search the files to find your man," said Alexander E. King.

"I will work up a list of requirements and have them to you by the end of the day. In fact, I'll have Schaeffer drop off the list on his way out tonight."

"Very good, sir. I'll await his arrival and plan on working late this evening with the hope of having a recommendation to you first thing in the morning." Mr. King departed as H. C. began to compile a list.

Schaeffer finally had a moment to enjoy his apple pie. An eventful day was close to ending.

H. C. was quick and direct in compiling a short list of attributes he deemed vital. The new director will be evaluated on a quarterly basis. He will be responsible for maintaining a minimum of three percent profit the first year and from five to seven percent thereafter. The final decision on employment, wages and yearly goals rests with H. C. Grant.

> To: Mr. Alexander E. King
> Fr: Mr. Henry Clay Grant
> Re: List of attributes for Director position
> Da: October 11, 1919
>
> The following is a list of ten items I deem necessary for consideration for a leader of the Grant Coke Company. All of these items must be met before I consider having an interview with the candidate.
>
> Relentless in the pursuit of profit
> Dictatorial style of Leadership
> Demanding
> Loyal to the Company
> Direct and decisive
> Will use force when needed
> Non-acceptance of unions
> Must be a Christian
> A serious no nonsense person

A copy was made for his file; the original folded, placed in an envelope and handed to Schaeffer for delivery to Mr. King.

At precisely eight o'clock the next morning Mr. King arrived at Grant's office.

"Thank you for seeing me at this early hour. Since I must be away next week, your willingness to meet early is appreciated," said Mr. King.

"You are prepared to honor my request, sir?"

"I have your man," said Mr. King to a surprised Mr. Grant. "I believe that Mr. Frederick C. Moses meets all of your requirements and more, sir."

"Tell me about him."

"He is presently the Chief Executive Officer of Midvale Steel, a small specialty steel company located in Ambridge. He has complete control of the operation including manpower, wages and work schedules. He oversees all facets of the company including sales and product pricing. He has attained a profit on average of..." Mr. King paused then emphasized, "seventeen percent per year since he took over. He runs a taut ship, has total control and meets all of your requirements. He is by far the best we have for your needs. He will be an excellent choice."

"Why, why, sir, would he want to leave a good productive situation?"

"Very good question, sir. The present position is not financially rewarding for the gentleman. He, like you, and me of course, wants compensation for the time and effort one puts into the job. He took a company with many problems in the labor area. He clamped down, got rid of the bad ones, readjusted wages and reorganized work teams. He managed to assign one less man per crew without any loss to production." Mr. King moved his chair closer to the desk. He wanted to make a point.

"Mr. Moses signed a contract, a five year deal that the owner will not renegotiate even though he performed well above expectations. He believes he should have been paid for his success in increasing the profit and now he wants out. That is why he is available."

"He signed a deal, that contract should be honored, and he could do the same thing to me. How will I know he will honor my contract and not leave me short?"

"First, he is all you ask for. He is perfect for your operation and basically wants paid for his work. He is good, one of the best, and I suggest in order to take care of the financial part, a new approach to his salary. I propose he be paid a percent of the profit, rather than a direct salary. There will be a ceiling, of course. He is confident that if he handled the brawny steel workers, he can handle the "hunkies" in the mines. Look. Sir, he has to make a profit to make money, he has to produce, and the more he makes the higher the profit for you. This is a good situation for both of you, and you retain complete control. Plus, you can feel at ease being away in New York."

"This is an interesting concept, Mr. King. At first glance I feel the need to speak to a confident here in Pittsburgh, and my bankers in New York. I need their council and guidance on this. I had a salary in mind, but this was unexpected, yet the concept appears workable. Yes, I will have to look at some figures and arrive at a ceiling amount, perhaps other things as well."

"It's a new idea, but fair for him and you. This relieves you of any worries like the ones that brought you back this time. You will be assured a top effort at all times, in fact guaranteed one since profit is tied directly to his earnings. To me it's simple: no profit, no earnings, but with profit comes great earnings for you, a good wage for him."

"You present an excellent case. Sounds like you are assured this man will succeed. I like your positive attitude, and you say this man meets all my requirements."

"Yes sir, every one trust me, he is a very good choice."

Mr. Grant, as he did many times before, walked to the window, leaving Mr. King sitting in the chair previously occupied by Hayes and Schaeffer. Changes were happening fast. H. C. felt comfortable at the window, his thinking, and decision making, crisp and clear at this spot. He reviewed the facts over and over; he finally decided to take the next step and act. After all Adelaide was waiting.

"He returned to the desk and abruptly asked, "When can I meet this man?"

"Tomorrow, or at your earliest convenience."

"Make it one o'clock, here in my office."

Alexander King excused himself, said goodbye, and left the office. He closed the door and walked to the front of the outer office where Schaeffer stood, coat and hat in hand ready to assist with the garments. Mr. King placed his briefcase on the floor and accepted the secretary's help He buttoned the coat, and picked up the briefcase.

He looked at Schaeffer, who offered the hat. Before accepting, Mr. King glanced around the office. Satisfied, he reached into his inside pocket and pulled out an envelope and handed it to Schaeffer. He put on his hat, gave the secretary a salute and left. Schaeffer quickly folded the envelope in half and placed it in his front pocket.

His boss was calling for him to report, "...and bring your notebook and pen with you," H. C. ordered.

"I will be meeting with Mr. Frederick C. Moses tomorrow at one o'clock. I want to prepare a list of questions to ask the gentleman. Once that is completed, I want to compile a list of directors for a meeting next Monday. Should I proceed with the hiring of the person recommended by Mr. King, I will introduce him then. Regardless, I want to inform them of the dismissal of Mr. Hayes. Now let's get to the list of questions."

Schaeffer wrote down the questions dictated to him by Mr. Grant. He was instructed to type the list and have it ready by the afternoon. Then he was to work on notification of District personnel for the Monday meeting.

"Today I will lunch at the Pittsburgh Club in a private room with the Director of U.S.Steel and visit the jewelers to get a set of diamonds for my wife." He exited the office before noon and went directly to the Club a short walk away.

Schaeffer typed the list of questions along with a copy he planned on giving to Mr. King on his way home from the office this evening. He was promised another envelope for the favor, and the secretary was eager to oblige. Mr. King was generous and paid well.

Lunch was over and the diamonds selected, Mr. Grant returned to his office where Schaeffer was waiting. A list of names and their positions in the Grant Coke Company were completed for notification of a meeting next Monday. "Make certain that the regional Director's, Baldwin, Blanchard, Houseman, and the labor agents, Erickson and Angelo are included on the list.

That should do it; I don't want to get overloaded with numbers."

Satisfied that the questions were developed and plans for a meeting finalized, Mr. Grant left the office earlier than usual. He had decided to leave Pittsburgh next Tuesday and wanted the servants to begin preparations for his departure. The more he thought about

Ridge Valley

the presentation by Mr. King the more he liked it. "This Mr. Moses sounds like an excellent replacement. The Director of U. S. Steel gave his approval, and the pay idea is appealing. I will sound him out tomorrow."

Schaeffer reported at his usual time in the morning and arranged the office. Mr. Grant arrived more cheerful then normal as he reminded Schaeffer of the one o'clock meeting and his decision to return to New York. Schaeffer's service would be terminated at that time. The morning passed quickly and ended with lunch for H. C. at the Club. He returned to the office to find a gentleman sitting in the outer office. The man's stature, looks and dress, except for the vest, were identical to that of Mr. Grant. He stood only five feet and seven inches tall with a dark well-trimmed mustache. He wore glasses so small and round that they barely engulfed the eyeball.

"May I present Mr. Frederick C. Moses to you sir," said Schaeffer.

"Good afternoon, you're a bit early I'd say…"

"Yes I try to be on time, and I will wait until you are ready and prepared, sir."

"It will be a few minutes."

Mr. Grant entered his office and closed the door. Mr. Moses and Schaeffer smiled at each other, both delighted at catching the boss off guard. Within a few minutes Mr. Moses was invited into the main office and directed to sit in the chair in front of the desk. H. C. noted not one wrinkle graced the applicant's face. He soon discovered a serious no nonsense person who was direct and specific in answering questions. He answered each question with understanding and knowledge of Grant's business operations. Of course knowing the questions helped.

"I assure you," Mr. Moses said, " I will earn my wages, every cent. I was successful at Midvale, as you know, and will do the same here. The wage arrangement speaks for itself, I must make a profit to earn money for you, and this arrangement will benefit me also …that was not the case in my previous employment. I assure you that I will do whatever it takes to be successful, I will succeed."

"I am impressed with your presentation and your reaction to my questions. You have given me much to consider. I do have one more item to pass before you and would appreciate your reaction."

"Happy to oblige."

"This is a copy of a lease signed by every worker living in a Company house." H. C. spoke slowly and emphasized his presentation with a slow precise diction.

"This lease is made solely between the H. C. Grant Coke Company and the employee, and shall under no circumstances be construed as a lease from year to year. The employee may rent said premises for the sole purpose of employment at a Grant operation. Failure to comply with this agreement will violate the lease resulting in immediate eviction from the house and…"

"Sir, if I may interrupt."

"Yes?"

"I understand that the house is there to provide labor for the Grant mines and the answer you seek is a simple one…no worker in the house, no house for any others to live in regardless of the circumstances. This is only good business and I assure you I will follow this agreement to the letter."

"I appreciate your frank reply, Mr. Moses. I have no further questions at this time. I believe we have agreed on compensation if you are hired, and discussed your duties. Do you have any questions, sir?"

" Not a question, but an observation, sir. I judge that the main reason for the lack of production, and of course lack of profit, is due primarily to manpower resources. You could be low in numbers of workers or simply lack numbers because rules and regulations are not followed. A new man must take the initiative to enforce the rules, and solve the need for workers. This to me is the major problem within your operation."

"Your judgment is accurate."

"Then may I suggest another position, an extremely important one to help solidify the rules and regulations of your company, and in turn your labor concerns."

A frown covered Mr. Grant's face. He was stunned into silence. He never expected a question, let alone a statement where another position is suggested. "This man isn't hired yet, and he is asking me to add another position. He is certainly confident, aggressive and demanding, but demanding of me?"

Mr. Moses took Mr. Grant's silence as an omen to continue. "I am suggesting that a Director of Security be hired by your company. He should organize a police force that will act fast, a force that will protect your assets and take the place of local constables. With company police presence, more regulations will be established to control the patch towns. You asked me about the lease situation, well, a company force is a way to take care of those not contributing to the labor force. You will have the power and force to get rid of them quickly. This is a good investment," he said.

Mr. Grant was overloaded, he felt bombarded with suggestions. He needed time to think, sort things out. He was impressed with Mr. Moses and actually glowed inside with the thought of adding a company police force. Anyway, even though he was impressed with the man, he wanted to play the waiting game.

"You once again present a good idea, Mr. Moses, I like your approach. I will need time to review your interview and all the suggestions you have made. Let's meet here in my office, say Thursday at nine o' clock A. M. I will have an answer for you then, but please allow me one more question? How would you implement authority in each individual patch?"

"Place the mine superintendent in charge. He will control and take responsibility for all facets of the operation including the Company Store and the new Coal and Iron Police.

The Director of Security will oversee all operations and report directly to me."

"Sounds like you have everything covered, gives me a lot to think about."

H. C. took time to review all options and came to the conclusion that Frederick E. Moses was the man to lead his company. He confirmed his decision with the President of U. S. Steel who knew of the success of Mr. Grant's choice. He would have Schaeffer draw up a contact and offer the job to Mr. Moses on Thursday. The request to hire a Director of Security was a different matter. The cost of having a police force in every patch was costly, very costly. Was it worth the expense? Yet, Moses made a good argument about quelling problems immediately and not let them fester. Furthermore, the superintendent would have total control, and if there was any grumbling or rumbling from the patch people he can turn the problem over to the Captain of the Company Police Department. He finally recalled the part that convinced him to allow the hiring of the Director of Security and the forming of the Company Police.

"You control the miners through your housing agreement. The one thing that must be done is to follow through on evictions when you have the police force to handle them. I tell you sir, things would have been much different at Homestead had a force like this been in existence."

Mr. Grant made the decision to 'take the next step.' He sent a telegram to Adelaide to expect him next week. He would notify Mr. Moses on Thursday of his decision and inform him of the planned meeting on Monday. He agreed with Moses about the hiring of a Director of Security. He would accept recommendations from Mr. King for the security position as soon as possible.

"We will meet with the directors, superintendents and labor agents. I will make a few remarks, introduce you, and a new Director of Security. I know the Pinkertons have someone capable. Being in the business, they should." said H. C. to Mr. Moses.

"They have some excellent candidates. I'm impressed with one Mr. Hood who assisted me at Midvale Steel. He tops the list as one of their best. May I cut through a lot of red tape and suggest him for your consideration?" said Mr. Moses at the Thursday meeting. I believe I can have him available for you to interview on Saturday. If he meets with your approval then you can return to New York without a worry.

The meeting ended with the two men exchanging pleasantries, and then Mr. Moses left the room. Schaeffer got up from his desk and walked Mr. Moses to the coat rack, where he assisted him with his coat. The new hire expressed his thanks with an envelope he handed to the secretary. He left the room smiling.

Those notified were gathered early Monday in the meeting room. They were surprised to be here. There were rumors that the Big Boss was in town, but that was pushed aside as simply that, a rumor. Then there was the Hayes question. Where is Hayes? The invitees did not know what to expect.

The door opened with all eyes focused on Mr. Grant and two other men entering the room.

"The short one is a spitting image of the boss, the other tall, muscular, rough looking; who and why is he here, and where is Hayes?"

Frederick E. Moses walked with Mr. Grant to the front of the room. Mr. Hood remained in the back.

"Good morning, gentleman." Said Grant who continued, "Due to production concerns, and other matters over the past two years, Mr. Hayes was duly dismissed from the director's position. Mr. Hayes is gone." The room buzzed. "I will not elaborate any further except to introduce Mr. Frederick E. Moses, the new Director of Operations, and the new Director of Security, Mr. Harold C. Hood there in the back. They will be talking to you shortly." More buzz and mumbling. "I have complete trust in these gentleman, and expect cooperation from you to accept their initiative to once again attain the profits this company expects." With that Mr. Grant left the room.

"This is all happening too quickly. You just don't move a person into the top position without any experience in mining. Where is this guy from? Why a new security position?" thought those assembled in the room.

The appearance of the new leader was in sharp contrast to those gathered in the room. A short, thin, queasy looking man stood over hardy, rugged men. They agreed with Hayes. "They were solving problems, making progress, but our leader is gone, wait, maybe this new man will listen to us, at least give us a chance to talk, then maybe that's why Hayes is gone, did he express himself and was fired for his belief."

" Gentleman I will not mince words with you. I expect you to produce, or join Mr. Hayes it's that simple. I will not accept excuses, I want results." He paused, and then motioned for Mr. Hood, to come to the front. He introduced Mr. Hood and explained his duties. The new Director of Security returned to his seat without saying a word.

"Now gentlemen, Mr. Grant presented two major areas of concern to me that he felt caused the decline in production and profit. The first one relates to you here in the room. Under the previous leader, he felt you have become lax in your duties. Instead of solving problems, you offered excuses. Take, for example, the check weight master. This position controls the accounting of all work and the amount of coal mined. How much coal is actually in the wagon, what percent slate, or waste matter, is it humped properly, are we giving too much credit and not taking the proper deductions? Is "labor larceny" going on here? When was the last time someone checked? Find out, I want to know."

A hand was raised, "Just a minute sir, you will have time to speak, but I have one more major concern and that is the manpower situation. It appears that we have become lax in replacing workers. There are families, I understand, living in houses without someone from that house working in the mine, widows occupying them, or houses that are just plain empty. People are dispensable, someone is always there to take the place of another, and to live in a patch house you MUST work for the Grant Company. Gentleman, it's that simple."

"Sir, sir, sorry for the interruption but I must speak to you about widows housing borders and the manpower shortage," stated Randolph Erickson a labor agent.

Mr. Moses frowned, stared at the speaker, and then waved his hand indicating to Mr. Erickson to proceed.

"Sir, a number of widows took boarders in so you must decide if it is permissible for her to stay under those conditions. Secondly, I have recruited in the Central European area as the labor agent for the Grant Company for years. We have been successful in filling the manpower quota for the mining and coke operations. The war changed everything. Men left and joined in the fight and governments expelled us from the continent. Secondly, our own government instituted immigration controls that slammed the door shut."

"We can get that changed, the war is over now, so let's resume our recruiting." Said Moses.

"Even if we could return to the European area the pickings would be slim, very slim. Over eight and one-half million were killed and twenty-one million more injured. Highly toxic gasses used by both sides in the war caused severe lung damage. Not many good recruits are left. Not many good choices, but if you want us to continue."

"No, of course not, we don't need more problems," interrupted Mr. Moses.

"There are more happenings that bit into our manpower woes. An untold number took their money to their homeland planning not to return knowing cheap land would be available after the war to start a farm," said Mr. Angelo the other labor recruiter, who added, "Beginning in the summer of 1918 and continuing through the next year, the Spanish Influenza hit our region hard, very hard. Our company doctor said the flu killed some half million Americans and twenty million worldwide. He reported that because coal dust weakens the lungs, when the flu hits, a miner never recovers. That Influenza stuff hit us hard. We lost a number of good men. Fact is it's still around.

Mr. Moses was caught off guard by what he just heard. He did not understand why the Director was unaware of the information just presented. Was he too preoccupied with thoughts of Art and going back to New York? Did he get forgetful in his old age? Did he know and not tell me? Where does one go? Europe is cut off from us; only hope is from miner's families who have a son available to work. But that supply is exhausted, most are already working.

"Time for lunch," announced Schaeffer. "We have to place the manpower problem as our number one priority for discussion this afternoon." Said Moses. That afternoon meeting ended without a solution so all agreed to return the next day for further discussion.

Mr. Moses, along with Mr. Hood, returned to the temporary office hastily arranged next to Schaeffer's. They reviewed reports, critiqued the meeting, and talked about organizing the security forces. Finally, talk returned to labor supply.

"Grant told me about the manpower situation, but I don't think he knows how serious the problem is. It's obvious that we have to find more workers somewhere. But where?"

The two considered a number of options but none seemed plausible. Frustrated Mr. Hood decided to call it a day. He left, leaving Moses to check the mail, review reports and plan tomorrows meeting. "Was it a big mistake to work for a percentage of the profit rather than a regular wage? Did the man know? Was I duped?" He finally decided to call it a day and leave the office for the elevator. He rang and waited.

"Good evening sir, going down." The operator, a tall black man said while holding the door for Mr. Moses, who delayed entering.

"Oh, sorry, thinking about something."

"No problem, sir, not many left in the building. Just to mention a bit of a chill in the air this evening, fall coming in a hurry. Then winter. Sure hate the cold. Sometime I wish I were back in my hometown, a lot warmer back there, yes sir."

"Where is that, what is your name?"

"Jimmy Washington, sir, but everybody just calls me Jimmy, yes sir, Jimmy will do. That is Carbon Hill, Alabama, sir. Yes sir, only work in that town was down under and I'm too tall to be a doing work there, so here I am."

The elevator reached the first floor; Jimmy quickly opened the doors and announced, "First floor, have a good evening, sir."

Mr. Moses exited the elevator and started toward the outside door to face the evening air. His heels clicked loudly on the marble floor. He reached for the doorknob but didn't turn it. He froze in place. He turned, clicking heels hurrying back to the elevator. He pushed the button; impatient he rang again and again, bells ringing for Jimmy. The elevator finally arrived, opening the door Jimmy stepped back surprised to see Mr. Moses. He apologized for the delay.

"Where did you say you're from?"

"Carbon Hill, Alabama."

"What do people of your color do there? I mean where do they work?"

"Carbon Hill Mine mostly, sir."

"Down under," Moses mumbled to himself. "You're saying that folks in Carbon Hill are miners, that they mine coal there?"

"Yes sir"

Ridge Valley

"I knew about West Virginia. Labor agents said the workers will not leave that area, but had no idea about mines in Alabama," Mr. Moses thought." Jimmy stood inside the elevator, looking quizzically at Mr. Moses who stood smiling. A bell rang calling Jimmy to an upper floor. The bell also jarred Mr. Moses from a stupor of deep thought, he looked at Jimmy, "you have a call, good night." He turned to leave. Jimmy closed the door and sighed. Mr. Moses would not feel the coolness of the fall evening as he walked down the sidewalk.

CHAPTER VII

HIS MOM'S SOFT knock on the bedroom door woke John. He was alert the moment he opened his eyes. He dressed hurriedly in the gray moonlight coming from the window. John left the room, closing the door quietly then reached for the "chamber pot" at the top of the stair landing and then pulled back.

"Hey, this is little brother's job now," he mumbled as he descended the stairs.

"Morning, Mom, looks like it's going to be a nice day for picking walnuts."

"Just be careful, and don't carry too much. Wash up and have a little something"

John went to the sink, washed, brushed his teeth and combed his hair. Sliced bread, butter and jam, along with a cup of coffee waited for him at the table. Since John was now the man of the house, his mom centered her attention his way. He got first choice at meals and with desert. He felt uncomfortable with this adoration, being one who strived to serve rather than be served. John slurped his coffee, ate the jam-covered bread, and slurped again. Finishing to the last drop, he rinsed the cup, dried it, and placed it in the cupboard.

"I'll be going now mom, hope to be back by noon."

John walked in stocking feet to the back entrance, slipped on his "clodhoppers" and exited the house into a brisk, cool gray morning.

True to form, Jerry appeared from around the corner to meet him and they began walking down the path to the cutoff.

"I'm glad you mentioned wanting to go for walnuts Jer. I been thinking about going but kind of set the thought aside with everything else happening. I gather they're one of your favorite treats."

"Got to have 'em, John, especially at Christmas."

"You know piccalilli is my favorite, and I worked extra hard to keep the garden going. The hail storm didn't leave any pickings, so my favorite winter snack is gone."

"Yeah but you'll have walnuts," said Jerry.

"Sure, right, for now, who knows about next year? This may be our last Jer."

Jerry stopped in his tracks, both hands on hips, legs spread apart. John went another step, stopped and turned to face Jerry.

"No way, John, we got to promise that as long as we live we meet at this time, at the company store the second Saturday in October to pick walnuts. You have to promise, John."

"Okay Jer"

"Promise, John, you have to promise."

"I promise, Jer okay."

The two walked down the path to the cutoff, where they turned, and continued walking on the road passing in front of the company store. Like those who made the trek previously to answer the call of the siren, the two followed the same path this early morning. The sun began peeking above the Blue Ridge Mountains sending rays to the top of the tipple as they crossed the railroad bridge. Men were seen working at the pit mouth.

"Patty Driscall told me that they're making good progress in shoring up the roof, and moving along much better than expected," stated John as they neared the junk graveyard.

"You still going down with him, John?" asked Jerry.

"Guess so Jer, I talked to him a couple days ago. Told me they could use workers but said to take time to help at home, relax as much as possible, then let him know when I'm ready. Said he wants a clear mind, one that will concentrate on the job "cause a cluttered mind can only spell disaster down there."

"I'm trying to get a job up top. I know it doesn't pay as much as a loader, but I'm not as strong as you, maybe when I'm older maybe gain some weight and muscle, but for now the top side looks like it for me."

The sun broke clear of the ridge and made a rapid climb in the sky. Fog that dominated the lowlands was reluctantly dissipating, trying to hang on in the low area near the creek. Sparrows increased their activity, darting, landing and pecking, darting, pecking, over and over repeating the routine. The clear morning allowed the two to see their destination in the distance beyond the heights.

"That's where I hid with my mom during the storm. Mrs. Mullin and the Dorek lady were with us," said John, pointing out the pit car to Jerry.

"She that young one who just moved in the second row?"

"Yep, her husband was lost in the explosion. Took it hard."

"May explain why that Tony guy is hanging around her house. He sure is a dresser."

They cleared the junk graveyard and approached a fence surrounding a large grassy area connected to the barn. Over the fence, moving past the barn, and now crossing the New Salem road to a path meandering along a shallow creek which was followed up the valley to a point where the waterway turned away from their planned route. They proceeded up a steep grade in the direction of the airshaft used to help air flow for the Ridge Valley mine. The full force of the sun warmed the two travelers as they moved beyond the shaft now advancing to the edge of the Glover farm. They climbed through a barbed wire fence. Wading through goldenrod and milkweed thickets they're movement roused a grouse hiding in the bushes. It scared Jerry. He jumped back, waved his arms, and stumbled about shouting, "What was that, did you see it, John?"

"Just a ruffed grouse, Jer."

A large and lengthy cornfield lay a short distance ahead. Entering, they progressed through dried leaves and stocks with ears of corn hanging down to dry. Soon the stocks would be cut and placed in bundles for shocking. They finally came to the end of the rows of corn and stepped out, finding themselves at the edge of the woods.

"Hold on John, got to go, bad, be right back," said Jerry as he hurried back into the cornfield.

John found a large rock, big enough to lean against. He gazed at the many yellow, red and orange leaves of trees in the woods. He relished the quiet and the sun warming his body while observing the beauty of the Heights. He reached out and broke a small twig from an Eastern Pine and closed his eyes while inhaling the piney fragrance. He heard the rustle of squirrels. Opening his eyes he saw them scurry about, snatching butternuts in jaws that stretched as though the poor things had the mumps. He watched one run in one direction and then another. Suddenly it stopped in his tracks, looked about, satisfied; now, the front paws moved so fast it was a blur; it buried the morsel, covered it, and then moved out to search for another. Looking in the sky, he viewed two crows circling, eying the cornfield. John now heard the rustle of dried corn leaves as Jerry walked up to John smiling.

"Feel better now?"

"I had to go worse than I thought, I just made it, feel much better except for the leaves, rougher than I thought, scraped heck out of me. I finally took off my shoe and used my sock It wasn't much use to me anyways 'cause it had holes in the front and back."

John shook his head and smiled.

"John do you know why I went in the cornfield and not the woods?

"Why?"

"Because there are NO snakes in a cornfield; did you ever see any in there?" Jerry said, pointing toward the field.

Pondering for a moment John finally answered, "Come to think on it, no, never"

"Remember that, John, trust me, it's safe in a cornfield."

"Jerry, you're a classic; c'mon, let's get going," said John, shaking his head, first smiling then laughing loudly. That was the first good laugh for John since the explosion last August, and Jerry provided the needed release for his friend.

They walked along the edge of the woods, telling stories, laughing enjoying each other's company. Together, the two delighted in reminiscing, about school, friends, their families and where the lassie at the Canteen lived. They would skip most of their teenage years and proceed directly to manhood. Dreams of John attending school was lost forever in the blast. The family comes first, and the family would depend heavily on both of them. This day, however, is one the two shares together as they look forward to finding the gnarled black walnut tree with green shells protecting the walnuts inside. Now passing a section of eastern pines, followed by a canopy of tall trees with brightly colored leaves that blocked the sun. A musty smell and heavy dampness produced a sweat in the stale humid air.

"Over here, John, this way. There's a spring beyond these rocks. Good cool water, and there it is," smiled Jerry happily, "C'mon lets go," he shouted pointing to water bubbling up from the ground, guarded by dark green ferns and a darker moss spreading over the area. Flowing down the hill the clear water collected in a small pond. The overflow spread into a lush grassy meadow.

"Look Jer, edge of the woods, across the way," whispered John, pointing.

"Yeah I see 'em, big buck peeking out by the maple, checking things out. Here comes the rest of the family heading for the pond, wow!"

Both forgot about a drink from the spring and just stood watching the deer meander to the pond. The deer drank their fill, then scattered about the meadow to graze. John finally poked his friend on the shoulder and motioned for them to get going. They drank heartily at the spring, then moved on; found the walnut trees and filled their sacks. They returned to the spring for another drink, and then started to walk back through the woods, over fences, struggling with the load. They arrived home where the walnut shells were placed on the porch roof. The shells needed time, along with a hard frost to rot, eventually releasing the walnut inside. John deposited his wares. Satisfied, he sat for a time on the roof alone, meditating about the past and contemplating the future. He checked the arrangement of the nuts, and, satisfied, left for the kitchen.

"Did you get a good supply?" asked his mom.

"Yes, mom, small this year, probably because of the drought."

"Hungry?"

"Not really, drank a lot at the spring, bit bloated I guess."

"John." She hesitated for a few seconds then added. "Mr. Driscall was by this morning and left a message for you to contact him as soon as you can. Said they needed workers, so" she turned away, not finishing the message. John walked over to her, took her shoulders gently and said, "Everything will be fine, you'll see, everything will be fine."

CHAPTER VIII

FREDERICK E. MOSES walked with a short choppy gait down the sidewalk to the entrance of the Grant Building. Schaeffer was already entering the lobby and soon descended the stairs to the basement to retrieve the mail. He was anxious to confer with Mr. Moses so he hurried to the elevator instead of taking the stairs. Mr. Moses paid well, much better than his old boss, and keeping the new one happy and informed was important to Schaeffer's financial health. He supplied information to his new boss, valuable information that helped in the Grant interview. He would offer more valuable advice to Mr. Moses for the superintendents and directors meeting later in the morning. Harry C. Hood was in the office, waiting for the secretary and the boss. There were plans to be made for recruiting men into the Company Police Force. The three gathered in Mr. Moses' temporary office. Hood was the first to speak.

"I plan on going to the Pinkerton's office to check the files for the North and South District Security Directors' positions. They will be responsible for overseeing all Captains in the mining towns."

"Patches, just to let you know that the mining towns are called patches. Locals will know you're an outsider if you don't speak their language," said Schaeffer.

"Nothing is simple in my business," said a flustered Mr. Hood. "O. K. I'll remember what you said." "I assure you, Schaeffer, that there is a new regime and a new chain of command will be established. The chain will extend to cover all facets of security in the patch. I will establish a curfew, keep an eye on visitors and double-check all strangers for possible union activity. Besides, we have the backing of the local sheriff, county police force and even the courts. Best I get started reviewing the personnel records available."

" Don't forget the meeting," said Moses.

"I'll be there." Hood said.

Schaeffer, unaccustomed to speaking to a superior until spoken to, vacillated between talking now or forever holding his peace. He chose to speak.

"Sir if I may. I feel it vital to suggest that Mr. Hood bears some watching. I truly think that he is an arrogant man who leads with emotion rather then with intelligent thought. This sort of dictatorship attitude…his need to intimidate, to create fear can only survive so long then…"

"He is direct, that is true, and you found that out, all that you said is true," interrupted Mr. Moses who added, "I need him in this position, he is indispensable because he will be my eyes and ears, or rather the Coal and Iron Police Force will serve that purpose, and they report to him, then me. I will take that information and make adjustments. He is loyal in that regard and Schaeffer; I want you to know that I also appreciate your loyalty and help. I am grateful to you for helping me get this job. The information you provided was indispensable. I also appreciate your concern with Mr. Hood. Your comments will be given due consideration, but for the moment we must move on to other things, like the meeting."

"Yes sir, I will go directly to prepare the room."

On this October day in 1919, Mr. Henry Clay Grant left from a rail siding in his personal railroad car for New York. Mr. Frederick E Moses would soon begin a meeting where he will become the power behind the company the departing Baron passed on to him. Mr. Hood would hire two Security Officers and instruct them to go immediately to Cleveland, Chicago and Detroit and recruit the future police force for the Grant Empire. John Ignatius would begin his first day of work in the Ridge Valley mine.

Ridge Valley

The philosophy of the leaders in the Federal Government early in the twentieth century was one of ignoring the working class. The top of the chain in Washington had their own agenda and preferred to let the industrialists handle the workingmen and women of the nation. The same could be said for the state and local governmental officials. The industrial bosses had clear sailing in utilizing force by accessing the state and local police units to quell any plan to organize union meetings. The working class was defenseless in efforts to upgrade the poor conditions they faced every day.

The Keating-Owen Child Labor Act of 1916 recognized the philosophy of government of the people, by the people and for the people. The Child Labor Act protected young children from the medieval working conditions found in the filthy slaughterhouses, garment districts, and in the coalmines. The law only lasted two years. In 1918, the Supreme Court struck down the Keating-Owen Act. That change would allow young boys like John, Bull and Jerry to work in dangerous occupations once again. Obviously the Robber Barons were instrumental in getting the Keating-Owen Bill reversed. They now had a stranglehold over working conditions.

Woodrow Wilson was president from the early teens to the beginning of the 1920's. In order to establish a Federal Department to oversee business practices in the United States, he established the Federal Trade Commission. One section of this commission was to investigate unfair labor practices brought to their attention. He also campaigned "to keep us out of war." The President soon changed his mind about the war. The United States entered World War I and tipped the balance of power in favor of the allies. Once the war was over, President Wilson became deeply involved in the peace process. He went to Paris to enter negotiations for, "a lasting peace." He became immersed in the peace process. Eventually he presented the Versailles Treaty, with his fourteen points that included a "Covenant of the League of Nations," to be ratified by Congress. The Versailles Treaty failed in the Senate by seven votes. The President was determined to override the Senate, so he embarked on a national tour to present his argument for acceptance to the people. He thought that by presenting his idea to the masses he could pressure the legislature to accept the Treaty. He suffered a debilitating stroke while on tour, ending any hope of success. The Federal Trade Commission's activities were all but forgotten. The industrialists were free to remain in power and run their companies with an iron fist.

This attitude allowed the Barons to do as they pleased to maximize profits on the backs of labor. These conditions allowed the leaders to continue their commanding authority and to dictate their philosophy over the Grant mining district.

What good fortune for the new Chief Officer to meet and talk with Jimmy, the elevator operator yesterday. The chance discussion solved a major problem for him and the Grant Company. They would recruit in the south and bring experienced workers into the fold. "No need to go oversees when workers were living practically in our back yard. Why didn't anyone, from Grant on down, think about this area to recruit for workers? I'll save this announcement until the end of the meeting and let everyone go home happy. They will have all the bodies they need. The only question is how soon can we get the flow of workers moving from the south to the Grant district? Will housing be available? Will the Company Coal and Iron Police Force be in place to help with evictions of people in homes where non-company workers reside? Have to discuss this with Hood," thought Moses as he sat in his office waiting for the superintendents to arrive.

The room was full, requiring Schaeffer to find additional chairs. He was unsuccessful, so a number of men remained standing as Mr. Moses entered the room. He was pleased at the number in attendance. After a brief welcome he asked all in attendance to introduce themselves and state the mine or district they represent. After all completed the introductions, Mr. Moses began speaking in a loud voice, almost a shout. The room was completely silent.

"Production is down, accidents are up; profit is down, expenses are up, transportation is a nightmare, replacement of manpower is nonexistent. WHY? Ask yourselves why, Gentleman. I assure you the status quo will not continue. Things will change I guarantee it. You will change it, or else! You in this room are responsible for where we are now, and you will be responsible for upgrading all phases of your operation immediately. It is as simple as that. I accept no excuses. Gentleman, my mode of operation is direct, to the point and demanding. I expect results. Now forget about any previous directives, the old regime is gone, you will follow directives exactly as given…at all times." He paused briefly to allow his message to sink in, then continued. "Now, my first directive is that every superintendent is not only in charge of the mining operations, but is in charge of all operations in his district. This includes the patch housing, the Company Store and labor assignments. You are totally answerable to my office regarding production and maximizing profit. Now, a new position has been added, and it is called the Director of Security. Mr. Harold Hood was recently hired to fill the post. He will be here a bit later to address this group."

A murmur began to reverberate among the audience. They wondered about the whys and wherefores of a private police force. Some thought it good, while others had questions they dare not ask at this time. A few saw it as a means to control the miners.

"Now let's get down to business. The biggest problem facing you remains the lack of laborers available for replacement of lost workers. This has plagued this company for a long time. I will address that point in a minute. However, another major concern appears in the transportation arena. We will work with the railroad executives to get additional rail cars and to attain much better scheduling of arrivals and departures. This will be a stopgap measure until a plan is developed to construct an underground conveyer belt system from the southern district to the river. The coal can be picked up and delivered by barge, saving enormous amounts of money.

"What the hell, I heard about that plan before, he stole that idea, I'm certain of that," mumbled one of the men in the back. Schaeffer, who stood on the side, smiled.

"The conveyer belt plan is down the road, for now we have to solve a more pressing problem that was brought to my attention. I was informed that because of the war, the flu outbreak, accidents and the new immigration laws have caused a severe labor shortage. Furthermore, the prime supplier of labor to us, the European theatre, is closed for further recruitment. Our shortage must be addressed. Gentleman…any of you who disagree with me on this?" asked Moses, one word at a time, emphasizing each one.

A hand rose in back of the room.

"You disagree, sir?"

" Oh no, sir, I agree, we need help."

"And help you will get."

"From where? There is nowhere to go for help."

"There is, and it comes from here in our own country." The room reacted with stares and mumbles as Moses continued. "Immediately following the conclusion of this meeting I will be sending Mr. Erickson and Mr. Angelo to Georgia and Alabama. They mine coal down there and that means experienced workers. Shortly you will have what you need."

"You understand that you will be introducing a new element into the patch," said a man from the back.

"Yes, and what about housing, where these new miners going to live?"

"Nothing is finalized at this time; we will work out the details regarding living arrangements when we start receiving the workers," answered Mr. Moses. He did not want to discuss possible evictions of families with this group now. He did not want any of this information out until the Coal and Iron Police were well established to back up that move.

"Time is moving on and I want to introduce Mr. Hood and call on him to present to you the role of the new security forces in the district."

Hood came forward and spent the remainder of the morning outlining his plans for the new police units. The men shuffled and squirmed in their seats but said nothing in response to the presentation. Mr. Moses concluded the meeting by reviewing his requirements and expectations. He then adjourned the meeting.

CHAPTER IX

THE DECISION WAS made. Leroy would accompany his father on the trip to Pennsylvania. Rufus talked to Bella countless times about going north but she fought him off each time. She could not accept the thought of leaving Momma. Rufus was persistent, bringing up the issue every chance he got. He thought he saw a possibility of her considering his pleas one day at supper when he mentioned, "Just think how much better it will be for Leroy." Then one recent evening he pulled out the last letter he got and showed her; "The Reverend done said it told of openings in a place called the Grant mining district, near a town called Uniontown."

Bella listened with patience, then thought of different ways to stall. One example was using the recent death of her mother.

"Momma ain't rested nearly enough. The dirt hasn't settled we just can't leave her here alone. Lord, forgive me for even thinking about moving away until she has a decent rest. Lord forgive Rufus for thinking it."

Once the Lord was mentioned, Rufus backed off. He knew he could not change her mind and going against the Lord left him discomforted. He didn't know why, but he felt ill-at-ease going against the wishes of Bella when it included the Lord. So Rufus bided his time and brought up the issues only when new letters arrived.

"A letter, came yesterday and I done run up to the church and have the reverend cipher it. There's work, good work and houses to live in, it says. The letter say if I come I can find a job right away in places called, Buff-in-ton, Or-I-ant or Rid-g-val-ee." Rufus announced excitedly. "The reverend said he has time to tell us more if we come today or we can wait until Sunday." Bella decided she would wait until Sunday.

"The letter from Lucas in September 1919, says that he is sure Rufus can find a job at this here Ridge Valley mine for certain. Says that a coal seam there runs to nine feet in height, all coal, and no waste. He says you can make up to four dollars a day, and there is plenty to be had," read the reverend to Bella.

"Why doesn't Lucas work there if it's so great? He don't work there, he works somewhere else, answer me that, tell me why he isn't there?" questioned Bella.

"Probably like here, I mean you work where you work, like Reverend Washington, he stays cause it's his place, and God placed him here and he is not going to change what God has planned." said Rufus, who grimaced for saying something that he knew his wife would use against him, and she did.

"Our place is in Alabama, so as you say we live where we live," said Bella who walked away with her head in the air.

Rufus had to wait for another letter to arrive to reopen the subject. The cause to breach the attempt came not from a letter but from a poster nailed to a tree along the road. Fact of the matter was, there were posters everywhere around Carbon Hill and their presence became the talk of the town. One bit of information found on the notice that aroused Rufus was that, "transportation will be provided for worker and family," so he tore the poster from the tree and brought it home to show Bella.

"How you know it says that?" asked Bella.

"Willie Towns tole me."

"I thought we settled this at church."

"I'm sure, real sure I can do well, make a lot of money doing' the same thing I'm doing'. The pickings just aren't good working for the Hawkes. They don't give us the best places to work in the shaft. Nine foot of good coal, wow."

"I'm happy here. Why leave, plus we be leaving a lot of memories, deep roots, family roots. I'm happy here in Alabama, and what about Leroy? I worry about him."

"Leroy will be better off there. He could go to school. Bella we done talked about this move many times and I honestly believe I can do better there. No matter how hard I work for the Hawkes we aren't going to be no better off than we are now. The big bosses give the good sections to their favorites; they give us what's left. I can't believe that a nine-foot seam of coal actually exists. A man can dig standing up in there. He's not bending or kneeling, or laying down for hours like we do here."

"I don't know about the weather. Hear it be cold there and we could be facing bad winters and they have snow; we have never seen snow."

"I think it would be something to see," interrupted Leroy.

"Maybe for you, maybe for you, not for me, Leroy," said Bella.

"Listen, Bella, we'd have a real house to live in, and they are two stories, four big rooms; one a kitchen with running water inside, no need to go out and fetch water. Preacher says according to the poster they will take care of and pay for our train ride there.

"Rufus, you are my husband and I love you and Leroy dearly. I will do anything to help you and him. I just worry a lot about someone wanting to give us things for free." Bella looked directly into Rufus's eyes then said slowly, "I say no…nooobody gives you things for free…nooobody does that, they always want something in return, and I mean nooobody." She gathered a dish from the table to take to the sink for washing. She hurried there and returned quickly looking over Rufus shoulder. Hands on hips she waited for her husband to look up at her and when he did she said with emphasis.

"You say it sounds good, real good. You say lots of coal to mine, and you say they have good schools for Leroy, and you say I can buy what I want at this Company Store, and a big house to live in for only how much."

"Poster says only three dollars a month to rent."

"Tell me one thing Rufus, why they down here looking for workers, I ask why? Why they giving us all this wonderful stuff? This being so good, why aren't they giving all these special things to white folks who live there, answer me that?"

"They is, Bella, they offering the chance to white folks too, poster says all are welcome, so it means everyone," said Rufus. Leroy sat and listened to discussions about going north for a long time. He knew not to interfere; yet he knew some thinking of other families, but he remained quiet. Rufus continued, "They must have found out that we work hard from those that went before, so they come to fetch us."

"I know you work hard, Rufus. Your sweaty clothes tell me that. I know you deserve more pay for the work you do, but again I say, it all sounds too good to be true."

"Bella, all I want is a chance. We deserve better than this shack. Listen, I'll take Leroy with me and you can linger here, get things settled with your momma's grave, and once settled I'll send for you," countered Rufus.

Bella got up from her chair and walked over to where Leroy was sitting. When she approached her son she placed one hand on his shoulder, then asked. "Will you mind your Pa? Will you go to school and learn to cipher?"

"Yes's, I promise."

She then moved to hug her son from behind, leaning over the chair with arms around his shoulders and neck tenderly squeezing his hand. She felt tears well up in her eyes at the thought of him being alone in a strange place.

"The boy will mind, Bella, he's been a good boy, don't see him changing now."

"I'll be good and go to school. It will be great cause I'll know another friend who'll be there," his parents looked directly at Leroy who added, "yeah my friend Billie, Billie Towns. I think his Pa is going up north, but don't want folks at the mine to know, I guess its okay to tell you."

"You say the Towns, Willie Towns, is a goin? I never thought he would leave, he has a good job at the mine, why would he go, and Billie said so?"

"Yes sir, Billie done said it, I guess it was okay to tell you."

"Would ease my mind a bit fin's others are a' going," said Bella.

"There sure must be others goin; if Willie's goin, got to be more." Said Rufus

"Be nice to have someone you know," Bella said looking at Rufus.

"You mean to say you agree with our going?"

She did not answer Rufus verbally; her look of a half smile and a slight headshake up and down provided the answer. While Rufus and Leroy smiled at each other, Bella released her son from the hug and walked over to the stove and began to clean the surface. It didn't need cleaning; she just wanted to get away from her men; she didn't want them to see the tears dripping down her cheeks. She dipped the washcloth in cool water and proceeded to wipe her face. The cool water helped to relieve some of the hurt she felt at the moment. Glancing over her shoulder, Bella saw Leroy and Rufus looking over the poster that provided information along with a crude map showing the travel route from Carbon Hill to the Grant district.

"The reverend said that according to the information on this notice that fin's we can get to any of the railroad stations listed and tell the clerk man we is going to this here Grant district, he will issue us a ticket to take us there."

"Maybe we should take this paper with us, just in case Pa."

"Good thinking, Leroy, see Bella, this boy is smart, and he will do just fine."

Bella turned away and scrubbed harder and harder on an already clean surface as her two men tried to figure out the map and where to go to catch the train.

"Seems you got a better understanding of this here map than I do Leroy," said Rufus who added, "You sure know the ins and outs of this poster."

The men continued planning and Bella her washing and cleaning. She felt better, at least good enough after wiping her face to ask once again, "I still wonder why we is blessed with this here opportunity. I really do wonder. Leroy, you say the Towns are going for certain?" asked Bella.

"Yes'm, Billie done said it sure, but he toll me to keep it secret, so you're not going to say anything to them, are you?"

"I won't cause you any problems, but it would be of ease to me if I talked to someone about this before you go. I do have trepidation in my soul, I do, and it would help greatly to talk to someone." She paused to ponder a bit then continued, "Why do you suppose they want to keep it a secret? Not to tell? Seems to me that there has to be a reason, because you think they at least be telling others, but then we've not said of our going to anyone except the reverend." said Bella.

"They don't want the mine owners to know," blurted Leroy.

"I want to see the Reverend Washington after church service tomorrow. I want to ask him to go over this here map and stuff again, just to be sure. Help if you joined me, Bella, so that you would get all the information." said Rufus

"I suppose I could, but it would sure ease my mind fin's I could talk to someone about all this. Leroy, I promise that I won't say anything to the Towns that you told me. Anyway I know Mrs. Towns and I think she'll understand after I tell her about my concerns," stated Bella.

"I suppose it'll be all right. Billie probably told a lot of kids anyway."

Rufus and Leroy continued to review the map on the poster. "Look, Leroy, I know this town, Eldridge, just down the road and it's one of the stations where we can get a token. We can walk there easy," mentioned Rufus.

Leroy took the map and began to look at other locations where they could depart. Rufus got up from his chair and eased over behind Bella. She was thinking so hard she did not hear him approach. He touched her shoulder, causing her to jump at the move.

"I didn't mean to scare you."

"Oh, Rufus, been thinking too many bad thoughts, I hope it's in vain, I really do."

"We'll make a new and good life up there, don't worry, everything will be fine. Leroy, it's getting to be a bit late, and we got church tomorrow, bed time, boy."

"Okay Pa. Can I take this map with me, do some more studying?"

"Sure can, but not too late you hear."

Rufus and Bella talked a bit longer, at least until Leroy got settled and then they moved to the bedroom. The time for reading maps, or talking about two story houses was over. The thoughts and actions would now be about each other.

Leroy who needed to be called two or three times to get him out of bed on Sundays, was first up, dressed and ready. This day he already visited the outhouse, got water from the well, washed, dried his face with a threadbare cloth, and proceeded to the back steps to sit with poster in hand. He was fascinated with the map, and determined to understand the contents.

"Good morning, Pa, been sitting here looking over the poster. Can't wait to get to church and see Reverend Washington. I think I got everything down pat and want to ask him if I'm right."

"That boy up before us? My goodness. Maybe he'll be all right up there if he is this excited about going," said Bella to Rufus as she began to prepare a breakfast of biscuits and honey. The three finished, and as Bella cleared the table, Leroy continued to discuss the poster with Rufus. Finally they walked out the front door, taking the same route they took every Sunday, meeting many of the same people as they walked to the Holy Gospel Baptist Church.

Rufus and Leroy quickly moved ahead, distancing themselves as Bella lingered, hoping to see the Towns. She met Mrs. Robinson who talked about family and friends to Bella, and about momma. "I know you miss her, especially on Sunday, going to church together and all, she was a fine lady," said her neighbor, "Oh look, there is Mrs. Lincoln, and she is by herself. I sure hope her husband isn't feeling poorly since I don't see him with her. I believe I'll see after her," and she walked away

Bella continued walking alone up the sandy road. "I wonder if this is the way it will be, walking by myself when Rufus and Leroy leave," she mumbled as she neared the spur in the road. Other families walking along formed a gathering as they siphoned from the wider road to the narrow rutted sandy one leading to the church. Rufus and Leroy were out of sight now as Bella lagged behind, looking for the Towns. She was getting concerned when she failed to see them coming. Finally she eyed them in the distance. She drifted in their direction.

"Morning, Mrs. Towns, a beautiful day we're having."

"Morning, Mrs. Johnson, it sure is."

"Mrs. Towns, I wonder if I could meet you after church for a few minutes. My men have always enjoyed your rhubarb pie and I just can't get the hang of it. Appreciate your going over that recipe with me." Bella lied

"Sure, be happy to do that. My husband has some business with the reverend after services so how about meeting in back afterwards."

"Thank you so much. See you after the preaching."

They arrived at the church; entered and took seats with their families. They sang with enthusiasm, thanking God for all his goodness bestowed on them the past week. They listened to the reverend praise the Lord and denounce the devil. He got "Amen's" from the congregation at special points in the sermon. Upbeat spirituals were sung at the conclusion of the reverend's preaching. A closing prayer and boisterous spiritual ended the service.

Leroy could hardly contain himself, urging his father to, "Get going" instead of talking to friends. Seeing that his dad was in no hurry, he decided to leave and wait for him outside. He immediately spotted Billie Towns talking to Georgia Jefferson. He moved without delay across the lawn to met his friend and talk to Georgia. He liked talking to her and if the opportunity came up, talk to Billie about going north.

"I saw you from the top of the stairs Billie, hope you don't mind my joining you in the shade."

The two-welcomed Leroy as three other girls, jealous of Georgia Jefferson getting all the attention, decided to move in and join the threesome. "Look at her, she's drooling over those two and look, nothing but a tease, c'mon, let's go and have some fun."

"Look Jessica Jones, you and your friends are here to cause problems, so why don't you and, and the two with you just leave us alone?" said Georgia.

"Why you treating us like that? We just want to be friendly, there is no law that says we can't talk to whomever we want."

"You and your friends are always butting in, and you're not welcome."

Ridge Valley

"Georgia," came a call from an observant mother who saw what was happening, "time to get going, please come and help me with Grandma."

Georgia said her good-byes to the boys. The three girls, satisfied, turned laughing to find another group to agitate. Leroy and Billie now had time to talk about going north.

The reverend was standing at the top of the front landing, greeting parishioners as they exited the church. After the last thanked him for a "special preaching" he walked down the steps and greeted youngsters in the yard as he made his way to the back entrance. Inside the sanctuary Mrs. Washington arranged the bibles and songbooks on shelves by the piano. She did not see two ladies talking in the back of the church.

Bella, as she talked, continually glanced about looking to see if anyone was near. Feeling secure, she abruptly changed the subject.

"Mrs. Towns, I do apologize to you. I used the pie question as an excuse, the real reason I must speak to you is about your husband."

"My husband, about what?" A surprised Mrs. Towns asked

"Frankly about going north."

"What makes you think such a thing?" came a blunt reply, "Where, I say where you hear such a thing like that? We have not said one word to anyone about leaving, so please don't suggest anything of the kind."

"Mrs. Towns, my husband and Leroy are going to Penn…ceil…vania, and want to go soon. We done got letters and now see the posters about jobs, good jobs in the mines up there," pointing to what Bella thought was north, "and all I want is some knowing that what is said about work, and houses and such is true."

"Why you asking me?"

"Your husband maybe knows more than what the posters are saying. Word is that he's one of the best at his mine foreman job. I hear he is highly respected by the white folks who run the Hawke mine. Him being in such a high position, well, I thought he might know some more things going on that we don't so."

"Mrs. Johnson, my husband is a good man," interrupted Mrs. Towns. "He is a good worker, and he knows how to get coal, looks out for his men, and yes, you is fully right, he does get some respect from those white owners, but not the pay. He does the same work as the white foreman, many say better, much better than they do. Mrs. Johnson he may know more than anybody about mining coal, anybody. There are times when he is called to solve problems no others can solve, including the whites. He done saved them Hawkes from disaster many times, but do they pay him like they should? No. Do they offer better work hours? The answer again is no. Well, let me tell you, what they do offer is more work and longer hours. He does what they ask. Then if something bad happens, who gets blamed, he does. And worse yet he gets money taken from his pay. That's how they treat him." Mrs. Towns turned away, walked a few steps, and then returned and continued, "Did we see the posters about work up north? Yes we certainly did. Did we get letters about work up there? Yes. Now all this been going on for a long time, and don't you know those mine owners see them posters, and I'm certain the Klan see them posters too, Mrs. Johnson."

"The Klan, the owners, my, the Ku Klux Klan, show' never thought about that."

"Listen, Mrs. Johnson, my husband hears a lot 'cause the Hawkes forget he is there when they is a talking. The big bosses weren't worried about losing a few but with the posters calling their workers they are real concerned about losing a lot of men. They think some of the miners will abandon them. The Hawkes can live with a few leaving but they're only talking now. Who knows what may happen if too many leave, it could get nasty."

"How can they stop em?"

"They find out things, they got ways of knowing. I judge my husband is one they do not want to lose. A few others I guess they will tolerate now let me tell you this could get serious."

"I see why you don't want anyone to know your plans. I'm sorry, but I had to know the facts for Rufus and Leroy's sake."

"Well since you're a asking, from what I know the sooner they go the better. Lots of talk now but if too many decide to go at once, they sure to clamp down on those left."

"Thank you Mrs. Towns, God bless you," said Bella reaching out grabbed her hand and caressed it, "My husband is meeting with the

Reverend Washington at this moment and he wanted me to be there so I think I better get on my way."

"You say your husband is meeting with the preacher? Well so is mine. I hope no one sees them meeting like that. Hear me, I'm saying to be careful; any change in the normal they will know and suspect there is planning in the air, they do find out."

"I see no need to fret. We see the preacher and Mrs. Washington a lot, doing some extra praying for momma, and now my family. Let's both go and join the men."

The ladies walked side by side to the doors at the front of the church. They took one step outside into a blinding sun; causing Mrs. Towns to retreat from the brightness, back into the alcove and shade.

"That sho' was shocking to the eyes, I believe I'm seeing spots," said Mrs. Towns to herself since Bella moved ahead down the steps. After a brief moment she moved once again to exit the church, cupping her hand over her eyes and looking sideways, away from the direct rays of the blistering sun. She could hear, but not see the children yelling as they played on the front lawn. She recognized voices, particularly the laugh of Mrs. Grant, a screech only she could render. Upon exiting this time her view was toward the thick shrub and pine forest. The church was built on scrubland at the end of a narrow, rutted sandy road. The road and church building adjoined a dense forest. Entangled with vines this section of woods, next to the church, was practically impossible to penetrate. No one except the parishioners ventured to the Holy Gospel Church. This was the place where the members of the congregation felt comfortable, a place where they sang as long and as loud as they pleased. They carried on their old-fashioned church and social gatherings without worry.

"What is that?" questioned Mrs. Towns who thought she saw movement in the pines next to the church. Not totally sure because of watery eyes, she squinted, wiped the tears away and concentrated deeply on the spot. A deer, no, can't be with all the noise and activity. She had to know. She retreated back into the church. Moving a short distance into the portico shade, she maneuvered to a position where she could view the area where the movement occurred.

"Are you all right, you're not ailing?" asked the pastor's wife, surprising Mrs. Towns.

"No, I'm fine, just want to get used to the bright sun, stay only be a spell."

With that Mrs. Washington walked away. Mrs. Towns stayed for a few moments, watching intently. "My, maybe I'm imagining things, but I swear I saw something there. Probably the sun playing tricks on me, can't be anyone in that thicket," she thought. Finally she decided to leave, but one more look. "Fooo sure," she said to herself and again, "fooo sure, foo sure."

"It's a man, he had a wide brimmed leather hat, small feather tucked in the side, a white man cause he has a brown colored beard, long scraggly hair flowing down his back," she mumbled to herself as he darted away.

"What's he doing here, in that shrub? He had to be there a long time. Got to be a good reason for him to be here, 'cause those mosquitoes will eat you up in there. Wonder if I should tell Willie? Wonder if he saw me?" she asked herself. Her suspicions, aroused earlier by Mrs. Johnson, were certainly compounded by this sighting.

"Does anyone else know of our plans about going north? Did anyone below see the man in the woods? No because I'm standing above the crowd. I was lucky looking into the brush. What do I do? Do I tell Willie? He should know."

Isabelle Towns, after one last glance toward the woods, protected her eyes, walked down the church steps, and once she reached the ground, began to make small talk with the ladies gathered on the lawn She continually checked the spot of the sighting. Because of the angle and foliage she was convinced no one could see the man from below the steps.

"We is talking about them posters, Bella, and we agree that they are not doing much good. Some talk, but no one here knows of anyone leaving," announced the first lady.

"I wouldn't go even fin's my man went," echoed a second with many others agreeing.

"Me neither. I do exactly like your momma always said, Bella, Lord put me here and here I going to stay," shouted a boisterous voice in the group loud enough for the man in the woods to hear."

Bella and Isabelle wanted to be with their husbands, but refrained from leaving. They always stayed after service, meeting on the front lawn with other ladies of the church bantering about happenings, and gossiping of course. Any change from the norm would be noticed. The talk would be magnified about the so-called problems of those missing from the lawn conversations. So the two bided their time when Mrs. Johnson finally said, "I need to see the reverend about my momma's grave, see ya'll next Sunday."

"I believe I will join you Bella, I need to see him also."

Mrs. Towns gave another look at the woods as she and Bella walked to the sanctuary. A pair of eyes watched from the thick brush, observing and listening to the people on the lawn. He viewed two ladies make their way to the back of the church. Once they entered the building, he decided to depart the area. He will report to Henry "Hank" Hawke of "no unusual happenings at the Holy Gospel Church this Sunday. Not a poster in sight, no labor agents about, and no talk I could hear about venturing north. I know because I was mighty close, close enough to hear. You don't have any worries from that church. I been there three Wednesdays and three Sundays straight, everything the same as always."

Mr. Hawke questioned if he may have been too close and might have been seen by someone. The man vehemently scowled back that, "Nobody seed the Possum Man fin's he don't want them to," then pounced angrily out of the room.

The church office next to the sanctuary was no larger than the size of a large closet. A small table and chair was all the furniture that fit and allowed the door to close. Three large men had to maneuver about in order to find enough space to fit. The privacy they sought was compromised by an ill-fitting frame, which allowed space enough for anyone close by to hear the conversation in the office.

This day, as soon as the reverend completed the final greeting at the front of the church, he returned immediately to his tiny office. Should anyone notice, and thank God they didn't, the preacher changed his routine this Sunday. He usually joined the congregation on the front lawn after services. He moved from group to group, talked and listened mostly to gauge the mood of his people. He often based his sermons on information gathered from parishioners on the front lawn

The Reverend Washington was a large rotund man with a deep voice. He possessed a wide mouth and full lips, chubby cheeks, dancing friendly eyes and a smile that showed pure white teeth. He had a knack of disarming those he met when he flashed that smile. A jovial man by nature, he enjoyed people as much as food and he was happiest when confronted with both. His personality, along with his status as a religious leader in the vicinity, permitted him to gain acceptance into areas not available to the average Negro in Carbon Hill.

"Get that preacher down here," was a first order of business when a black worker was injured or killed in a mine accident. While tending to and praying over the body he listened to conversations by mine personnel. This way he gained insight into happenings occurring at work. The administrators ignored the man, and talked in his presence. This was how the reverend learned about the feelings of the owners at the shaft.

"They is worried, real worried since those posters arrived. Heard them say they lost seven good workers to those damn northerners, their words exactly. They show' don't want to lose more and could do something drastic to warn anyone thinking of leaving. "

"All they got to do is pay better and give us some good areas to mine," said Rufus.

"Boss mentioned the need to have men work extra since they got a large contract to feed those big ships sailing out of Charleston and Savannah. Mr. Hawke said they're now in position to make a lot of money and don't want any problems. What about you all, what have you been privy too?" asked the reverend.

"I is not heard anything," said Rufus, "Fact is that I go in and do my work, don't see any bosses. Just hear what working boys are saying. They're thinking about those posters 'cause there be a lot of talk about em. What about you, Willie?"

Willie Towns, at six foot, five inches tall possessed a muscular well-proportioned body that emitted strength. Light brown in color his facial features of high cheekbones, sharp piercing green eyes and a white man's type of nose placed him apart from others of his race.

He could read and write, was adept at ciphering numbers and was a master at solving mine problems. His canny sense of direction was used often in leading workers to the best seam of coal. The Hawkes liked Willie for his quiet hard working attitude and appreciated his abilities to find the good coal. The owners first noticed Willie when his crews out-produced all others. "That Willie Towns was right again," his fellow workers bragged to other miners. The mine bosses overheard the bragging. Checking his work section they found elaborate brattice walls well situated to provide an excellent airflow into the working face. The work was organized and resulted in good production. He was quickly promoted to section boss, eventually reaching the position of assistant mine foreman, a position he presently held.

"I hear some rumblings amongst the Hawke bosses who seem to be a bit more jived up lately. There was talk about losing workers a while back for one reason or another. Now comes the posted signs and labor agents. The mine owners, even the sawmills are worried, but mostly quiet for now. I know one thing, the labor agents better not get caught by any of the deputies or Klan members, and believe me they are looking. They also hear about labor guys recruiting in black churches. They are watching, so be careful whom you talk to, reverend. One thing more, they're watching train stations, especially those listed on the map. You know I'm a going, that's for sure. Please, don't speak of this to anyone about my plans," said Willie. "Who's to know what the Hawkes will do if they find out my intentions?"

"I'll not tell anyone," announced Rufus.

"Nor I," said the reverend. "If you don't mind, I suggest that the sooner y'all leave the better. Men can go first, get things settled and then send for the women."

"I think he's right. The longer I stay the better chance the Hawkes will find out about my going. Yes, take Billie with me, and pastor, may I send money for Isabelle to you to pass on to her?"

"Why you doing that?" asked Rufus.

"Couple reasons, I'm thinking. No one will suspect the letters are from me and trace me to where I'm located. Secondly, the reverend can take out the tithe to the church for his help. Remember, sir, only accept letters with your middle initial as part of the address. Discard any of those that do not have that initial."

"Seems to me that's a roundabout way of doing things, and why so secretive?"

"Look Rufus, the first thing in learning Willie's location is to intercept his mail. Those Hawkes are mean spirited when they are crossed. They may want to find out where he is and send some Klansmen there and do him harm, maybe even bring him back. Let any others to think hard if they are planning on leaving. Yes, this is the best way to communicate with Isabelle and send her money. I suggest you do the same. I think you two better do some planning fast. I say that what starts as a trickle can quickly turn into a flood of workers leaving and believe me the Hawkes will fight back to stop the desertions. I say go as fast as you can."

"Reverend Washington, Willie, I'm going that's certain, but I'm also getting confused some. I can't cipher much, or read well either but I know I can do better up there. Listen, no one can keep you here fin's you don't want to stay."

"Rufus, calm down. I'm just trying," Willie stopped and held up his hand. "Heard something, listen."

"Willie, I know you're in there, we can hear Rufus clear down the hall, open up." Said Isabella, "and let us in."

To accommodate the women the table and chair was moved into the hallway. The ladies entered maneuvering for room in the small office.

"Mrs. Johnson is with me and she knows about your plans, so speak your mind. I'm afraid if they know, surely others know. I must admit I'm a bit frightened."

"How did you find out about our plans, Mrs. Johnson?" Asked Willie.

"We had a good idea is all, and had to find out one way or another, we needed to know," lied Bella.

"I found out an important thing in all my years preaching the Gospel. That is that walls have ears and the more said gets out to someone. The Hawkes are watching and listening. You must not repeat what is said here. All this talk worries me. I fear the mine owners have a big concern about losing workers. Labor Agents, posters, some having left already; put them on edge. I say if you're a' going, then the sooner the better," said the preacher.

"I'm thinking on leaving tomorrow, Monday. Thinking hard on it 'cause time a passing fast and like the reverend said, the time is now," said Rufus

"You're taking Leroy?"

"Yes"

"Would you consider delaying until next Monday? I'll take Billie and that way we can go together. Boys will like being together. Like you, I'll send for Isabella when we get houses then the wives can travel together, what do you say?"

"Well, that sounds okay I guess."

Isabelle Towns kept quiet about her sighting a man in the scrub. She felt a disclosure would precipitate an earlier exit, so keeping quiet allowed her to have her husband another week. The time was set. Reverend Washington motioned for all to hold hands and once done raised his head in prayer.

Mr. Henry "Hank" Hawke on this Sunday hired some men to find and tear down every poster in the tri-county area. He would pay handsomely for each one returned to him. The local sheriff was contacted and was asked to have his deputy's patrol the railroad stations in Hilliard, Carbon Hill and Jasper. A sizeable financial reward would be given for every labor agent found at any of these sites. They were not to bother or address the agents, just simply inform the Klan of their presence. I will instruct them on how to take care of these intruders.

After leaving the mine office Mr. Hawke would pick up a bottle of local homemade corn whiskey. He'll take it to the Possum Man for payment of past favors, and request his continued surveillance of local churches. While traveling to the Possum Man's shack he'll think of a good excuse to send for the Reverend Washington to sound him out. The mine owner wanted to observe the preacher's reaction to questions about the posters and ask if labor agents contacted him for recruiting men at his church. He made a mental note to talk to Willie Towns.

CHAPTER X

JOHN TOSSED AND turned throughout the night in anticipation of starting his first day of work at the Ridge Valley Mine. The explosion last August completely changed his life from thoughts of attending school to now being the man of the family. Patty Driscall instructed him to call on the alderman and secure the necessary papers for work. He was told to present his working papers to the mine foreman. A meeting with the superintendent was the next step in the process. Once cleared, a work assignment would be made. Patty made a request to have John assigned to his crew. Since he was collecting favors owed from those who made personnel assignments, he also asked that Jerry Burdock be assigned to the job opening in the lamp house. The requests were honored and the deal done through the assistant mine foreman. A shot of whiskey and a glass of beer sealed the agreement at O'Malley's.

John's final task was to set up an account at the Union Supply Company Store. The store manager issued a check number and marked the date of October 14th, 1919 for the beginning of charging purchases. He could now buy the clothes, work shoes, gumboots, hardhat, carbide lamp and any other supplies needed for work. He signed to give permission to his mom to use his account to purchase items at the store.

John finally gave up the fight to sleep. He got up from the bed and checked the Big Ben clock on the dresser. It read three-thirty. Glancing at the window he saw the wetness on the panes. A pattering on the roof announced the rainfall. All others in the house were asleep. From habit he automatically reached for the "thunder jug" but immediately pulled back. "Mike's job now" he mumbled.

Like his father before him he walked quietly down the stairs and into the kitchen. He flicked the cord extending from the light fixture to turn on the light. He proceeded to stoke the hot coals in the stove and added lumps of coal to red embers. The coal caught, sending fumes and smoke into the kitchen. He quickly returned the lid and adjusted the damper.

"I got to do better than this smoking up the whole kitchen. I'll have to ask Patty or one of the guys how to keep the smoke from getting out."

He filled a pan with water and placed it on the stove to heat for coffee. Once done, he exited the back door and proceeded to the outhouse. The cool autumn rain felt good and refreshing. The fresh air tasted much better than that rancid stuff in the kitchen. "I got to remember to talk to Patty," he reminded himself again. He returned to the sink in the kitchen and washed in the cold water flowing from the spigot. He then retreated to the bedroom to finish dressing. He heard his mom descending the stairs. He could hear her grinding coffee beans, the results she added to the boiling water. The aroma aroused John's taste buds so much he hurried downstairs to dip a cup into the pan even before the coffee grounds settled. He sipped the tasty brew, along with some of the grounds, accepting fragrance and taste like a bee sipping nectar from a flower. He would regret later in the day at work his not accepting a full breakfast offered by mom.

"Please be careful and listen to Mr. Driscall. I have some pork chops, and bread in your bucket, check to see if you want more."

John took the top cover from the circular lunch pail and checked the contents. He removed the attached middle section of the two-tiered container and his mom poured coffee into the bottom section. He replaced the middle section that contained the food, then the lid. Finally, John kissed his mom on the cheek and walked out the back

Ridge Valley

door. She watched him go, holding back tears. John no sooner left the house than Patty appeared from around the corner.

"Morning John, I see you got your bucket, so it looks like you're ready to go. You have two good things going for you. It's Friday and beginning a job on that day brings the new worker luck and good fortune. We have rain and that is a good omen, besides washing everything clean, it strengthens the soil, and brings good luck to new ventures. I feel good having you as part of the team. Let's do some work," stated Patty as he slapped John's left shoulder.

They walked briskly, accepting the cool rain with refreshing delight. Other workers joined them as they walked to the mine. Each new entrant to the group was introduced to John as they moved along. They kidded him about being assigned to that lazy bum Patty.

"He didn't get the beer belly from work," one man said. "You do the work and he gets the credit," stated another; that got a good laugh from the crowd.

When John entered the lamp house, Patty went ahead and instructed John to wait. He returned in a few minutes, hardhat in hand. He handed it to John who saw the letters "Iggy," short for Ignatius painted on the front. This was his father's nickname passed on to him by Patty. John was official, a working member of the crew. He had a nickname now, as did every other man in the patch. Rarely was a male called by his real name in the mining community. All men had nicknames and were always addressed by those names.

Patty checked John's dress, told him to button the top of his shirt and to secure his trousers by tying a rope over the pant leg around his ankle.

"You want to keep out as much dust as possible. If it gets on your skin it'll itch the hell out of you, so tighten up." They collected the carbide lamps, attached them to their hats, grabbed the lunch pails and walked to the elevator, called a "cage." The reason it was called a cage was because it was built with fence like material and was an exact replica of a square birdcage. Patty took the lead. He pulled up the gate on the front and the men entered. After closing the portal the hoist man lowered the men six hundred twenty three feet slowly to the bottom. A bell sounded, the gate opened and the workers exited. John noticed a distinct change in the demeanor of

Bob Menarcheck

the men once they entered the haulage. The joking was replaced by a quiet serious attitude toward the task at hand. Patty gathered his crew to give the orders for the day He was stern and to the point in addressing expectations for the shift. Part of the crew was assigned to the timbering segment while the others, including John, would lay track.

"We got a new man here today," announced Patty after completing the work assignments. "He'll be working on track this morning. Maybe I'll do some shifting after lunch, we'll see. Now let's help him out and break him in right. O.K. lets go to work."

They checked the carbide lamps on each other's cap, and then followed Patty, walking about a half mile down the haulage. They moved briskly and kept a steady pace. The mine was cool. A slight breeze was felt but it did not halt the beads of perspiration on John's back and forehead. They reached the dinner hole, a dug out area, about five feet deep and about a dozen feet wide. A bench-like structure was carved into the wall. The crew placed lunch buckets on a dug out ledge, "Be sure your lids are on your bucket tight, John, if not the rats will get in there," said Patty. They all checked the tightness of the lids, then headed for work.

"You're with me," said Patty to John. Once they arrived at the workstation Patty saw that more cross ties, along with additional track were needed. He ordered the other crew members to begin digging for cross tie placement while he and John fetched more ties and track. Patty was disgruntled because the previous crew chief failed to tell him supplies were low at the worksite.

"Could've taken 'em in with us on our way, wasting time this way," mumbled Patty.

Returning back to the cage drop site John and Patty being ultra cautious, loaded the flat car carefully in order to equal the load. They worked steadily for two hours. John sweated heavily and his arms felt weak from the lifting and loading of ties and track. The mule pulled the wagon as the two followed. Soon they approached the dinner hole area.

"Mind if I get a drink, a bit thirsty, sir."

Patty waved an all right. John ate a few bites and drank, finishing about half of the cold coffee. The crewmembers left behind dug enough trenches to accept most of the railroad ties. They were placed into position and carefully adjusted to be certain each tie was level.

"Can't have loaded cars tipping over; take time and double check to be sure the placed rails are level," said Patty.

The routine of placing ties and attaching track moved along at a steady pace. Occasionally Patty left to check the progress of the timbering gang, allowing John to sneak back to the "lunch room" for a bite and a swallow of coffee. Paul Houlka, the oldest member of the timbering crew, and a section leader were in a serious discussion regarding the quality of the timber when Patty arrived. He settled the concern.

"Order a new supply of timber, it'll delay things a bit, but you can't take chances, you got to do things right or it will come back to haunt you." They secured the necessary timber, and moved along. Patty's steady and sure attitude won the appreciation of the men, especially for looking out for their safety.

That settled, Patty returned to the area where all but one section of track was laid.

"Finish that last one and we'll break for lunch," said Patty. He sent John to fetch the mule driver to retrieve the flat car. John followed orders quickly; he was ready for lunch. By the time Patty checked the section and walked to the dinner hole to eat, he found the crew was well into emptying their buckets. John already did just that.

"Got a few pieces of good chicken, John, how about it?"

John initially refused but a second offering was accepted. Patty continued to offer more and John took the offerings. It wasn't until lunch was finished that John realized how much he ate from Patty's bucket.

Patty announced that the men would switch work assignments after lunch. He told Paul that more rails and ties were needed since the morning group placed all that were delivered. The men continued to work steadily for the remainder of the shift. The timber placement was a bit slower than usual since each one was checked carefully. A number of inferior logs were discarded since they didn't meet Patty's approval. Later John found out from Jerry that a problem existed in finding good timber for use in shoring up the roof. Jerry's job in the lamp house made him privy to overhearing discussions between

Bob Menarcheck

the big bosses without their knowing. Jerry passed on all of what he heard to his friend.

The last track was laid, and the last timber placed and the ten-hour shift was over. John made it, he kept up with the work demanded of him and this made him feel good. He would eat a good breakfast tomorrow and add more food to the bucket. He walked up the haulage with his new working buddies to the cage. They rang the bell to signal the hoist man, and were lifted to the surface. The late evening air felt good, smelled good and tasted good. He spit and a black glob of saliva splattered on the ground. John looked in dismay, he spit again, as the taste of carbide smoke and coal dust lingered.

John observed the change in the personality of the crew once they reached the surface. Patty regained his easygoing personality. Talking exuberantly about the success of his new boy.

"He outdid you, big guy," a crewmember interrupted, "Leave him with us all day tomorrow and we'll show him the right way."

Patty walked over to John and like a proud father patted him on the back as they walked together to the lamp house.

"Brought you here lad and intend on taking you home," said Patty

After turning in their lamps they began walking for home. "You did good today, John. Your daddy would have been proud of you; he told me many a time how he thought you to be a smart lad. Thought you'd go to school instead of the mine. Things happen and you're here, working, and you kept up, yep you did and I'm mighty proud to have you. I do believe the crew feels the same and that is important," said Patty.

"Thanks, Mr. Driscall, sir. I thank God for you being there. I'll keep trying to do my best, and thanks for the chicken at lunch. It hit the spot."

"No problem my boy, I suspect you may be a bit sore come tomorrow, but that will pass in time. Remember when working, get in a regular pattern, set your pace and follow it. Now don't compare yourself with others, do your best and when tired, take a break because most mistakes happen when tired or when one overworks. Take heed, one little mistake could spell disaster. That's why I checked the timber so close today; don't take chances no matter what the bosses say. Now listen, John, when trouble comes, it comes in a flash, you act fast and you take care of yourself first."

"Now I know why they're so serious down there," John thought as Patty continued talking or more like preaching.

"Remember if trouble comes a knocking, your first inclination is to help your buddies. No, you keep away until things are settled. Saw it happen, a roof fall, man trapped, buddies come running, fall wasn't over. Remember, always test the roof by tapping and if it has a hollow sound then go and report it. Be careful of dripping water, loosens the shale above, stay away, mind my word, test, check, look and listen." They walked in silence as Patty thought about losing a buddy who rushed to help; the person survived, his buddy was lost. John wondered about what it would be like when they actually start mining for coal.

"Well, was it what you expected?" asked Patty.

John didn't hear the question, he was thinking hard, still digesting what Patty said about helping. What if it were Patty in trouble? Could he hold back?

"Well how did it go today, John?" he said again.

"Went fine, good, I'd say, a lot to learn. But I been thinking hard about all you said and wondering if it's easier to just work and leave happenings up to the Lord?"

Patty stopped in his tracks, turned to John with a scowl on his face that would stop an elephant. In a stern voice he lashed out, "Look John, There aren't any shortcuts in the mine. I heard others say exactly what you just said and their wives and kids pray over their graves. You make certain, always, be sure you do things right, always."

"I didn't mean to say."

"I'm telling you," interrupted Patty, "When a roof fall comes there is blinding dust everywhere, get away to a safe place. Now, an explosion, get down fast. Close to the ground, then try to get out or find good air. Follow the rats. All I got to say now is that your father is up there," he pointed to the sky, "looking down and telling St. Peter how proud he is of you this day. Now I'll leave you, get a good rest, and remember no shortcuts."

Bob Menarcheck

They parted, with John heading home and Patty taking the route to O'Malley's for a shot and a beer. John thought deeply about what Patty said. He wondered how he would react in an emergency? Some doubt crept into his mind.

Patty continued down the road heading toward the tavern. John cut across the road and took the path home. He stopped at the top of the hill and looked back. He strained his eyes, squinting, could it be, yes it was, Patty was carrying two lunch buckets. John smiled, shook his head then walked chuckling to his house.

CHAPTER XI

HENRY "HANK" HAWKE delivered the bottle of corn whiskey to the Possum Man. A grunt was his expression of thanks. He wasted no time after grabbing the bottle; he quickly twisted the cork from the top, a look, a smile, then a long slug, a wipe of the mouth with the back of the hand and a return of the cork. The Possum man knew why the boss was in his cabin, and answered the question before being asked.

"Been to that church every Sunday and Wednesday. Ain't seen anything suspicious."

"What you see?"

"I saw a lot of Negro folks, coming to church, then talking, seems for hours after preaching. Kids running around, playing," he stopped to take another slug of booze, "nothing out of line that I saw, chief, nothing.

"Too easy to think that labor agents been all over the area, and none been to Holy Gospel. I know what you're saying, Mr. Clagg, but something tells me things can't be like they appear. I don't feel good about things at that church, I just have that bad feeling."

The senior Hawke left the cabin and, although assured by his spy that all was fine, continued to have doubts. He needed to speak directly and alone to the Reverend Washington. He had to be certain if labor agents visited and preached at the church.

Both men, one a minister, the other a mine owner, had a desire to meet and sound out each other regarding the Negro miners. The owner wanted to keep his workers; the minister wanted to assist members of his flock in moving north. They both bided their time. A day went by, then another. Time was of the essence since the Negroes were anxious to go. The reverend had to do something to get to the mine without the Hawkes suspecting his motive. So early the next morning he approached the front steps of the church and after looking about, he pushed, looked again, pushed and pushed until finally the steps partially gave way. Satisfied, he returned to the office in the church. He dressed in his preaching clothes. He secured the church door and left. He walked slowly down the sandy road towards Carbon Hill.

Hank wanted to get the reverend to the mine so badly that he considered causing an accident to get him there. He finally decided to arrange something for the afternoon.

"Hey boss. Look outside. Would you believe who done dropped in on us?"

" It's the preacher!"

"What? Are you kidding? That preacher done come down here for no reason? Don't recall him doing that before," said Hank.

"Let's go out and shake him up a bit," said Lester, who added, "look he's nosing around all right, and he's coming this way."

"Everyone stay in here, all of you, do not leave this room. I want to confront this preacher myself, and check him out alone. That way I can get a good read on the man, and it may take some time. I want no interruptions for any reason." He left the office to meet the reverend.

The preacher felt tense the moment he walked on to the Hawke mine ground. "Maybe a mistake to come down here," he thought. "Should have waited, but waiting doesn't help my people, had to take a chance, so it's now or never."

"Preacher, Reverend Washington."

"Yes sir, Mr. Hawke, sir."

"What brings you here?"

"Well, sir, the steps at the church busted, needs them fixed before preaching on Wednesday. Guess they rotted and finally gave in. Came to see if I may have your permission to speak to Rufus Johnson or Walter Ponds. See if they can come to fix the broken parts."

"You know anything about them recruiting men for work up north? I know there are labor agents about and lots of bills posted," said Hank, ignoring the request.

" No, sir, not seen any, saw a lot of signs yonder but gone now, thought all those labor people done left the area, have you seen them?"

"We seen them, they be planted," said Hank. One of the boys in the office who overheard the statement laughed loud enough for those outside to hear.

"Couple of my boys got themselves a reward reverend, told us where some of those agents been staying. We went after 'em but they left 'fore we got there. And you know what else? They say these here agents been inside the Church at Eldred talking from the pulpit, any been to your place reverend?"

"Holy Gospel is a way back in the scrub, way off the beaten path, not an easy place to find, sir. I haven't seen or know of anybody from our church that have even seen an agent."

"So none of those labor agents has been to the Holy Gospel? Funny, hear they been paying good money to preachers to talk from the pulpit, and you're not getting any cash? Tell me have you seen any of your fellow pastors lately?"

"No, but did see a lot of them posters around a while back, not seen any lately, thinking the labor folks left since all the posters are gone."

The sheriff along with Earle his deputy and two of the Hawke boys left the mine office and sat under the overhang outside. Their thought was to intimidate the pastor. Hank was furious at the move. They did not intimidate the preacher but frustrated Hank who lost his concentration on the man. His questioning was over.

" Your men over there. Take only a few minutes talking, they have work to do."

The reverend walked toward the group. The black workers turned their backs, hoping he'd simply pass them and go on his way. Talking to him led to trouble. "When he comes down here somebody's hurt.

Had a problem that I know. This is bad luck for sure," said a black worker.

"Not to worry, soon the bad luck be on them for a change," said another.

The reverend walked directly to Rufus as the others standing near by meandered away. The black preacher finished the conversation quickly, turned to Hank, bowed, tipped his hat and began his walk toward town. Hank watched him go until he turned the curve and out of sight. He started toward the office, stopped before entering, stared at the group, pointed to the youngest Hawke and said in a stern voice, "Come in here, I have a job for you."

"I want you to go to the Holy Gospel Church, do you know where it is?"

"Yes, I do."

"Run up there as fast as you can, look at the front steps going up to the church entrance. I want to know the condition of those steps. Do you understand? Look at the front steps and come strait back here and tell me what you see, now hurry up."

The young Hawke left, jogging past the group shrugging his shoulders as he passed. Wondering, the group drifted into the office. The boss was not in a good mood, he didn't get the answer he sought, and they were responsible.

"You boys don't know your ass from nothing, there is something up, by God I can feel it. You interrupted me and he clamed up, now get the hell out of here, leave me alone."

"But boss."

"But boss, bullshit, leave…now."

The Reverend Washington, after seeing the young Hawke boy running up the road, decided to take a shortcut across wasteland and return to the church. The section he would cross was a known haven for rattlesnakes; a misstep on a rattler and you are gone. He had to take a chance and trust in the Lord. He crossed the scrub without a problem. Perspiring heavily, he entered the Holy Gospel graveyard directly across from the front entrance of the church. He placed himself out of sight behind some bushy pine, and waited.

"There he is, coming down the road," he mumbled to himself.

He watched the young man take a route through the woods and approach the church from the rear. He stopped, looked around then inched his way to the front. Turning the corner he jogged to the steps. Looking, then pushing, he almost knocked them off their anchors. Satisfied, he retreated back around the church and started running, down the road.

The reverend left his hiding place knowing that the Hawkes believed him for now. But he also knew it couldn't last. "The exodus must be soon, we must move while the mine owners are off guard," he thought. "They'll be watching us closely. Get as many as I can to help with the steps and suggest that all going north go next Monday. The Hawkes and their clan will be mad as hornets whose nest was destroyed. The loss will devastate the mining operation. We can expect retaliation for sure. But we won, we won for now," mumbled the reverend.

CHAPTER XII

HENRY CLAY GRANT returned to New York to pursue the purchase of world-renowned art and join his wife on the social circuit in Manhattan. He had relinquished the power of his company to another, and would check on progress with reports from his accountant. He was confident that the new man would improve the profit margin for his company. He has to produce because of his contract, based on company earnings, or else he will lose money. "The Coal and Iron Police, an excellent idea, I should have thought of that move myself, a long time ago," he smiled to himself.

Early reports mentioned that labor agents would be sent with utmost speed to the southern coalfields to recruit experienced miners. Since the European theatre presented too many obstacles for recruiting this was another excellent decision. This pleased the New York resident immensely.

"I am happy to hear talk of revising the plan to transport coal by an underground conveyer belt system. That move alone will save millions. In addition, it gives me great pleasure to know that I will not have to use Rockefeller's railroads to haul the coal," he told his beloved Adelaide.

The mansion glowed with activity as guests began to arrive for the viewing of his most recent purchase " *THE PURIFICATION OF THE TEMPLE*" by El Greco, an oil on canvas painting from the early

1600's. The guests oohed and ahhed in wonderment while viewing the many masterpieces on display in the mansion. The richness and elegance of Renoir, Whistler and other world-renowned painters were well represented throughout. The stunning architecture of the mansion itself was enough to enthrall the attendees, but the added collection of art was beyond belief.

"What a splendid collection, must be worth millions. What does this man do to gain such a fortune?" asked one guest of another.

"Mr. Grant owns mining villages and other industrial conglomerates associated with the steel making industry in Western Pennsylvania. He became a millionaire by the time he was thirty."

"Goodness that is, yes, let's see he's about seventy I'd say so that was forty years ago. He must have amassed hundreds of times that amount since then judging from the accumulation of art displayed here," said a third guest.

"If I may, please?" interrupted a gentleman.

The group turned from viewing a work by Bellini to listen.

"Mr. Grant originally made a lot of money by organizing a company that produced a high quality of coke, then made many millions when his company became a subsidiary of United States Steel in 1900. He moved to New York in '12 and been traveling the world since then acquiring these treasures."

Other notables from New York society arrived and were directed to the drawing room. They mingled talking and drinking waiting for Mr. and Mrs. Grant to enter. Meanwhile, Mr. T.J. Hathaway, an organist, entertained. One invitee to the unveiling was a Broadway producer. He meandered over to the organ, "Sir, the gentleman apparently enjoys the arts and I understand attends the opera and symphony. To your knowledge, has he ever backed a play or musical production?"

"Not to my knowledge. Fact is I'm not familiar with the master of the house. He is an ultra private person who maintains his distance. My dealings are always with Mrs. Grant, never with him. Fact is he may not stay long after the unveiling, more than likely he'll arrive, pull the curtain, and say a few words and leave. He's become an enigma, difficult guy to judge, others say he's a cold calculating businessman, never social or at ease in a crowd. I doubt his ever being involved in show business, probably too risky for him."

"He would have a big say in the production,"

"Has to have total control. I understand he emulates a dictatorial style of management it has to be his way. No, too much uncertainty in theater to make money. Well, I best get to the organ."

Mr. Hathaway played, the guests mingled. The Grants appeared along with the wine and hor'dourves. They mingled briefly greeting the guests as the music played. It was obvious to those who knew the Grant's well that Henry Clay did not look well. The guests were gathered quickly for the unveiling of "The Purification of the Temple." After the unveiling the hosts thanked their guests and bid them farewell for the evening. The organ played until all departed the premises.

> For release to all news services----December 2nd, 1919
>
> Henry Clay Grant died in his home at 2 West 51th Street today in New York City. His wife was present at his side at time of death. No details of the cause of death were given. Rumor persists however that Mr. Grant died from heart damage resulting from an undiagnosed illness. Although final details regarding burial are not known at this time, close associates of the family stated that the body would be interred at the Homewood cemetery near Mr. Grant's former residence in Pittsburgh.

CHAPTER XIII

JOHN WAS SLOWLY getting the hang of things at work. He set a pace for himself as Patty suggested, working in a steady manner throughout the shift. The only breaks from work came at lunch and for answering nature's call.

"Never knew one could get so sore, everything hurts, everything even my toes."

"That's a new one, John, your toes?"

"I'm telling you, I got a cramp in my middle toe yesterday, it stayed hurt the whole day. I couldn't sleep because of it hurting so bad," said John to a laughing crewmember.

"You're using muscles you never used before, hurting means you're getting stronger. The hurt will slow down give it time. You get over the soreness but never the dust. That gets to you and stays with you. Breathing the coal dust only gets worse. When you start coughing up black in your spit, you know then you're a miner, and it doesn't take long."

Clearing the colossal pile in the curve proved a time consuming task. Men worked ten-hour shifts to complete the project and the pace took its toll. During one week twelve miners were injured when the pile shifted, catching the men in the fall. The injuries ranged from broken bones to cuts and bruises, but no fatalities. Work parties were further reduced by individual accidents. Replacements consisted of young untested boys who needed to work because of the loss of the breadwinner in their family. They tried to fill the void, but the workers were boys doing a man's job. The "gray beards" watched every move the new workers made for fear of them "doing something stupid to get me killed." Slowly, the pile diminished and once the debris was cleaned up, the crews would have clear sailing in restructuring the mine. Every inch of haulage needed new rail ties, new track and timbering throughout. The track laying, brattice work to adjust airflow and timbering would soon begin. The only thing holding them back was additional workers and necessary supplies.

"We plan on delaying a mine opening in the northern section of the district and divert rails and ties from that shaft to Ridge Valley. Ridge Valley is our main priority. Pittsburgh wants this place in operation by the end of the year," stated Patty.

The crews worked with the supplies they had available. The delayed deliveries in rails resulted in the crews placing timbers full time. The lot storing the posts was quickly emptied.

"Salvage timber from the woods above the valley," came the call from the District Office. Orders to restock the logs were sent out and top prices paid for quick delivery. Soon truckloads of timber arrived at the mine. The trouble began when Patty Driscall and Paul Mankovich were sent ahead to retest the roof. The mistake made by the superintendent was assigning these experienced leaders to this job. No one expected a roof to give way, especially since the sounding came back as a solid firm reading. Luckily, they sensed the weakness with a roof tap and scrambled out of the way before it all came crashing down. They suffered deep cuts to shoulders and upper arms.

"Probably be out a week, but we must carry on without Patty and Paul. Have the crews timber up to the fall, draw back, lay track to the roof collapse area and get rail cars up there and clean up the mess, then begin timbering again," said the assistant superintendent.

Secure with the thought of sturdy support above their heads, the men worked to advance the rails. They wanted to serve notice that they could do the job without supervision. However the leaders of this young crew, in their haste, failed to check the tone of the logs. Some timbers with hollow and soft areas were inadvertently used to support the roof. A price would soon be paid for the bad selection of timber. A shift of men were laying track in the haulage when timber cracked and the roof gave way. Later, blame would be placed on the crew, not the poor timber that was used. The result of the fall killed two and maimed six others. The crew that Bull was working with in another section was diverted to rescue operations. A full shift was required to retrieve bodies and secure the area. The cleanup taxed John's soul, especially when the crushed dead bodies were found. He never fully accepted the horror of the scene but continued assisting the fallen.

Bull joined in but as usual had a difficult time keeping up. The mine buddies were on Bull unmercifully. "Do your part, do this, hurry up, c'mon fat boy do that." They never let up on him. Bull had enough and could no longer tolerate the hazing. He left and started for the cage as laughter and guffaws were directed his way. John understood Bull's feelings but not his actions and wondered why he didn't stand up to them. He had to talk to Bull. John got permission from the straw boss to leave. He reached Bull as he belled for the cage.

After departing the cage they walked to the lamp house and turned in their carbide lamps to Jerry. John told Jerry about the accident and because of the deaths, as is the custom when someone is killed, they will have the next day off. Bull stood by, relieved at being topside, away from the pit and crew.

"Since being off tomorrow to honor those killed, I thought of going to pick more walnuts. Patty mentioned his taste for 'em so I thought about getting him a good supply. You want to go along, Jer?"

"Let me check."

"Sorry, John, can't go," said Jerry on his return.

"Why not?"

"Got to work, Shaun said we don't get off like you. Said no one died up here so we work. We have to get more lamps ready for additional men. Heard other things," Jerry looked around them continued, "Big shots from Pittsburgh been in the office and I heard them say they wanted more control, like appointing new bosses, new rules, new pay scale, and something about a police force of some kind. They are doing some recruiting for new workers too."

"Really, you sure, where they going to get them?" asked Bull

"Hear of getting Negroes from the south."

" You keep hearing things, but nothing happening," said John.

"Get a move on and quit doing all that talking. Pick up those lamps and bring em back here, move boy," came a shout from Shaun in the back.

"Can't talk now, meet ya at the store tomorrow about six o'clock," whispered Jerry

John nodded an okay and turned with Bull to leave.

"I feel a lot better now that I'm out of there. The guys on my crew are always on me, John, they never let up, I just couldn't take it anymore."

"Hard for anyone to take. I mean it got to me too Bull, God a man smashed, the other one's belly torn open," said John, trying to offer an excuse.

"Mind if I go nut picking with you tomorrow?" asked Bull, changing the subject.

"Love the company, see you at the store at six, we'll get an early start."

"Be there," said Bull. The two walked the remainder of the way home in silence, keeping thoughts of mines and accidents to themselves.

The bed was welcomed, for it was the first time all day that John felt relaxed. He snuggled under the thick blanket, thinking on what Jerry said about new Negro workers. A smile came across John's face as he recalled the lassie at the canteen. He vowed again to find out where she lived. "Dolly and Tony, haven't seen them in a long time; just can't imagine those two being together." He wondered about Patty and how he is doing. He can't wait to see his face when he takes him the nuts. Mom looks like she's aged considerably since the explosion. I'm sure she misses Dad, she doesn't say much, so sad. I sure would like to do something to cheer her up, a good Christmas gift maybe. Hey what about a stop at Glover's farm tomorrow after nut picking to order some sausage, kielbasa, and a ham and surprise her for the holiday. I'll see Tony later for a loan. Bull and Corky have changed, Bull especially. He lost that cocky attitude, seems kind of docile anymore. Corky, never see much of him anymore since he began working at the Company Store. He turned over to his side, burying his head into the pillow, again trying to recall the lassie's name. He fell asleep promising Dad to do his best at work and in helping the family.

Bull also lay awake in his bed, and like many nights in the immediate past, began to break into a cold sweat. Constant agitation, kidding and hazing by members of his crew played on his brain, robbing him of sleep. A man's masculinity is his trademark in mining lore. Strength, perseverance and endurance were a man's badge of honor and these traits meant either acceptance or rejection by members of a crew. Bull's physical appearance alone ruled his peers only a few months past. Expectations by fellow workers in Bull's crew were high when he got his assignment. But fat is not muscle and regardless of his size, Bull could not handle the work. His badge of honor was tarnished badly. The insults and guffaws started and he did not know how to handle the rejection. He needed some help and decided to talk to John tomorrow.

John arrived early, surprised to see Bull waiting.

"Morning John"

"Hi, Bull, see you're ready to go."

A misty vapor danced about the two as they walked down the dirt road away from the store. A heavy fog hugged the creek. Only the cattails peered above the low cloud in the valley. A train could be heard bearing down from the east. Black acrid smoke from the engine intermingled with the fog and spread throughout the valley. The train finally chugged on by. They crossed the tracks and headed for the junk graveyard

"John, I ain't worked before going down the shaft. I didn't think I would have any trouble but right off the bat they started on me; didn't give me a chance. How did you do it, John?"

"I've been a' picking coal on the slate dump since I can remember. Doing a lot of scavenging for every lump. Lotta days I wanted to quit, but I stayed with it till I had enough to carry home. Shucked corn at Glover's, loaded hay, lots of garden work but none of that compares to mining. I kind of follow what Patty told me, set your pace and follow it. That's what I decided to do, got to help the family, plus too much stubbornness in me to quit I guess," said John as they walked along.

"I tried, I really did, but, John I can't go back to working with that crew, I can't. John, I made up my mind, I can't go back to working with that crew."

"Look Bull I know you're a good worker. Listen, all crews do things to test the new guy, one guy starts kidding around, and if the others see it's getting to you they all join in to get their kicks. If they see it bothering you, then they never let up."

"Can I get on your crew? Will you ask Patty for me?" pleaded Bull who added, "I can't sleep thinking about going back to that crew."

John continued walking slowly with Bull at his side, hands deep in his pockets, head down, thinking of what to say. Bull looked at John, waiting for an answer.

"Here is the facts as I see 'em, Bull, here's the facts. You can't leave your crew, it's as simple as that, 'cause you're doomed if you do, you'll never, never live it down. You have to go back and show em what you're made of, or your life will be miserable."

"I am not going back, I've made up my mind, I am not going back," sputtered Bull as a tear rolled down his cheek.

"Bull, I'll take you to see Patty, I will," said John seeing the wetness on Bull's face. "You can talk to 'em, I'll do what I can, but I'll take you sure." Bull looked directly at John, uncontrolled tears dripping down his cheeks. He stood motionless, staring. John stopped, looked Bull in the eye and said, "I'll take you, when we get back, I'll take you."

Bull did not answer, he turned and threw the empty sack over his shoulder and began walking. John delayed for a moment, and then hurried to Bull's side. They moved across the junk graveyard toward the horse barn and fenced pasture.

"Wow, look at those beauties, Bull."

"What?"

"The horses, those are riding horses, not working ones, sure not for pulling wagons."

Bull ignored John and walked on ahead. John caught up again. They followed the lower road, then up the path passing the airshaft finally reaching the woods. A stop at the spring for a drink, then on to the walnut trees, where they filled their sacks to the brim. Clouds began to gather, covering the late morning sun as the two started to leave the woods.

"I want to stop at Glover's farm and order some kielbasa and a ham for Christmas. It's on the way, just a short trek across the cornfield. Do you want to go with me?"

"Think I will, may put an order in myself."

They lugged the sacks on their shoulders heading for Glover's as the wind kicked up dust from the dirt road. The smell of dampness was in the air. They turned now, walking between fields of corn and wheat, down a hill to the farm. A drop of rain soon turned to sprinkles. They quickened the pace.

"Head for the barn, over there, go up the ramp," yelled John.

He pulled the sliding door open far enough for Bull and him to enter. They moved inside and placed the sacks on the floor. John on his return to close the door saw Mr. Glover whipping his horses pulling a wagon of hay.

"Bull, help me open the doors all the way," shouted John who added, "Mr. Glover is coming fast to beat the rain. He doesn't want to get that load of hay wet."

Mr. Glover charged down the rutted road, directly into the barn as a shower began.

"God was with me this day, you boys saved the hay, thanks," said Mr. Glover as he climbed down from the wagon. Once he reached the floor he asked, "What brings you boys here anyway?"

"We've been up in the woods picking walnuts. I also wanted to tell you that I'm now working in the mine, can't help you this fall. Send my brother up if you need someone."

"Sure, send him up, I can use him, and John, sorry about your Dad."

"Thanks, Mr. Glover, appreciate your concern. Sir, I want to get a ham and kielbasa for Christmas. I wondered if you'd give me an idea of the cost, and maybe I'll consider some homemade sausage."

"For you, John, consider it done, I'll give you a good price, don't worry. I'm glad you came early to give me time for butchering. I'll need the time 'cause I'll be losing George Jr. soon.

"What you mean losing George, Mr. Glover?"

"He's leaving for a job in a place called Detroit, place where they make automobiles."

"That's the name of that town. You say they make automobiles there? When is he going and how is he going to get there? Can I talk to him?" asked Bull excitedly."

"He's somewhere about. The rain will bring him in to help unload these bales."

"C'mon, John, let's give him a hand unloading, till George gets here. I got to talk to him about his going to ah, what's the name of that town?"

"Detroit, and I'll never turn down help, that's for sure."

Mr. Glover climbed to the top of the bales of hay on the wagon. He showed the boys how to use the hooks, and then began passing the hay bales to Bull, then to John, who stacked them in rows in the hayloft. The bale, being heavy and cumbersome to handle, taxed the strength of the handlers. Dust from handling the dry hay stuck in throats and itched the eyes but the work continued. John noticed that Bull couldn't keep up, since he had to wait longer and longer for Bull to pass on the bales. John jumped down from his perch to help, then back up, stacking the loads. Mr. Glover recognizing the situation called for a break. Bull was thankful as he slumped down on a bale, sweating profusely, breathing heavily. John was fazed by the heavy work but nowhere near as exhausted as Bull.

"I'm going to check the rain," said John, climbing down from the loft. He opened the barn door to a steadily falling shower. The cool breeze felt good.

"Bull's worse off than I thought. Maybe it's his size working against him, he still has a lot of fat on his frame," John thought to himself. "Sounds like the crew is on him pretty bad. Patty surely knows about Bull, the crew leaders talk, brag up the good ones and complain about the bad. An unwritten rule with every crew chief, is they keep they're own and one doesn't pass on slackers to others. Patty won't consider him, he can't, and it just won't work."

"Ho, John, whatcha doing here?" Asked a six-foot muscular young man who appeared from around the corner of the barn.

"Hi, George, was picking walnuts and stopped to order a ham for Christmas."

Ridge Valley

"Listen, I'm sorry about your Pa and I'm glad to see you, 'cause I'm leaving tomorrow. Going to make cars in Detroit, Michigan."

Bull, seeing George, walked over to the doorway.

"Hey, Bull, good to see you. I was telling John here I'm leaving tomorrow for Detroit, taking the train from Brownsville all the way."

"Your dad is sure going to miss you George, why you going anyway?" asked Bull.

"Be tough for a while on him, but I have plans. They pay five dollars a day so if I work a couple of years and send the money home, Dad can use it for buying a tractor. Can you imagine what he could do with a tractor instead of horses? He can buy new equipment, fix up the place, maybe buy some land, and expand the farm."

"Tell me more about this here Detroit, George," said Bull.

"How about it, boys, George, what do you say we get this load of hay into the loft? With all of you pitching in we can get it done fast. That is if you boys don't mind giving us another hand."

The four worked diligently to finish stacking the bales of hay. Bull, with his adrenalin kicking in, hustled as never before to get the job done. The sooner they finished the sooner he could hear from George about this Detroit place. The rain pelted down on the roof as they placed the last of the bales. Mr. Glover left to visit the milk house and returned with a cold pail of fresh milk. The dipper full of the cool sweet liquid was passed from one to the other. The last of the milk drunk, the three sat together in the open doorway, accepting the refreshing breeze. They accepted the windblown drizzle to cool their sweaty bodies.

"George, tell me about this Detroit place again, "said Bull.

CHAPTER XIV

INDUSTRIALISTS IN THE late nineteenth and early twentieth centuries maximized profits with no regard for anything or anyone who stood in the way. Labor, for example, was simply another factor of production, the same as raw materials, and the cheaper the labor cost the better. To hold or reduce wages paid for work was considered a good business practice by the barons of industry. The unfeeling thinking of these men led to ruthlessness on the part of management that created grave hardship among the working class. The search for more and greater profit was laid on the backs of labor. The industrial barons ruled with dictatorial powers and in most cases were backed by law and supported by governmental officials.

Henry Ford was an industrialist caught in the ruthless attitude of treating labor as just another piece of machinery. He also reached the pinnacle of production by developing a new process of manufacturing. He would forever become synonymous with the automobile and the assembly line to build them. The assembly line revolutionized the method of making cars. The process also provided two additional things: a quick, cheap, efficient method of production that offered affordable automobiles for the common man, and the opportunity of jobs for thousands at Ford plants in Detroit, Michigan.

Mr. Ford created the idea of running a chain along a line, stacked with parts where men stand on station to add the parts when the section of the automobile reached their station. The chain ran at a pace requiring workers to remain at their assigned point along the line and continuously add parts throughout the shift. The chain would not stop for anything or anyone. The worker has to keep up with the chain, leaving the line was forbidden, and breaks nonexistent. The seemingly never-ending work period became a tiresome, backbreaking continuous movement for ten hours. For his efforts a worker earned two dollars and fifty cents a day. The longevity of a laborer on the chain assembly line was a short one, a very short one. Many failed to return for a second day of work. Keeping workers under assembly line conditions taxed management constantly. A thousand men were hired in order to retain only ten percent of that number on the line. Adding to Company woes, a growing union movement concentrated on assembly line workers. Pamphlets distributed by union recruiters featured sayings like, "The hours are long, the pay is small, let everyone take your time, and buck em all." The absence rate and union efforts worried the leader of the Ford Company.

"We must maintain a smooth consistent assembly line operation in order to attain a thirty car per hour output. Anything below that number cuts into our margin of profit considerably. Also, gentlemen, we must look at adding more assembled parts, and then we can increase the speed of the line. The outcome obviously is more car production," said Mr. Ford at the director's year-end meeting.

"Frankly, gentlemen," Mr. Ford continued, "I am deeply concerned with the union movement in our plants. I fear that many problems will result if the workers are unionized. I dread that more than anything else. I also must recognize that to maintain a high workload from labor at the cheapest rate is good business. On the other hand, we cannot continue losing workers on the line everyday. The loss is costly and troublesome. We must give the labor issue immediate and due consideration. A solution to maintaining our manpower must be found or we will face serious consequences in the future. I expect you to give this issue deep thought and return with suggestions at our next meeting." The director's year-end meeting closed with expressions of enjoying the holiday, and ringing in the New Year with vigor and excitement.

There was little for the laborers to cheer about now or look forward to in the New Year. They and their families survived with barely enough in wages to subsist. The beginning of 1914 found no significant change in this philosophy. The barons of industry lorded over everybody; even the government bowed to their requests. The norm of keeping wages as low as one would accept, and to have prices as high as the public would pay was the code of conduct carried on by the robber barons in the early 1900's.

Henry Ford, after considerable thought and deliberation concluded that drastic changes must be made for his company to prosper. He understood that to reach new heights, improvements in labor conditions and higher wages were needed, and needed soon. He had designed the assembly line, an excellent productive technique. Now improvements for the men who work the line must follow. With this in mind, Henry Ford called a meeting of his top executives, and the Board of Directors on Tuesday, January 5th 1914.

"From this moment on, the minimum wage for assembly line work will be doubled to five dollars per day." The group at the meeting sat in disbelief. They turned to each other mumbling, "Did he say? Did you hear? Double the salary?" Before they settled down, a second announcement came.

"Gentlemen please," said Mr. Ford while holding up his hand. "Furthermore, the work day will be reduced to eight hours per day. This move will allow us to have three shifts working around the clock, thus increasing production."

The executives joined the directors in shocked silence. Again Mr. Ford paused to let his words play out as those in the room gasped in astonishment. Little did they realize that more announcements were forthcoming? After a few minutes the speaker held up his hand and asked for silence.

"I want you to know that I took time to observe happenings in the shops, and watched the workers on the assembly line for three days. I have also taken time to travel about the city, viewing the overcrowded tenements where many of our employees live. They are not sharing in our good fortune and have not been fairly rewarded for their hard work. I believe they should share in our success; therefore

Bob Menarcheck

I will install a system of profit sharing. The plan will be introduced soon for all workers and management," declared Mr. Ford.

The room was aghast. Had he gone mad? What was he thinking?" "He'll ruin the Company, he doubled the salary, eight hours of work instead of ten, sharing in the money he makes, wait, did he say management will share the profit also? That means us. The man is either a fool or a genius," said a director. The room buzzed with talk, gestures of excitement never seen before as the room changed from a mundane atmosphere to one causing boisterous exchanges among the occupants.

"Gentlemen, gentlemen please." Mr. Ford repeated, trying to get the attention of the group. "Gentlemen, please, I assure you that I have given these announcements much thought since our last meeting. I am convinced that this change in policy will result in increased production and lead to higher profits. We eliminate absenteeism, and foil the union movement in one quick swipe. Labor will respond with better work attitudes. The money paid will upgrade the economy and eventually lead to the purchase of Ford cars, and on it goes.

The news of Ford wages finally reached George Glover in late 1919 in the isolated patches and farms in Ridge Valley.

"George, you're telling me a powerful story and I have to ask once more about the pay, are you sure about the five dollars a day?" asked Bull.

"Certain of that, fact is it may be a bit more 'cause they paid that a while ago."

"Who you going with, George?"

"No one, going by myself. I checked it out, catch a freight out of Brownsville to Cleveland, connect up there for Detroit."

"George, I'm going with you. Where can I meet you and what do I need?" said Bull.

"You're welcome, but are you sure? I have been planning this move for a long time."

"I'm sure George, I'm going and that is a for sure."

Well I plan on catching the first streetcar to Brownsville tomorrow. You need to bring some clothes and eats in a gunny sack, 'nuff to get you there."

"Bull, listen, think about your family. What about them?" said John.

"I'll send back money like George, and my mind is made up. John, like I told you before, I can't go back into that mine. John, this is a Godsend, you see that, don't you?"

John did not have an answer. He got up from the bale they were sitting on and walked to the barn door to check the weather. "If he's a' going, he's going," mumbled John as he opened the door.

"Looks like we're going to get wet, still raining," John shouted back to a non-listening Bull. He and George were deep in discussion about their upcoming venture. John stood at the door wondering what he would do in Bull's situation.

"Let's go John, got things to do," said Bull, shaking John from his thoughts. They quickly mounted the sacks and stepped out into the rain

"To hell with all of them, John. I'll show .em, yeah I'll show 'em damn it. You say I got to face those asses and take their shit, no way, John. I don't have to beg your buddy Patty to go on his crew either. I don't need anybody."

They trudged on, both getting drenched with the sacks of nuts gaining weight from the added moisture. They moved past the stables, traversed the junk graveyard, across the bridge and up the road. John stopped briefly as he saw boxcars and a caboose being disconnected from a locomotive on a spur of track behind the Company store.

"Funny," he thought, "why drop off a caboose?"

Bull moved ahead breathing heavily. He opted to take a shortcut up the hill.

"He won't make it with that sack," said John to himself. Bull was slipping and sliding trying to make the grade. He lost the sack and it rolled to the bottom of the hill. Bull continued the struggle to climb. On hands and knees he succeeded in making it to the top. Once there he looked at John and glanced at the sack of nuts below He gestured a sign of defiance, turned and walked out of sight. John walked up the road to his home. He dropped the sack near the back door. Entering the house he welcomed the warmth of the kitchen.

"Better get them wet things off and hurry, catch your death of cold," said Mom.

"I've got to do something first, be back in a minute."

John went back to the bottom of the hill to retrieve the sack of nuts left by Bull. He returned home and explained to a waiting mother, "Bull left his sack at the bottom of the hill. I went back to get them for his Mom. He's leaving with George Glover tomorrow for a place that makes automobiles, Detroit; it's called. He's going to work there. He'll make five dollars a day."

"Leaving his family isn't worth the money and besides, work is work, here or there. Your Dad always said that you're either a worker or not, don't make no difference where. Now that George Glover, he'll be all right, he's a worker. Bull, just wait and see."

"Mom, I hope they both do well, I really do."

Jerry stood waiting in the same alcove where Bull stood in the morning. The rain eased into a light drizzle. John, hands in pockets, collar turned up, moved in quick choppy steps to meet Jerry as planned

"Hey, Jer."

"Hi, John"

"I've got something to tell you, Jer, Bull is leaving with George Glover for Detroit, Michigan to do factory work. He's going tomorrow. He had a lot of trouble working in the mine. His crew was on him all the time, so he's leaving."

"Word's been out a long time about Bull, big as a bear, weak as a kitten. I think his size worked against him. Fact is, I almost feel sorry for him but he brought a lot on himself. You know maybe with a new start in a new place, who knows?"

"We'll see, but right now he's mad, real mad. Tell me what's happening at the mine?"

"Hear em talking, John," Jerry said as he began pacing, "Big shots coming and going all the time, I'm in and out of their meeting, delivering stuff and I hear bits and pieces. There's a lotta talk about getting more miners, a whole shift of em."

"When, Jer?"

"Sounds like they plan on doing something soon. You see those box cars in back of the store? Do you know what they're doing there?"

"I guess waiting, but why a caboose? Don't make sense to leave one of those."

Ridge Valley

"For feeding, that's why."

"Feeding?" questioned John.

"Those boxcars back there are going to be fixed up to make something like a rooming house in each one. Sleep maybe twenty in each car. Listen, word is if they get enough they can double up. When one is sleeping the other is working."

"And the caboose is there to prepare food, wow, tell me, Jer, how do you learn this stuff? How do you get into the room with them?"

"I'm the go for person. They need something, I get it, bring it in. I stay around, clean, and listen. Heck, John, I hear a lot more like 'em sending labor agents to get workers. They're worried about the union coming in and about adjusting the pay scale. They talk about evictions of people in houses that don't have someone working for the Company. They claim they can't do anything until they get their own police force."

"A police force, the horses, the horses at the barn, they'll use em for mounted police. That's the answer, Jer, the box cars, caboose, it's all building fast."

The light rain turned into a fine mist that found its way into the alcove. Fog began to develop in the bottom above the creek. It drifted into the valley soon to reach the store. John and Jerry stood in silence, pondering what each said, watching the Kolinsky brothers stagger up the path together. They finally had enough to drink at O'Malley's.

"John, one more thing," said Jerry, breaking the silence. "Heard talk from some of our fella's about doing something to form a union, no real plans though, just talk for now." John now did the pacing as Jerry added another statement for thought. "I think someone is giving them information about us. No proof but they seem know a lot." John stopped pacing as Jerry continued. " I also heard them say that Patty Driscall is one to watch since the men listen and follow him. They're saying that he could easily lead the men in joining a union. They want to knock him down a notch as they say it. Problem is they need him for now so I don't expect anything to happen soon. I also heard it said any move now may cause the men to revolt."

John looked at Jerry, who looked back without flinching. The reaction concerned John, his friend didn't back away, and he was serious. A concern now evolved into a worry.

"Jerry, let's keep in touch, and be careful snooping around. I think we better get going for now. Got to work tomorrow and a lot to think about. Be careful."

"Don't worry about me John, I'll be careful."

They stepped from the alcove into the misty night.

CHAPTER XV

THE POSSUM MAN watched from the scrub. He'd observed the step reconstruction on Tuesday, and the church gathering the following Sunday and reported as before, "There are no suspicious activities seen or heard," to a doubting senior Hawke.

The exodus of black men migrating north years ago began as a trickle. The meager number moving above the Mason-Dixon line in the early 1900's opted for big cities like Detroit, Chicago, Cleveland and New York. A few found their way to the coal mining towns in Pennsylvania. These few often sent letters to relatives and friends inviting them to come. Only insignificant numbers responded at first to the call. Rufus Johnson received such letters. He wanted to join the trek north, but because of Grandma Smith and Bella's insistence on staying he had to bide his time. He did and now his patience was rewarded.

Great excitement prevailed in Southern towns as the recruiting man spread his alluring tales to all who would listen. The response from his new friends was quick and decisive. A large percentage of the black workers in the Hawke coalmine were anxious to answer the call. They got the message from the labor agent, and caught the fever to move to the "promised land."

The moment came on a Monday morning in early October of 1919. Getting word that the Klan was watching the rail stations in the Carbon Hill area, and to avoid them, the Negro workers including Rufus, Willie and their sons, decided to walk miles west to Lowellville to catch the train. Further south, Negro field workers learned of the labor agent tales. The past year had brought floods that destroyed thousands of acres of cotton. The boll weevil added to the misery by ravaging acres of good growth. With crops short, the Negro field worker was left dirt-poor and penniless. They would be the first to board the trains north. The black miners from Carbon Hill could only squeeze into the overcrowded compartments. Rufus, Willie, Leroy and Billie found a place on the floor in the corner of the third car. After a short time they had a breakfast of hard tack and biscuits garnered from the knapsacks. Occasionally the boys walked the length of the car while Rufus and Willie, not wanting to give up their spot, accepted the bumpy ride in position. Passengers who worked at the Hawke mine stopped to talk. The conversations usually ended with expressions like, "Wonder what those Hawkes are going to do now? Good for 'em, we showed 'em, let them dig their own coal, see how they like it."

The train rumbled on to Cincinnati, then to Pittsburgh. It took three days to reach Scottdale, Pennsylvania, the central marshalling station for new arrivals. There they would be processed and dispersed to various coal mining towns in the Grant Coal District. Rufus and Willie, along with other men were handed a numbered tag as they departed the train.

"This is your identification tag. Use this number when signing in, keep it with you at all times," shouted the porter over and over.

"Number 1467 report to the registration table for processing and assignment," repeated a boy carrying the same number on a sign. He walked slowly on the overcrowded platform, repeating the number again and again.

"I got number 1829, what's yours Rufus?"

"1830, looks like we got a long wait, more people here than they expected, I reckon."

"Number 1468 report, this is your identification tag number 1468, keep this tag until registration," the announcements reverberated

Ridge Valley

from the platform walls calling to the hundreds of Negroes circulating about. "New arrivals sign in at station number six, new arrivals, that means us, let's go," said Rufus.

"We is got more than we expected, take a bit o' time to take care of all of you' all. Have soup and bread on the other side of the station. Sleep on mats in back; we hope to get you assigned tomorrow. Wash or bath if you want after dark down at the river, water may be a bit cold but it's the best we got. The outhouse is in the woods. Next please."

The process for getting the overflow assigned slowed considerably. Boarding houses in the mining towns were full. A few cots became available due to deserters, but not enough to handle the onslaught. The numbers multiplied as more trains arrived taxing the facilities. The Scottdale rail depot became a human stabling area with hundreds of men milling around, waiting. The head of the Grant Empire called a special meeting of the directors to discuss and finalize plans for housing the new workers. The decision was made to billet the overflow by using boxcars.

"I understand we are making bunkhouses out of boxcars. All the patch towns have out of the way railroad spurs to accept the cars. A caboose has a stove for cooking meals. Double up if we have to, one works while the other sleeps. That's the decision and we start with Ridge Valley, so get moving gentleman," said Mr. Moses at the director's meeting. They all left except Mr. Hood who was asked to stay.

Railroad boxcars and cabooses were moved into position. Carpenters and cooks were hired; and the assignments of black workers intensified. Designation of numbers 1829 and 1830 were assigned to The Ridge Valley complex in bunks 11 and 12, boxcar C. "Mr. Hood, we have the workers, the agents did an excellent job recruiting, now we must move to get the Grant Coal and Iron Police organized. We can house the new folks in the boxcars temporarily. Winter is coming on and these Negroes lived in warm weather, don't know how they'll adjust to the cold. They have to be placed in more secure quarters as soon as possible. We need to begin planning on evicting those from houses who do not have anyone working in the mines, and we need the Company Police to complete the job. When can we expect a force to be in place?"

"My men are looking in towns like Chicago and Detroit for the type of, well the right kind of men we want. It takes a special person, big, mean and one with an attitude. We have to give some training; all this takes time. We'll work as fast as we can but you may have to use those boxcar hotels a bit longer than expected. I'll do all I can to hasten the process," said Mr. Hood.

"I want you to hasten your recruiting. We need that force in place as quickly as possible. The sooner the better," said Mr. Moses.

Ridge Valley was the first on the list to get the boxcar bunkhouses. The cars, the ones John saw, were placed on a spur behind the Company Store. A contingent of carpenters converged on the scene to build wooden bunks. Straw filled sacks would be used as mattresses. They wanted to accommodate twenty men per car. Soon about sixty black miners would descend on Ridge Valley. The new workers would go directly to the Union Supply Company Store to open charge accounts using the number assigned at the registration desk in Scottdale. After purchasing work clothes the men would report to the mine office for assignment. Cooks from the railroad were hired to prepare meals. After supper the new laborers finalized bunk assignments would began working the next day. The local superintendent, after viewing job applications completed in Scottdale, assigned Willie as the section leader. His job was to divide the men into six crews and allocate jobs. The last chore was for all to report to the store for shovels, picks and other work supplies furnished by the company. Coal mining patches in selected sites, would follow the Ridge Valley lead with boxcar hotels and a caboose parked on railroad spurs close to the mine.

The cool, damp weather and the Negro workers arrived simultaneously. October in Western Pennsylvania is a time of change. Leaves turn their green colors to bright orange, red and yellow. The daylight minutes become fewer each day. The rainy season enters its height in October, bringing along cooler temperatures. Sweaters and shawls would become the outer clothing of choice for patch inhabitants to combat the climate change. Coal burning kitchen stoves in patch houses provided heat to keep out the chill.

The boxcars provided little protection from the cool winds. Rags and old rope were stuffed into openings between the slats. The procedure kept out the wind, but not the dampness. Soggy sweaty clothes hung inside the cars on nails, adding moisture to the room. Without sufficient heat or air movement, the apparel never dried. A dank stench from the sodden clothes intensified. The Negro's tolerated the conditions mentally but not physically. The long trip north on bumpy, crowded rail cars took its toll, tiring the men considerably. The wait in crowded Scottdale with no sleeping accommodations added to the strain. The food although very good, was not tolerated well by the new arrivals. They carried their stomachaches and body aches to Ridge Valley. Regardless, all were anxious to work and put forth the effort to make the good money promised. The hard work sapped their strength quickly during the first three weeks of work. Mostly working for ten hours a day, they endured until sore throats, colds and flu-like symptoms began and spread quickly to the bunkhouse inhabitants. All kept quiet about their physical ailments believing the sickness would pass. Although ill, they went to work until it was physically impossible. Days of work were lost when dysentery hit with a vengeance. Loose bloody bowel movements affected every boxcar worker.

"The labor man never told us about the weather. Never been this sick in all my life," said Rufus to Willie. "I am so cold, and it's said that it's going to get colder. I feel so weak and hot I can hardly move. How are the boys?" asked Rufus.

"Both are good, working and sleeping in the caboose where it's warm."

"I have blood, a lot of it when I go, it just runs out of me, can't stop it."

"A lot of the boys have the runs, and fever, they're weak but still try to work."

"Sorry about the shivering, can't help it, feel so cold, thirsty."

"Let me get you a drink, be right back."

Willie returned to find Rufus shaking and moaning. A green slimy vomit lay on the floor near his bunk. Closer inspection revealed more on the other side. The smell, like rotten fish, permeated the

Bob Menarcheck

room. Willie gagged, covering his mouth and nose with his hand; he retched, holding back the vile taste in his throat.

"Rufus, Rufus," Willie said as he shook him. Rufus did not respond. Horrified, he soaked a rag with water and wiped Rufus's face and cleaned the remnants of green puke from his cheek.

"He got a deep heat in him. He's burning up inside, talking out of his head. Rufus, I'm going to get some help. We need a doctor." Willie cleaned up the area as best he could, then covered Rufus with a second blanket and walked to the caboose. He sent Leroy to the mine office to ask for help.

"Man said company has a place for injuries. They don't have anything for fevers and such. Said we have to help ourselves." Leroy reported on his return.

" Who is this man you saw?

"Man who sit at a table in a room?Couldn't have been the Superintendent he saw thought Willie who checked the other cars and found many sick. The sleeping area reeked with the smell of sweat, bile and vomit. He decided to go down early the next morning to talk to the Superintendent.

"You're telling me most of your men are sick? They're not slacking off are they, Willie?" asked the superintendent.

"Came to tell you they are sick. Doubt if I could have one crew available for work. We done worked when not feeling good, now most have colds, fever; dey is flushed and parched, puking a lot. Where we are living is not good. One gets sick and it spreads to everyone else. I'm asking for the men, sir, we need to get a doctor and when we going to get us those two story houses? Labor man told us we would live in them. That sure would help."

"Don't know what the labor agent said, right now we have no houses available. Have to do the best you can and get your men well and back to work. I'll send the Company doctor over soon as I can to give your boys a look. You just worry about you and your men doing the job. See you and all that can work in the shaft. We'll get the doctor over to your men this morning."

Willie left the office dejected, and for the first time felt that maybe the move north was a mistake, a big mistake. Many came because he came, and they trusted his judgment. He was their leader, they trusted him and now he felt the pressure. Doubts crept in his mind about promises made by the labor agents. "Are these owners the same as the Hawkes? The men are sick and all they want to know is, how many can work? We already owe the Company Store money, they're charging for rent in these boxcars, no houses, worse than in Alabama. I'll do the best job I can for now and hope the bosses soon understand our plight." He mumbled to himself. Willie went to the caboose and told Leroy about his dad being sick and not going to work. He also told him not to go into the boxcars for fear of him catching the fever.

"I'm going, I'll take his place. We need the money. I'll use his name and check number. They won't know the difference." Said Leroy on hearing about Rufus.

"No, Leroy, I can't let you do this, Rufus will never forgive me. NO."

"I'm going with you or someone else, but I'm going."

Willie felt that further talk to discourage the boy was fruitless. Actually, down deep he was proud of Leroy wanting to take his dad's place. "After all he is fourteen, and I started to work at that age. The doctor will come soon and get the men on their feet, so it'll only be a few days; work him a bit, he'll be glad to get back to helping in the caboose" thought Willie hopefully. "All right, tomorrow. Get ready to go in tomorrow."

Leroy couldn't sleep. He pondered about his decision, wondering if he could do the job, and about Rufus's condition. He decided to get up from his floor bunk in the caboose and check on his father. The time was two o'clock in the morning.

"Close the door," yelled an inhabitant in the boxcar, Leroy quickly obliged. Two candles in opposite corners provided the only light in the room. Leroy stood by the door waiting for his eyes to become accustomed to the shadowy surroundings. The place reeked, there was no air and it was hard to breath. Coughing rang out continuously and the men moaned from the fever. The heavy atmosphere, and the dampness could be felt in his bones. "I've got to get him out of here, and now," thought Leroy.

"Pardon me, sorry," he said to men he walked by to get to his dad's bunk. "I'll take him to my place in the caboose, at least he'll be warm, and away from this wretched place," he mumbled to himself. Leroy became alarmed when he reached under the blanket to lift Rufus from the bunk. He was burning up, dry heat radiating from his body. He knew from Grandma's ills that this condition needed treatment. He remembered hearing the midwife lady say that heat kills the brain. First thing to do is to cool the head and the body will follow. Leroy tended to his father for the remainder of the night in the caboose. By early morning Rufus stopped wailing and settled down to a deep sleep. Leroy, happy with the progress, decided to take his dad's place and go to work.

Billie joined him in the shaft. He slipped in, using another man's name without Willie knowing. The toil of laying track, timbering, avoiding leaky roofs, carrying, digging and retrieving supplies taxed all. The exertion to keep up showed as the two slowed considerably and rested more often as the shift neared the end. They were elated when the time came to trudge to the cage and exit the mine. They were exhausted but pleased that they held up with the others. They would return with pride from the mine complex to the boxcar hotel. Walking from the opposite direction was John, along with other members of his crew heading for work. The groups crossed paths as John, Leroy and Billie eyed each other briefly. All three wondered about the age of the other.

Leroy hurried to the caboose to see Rufus. "He's not here. The Company doctor ordered him back to his bunk," said the cook who added, "We can't have a sick man spreading germs maybe contaminating the food in here." Leroy dashed to boxcar C and found Rufus flushed with heat.

"Despite the efforts of the doctor, he's worse off than when I left him this morning. His eyes are rolled back and he's hotter," Leroy said to himself.

"Been talking out of his head since he came back. Nothing makes sense in what he says," said a black man in a bunk next to Rufus. Leroy sponged him down with cold water and offered drinks that Rufus refused. Without warning he started to rave, flailing his arms and shouting incoherently, then instantly quieted down breathing heavily.

"Been doing that too, only goes on longer, wearing himself out, he won't last long in that state. Doctor gave us all some kind of medicine, he refused."

Rufus continued in his delirious state during the evening. Willie came by to help and provide time for Leroy to eat and rest. "I'll sleep in the caboose, Willie said, you can use my bunk and bring it next to him. Remember you have to get rest yourself if you plan working. Do what you can, but get your rest."

Leroy lay on the bunk. He felt the dampness, heard the hacking coughs and the occasional deep moans. He slept deeply for a short time, only to awaken and check Rufus. The process lasted throughout the night. Willie was hesitant when the time came to awaken the lad for work. "Best he go down with the crew, take a break from this." Rufus was resting and in a quiet state in the morning. He felt warm but not as hot as before. He decided to go to work. In addition, Willie needed him for two men that worked yesterday, were too ill to go in today.

The bright colored leaves in early autumn were now gone. Browns of various shades replaced the gorgeous hues. Losing their grip to frost and wind, the leaves drifted to the ground. Trees stood bare to face the onslaught of a bleak cold season. Winter weather was approaching and it would arrive with a vengeance. It was now November tenth and the day began crisp and cold. The breeze shifted nonchalantly throughout from the west to the north. A fresh wisp of wind carried a hint of biting frigid air. The damp warmer air that lingered in the valley clashed with the new colder current. They danced together until hitting the ridge where they meshed and turned back into the valley. Gathering momentum with each turn, the conditions worsened as the day wore on to evening. Gray gunmetal colored clouds assembled, the kind that the locals knew brought snow. The white flakes came and accumulated until bitter cold took over, chasing the damp air to another location. This was a time families gathered in the kitchen near a warm stove. The new arrivals that were not accustomed to the snow and cold suffered. The doctor tried all he could to counter the flu and fever but the living conditions in the boxcar allowed the illness to linger. The flu was passed from one to another it never abated. They all suffered, except for one who no longer felt the pain. He was Ulysses.

"I don't think he had a last name."

"When did it happen, does anyone know?"

"Naw, jest found him back in the corner bunk, must been burning up with the heat, hardly any clothes on, probably froze, I recon. We can't let him just lay there like that. Willie done went down the shaft, won't be back for awhile."

"Didn't that Company doctor say to notify the mine office fin's we got worse? I reckon this calls for a trip to the office. Who's to go?"

Alonzo Jones, a crew leader, and one of the older men who broke his fever, was chosen as the spokesman.

"This boss man was not happy about Ulysses dying. He is sorry all right, but I think only cause a worker is lost. That Company doctor said we would be fine once the fever passes. The mine foreman said he needs workers, not sick or dead people. I asked about Ulysses and he say for us to go and see a Reverend Jefferson in Brownsville. Place about twelve miles away. Gave me streetcar tickets to go and bring the preacher back here. Said to go right away so we can get on with planting the dead man so we can think about work."

"You sure he done said to plant Ulysses as soon as possible so that the rest of us can get well and go back to work?" asked one of the men.

"He said that exactly."

"A man is dead, and the man say plant him, like he's a nothing. That means then that we all are nothing. The doctor done tried to help but a lot of us too weak to mend. Some of the mine folks don't care about us except to dig the coal and dig some more. We can't live like this, cold, sick, bad food. Alonzo, what we going to do?"

"I'll go and fetch this preacher, first things first, bury Ulysses proper like, then we got to do some talking, we are doomed if we don't do something."

"I think we talk to Willie when he comes out. Make some decisions then. Now let's remember we have a dead brother to tend to and not act like them, we got to do right." Said Alonzo who added, "Now I'll go and fetch this Reverend Jefferson and get him here. You' all tell Willie about things when he comes out of the shaft."

CHAPTER XVI

"THE LORD GIVES and the Lord takes away," said the reverend in a booming voice upon entering the boxcar. "Seems he takes more 'cause we done got one to "plant" like them bosses I hear say."

Reverend Jefferson walked to the center of the boxcar and stood silently for an entire minute, looking around saying nothing. A huge head with a wide flat nose dominated his face. Full buxom lips, a rounded chin and puffy cheeks added to his features. A long overcoat hid a pear shaped body. Half-dollar-size eyes were used to stare down an entire congregation. He used the technique now to settle about fifty men in a boxcar. He succeeded in gaining their attention, their complete attention.

"I come here to honor your request. I bring the Lord and Savior to your presence. I come to pray for the dead, honor their soul, give a proper burial then, then, then I say, when that is done, I bring you help to save your soul, for those who listen to my preaching will be saved," said Reverend Jefferson in a booming voice that reverberated off the walls of the closed boxcar. "You, sir, what is your name?"

" Ezra Smith."

" I ask you and your fellow workers to trust the Lord. I am his representative. If you trust in him, then trust in me. That's all I ask.

Let us together do what has to be done. We bury your friend, then we will talk about give and take, Mr. Smith," announced the preacher.

Willie convinced the superintendent to give the men a day off to bury and grieve for the deceased. The services would be held in the Southern Baptist Church in Brownsville. Burial would take place at Laurel Cemetery. Willie, along with Leroy and Billie, volunteered to stay back and take care of Rufus and six other severely ill black brothers. All others, some weak from the fever but able to go, would board the special streetcar to take them to the funeral. For this Willie promised to have four crews at work the next day.

A quick burial service took place at the church. The burial will take place at the cemetery about a mile away. Once the burial ceremony was completed the Minister joined the men on the streetcar.

"We will not be returning to Ridge Valley immediately. Instead, we will return to the church for final blessings and remembrances," announced the Revered.

They rode the streetcars back to a makeshift church in a converted rundown vacant one-room school. On the lawn in the back of the building a fireplace roared, with red wood coals heating a pig carcass on a spit. Two black boys turned the pig slowly, searing and cooking all sides. A cauldron of chit lings boiled in the corner. A pot of beans that hung on a shard bubbled near the fire. Two women were baking bread in a Dutch oven. A huge pot of coffee hung in another corner over hot coals. The Minister welcomed the Negro miners back to his church as they exited the streetcar. He then led them to the back of the building to see and smell. The sight and fragrance of the food overwhelmed the crowd. A miracle happened. They all smiled and to a man they felt physically better about the cold and their ills.

"We will eat soon. The cooking is not quite done. Until it's finished I ask that you please join me in the church," boomed the preacher.

They entered and sat on benches gibbering excitedly to each other, gesturing and pointing to the area where the food was cooking. They couldn't believe their good fortune seeing and smelling the roasted pork, chit lings, beans, and fresh bread and coffee. Their mouths watered at the thought of gorging themselves on food they hadn't had for a long time.

The reverend closed the door and walked up to the pulpit and raised his hand for quiet. The men obliged. As was his custom, the preacher hesitated in speaking. He took a while, as the audience became edgy waiting, he now had their attention.

"We have a demon among us this day, and that demon is Greed. Greed, I tell you, and you, yes, you are helping that demon." The reverend's voice reverberated from the walls of the church. He hesitated again, letting his remarks sink in.

"I am not helping no demon, how you figure that, preacher?"

"You are helping those money- hungry monsters, you is a' mining his coal for him, and that is helping the greedy."

"I am not doing no such thing. I am not, all I want is to do the right thing, to work and earn good pay for my family. I come north for a better life, we believed the labor man, promised houses but where are they? You, reverend, you say we are demons, well, you are wrong," said one of the men in the crowd.

The others in the room murmured in agreement. Some just sat, not fully understanding the preacher's message. A few, anxious to get to the food, were heard asking, "When we going to eat?" The reverend waited and watched. After a time he held up his hands asking for silence.

"My good man, if you are not wrong then I am. A true Shepherd cares for his flock, and you are my flock and I care for you, all of you. The harvest is abundant, Jesus told the seventy-two, but the workers are few." The reverend then told the story of the good Shepherd. The group listened intently. They answered at times with "Amen" and nodded heads in agreement. They wanted more and the preacher told the story of the Good Samaritan. He described the situation in graphic detail.

"The man was beaten, robbed and left by the side of the road, lying in blood, wounded badly. The Samaritan stopped to help. He saw to the person's needs and paid for his care. I tell you that I am a true Shepherd who cares for his flock. You are my flock. Like the Good Samaritan I will not abandon you. I tell you I am the one who provides food, shelter and GOOD JOBS with wages to match."

A tall distinguished looking white man walked about outside checking the food preparation. He was dressed in a brown wool suit with a matching topcoat, black leather shoes and a derby on his head. His dark bushy eyebrows, sharp nose and protruding chin dominated, along with his dark piercing eyes. All those preparing the food obeyed his directions. Two Negro boys about twelve years old stood directly in front of the man, listening to him intently. A wave of the hand sent them scurrying to the woodpile. They gathered all the firewood they could carry and moved to the back door of the church. They knocked; the preacher answered.

"We is got wood for the stove and the "master" says the hog is ready."

Those inside that heard the announcement began shuffling about.

"Gentlemen, hold on please, first let us give thanks to the Lord for what he has provided. After grace you are to proceed, and please be orderly, to the ladies who will give you a tin plate, cup and utensils. The food will be served to you. Please return here, where it's warm, to eat. I will have more good things to say to you later."

The men jockeyed for position and filed out in good order. The reverend followed. He went directly to the white man standing near the fireplace. He called him by his first name.

"Mr. Kenneth, sir, there they are, how many can you use?"

"I need them all, for as you know the railroad needs help. I'll take the lot and pay handsomely for each one, less the cost of this feeding, of course."

"Of course, Mr. Kenneth." They both laughed.

"What say we get some food, then talk to these boys about working on the railroad reverend?"

"You first, Mr. Kenneth."

CHAPTER XVII

THE STORM CLOUDS began gathering in the west during the early morning hours. Billowing white clouds curled higher and higher, building huge White Mountains in the blue sky. They pushed to their zenith and with no place to go began pressing downward. Gently, with a wisp of wind, the gathering fleece moved slowly, covering more and more of the once azure sky. Aging quickly in the distance, the overcast darkened into a leaden cover. Throughout the day fluffy whites moved faster and faster to the east. They raced ahead of the ominous darkening storm clouds in the distance.

"Wind a' picking up, look at them leaves a' turning," said Bella to herself as she made her way to the outhouse.

The leaves of the gum tree turned up in the stiff wind, pretending to watch the cloud racing competition above. They flipped back and forth, holding on against a steady wind. Should they have a voice, no question cheers would erupt loud and clear for the whites to outrace their dark pursuer to the horizon.

"Big blow a' coming, likely rain be here by late afternoon," Bella said to Brownie as she left the toilet and started walking to the house. "Best we go in and close up the place before I leave to see the pastor." She latched the back screen, and secured the back door. Shutting all windows, Bella moved to the front door. The outside screen, besides owning a long tear, also lacked a proper hook. A strip of cloth, torn from an old rag, was used to fasten the front screen door. A sudden burst caused Bella to retreat quickly, closing and bolting the wooden door.

A month passed since Rufus and Leroy left. She received two letters sent by Rufus that were passed on by the Reverend. The last letter was sent from a place called Ridge Valley. They are doing well, living in a boarding house until a house becomes available in the "patch." The letters did not mention the cold weather or their living in boxcars.

Bella anxious for more information walked to the church everyday, usually in the afternoon. Mornings were not good times for the Reverend Washington, and since the mail was delivered to the church in the afternoon the best times for her to visit were late in the day. So Bella walked to the church this windy day, hoping for a letter. There was none. To avoid walking back in the afternoon heat, Bella stayed until dusk. Today she lingered a bit longer since she decided to stop at the grave and talk to Momma.

"Always had someone around but all left me Momma, you, Rufus and Leroy. I sure do miss you Momma, I sure do," she said in a whisper with tears welling in her eyes. " I thought people would come over to visit more often, but I guess they have enough to keep them busy without worrying about me. Anyway I still have you to talk to. Don't know how I'll survive without you up north. Things are changing fast, sometimes too fast Momma. You should be glad you're gone fer people are getting fidgety and fickle. Yep, folks leaving and mine owners all fussed up about losing workers. Talk is they got caught off guard, and without Rufus, Willie and others they is awful mad those Hawkes. Yes sir Momma, only we women folk are left to fend for ourselves," said Bella glancing at the sky.

" Heard the Grain Mill lost every working soul Momma. Saying goes the Boss men went to lunch and a train came by and slowed down enough for every man from the Mill to jump aboard. Dem white folk owners are sure those northern labor agents planned the move and they are as mad as roused hornets. Been talk of them doing something cause they can't keep losing good workers." A gust of wind picked up dust causing Bella to cover her face. " Well time is getting on Momma. Wind a kicking up a storm for sure. Clouds are moving fast, a good blow be here soon. Be a heading home now. Life is a coming and going awful fast anymore. I sure miss those Sundays when we had time for everyone. Believe me Momma, those days are gone and now it leaves me missing someone all the time."

Bella stood and took time to say a silent prayer. Finished, she bent down, patted the ground turned and began to walk home Large drops of rain began to fall as she reached her back door. She entered the house and closed the door as the rain arrived hitting hard. The sky darkened. Jackhammer sounds pounding against the side of the shanty from driving rain rattled the brain. The dog retreated to a spot under the table.

"Brownie you ole scaredy cat. It's just a bit of wind. I show' don't mind that, but that pinging from the roof, that's another story. Must be some hail mixed up in the wet stuff," she said bending over the side of the table looking at a frightened mutt. The old rag binding at the front screen started to give way against the onslaught. The screen door, now loose rattled against the house. Damaged from the pounding the screen finally gave in and joined other debris in the yard. A growing gale whistled through slat openings causing ole Brownie to retreat back into a corner. He got up once to roam, looking for Rufus or Leroy. Not finding them, quivering and shaking from the onslaught he cowered in a corner. A loud crack of thunder finally sent the mutt to the bedroom to seek solace under the master's bed.

Bella lit oil lamps in the living room and kitchen then began a fire in the stove. The fuel she added caught quickly. Burning hot from the pull of the breeze, gusts of wind gave the flames more and more oxygen causing the fire to burn even hotter. The top of the stove turned into a red hue. The central section became a crimson red. The lightning cracked, thunder rumbled and the wind banged debris against the side of the house. Bella cleaned up the kitchen after supper. Following her routine since her two men left, she sat in the living room and read her Bible. The low-hanging clouds produced a steady rain and created an early dusk atmosphere. Bella concentrated so deeply on reading the Bible she totally ignored the happenings outside. The wind picked up, pushing clouds, driving the rain in gusts, tearing at loose boards and roofs. The bottom section of the front screen door latch finally gave way freeing the door to bang against one side of the porch wall, then the other. Back and forth the door swash buckled at the mercy of the wind.

CHAPTER XVIII

"GOD DAMN IT, let's cut out this sneaky crap."

"Just shut up Billy."

"Waiting around here, getting sloshed in this rain, man, let's go."

"Either we go or forget it. Why the hell not? And if we don't get going soon we'll drown in this field."

"Can't go yet."

"Well, why not?"

"Just can't, got to wait."

"What is so important about tonight anyway? Why not tomorrow?"

"Listen, it's all set for tonight. I've been watching, she's alone, no one around, and the man says its tonight, he's expecting it and what he says goes."

"God Damn it anyway, he's not getting drenched in the middle of the corn field, and besides old Rufus and his boy are gone so she's in there by herself. C'mon, what do you say deputy?"

"Don't call me deputy, no names are to be used, everybody remember that."

"Been told we go in, mess her up a bit, scare hell out of the bitch, and bash in some stuff, let them other niggra women know what's in store for them 'cause their man left for up north," said Lester.

"Yeah tear up the place," echoed Johnny Paul, "I say we go, what say, Lester?"

"Damn you" said the deputy, pointing at Johnny Paul, "For the last time, I said no names, do it once more and I'll crown you. Meantime, just shut up and wait. Listen, we follow orders and as soon as we get the signal we move and not before. We'll get the job done, take care of things then go to Red's to celebrate."

"Yeah that's right, he's got beer stashed in iced tubs and real good "shine to sip on," sputtered Lester while wiping wetness from his face. "You coming to celebrate with us, deputy?" asked Johnny Paul, using the name deliberately in order to agitate the deputy.

The deputy stared in contempt, not answering. Lester reached into a side pocket under his canvas poncho, pulled out a pint and took a long pull. He swiped his mouth with the back of his hand, smiling at the deputy. The force of the rain and wind pelted the cornfield resulting in a crackling noise as it struck the stocks. Once soaked, a dull thud reverberated in the field as the men crowded together inside the fifth row from the edge of the planting. Total darkness now engulfed the area. A blinding rain limited the vision to only a few yards. Beyond the field, about five yards from the edge, the deputy located the one-person outhouse used by the Johnsons. A path worn through the years of trudging back and forth from shack to outhouse was filled with water. Something to avoid, thought the deputy. He squished his eyes to find the back door, wondering which room the women inside was located.

"Damn it, deputy, the Possum Man left, just left, and I'm leaving unless we move, so either we go or forget it," sputtered Lester

"Leave and you're in big trouble and you know it. I got special orders to wait for a signal, and I'm waiting," said the deputy.

Lester Polk mumbled to himself as he spit a glob of tobacco juice from the corner of his mouth Lester, a part-time rumrunner and whiskey still operator, occasionally ran the saw at the mill. He loved to do the dirty work for the Klan. Shabby long black unruly hair topped a cruddy-pockmarked face that got that way from a bad case of childhood measles. Dark brown teeth, stained from years of chewing, added to Lester's shady character. He had lost his incisors from a fight, causing him to spit on a person when he talked. His main activity in the Klan was cross burning. "Soaked den logs with my own whiskey juice, make em burn for hours." All he needed was to be asked. The more he lingered in the cornfield, the more mean-tempered he became. He felt caged, he wanted to go…and now.

Billy Ray, a handyman for the Hawke Mining Company, was along to report all happenings to his boss. A Bible totter, he was totally loyal to Mr. Hawke who accepted his report as gospel. Only five feet, four inches tall, he looked out of place with the rest, neatly dressed, every hair in place, accepted by the Lester's of the world because Mr. Hawke said so. Billy accepted the conditions calmly, mentally remembering every detail.

Johnny Paul was the youngest of the group at only nineteen. He was thrilled to be here and serve the Klan. He quit school and hung around the mine office running errands for the boss, and the boss loved the attention. His father was killed in a mine accident and with his mother working; Johnny Paul was left to fend for himself. He got in with the Klan when he stole an outfit and attended a rally. He was hooked, especially by the ranting of speakers at meetings that created frenzy in him he could not explain

Deputy Earle did all the Klan and "the Man" asked of him and often it was what Sheriff T. G. Potts didn't want to mess with. A heavyset person, who some considered fat; he got that way eating free at the three restaurants in town. A non-decision maker by nature, he allowed events to happen without control. His order this night was to wait until after dark in the cornfield. The sheriff would drive by, make certain all was in order and if he dimmed the car lights, they would go as planned. The deputy and his helpers were to leave an unmistaken message, through Bella Johnson, that the Klan will not tolerate any more black miners moving north.

The sheriff would proceed back to the mine office where he and the mine owners would be seen by the black miners at the shaft. The entire county, including the blacks, knew the Klan members, so an alibi was always planned when something was coming down.

The continued cranking of the car engine and using maximum spark was to no avail as the patrol car's engine only sputtered and coughed; it did not start. Dampness in the electrical system would not allow T.G. to make his rounds this night. He could not show to give the signal for those waiting to move in on the Johnson house.

"This is plain horse crap, is we a' going or not? Well, I'm not waiting anymore, I'm going, is anyone else coming with me?" shouted Lester.

"I'm for going, me too, let's go."

The deputy was outvoted. He ignored the group and continued looking for the signal. "Wait, with all the rain maybe I missed it, yes that's it, I missed it," he thought.

"Okay, let's put on the hoods and robes, make sure you're covered."

The hoods normally stood stately and tall but being soaked from the rain hung limply to the side. The pelting rain played havoc with the robes. The four turned, gyrated and jumped in an effort to cover themselves by placing the wet robes over soaked clothes. Except for the deputy the others cursed, swore and dammed their maker as they comically maneuvered in weird contortions to don the apparel.

"Let's go without em, who cares if she knows who we are?" said Lester.

"Get 'em on, now, do it and shut up, get it done," said the deputy.

They did it, they succeeded somehow as the hoods drooped, robes muddy and wet stuck to damp clothes, and clumped about the knees; a motley looking crew.

"I'm ready, let's go," announced Lester.

The lightning cracked, thunder rumbled and wind gusts continued to bang debris against the side of the house. Bella ate her meal, cleaned the table and retreated to the living room where she was reading her Bible. Suddenly she raised her head from the book and looked quizzically at the window, and she listened. Call it instinct, or a sixth sense but she felt it, there was someone outside the house.

"What or who is it?" she questioned, "Can't be any one out in this storm."

Quickly Bella went around the house blowing out all the lamps. The only light in the kitchen came from the crimson glow at the top of the stove. Lightning on occasion added some luminous flicker, but it ended as fast as it came.

They moved toward the shack, shadows that passed around the outhouse into the watered rutted path to the back door. Johnny Paul hesitated, letting the others go ahead. Once they reached the door, Johnny Paul exited the field next to the outhouse. He hesitated and pushed. Assisted by the wind and rain, the building toppled into the mud. Smiling, he hurried to catch the others. The deputy turned with a questioning look.

"The wind, I swear, the wind, you could see it leaning, just put my hand on it and."

"Oh hell Johnny Paul, wished I'd thought of it," laughed Lester, who imagined a big toothy grin under his friend's hood.

Billy Ray was the only one alert enough to notice that the lights that were on in the house earlier were now out. He mentioned it to the deputy.

"Something is wrong, move now and move fast," shouted the deputy.

Bella's intuition was answered with reality as she saw the white clad trespassers in a flash of lightning outside the back entrance.

"Lord," she muttered to herself then added. "Got to get out."

Bella hurried through the kitchen, into the living room to the front door. She called Brownie who was reluctant to move from under the bed. She grabbed for the doorknob but missed. The noise from the back was unmistakable; the white hooded intruders were bashing in the back door. She found the knob but the door would not open. She forgot about the lock she secured earlier.

"Where you a' going, bitch? We is here to set you straight," said Lester.

Bella reacted as quickly as a cornered cat. She whirled in the dark around Lester and broke toward the kitchen hoping to exit through the back door. She encountered the deputy on her way, in the kitchen. Earle saw her coming and shouldered her, knocking Bella off stride. The hit caused her to stumble and topple toward the red-hot stove. A high pitched piercing scream came first; then the acid smell of burning flesh accompanied by a sizzling sound like bacon frying in a skillet. The blow by the deputy sent Bella skidding across the molten red stovetop, severely burning her arm, shoulder and back. She stumbled to the floor and rolled under the table, shrieking from the intolerable pain. She screamed and wailed, calling to the Lord for help. The deputy searched but could not find Bella in the dark. The old hound, now ignoring the lightning and thunder, charged toward Bella's Lordly call. Brownie bounded past Lester and Billy Ray to Bella's screams. The protective instincts kicked in as the animal jumped the unsuspecting deputy, knocking him off balance and toward the stove. Stumbling out of control, Earle reached out to steady himself from falling. His right hand hit hard and flat on the red-hot stovetop. He reared back against the wall, yelling and cursing. Brownie was unrelenting, biting the officer's legs and ankles.

"My hand is burning, my hand's burning," he cried, "Oh my God, help, somebody help," he yelled in a pained voice holding his right wrist of the smoldering hand. Brownie danced between Bella and the deputy, first licking the master, and then baring teeth and nipping the officer's heels, keeping him at bay. Earle, tightly grabbing his wrist, shed tears, squeezing his wrist trying to deaden the pain, pleading for help.

Lester reached out to catch Bella but failed. He tripped and fell hard, hitting his head on the corner of a table. Dazed from the blow, Lester staggered, and then fell to the floor. He heard screams coming from the kitchen but could not comprehend what he should do. Brownie, hearing the noise in the living room, ran to investigate. Satisfied that Lester was not a threat, he returned to the kitchen and attacked the deputy, who lurched futilely toward the door. Once again Brownie backed him against the wall.

"God, help. Somebody help me please, and get this dog off me," pleaded the deputy.

Billy Ray followed Lester into the living room and moved to check the bedrooms. In the darkness he felt his way around the corner of the first bedroom when Brownie brushed by him. Thinking it was a person he warned the others shouting, "He's heading your way."

By this time Earle had already knocked Bella into the stove. The dog attacked, and Billy Ray, hearing all the screams from the kitchen, assumed it was the boys taking care of the woman. He felt his way around in the darkness to the second bedroom and not finding anyone hurried back to the kitchen. He tripped over a book, the

Bible that fell to the floor from the table Lester's head found earlier. His hood flew from his head.

"Lost my covering, lost my covering," Billy Ray shouted as he searched the floor in the dark for the hood. A flash of lightning showed a lamp in the corner of the room. He decided to make his way to the lamp.

Because of his antics with the outhouse, the deputy had ordered Johnny Paul to remain outside and check around the house to be certain no one was about. He walked to the east side of the building; protected from the wind and rain he stood sulking. He did not hear Bella's screams or Earle's pleading calls.

Lester staggered to his feet, found his balance and stood erect. Not fully recovered, he wondered aloud, "What the hell is Earle cursing about?" He moved slowly to the doorway between the living room and kitchen. A lightning flash showed Bella on the floor under the table and Earle against the wall. He heard the dog growling but failed to locate the animal in the dark.

"Get the dog," Earle pleaded over and over.

"Where is it?" asked Lester.

"At my feet, Les." Catching himself from calling Lester's name, "Listen please" shouted the deputy. "Get my gun, and shoot at the floor, scare him or kill him, he's chewing me up," cried Earle. The officer was helpless. His left hand could not reach the holster, his right so badly burned it will never grasp the handle of a pistol again. A lightning flash solved Lester's problem. He located the dog between Bella and Earle. The dog snapped continually at the deputy, standing his ground protecting Bella, who quivered and whimpered from the excruciating pain. Lester waited until lightning illuminated the room once again and he located the dog. He moved closer to the animal. Certain of the dog's location, he brought a swift kick of his pointed boots, catching Brownie under his chin. The blow dislocated Brownie's jaw and scattered broken teeth about the floor. Blood poured from the dog's nostril. Battered but not broken, with blood dripping from the mouth, Brownie had fight left. He charged his new adversary. A flash allowed the hooded Klansman to see the dog charge. The raging animal leaped. Knife in hand, retrieved from his boot, Lester jabbed it in the direction of the leaping dog. The razor sharp blade struck home, slicing the dog's stomach deeply from front to back. The charge knocked Lester backward into the wall near the stove. Killed instantly, the dog was impaled on the knife and Lester's right arm. Blood and intestines splattered over the front mask and robe made Lester look like the one injured. The shocked Klansman grabbed the dead dog with his free hand and with all the strength he could muster threw him from his arm. Brownie landed on then skidded across the hot stove, depositing hair and intestines on the hot crimson surface. The sizzling hair and guts sent stink and smoke into the kitchen.

"What the hell is going on?" coughed Earle. "What's that smell? Lester, where are you?" said the deputy, breaking the no name rule. "Please get a lamp in here."

Lester, recovered from the encounter with the dog, located Bella. He moved the table and stood over her, knife in hand, dripping with blood, shouting, "Where's the lamp, bitch, where's the lamp?" Bella answered by coughing and choking. Intense pain racked her brain; it intensified further with a grab of her burned arm by Lester.

She wailed and bellowed to God, "Save me Lord, and take these devils away."

"Where's the lamp, where's the lamp?" Lester repeated, grabbing and shaking his victim. Bella could not tolerate the torment any longer, and passed out. Lester finally threw her to the floor.

"Lester, get a lamp…NOW! I got to see my hand," Earle choked.

"I hear you, I hear you, I been looking and found one," yelled Billy Ray.

Billy Ray grabbed the lamp and threw the chimney from its base. It landed on the floor, shattering the glass. He dashed toward the kitchen and entered as a flash of lightning illuminated the room. He removed the lid from the top of the stove, exposing the hot coals within. Ignoring the smell and smoke he touched the wick to the red coals; the lamp burst into flame. The light revealed a gruesome scene. Earle's hand was raw meat in the palm with fingertips burned to the bone. Bella had penetrating burns to the shoulder and back. Seared flesh hung from her arm and side. She was unconscious. Smoldering intestines and dog hair produced an acid smoke and a choking stench. Breathing the polluted air created a strangling suffocating feeling. Lester was splattered with blood and specks of dog innards.

"Is you hurt too, Lester?" asked Billy.

"No, and where have you been? Forget it, take that bucket and go out to the rain barrel, fill it up and bring it here for Deputy Earle's hand."

Johnny Paul, who stood outside, saw Billy filling the bucket and decided to follow him into the kitchen. The deputy knelt and plunged his hand into the cool water.

"Wow, what a mess what happened to her? Boy it stinks in here, the dog, how'd that happen? And you kept me out cause I pushed the shithouse over. Lester, you okay man? Where did all that blood and guts come from?" bantered Johnny Paul.

"Shut up, open that window and help Earle," coughed Billy Ray.

Johnny Paul hacked, "Look, my God look at that hand, it's all black and you can see some red, what's that white stuff? Ain't ever seen nothing like that."

Lester checked Bella, hoping she would come to so he could tell her why they came. Bella did not respond to his jabs and shaking. He finally gave up and joined the others near Earle.

"Look at that hand, he'll never shoot a gun again," said Johnny Paul to Lester.

"We got to get him to Doc Gibbs, so you, Lester and Johnny Paul take him over there right now." Billy Ray took over. "I'll go back to the Hawkes and report what happened here, c'mon Earle." He grabbed Earle and pulled him to his feet. Earle held his wrist, bending low and stepped forward. He stumbled over Bella's foot and pitched hard toward the door. The screen gave way as he tumbled through the doorway and fell hard into the watery, muddy outhouse path. Johnny Paul was close behind, but Lester returned to Bella. She moaned as he grabbed her.

"Remember this night, pass it along, that we will not have Negra miners a going anyplace but the Hawkes to work," said Lester as he shoved her to the floor. He then joined Johnny Paul in the rain to help remove Earle's robe. The two dropped Earle off at Doc Gibbs and hurried to report what happened to the Hawkes. They arrived at the mine office, wet robes in hand, smelly from the smoky kitchen.

They reached immediately into the icy tub for a drink, and gulped half the contents before sitting down.

"Where's the deputy? Billy here says he's in bad shape," asked a Hawke.

"Where did the Possum Man go? How bad off is Earle? Billy here said the dog is dead and the women bad hurt? "The questions continued, one after the other.

"He's staying at Doc Gibbs, he'll not be handling a gun, ever."

"This may end up being better than a cross burning we tried over at Willie's, " said one of the Hawke boys. They'll know now we mean business. Towns' woman knows what we mean too, yep, may be better," said the boss man, Hawke.

They all had a good laugh.

The words from Lester gnawed on her brain. She could not recall the things said, only that someone talked to her. She stirred, tried to get up but collapsed to the floor. She crawled to lean against the wall. The stench overwhelmed her, eyes watering profusely, she sobbed, tears flowing; now dizzy, confused and so much pain.

"What happened? She asked herself. "Yes, a warning about going north, oh my, does it have to do with Rufus? Is he safe?"

She started to get up but fell back against the wall on her burned shoulder. Pain, indescribable pain, shot to the brain, then no pain at all, tears welled as she grabbed a corner of the table, slowly getting to her feet. One moment extreme pain, then none at all. The nerves in the deepest burned area were exposed, one time sensitive torture, another moment no feeling at all. She found a chair and sat down; in a stupor; she somehow tolerated the hurt. The room wreaked of singed hair and smoldering innards. Bella just sat in a semi-conscious state for an unknown period of time. The storm abated into a steady rain, singing its unrelenting song on the roof.

Bella slowly recovered, awakening to the burning pain; she summoned enough strength to make her way to the door. She exited into fresh air and sat on the bottom step letting the cool rain strike her body. The drizzle provided some relief, gaining more of her senses; she looked at the downed outhouse.

"Where's Brownie? BROWNIE! BROWNIE!" she called.

Bella stepped back into the kitchen, again facing the acid smell and smoke. Looking up, a new fright caused her to back out the door in fright. A noose hung from the doorway leading from the kitchen to the living room. She failed to see Brownie's body on the floor.

"Oh my God, did they go to the Towns'? Got to warn Isabella, I've got to go."

She moved stooped over, stumbling toward the road. Fortune was with her as she moved with the drizzle and wind. Reaching the Towns', Bella stopped short in the front yard facing a large cross, set for burning. It was never ignited because of the wetness. Instead, a noose hung from the left arm.

She hurried, staggering through an open front door. She found Isabella sitting on the floor sobbing incoherently. Her clothes torn, it was obvious she had been beaten, her face swollen, one eye closed, the other eye puffed to the size of a small tomato. Although hurting, Bella sat down on the floor next to Isabella. She gently lifted her head and placed it on her lap. She placed the bottom of her wet dress over Isabella's face to ease the pain. Bella remained in this position during the remainder of the night, worrying about Rufus and Leroy, caressing her friend to her breast, humming hymns, and rocking with the melody.

CHAPTER XIX

"THEY JUST DISAPPEARED, sir. They took a streetcar from Ridge Valley to attend a funeral in Brownsville. I tell you there is no trace of them."

"You sent no one with them, why?" asked Mr. Moses.

"Didn't have anyone available. More reason to have our own security, don't have our own, yet."

"Well, where is our police force? What's the delay, why aren't they in place?"

"Had to go as far as Chicago and Detroit to recruit the type we wanted. Slowed us down."

"Well, let's get them in place so we can move on this housing thing. Those boxcar hotels left us vulnerable; abandon them, and the sooner the better. Lost a lot of Negro miners, good ones and we don't want to lose them again," said Mr. Moses.

"You plan on getting more?"

"South is the place to go, and I want to be ready the next time. We must have our own security to finalize evictions. Do you understand, Mr. Hood?"

"We'll have everything in place by the first of the year."

Only ten remained out of the sixty-five that lived in the boxcar hotel. A house became vacant on the number two side for Willie, Rufus and the two boys. Because of transfers and by squeezing bunks together, the six others were integrated into the boarding house. Within a week the boxcars and caboose were removed from the spur. The initial introduction of Southern Negroes into the Ridge Valley patch ended with more desertions than workers.

Work in the mine progressed through Thanksgiving and into December with the men available in the patch. The headway in completing repairs was steady but slow. Working six-days a week was the norm. Due to a fatality and four severe injuries, Leroy and Billie were pressed into service. They will begin working a full shift in the mine.

Rufus's fever finally broke, leaving him weak and bewildered. He talked out of his head, not making any sense, baffled regarding his whereabouts. He left the house one day and got lost. He was gone well into the night; confused and not knowing where he was, he roamed the woods. Chicago John, a recluse living in a cabin in the woods found him and took Rufus back to Patty, who then took him to Leroy. Rufus rarely left the house after that, spending the day doing house chores, afraid to leave.

Christmas thankfully provided a break in the work schedule. Following church services on Christmas day, John and his family celebrated with a noon meal centered on the ham purchased from Mr. Glover. Presents were opened; a treat of chocolate cake with butter icing and an orange completed the festivities. Michael, John's brother, joined friends for sledding on a steep hill over at the number two side. A fire was started to warm the riders. John later in the evening decided to walk over to the sled-riding hill to check on his brother. While warming himself at the fire, John noticed Leroy and Billie a short distance away. They looked cold.

"Come on over by the fire," John beckoned. They hesitated then accepted the invitation.

"Warm where you come from?" asked John.

"Never saw any snow in my life till now. Looks like fun going down the hill. Like to give it a try. Could all three of us fit on one of those sleds?" asked Leroy.

They rode together over and over well into the evening. Others left, the fire died, the last ride made, the evening of fun and excitement was over. The days of being boys ended this Christmas night. There would never be another like it again. Boys became men quickly in Ridge Valley, and men tended to their families and their work.

The routine of ten hour days for six days a week started again for the sled riders after the Christmas break. They continued through January and February of 1920. The workers were nearing the completion of repairs, approaching the time when the pit would be producing coal.

"Changes are coming, I tell you sure," announced Patty to John and others in the crew at lunchtime in late February.

"What are you saying? What changes, Patty?"

"Work changes with new rules, new people, they have to be in charge, it's their nature. You heard about getting a new super right?"

"Sure we did," the men agreed in unison.

Patty looked into the faces of the men. He rubbed the back of his neck. He spit on the floor then began speaking.

"His name is Winegartner, Marcus Winegartner, and he's been headman at Taylor and Revere. He's a Company man all the way. The decision is not final as yet but I'm sure he'll be the one assigned here.

The process of gaining complete control of all operations of the H. C. Grant conglomerate was now in the hands of Frederick C Moses. Changes eventually would be made and they would begin in the Ridge Valley complex. Eventually the Moses dictatorial concept would be passed on to the District Officer's and Superintendent's involved in mining operations in the Connellsville Coal District.

He planned biding his time for now letting the local men on their own, with local leadership working the mine.

CHAPTER XX

BELLA STAYED WITH Isabella since her encounter with the Klan. She remained bedridden and very weak from her injuries. She ate only when fed by Isabella. She improved slowly until a change of bandages brought screams of pain from tearing flesh that stuck to the cloth.

"I got to go to church, I got to see the reverend, get my letters. I got to go and talk to momma," she repeated over and over until exhaustion took over and sleep intervened. Even in her sleep she called for Rufus.

Days passed slowly for Bella as salves, root extract and drippings from the gum tree, were used to treat the burns. Sassafras leaves soaked in an excelsior mixture worked in adding a white colored skin graft to cover the burned area. It repaired the skin but not the nerves under the graft. The process helped in mending the body but not the mind.

Mrs. Washington and the reverend visited Bella frequently early on, prayed over her and offered God's grace to Isabella. Bella in her often-delirious state of mind failed to recognize the preacher and to accept his blessings.

"When she's better, let me know, however, should she ask please tell her that I have not heard from Rufus for some time, no letters and no money It worries me a bit not hearing from him, hope he's all right. Should I get a letter, I will pass it on like I've been doing for you Mrs. Towns." He looked closely at Bella. "It seems that potion and salve is working fine but remember the Lord will prevail in the end. Bless you child, bless you." He said his amen and departed the bedroom.

The Washington's accepted a meal of ham, potatoes, and greens. During the meal Isabella opened one of her letters from Willie and gave the preacher her tithe for the month. He thanked her for the meal and before desert mentioned, "Now that I ate I can go directly to the church. Been staying over night, sleeping on a cot in back. There have been some church burnings going on close by like at Harwell and Orrick. They had to be set 'cause the pastors done went north with their flock. So us ministers that be left are sticking close to our churches."

He finished his sweet potato pie, thanked the hostess, gave his blessing and left. Dusk greeted him with the darkness of night soon to follow. He left later than he wanted but he could not resist the good food. The reverend felt uneasy as he trudged up the sandy road. "Lord," he mumbled to his wife, "I know someone be watching me from the brush last Sunday. All those noises at night can't be coming from animals banging against the church, just can't." The preacher checked for danger from behind every dozen steps as he upped the pace. He walked his wife to their home then went directly to the Holy Gospel Baptist Church. He continually checked if anyone was following him from behind. He didn't find it from behind, but in front. He stopped with a jerk, perspiration forming on his forehead.

"Is that someone up the road by the spur, sure is and he's walking this way," he mumbled to himself. He thought about calling out. "No better not" he thought. "Wait, that, that someone is gone. Was he there or am I imagining things? Nothing there now."

The reverend, uncertain about the sighting, quickened his pace up the road. Back in the scrub and wispy pines a pair of eyes watched the preacher scurry up the road looking back often, a handkerchief in hand, wiping his brow as he went.

"Got your attention, fat man," the Possum Man said to himself, "your time is coming."

Those same eyes had been watching the preacher ever since the mass exodus of blacks went north. The Hawkes cohorts shamed the Possum Man every time they saw him. "That ole fat preacher done outfoxed the great hunter and tracker," the boys said to aggravate the man.

"That man will pay, and pay dearly, I say to you. Give it time, it will be done."

"When and if, you got to let me know the time." Said the Sheriff. Do you need the Klan on this one?" he asked.

"Don't need anyone."

"No cross burning?" asked Lester wide faced, hoping he'd be asked to help.

The Possum Man looked directly at Lester, staring him down. Lester's smile left his face and disappointment appeared.

"I'm just biding my time is all, when it happens you'll know, you all will know."

"Hold it, boys, I believe I see Ezra Pennington coming this way," said Mr. Hawke. The sawmill owner that was hit hard with worker losses came calling. In one afternoon they had all left, just vanished. He couldn't operate the mill and had to close down.

"What brings you, Ezra?"

"I was recruiting new workers over in Hadley. I know it's a good piece away, but if I get em to come they could move into the abandoned shacks down on Sandy Road. Then out of the blue I see a number of boys who left are now back, a lot of them.

"Well, how about that."

"Yes, and would you believe I ran into big George who worked for me? He asked to come back. Lord knows I could use him, plus he might bring others with him, but I been wondering.

"Wondering, wondering about what?"

"Well, I suspect a lot be coming back cause ole George said they couldn't stand the cold. They got sick from bad food, stayed in boxcars, and some even died from the chills, so they left. The reason I'm here is asking if I should take them back, and if so, how do I guarantee that the next time some new offer comes their way they won't bolt again and leave me high and dry?"

"Why don't you come into the office and talk about this." Mr. Hawke asked if Ezra saw any others in addition to his own workers? He confirmed that " yes he did, thought he saw some miners he recognized when he used to deliver timber to the mine. Mr. Hawke pondered for a minute thinking, he finally answered.

" First, Ezra, I recommend you take them back. It's only good business 'cause they know the mill and how to work it. But two things, Ezra; they take a pay cut and sign a contract."

"A contract?"

"A lifetime contract .If they leave without your permission, you take possession of their house and property. No contract, no work. That will make em think twice before leaving again."

" What about you? Are you going to do the same?"

" Yes Sir, pay cut and a lifetime contract. No contract, no work."

"Thanks sir, I believe I will do that. Yep, that answers it for me, much obliged, sir. I know we have been lax in getting timber to you, be assured it will arrive on time in the future."

They shook hands, Ezra nodded to all in the room turned and left.

"Well, what do you know, what do you know" repeated Lester who continued, "Can you believe that?" now in a loud voice said, "what do you know."

"I know this changes things Mr. Scrags," Mr. Hawke said to the Possum Man, who was surprised to be called Mister; he jerked his head up to look directly at the speaker.

"What do you mean by that?"

"I don't want anything done to that preacher."

Mr. Scrags interrupted, "You're a' squashing me, man, you and the boys been on me about this man getting the best of ole Possum Man. I been a' taking it, saying nothing back but I been a' planning and now you're squashing me."

"Lay off. We may need him for some answers. I told you before that man knows what is going on, see who he's talking to, where he goes. Keep on hounding him like you been doing, keep him on the worry, keep harassing, get him shaky, worried and shaky, sooner or later, those kind make mistakes."

"I'll give it some time and thought like you ask, but its sweaty work waiting and watching. A body gets mighty thirsty doing that, you know."

"Do as I tell you, and you'll get your due in time."

The blacks that jubilantly headed north filtered back into all parts of the south. They came mostly in small groups of two or three, tired, hungry and downtrodden from the trek back. They staggered across fields and up roads in tattered clothes to homes including those in Carbon Hill. Their hollowed look told the story of a long road back.

With constant care Bella recovered from her burns. She managed to walk alone around her bed, soon to venture to the kitchen. Another week found her walking outside. She gained enough strength to travel to the outhouse and return. Determination overcame the occasional setback as Bella improved everyday. Her one major problem was the stinging prickling sensation she felt to the burned area when in the sun. The salves and leaves used to cure her burned skin left it snow white, a condition that did not protect the nerves from the heat. Each day now she asked about the Reverend Washington.

"Where has he been? Why doesn't he visit? Did he get any letters? I've got to get to the church to see him. If he won't come to me, then I'll go to him."

She continued her rehabilitation, gaining strength, and by mid December found the type of day she was waiting for to venture back home. It was cool and cloudy. She had not been home since that fateful night and wanted to return for a visit. Others told her to forget about coming back, but she had to go and today was that day.

She wrapped a shawl around her head and a loose covering over her injured body. It was vital for her to cover her injured parts in order to protect them against exposure to the air and sun. Down the road she hobbled, going a short distance, resting, then moving again. She progressed slowly, each step bringing pain from unused muscles. She stopped to rest.

"BROWNIE!" she shouted to no one, "I forgot about Brownie, and he may be waiting for me." Bella recalled many happenings that fateful night but forgot about her dog. She hastened her stride thinking about Brownie waiting for her at the house. Finally she turned a bend in the road and there it was, the shack she called home, front screen door missing, slats broken and the corner of the tin roof over the living room peeled back, leaving an opening into the room from above.

"Surely rain done found that part of the house," she wondered. "Oh my," she cried seeing the front door open and hanging by one hinge. She moved to the back calling for Brownie, now seeing the outhouse down on its side. Mrs. Jones, the next-door neighbor, hearing some talking outside, came out and looked in disbelief at what she saw.

"Dat you, Mrs. Johnson? Oh my, yes, it is you. Oh my God, how are you?"

"I am fine, considering."

"Show' missed you, worried about you sure," towel in hand, Mrs. Jones carried it with her as she waddled over to Bella.

"My, but you do look a bit peaked, are you sure you're okay?"

"I got some bad burns, still a mending."

"It show' has been a long time, and where have you been a' staying, and where be your man and Leroy?" knowing the answers but pretending otherwise.

"Rufus went north. I've been staying with Mrs. Towns. Mended enough to come back for a visit and look for Brownie. Have you seen Brownie about?"

"No, not seen your dog Mrs. Johnson," she lied.

Mrs. Jones had seen the damage to the outside of the house, investigated the open door in the back and went inside. She saw the carnage. Innards oozing from Brownie and the maggots, along with the choking foul smell, chased her from the kitchen. She decided to go through the front entrance. She looked through the window first and retreated quickly when she spotted the noose hanging in the doorway between the kitchen and living room. She left never to return. The sheriff came by a few days after the storm. He asked a few questions about the Johnson's, and told Mrs. Jones that he was investigating the damage next door. He instructed her not to reveal his presence and tell no one about happenings at the Johnson house. She followed his orders.

"Is you coming back to live?" her neighbor asked.

Bella looked sternly at Mrs. Jones, she did not answer. With her neighbor following, Bella walked gingerly to the back door. The stink hit her first as she entered the kitchen. She searched for something to cover her nose and mouth, and wipe away tears. Mrs. Jones handed her the towel. The blackened intestines on the stove, Brownie's skeleton crawling with maggots, broken furniture, the stench of rotting wood and termites, millions of termites munching on the rotting living room floor.

"I got nothing now, nothing, no money and no men to help." Tears flowed from sunken eyes as she sobbed, "Just because of letters about two story houses."

Bella was led out of her house to the Jones porch. She was helped into a large rocker.

"You rest now, I have some good jowls on the stove. A good meal is what you need. You rest now," said Mrs. Jones as she departed for the kitchen.

Bella's rocking motion became slower and slower. The walk left her spent, and viewing her home exhausted her both mentally and physically. She slept only intermittently, her mind turning over and over. She dreamed about Rufus, her momma and white hooded men in her house. She dozed and in one of her restless periods half opened her eyes. In a dream state of mind she saw two men she knew walking down the road, it was Oliver Smith and Cooney Wilson. "No" her mind said, "they went north with the others, can't be them." She cast aside the thought and rejected the dreary vision as she relapsed back to sleep.

"Its time for supper, can't hold it any longer. I figure the best remedy for you was rest so I done let you sleep as long as I could; now how about some good eats?"

Bella ate heartily, forgetting about her ailments and eating the most food she had consumed for a long time. After finishing she thanked and "God Blessed" her neighbor and began her walk back to the Towns'. She only looked back once at her old homestead.

She ambled along at a snails pace, finally arriving at the Towns' as evening settled in. Bella felt tired yet wanted to talk.

"Been resting in a rocker and must have dozed off. I dreamed I saw Oliver Jones and Cooney Wilson. Show' wish it were true, and then I could ask about Rufus and Leroy. But I know they went north with the others."

Isabella looked with a questioning stare. She hesitated in saying anything for the moment, knowing that many of the men who left, had returned. She did not mention this to Bella.

"You had a heavy day, its time to rest now, we'll talk more tomorrow."

CHAPTER XXI

LIKE THE FIRST radio station established in Pittsburgh in the new year of 1920, so would there be new happenings coming to Ridge Valley. Willie's crew, like all the other crews, worked hard to repair the mine so that coal production could start soon. Their efforts continued despite the lack of upper management leadership. Superintendents, along with their assistants and the Company store manager in various mine complexes, were released en masse. They were not immediately replaced. Ridge Valley was included in that decision. The man who took on the leadership task at the Ridge Valley mine was Patty Driscall himself. There was no one else with his years of experience working in Ridge Valley. Many of those who were equal to him had died in the blast. The dead miners took with them uncounted years of skills that would have been passed on to the next generation. Their loss produced a huge gap in experienced men, working the mine. Patty took over and assigned crew leaders, organized work schedules, and conducted training for new workers. He was insistent that the new and inexperienced learn all the nuances of the mine and always work with safety in mind. He urged all to work hard and do their best to put the mine back together in the proper manner.

A miner after a few shots of whiskey and a couple of beers at O'Malley provided the courage to speak, challenged Patty. "Why do you work so hard down under, man? You know in the end you're only helping the Company make more money."

"Yeah, why you pushing us so hard? You're not kissing up to, em, are you, Patty?" said another as more chimed in with alcohol doing the talking from a well-soused group. The men listening chuckled their agreement with the speakers. Patty sat silent, sipping his beer. He let all who wanted to have their say, accepting the comments without a remark. He emptied his glass and walked to the bar and ordered a shot and a beer. He downed the whiskey, took a swig of beer, turned and faced his fellow miners and called for silence. The scowl on his face told all to be quiet for Patty was to have his say, and God help anyone who interrupted.

"I was there to see the charred bodies, black as the coal we mine. I was there to see guts oozing from bellies and sizzling from the heat. I was there to see hard hats welded to heads, eyes gouged out, and I was there to see wives and children pained and scared. I went to wakes, attended funerals, and helped bury friends and fellow workers. They were all family to me, for in our work, we are all family. Yes, I work hard to put the mine back together in the right way, and I do it because I don't want to see last August again. The owners, Grant or whomever, lost money, I lost family." He paused; sipped beer from his glass, all in the room remained silent.

"I work for my family beyond all else, and I work for YOU. We have only each other, for when the chips are down we must trust our fellow worker. Remember we have only ourselves. The mine is our work, good or bad it is what we have, so we must do our best. I know this mine, it's gaseous, a nine-foot seam emits methane in quantity, and therefore extreme caution is vital. I also know that too much whiskey and beer loosens tongues and closes minds, and causes erratic thinking, yet you are right. I do work for the Company and I also work for you. The main reason I work hard is to do all I can to avoid seeing any of you as I saw my buddies." his voice faded into silence.

Patty drained his beer, placed the glass gently on the bar, turned, looked around the room, and walked out the door into the cool night air.

"God knows," he mumbled as he walked up the path, "God knows all I want is to do my job and leave the running of things to someone else."

Henry Clay Grant selected Frederick C Moses to lead his company in early fall of 1919. Mr. Moses immediately faced the need to find manpower replacements. The Negroes recruited to solve the labor problem came and left. Now there was talk of union organizers in the district. The security concerns and productivity issue needed attention. To face these issues, meetings by the top echelon of the Grant mining conglomerate began in the fall, and continued into early winter. The decision to begin the New Year with a strict operational philosophy led by rigid directors would start in Ridge Valley. Marcus Winegartner was selected as the superintendent over all operations for that complex with instructions to use whatever means necessary to get production started.

"We can't afford delaying operations at Ridge Valley any longer," stated Mr. Moses. "The seam there is nine feet of pure coal, no slate or shale in the whole lot. In addition the security forces, the Union Supply Company Store and housing assignments all come under your jurisdiction Mr. Winegartner. You have total control of all phases of the operation. To assist you, I have assigned Lloyd Barnes as Chief of Security. Mr. Hood will soon have sixteen-coal and iron policeman available for his use. George Boyle will be your assistant and Solomon Judah your new store manager. The "Bosses Row" of houses is ready for immediate occupancy. You will be located in house number one, Mr. Winegartner, your assistant, George Boyle in house two, Mr. Barnes in house three and Mr. Judah in four. The security forces will occupy houses five and six. All of these houses have four bedrooms so assign two policemen to a room. Oh, one more thing, we both know that the weightmaster is the key to getting the most profit, choose wisely."

On January 16th, 1920, church bells rang to celebrate the beginning of the prohibition amendment in America. There was no celebrating in Ridge Valley. They loved their whiskey and beer. They worked hard in a backbreaking job. They asked for little in return and only expected a fair wage and that shot of whiskey and a beer after work to wash down the dust. The law of the land took the whiskey and beer away from them.

On this same date the new regime planned their move into houses on Bosses Row. Mother nature spoiled the move. Heavy snows stopped trucks from getting through, delaying the move for over a week. The storm also postponed the planned organizational meeting for the Ridge Valley mine until the first week of February. Marcus Winegartner finally organized and led the group meeting. Those in attendance consisted of Lloyd Barnes, George Boyle, J.P. Whitaker and M.L. Blanchard.

"Who has been in charge and where do we stand in completing the repairs?" asked the new superintendent to open the meeting.

"A Patty Driscall, one of the old timers, took charge when the last superintendent left and there was a delay in naming you as the successor. He says that all will be in place to begin operations by the end of the month except for the Bottom.

"Why the delay there?"

"Says he didn't have the manpower to do both the repairs and complete the Bottom. Chose to work the interior of the mine and then concentrate on the Bottom."

"What do you mean by the Bottom?" questioned Mr. Hood, who was in attendance and representing the home office.

"Place where everything comes together, like a communications center for example. The boss's shack, machine shop, pump rooms and emergency medical location and a supply storage area needs constructed. The area, like the main haulage needs "rock dusted" to seal the ribs against possible gas seepage.

"All that needs done before mining can start?"

"Yes sir."

"How long?"

"Couple of months I'd say."

"Best we get started

"Mr. Boyle, I want you to take charge of constructing the Bottom immediately. Work overtime, even Sunday, to get this done. Keep me updated on progress. Now, one more thing to consider, and that is identifying all the people living in the patch. We have to get a handle on our available manpower. Mr. Barnes I suggest you begin by checking the Company store charge cards. They should give you the identity and the house number of everyone living in a house in Ridge Valley. I believe that's all we have for now."

Winter refused to give up its hold on Ridge Valley. The heat of the past summer was now replaced by weeks of bitter cold and snow. Frigid winds, accompanied by flurries and occasional squalls, blew hard down the hills into the bottom of the bowl. Temperatures hovered below freezing during the day, plunging to near zero at night.

"Coldest winter I can ever remember, so cold I have to keep the spigot dripping all the time to keep the water pipes from freezing," said one patch woman to other patrons at the store.

"We got to bank the stove early at night to save on coal," said another.

"Pickings are slim at the slate dump, always some coal mixed up with the waste dumped there. Not much available since the mine hasn't worked and we had no fresh dumping to pick from since last August. Nothing down along the railroad tracks falling from overloaded coal cars, those droppings have been gobbled up a long time ago. Hope the weather breaks soon or we'll be in a fix may have to buy coal."

"Cost too much," interrupted another woman waiting at the counter.

John's younger brother Mike accompanied his mom to the store to help carry packages home He overheard the conversations between his mom and the neighbor ladies. He tried to help out and do his share at home, and one way was to pick coal, but had little success at the dump, and down by the tracks. He also went to the pit area but was chased away.

"Mom, you going to be a while?"

"Why, what's your hurry, what you got to do?"

"Thought about something I have to check on, I'll carry what ya got so far and come back if you need me."

"I have a few more things to get and a bit more visiting."

"Something I got thinking about and I sure would like to check it out."

"Well, go on with ya then and take the flour and sugar, I think I can handle the rest."

Mike grabbed the two items and hurried out of the store, quick stepping as fast as he could up the path. Through the back door and into the kitchen he placed the flour and sugar on the table. Quickly out the back door he ran up the back yard to the empty coal shed to get a coal bucket.

"I've got to do this before somebody else thinks about it. There's got to be some for sure. I been up and down that alley a hundred times, seen it," said Mike, talking to himself.

He grabbed the bucket and ran around the building into the alley. Behind the coal bins he found his treasure. He located lumps of coal lying about that were probably dropped there from misplaced or overloaded shovels that carelessly missed the back coal bin door while filling the coal shed from a truck. Small in size but plentiful, he filled the bucket by picking up the black stones from both sides of the alley. Hurrying to the house, he opened the cellar door and dumped the contents in a corner under the steps. He grabbed a pick on the way out to dig out the imbedded buried lumps he saw in the groves of the alley road. The lumps, large ones, were buried over the years in tracks from rolling trucks. Happily he dug out the coal, filled his bucket quickly and dashed once again to the cellar to unload his wares. Mike's mom, home from shopping and hearing a noise in the basement, went down to investigate.

"Where are you getting all this?" she asked pointing.

"The alley, mom."

"Alley?"

"Yes, mom, dropped when filling coal bins from trucks and such."

"You're not taking from anyone are you?"

"No, mom, NO"

"Seems like a lot to be forgotten about."

"I'm going back to find more, maybe get enough to last a couple of weeks."

He walked up the steps, closed the cellar door and trudged up the back yard. He walked up the alley and stopped between the Mullin and Dorek's coal bins. He began picking then digging, working hard to fill the bucket. He was concentrating so hard he did not hear or see a person approach from behind.

"Whatcha doing, Mike?"

The voice sounded familiar, he had heard it before. He turned and looking up from a kneeling position could not believe what he saw. Standing before him was none other than Bull in some kind of uniform.

"Bull, it's you, I'm picking coal, whatcha doing yourself?" said Mike as he started to stand, "Thought you be in some city somewhere. John told me the name, forgot it but I think it was where they make cars."

"Detroit is the name, been there, now here."

"That uniform you got on, never seen anything like that before, is that some kind of police uniform? Are you a cop or something, Bull?"

"Yep I'm a full fledged Company Policeman."

"Are there others?"

"Yep, sixteen total including me."

"I don't have any idea why we need to have police people in the patch, Bull. Now you say we have Company police, what will you be doing?"

"Guarding and protecting owners' property. Make sure no one takes anything from the owner and things like that."

"Does taking this coal count, Bull? It been laying here and nobody wanted it, so I say it goes to the one that finds it, like free stuff I say."

Bull thought for a moment, he didn't have an answer. "Fill your bucket and get going. Getting to be dark anyway and you should be home by dark. Remember though, if I see you doing this again I'm obliged to turn you in, it's my job like I said and I'll do it Mike."

Mike went directly to work at digging and picking. While doing this he kept an eye on Bull who stood his ground, watching.

The Dorek residence sat directly up the hilly back yard from where Mike and Bull were located. Since darkness was approaching it was time for the Ignatius girls, who were visiting Dolly, to go home. Tony, who was also visiting, volunteered to accompany the girls. They called on Dolly often, ever since meeting in the junk graveyard last

August. They enjoyed each other's company, and Dolly loved having them visit often, especially after having a miscarriage and loosing her baby. The loss happened from stress the midwife said. "Loosing a husband, being young and alone in a strange place and now having to fend for herself was just too much to handle," the midwife stated. Tony had became a friendly companion following Dolly's husband's funeral but drifted away when he learned of her pregnancy. The girls filled the void. Tony renewed his friendship with Dolly after finding out about the miscarriage. His visits, strained at first, were slowly accepted since he was the only male acquaintance to offer assistance to her. Their acquaintance became solidified when Tony mentioned to her that, with the prohibition amendment taking the liquor away from the men in the patch, if he knew how to make whiskey and sold the moonshine to the miners he could make plenty of money.

"God knows they work hard and drink just as hard. They need to have their shot of whiskey after work. It's a ritual, a habit that sticks with them. I know. I lent them a lot of cash to buy the drinks. That lending can set one back like happened last August, and. I haven't recovered yet. They will get the stuff somewhere and whoever supplies the whiskey can make a small fortune."

"You talking about making drinking whiskey, the kind my father and uncle made from the extra corn they had left over?" asked Dolly.

"Your family made moonshine?" asked Tony excitedly.

"I don't think they made that moonshine stuff you talk about, but they made this drinking whiskey for themselves. Must have been darn good 'cause it was the talk at the grange socials."

"We call it moonshine, when you make it yourself its called moonshine whiskey. You telling me your folks made this stuff?"

"Yes. Every year."

"Listen, Dolly, did you ever see them making the mash?"

"Sure, on a farm everybody helps with chores, and making whiskey for home use was no different. I helped with the distilling all the time. Fact is I was the one doing the measuring and watching. That was no big deal cause the men folk were usually busy with the farm work. The entire process takes time they didn't have so I was the one. Like I said no big deal," said Dolly in a nonchalant manner.

Tony could not believe what he was hearing. Excited by what Dolly said, he stuttered in a high pitched voice, "You, yyyou, hhhelped with making the booze, you said you know how to make the mash, the whiskey, and it was the good sipping kind?"

"Well, like I said, everybody that tasted it said it was smooth stuff for homemade."

"Dolly dear," taking her by the shoulders with both hands, looking her straight in the eye he asked softly, "Can you make this drinking whiskey?"

"Sure can, I don't think I'd have any problem. All I need are the ingredients and I'm certain I…" He interrupted her with a long hard kiss.

Tony, along with Hanna and Joanna, were leaving Dolly's back door, " I'll walk em home, be right back to help with." He stopped short of saying to help with the distilling. Dolly did not want the girls to know what was going on in the basement. The girls politely thanked Dolly for the visit. They walked with Tony down the back steps toward the alley. Dolly remained outside on the porch, watching the three walk together down the back yard. She waved as the trio turned, then disappeared around the corner of the coal shed. Dolly waited and waited to see them exit from the back of the building but they never appeared. Puzzled and concerned, she walked down the yard wondering what could have delayed them. She turned the corner and was startled to see Tony, the girls, little Mike and, taking a step back asked, "Is that you Bull, what are you doing here? We heard you were in?"

"I was in Detroit, learned to be a policeman, and now I'm back."

"Oh." she searched for something to say. Finally addressing the girls, "Best you two get along. I'm sure your mom is waiting. We'll watch from here 'till you get home."

Mike went back to filling his buckct as Tony, Bull and Dolly watched the girls walk down the road. Three contrasting figures stood in the alley, focused on the girls walking home. There was Tony in his long coat, slick black hair and shined shoes, Dolly in her cotton dress and shawl, Bull in his dark gray jacket with matching pants. He wore a fur cap with the brim turned up. A badge was attached to the front. Earflaps made of fur were tied at the top of his head. The three watched until the girls entered the house.

"Glad to see you Bull. I'm sure your mom is happy to see you with a job and back home," said Dolly, breaking the silence.

"Yes, she's happy."

"What is your job exactly, what do you do?" asked Dolly.

"Patrol work mostly, at the mine, in the patch, down at the store, but mainly down at the tipple to protect the mine."

"I don't recall any trouble here a bouts, most folks don't even lock their doors."

"Well I know its been planned for some time. They brought horses in a time back, learned to ride and we'll be issued weapons, a rifle soon."

"I still don't know why we need police protection but I guess if the mine owners think it's a good idea then so be it. I'm a getting a bit chilled and got some things to do at home so I'll be a going. Good luck on your new job, Bull and tell your mom I said hello," said Dolly. Tony and Bull watched Dolly amble up the yard.

"C'mon Mike, I think you got enough, how about you head for home now?" Said Bull

Tony saw Dolly enter the back door about the same time Bull viewed Mike turn the corner around the coal shed. Only Bull and Tony remained in the alley.

"How you do it, Bull? How did you get on this Coal and Iron Police force?"

Bull looked at Tony, and looked, he did not answer. He was trained not to answer questions. He was trained to take charge, use scare tactics if necessary. More importantly, an officer never revealed anything to anyone about the force. Certainly Bull will not reveal that he could not keep up with the work in the factory, losing his job on the assembly line shortly after his arrival in Detroit. He tried a number of jobs but never fit in. The only work opportunity left to him was the slaughterhouse. The job was working in the blood and guts section known as the killing zone. He lasted only one shift. While leaving the building splattered with blood, guts and sinew, he was spotted by a Pinkerton recruiting agent. The recruiter saw a huge specimen of a man, obviously working in the killing zone.

"We need your kind," said the agent.

Bull answered the call.

"Where you say he's from?" asked the Captain.

"Like I said, Ridge Valley, in Pennsylvania, Ridge Valley," repeated the agent.

"What a coincidence, he'll fit in perfectly because this is the area we're assigned," replied the Captain."

Bull stood in front of Tony, not saying a word. Tony decided to ask another, "What about George Glover, did he come back?"

"No, he stayed, got lucky he did, got a job at the Ford plant making good money."

"Let me ask one more thing? We know about the old bosses being fired; what do you know about the new one's assigned here?"

"I'm glad those old bastards are gone, they did me wrong but a few are still around. I'll let them know that Bull is back and in charge, now no one can push me around, Tony, and you can pass that on."

"How many of your kind are here?"

"Sixteen total counting me, and we live in houses five and six. Can't believe I'm there where the big shots used to live."

"Where are these policeman from and what kind of men are they?"

"Mostly from big cities like Detroit, Chicago and such. Big guys, most of em bigger than me, and they grumble a lot saying that there is nothing to do here. Heck, we're not even settled in yet."

"Who's in charge of this outfit, Bull?"

"Captain Ross, Charles is his first name. He's in charge by rank but the real boss is the Sergeant. "Bear" Grossman is his name and he is just that, Tony, a bear. He has a mean streak in him for sure. Most of the others are nasty people but he is a mean-tempered one and doesn't take any guff. Got to be careful with him."

Tony and Bull talked a while longer until full darkness set in. Tony watched as Bull walked down the alley and sure enough he turned to enter house number six. Snowflakes began to fall as Tony made his way up to Dolly's. He thought about what he heard through the grapevine from banker friends in other patches. One of the main reasons for people like Bull was to guard against anyone trying to organize a union. The other was to carry out evictions. They are probably making lists and since Dolly does not have anyone in her house working for the Company, her name has to be high on the ledger.

"One good thing," mumbled Tony, "was that the Negroes left, so unless they transfer from other mines, no, that won't happen, others shafts need workers also. We got time on our side for awhile."

The snow fell in large flakes as he reached the back door of Dolly's. The pungent smell of mash working greeted him as he entered. Dolly was in the basement working on her second attempt in the distilling process. Tony spread the word earlier about the availability of good booze at Dolly's. He invited some to a taste when the first batch was made. Well into her first attempt at the distilling process, Dolly discovered that the wrong yeast was used. A harsh bitter taste resulted. To the dismay of Tony she had to discard it all and begin again.

"Try this," she said, handing Tony a pint jar filled with a small amount of new freshly brewed liquor.

"Dolly, you certainly did it this time." Taking another sip, he looked into the jar and pronounced, "This is good sipping whiskey, tastes as smooth as Old Overholt. You did it this time, you certainly did, what did you change?"

"Special yeast I asked you to get. Forgot you can't use bakers yeast for brewing."

Tony took the jar over to the steps, removed a white handkerchief from his vest pocket and placed it down before he sat. He sipped slowly, sitting in silence, watching Dolly fill and cap the pint jars.

"What do you think about Bull coming back as a policeman? Quite a shock I'd say. Then there are the new ones, the Company cops as you call them. Could they close us down?"

"No don't think so, I believe it has to be public police. These are private."

Tap Tap Tap Tap

The sound came from outside the small basement window.

Tap Tap Tap Tap

Dolly, without thinking, walked over to see who was there. A man kneeling in the snow with his face close to the glass motioned for her to open the window. Dolly looked at Tony for advice.

Tap Tap Tap Tap

Before Tony answered, Dolly unlatched the bottom of the window and pushed it up hitting the man on the chin. He recovered, then quickly stuck his face in the opening and said, "Madam, I've been told about you, and saw the light in the cellar, hope I didn't scare you. I'm needing a drink real bad, only got nineteen cents and I'm wondering if you'll allow me nineteen cents worth?"

Relieved, Dolly recognized Jimmy, a broken down old miner who lived in a shack on the hill. Frail from injuries accumulated over the years he simply could not carry the load anymore. He lived by doing odd jobs for food or money.

"I just finished making a new batch," said Dolly. I need someone to give me a straight answer. Tell you what, Jimmy, give you this pint for your nineteen cents, if you give me an honest answer as to how it tastes."

Jimmy was all smiles. They exchanged money for the jar. Jimmy quickly unscrewed the lid, gulped a good amount, shivered from the jolt to his system, smiled and then took a sip, savoring the whiskey.

"Gives one a jolt, yet it be mellow, washes down good, very good, lot better than what they got at Chubb's Place. Recommend you to my friends."

"Thanks Jimmy, you keep warm and come back anytime."

"Happy to be your tester."

Jimmy left and Dolly closed the window, thinking that she had to place a curtain over that window.

Tony watched in silence thinking to himself that all men liked two things more than anything else in the world. One of them is good sipping whiskey. No matter who they are or where they work, they all like a drink now and again, even policeman.

CHAPTER XXII

FEBRUARY WAS ALMOST gone, yet the Bottom was only partially completed. A number of problems plagued the project from the start. The new bosses acted without seeking advice thus made mistakes in assignments. Late winter snows that produced slippery roads caused delays in delivery of vital supplies. Communication problems between construction crews slowed the project to a snail's pace.

"Too many languages to deal with, it's difficult, if not impossible, to make them understand what you want them to do. We can't get what we need on time," were two excuses used by George Boyle as to the reason for the delay. Fact of the matter was that Mr. Boyle never constructed a bottom. He was out of his league.

Winegartner began to get pressure from the main office in Pittsburgh. They expressed their dissatisfaction with the slow progress and demanded to know why production was delayed once again. Mr. Moses would not accept any more excuses. Three weeks, or else changes would be made he warned. Joseph P. Waters, the district manager was sent to Ridge Valley to take a look at the problem. He immediately called a special meeting with the superintendent, Assistant Superintendent Boyle, and other members of Winegartner's staff. After a lengthy session, where excuses, often exaggerated by

Boyle, countered any new suggestions, Mr. Waters finally asked a vital question.

"How did the mine repairs get done? Someone had to be in charge of doing that. Who was responsible for completing repairs? Find out who it was and put that person in charge to work on the Bottom. He did that job, no doubt could do this one."

"I hesitate in giving a local man a position of that magnitude. Seen it happen; the men go to trust that person's word totally. What he says becomes the law in the workplace. The men place total confidence in that person and in turn he can make demands of us. If we don't comply he could call a stoppage and then we are stuck".

"You have to get this Bottom work completed, and soon, or else we're all in trouble. Let them do the planning and the work. Keep George Boyle here as the overall director. He'll be your eyes and ears. Once completed, retain the man as the mine foreman until production is under way. You can make changes later but right now we need a Bottom constructed, and production started.

"Captain Ross I want you to get me information on who we can consider for the job other than this Patty fellow. Start with that big boy Bull, then go from there. Now get going."

Tony wasted little time in calling on the new arrivals to the patch. He walked down to Bosses Row the next day and selected house number five, hoping this is the one occupied by the captain and sergeant. Dressed in his greatcoat, linen shirt and black shined shoes he knocked on the door. In his pockets rested two pints of Dolly's latest blend. It had been about a month since the bars closed due to the prohibition law. They may have tried the rotgut at Chubb's, the new local speakeasy that just opened, but the bet is that none tasted as good as Dolly's. Tony, hat in hand, knocked louder the second time. The door was answered by a man dressed in the same trousers as Bull, and a long john top with suspenders hanging on each side of his waist. The trooper scrutinized the dude standing before him with an open mouth, looking without saying a word.

"Who is it, Grump?" came a call from within.

Grump remained silent; mesmerized, he just looked at a person dressed in a way he never saw before.

"Grump, who is it?" came the question the second time.

"You got to come and see this, Harry, I ain't ever seen anything like this," said Grump.

Harry guffawed when he saw Tony.

"Would you get a load of this? I mean, I've been to a lot of places and never seen anyone dressed like you, you got a name?" snorted Harry.

"Tony, Tony Baritone. I would like to speak with your sergeant please."

"Get the sarge, just tell him he's needed at the door."

"Bruno "Bear" Grossman came as requested. Walking past Harry, he went directly to the open door, a scowl on his face.

"Goddamn it, who the hell are you, and what do you want?" Before Tony could answer Bear continued, "It's getting cold, I'm going to close this door, you either come in and state your case, or get on your way."

Tony quick stepped through the back door into the kitchen. By this time other officers in the house came to see what was happening. Some stared, others chuckled. Grump and Harry stood back, hands folded, waiting to watch the fun the boss is going to have with this creature.

"Well, you're in, what the hell are you and why you dressed that way?"

"Like I said earlier, my name is Tony, I'm what they call the banker for Ridge Valley. I lend money to men in the patch who need cash money to buy a whiskey and beer. Because of the new law they'll need money for moon…err, drinking whiskey, that is homemade drinking whiskey," said Tony emphasizing the drinking.

"What the hell all that got to do with us, Dude? Yep, I think I'll call you Dude, yes sir that's your name, Dude." The group agreed repeating "Dude, Dude," while chuckling and laughing.

"Well, I called on you to offer my lending services to all of you, and of course present you with a welcome gift."

Tony reached into his pocket and retrieved a brown paper sack. One of the policemen in full uniform placed his hand on his holstered pistol. The others stepped back. The sarge held his ground. The paper sack garnered the full attention of all present. Tony, sensing the curiosity displayed by the men, slowly opened the sack. He lifted the pint jar gradually. All stared in silence, watching. Tony finally displayed a pint jar containing a clear amber liquid. He lifted the jar, turned it in his hand and licked his lips.

"This jar contains the best, and I mean the smoothest drinking whiskey to pass your lips." Tony stretched out the moment as long as he dared, at least long enough to see the men licking their lips. Now he felt they were anxious to taste the brew.

The Bear grabbed the jar out of Tony's hand. He unscrewed the lid, threw it aside and raised the pint to his nose. All watched intently as he lifted the container to his mouth, took a tender sip, swallowed, smacked his lips, shook his head from side to side, and smiled. He sipped again, exhaled, licked, smacked then lifted the jar to eye level and declared.

"Goddamn, this is good stuff, one of the smoothest I ever tasted."

All in the room, smiled broadly, Tony included. Hands reached out, hoping against hope that the jar would be passed their way. Tony, savoring the moment, opened the second jar he brought, unscrewed the lid and passed it on to Grump who outreached Harry. Another officer wisely grabbed a glass and pushed it forward for a pour. He was accommodated and others soon followed.

"Hold it, now hold it," the sarge shouted. "You, Paul, go over and get the captain and be sure to save a sip for him, he's got to see this guy."

A brief explanation brought the captain. He eyed Tony up and down. The sergeant explained Tony's presence with Tony himself filling in any left out information. Captain Ross sipped the whiskey from a glass saved for him. He agreed that it was good and smooth tasting for homemade brew. He invited Tony and Sergeant Grossman to sit at the kitchen table, and then asked the others to leave. They complied, closing the door behind them. Two empty pint jars rested on the counter.

"Now, Mr. Baritone, tell me why you're so generous with your liquor. This is a good drink and could be sold easily, why so generous?" asked the captain.

"I told the sarge here that I wanted to extend a welcome to you and the police force. I also wanted to let you know that in case anyone here is in need of a loan, I'm available. Also, a widow lady who lives in the patch makes this drinking whiskey. Her husband died in the explosion last August. I heard rumors about the possibility of evictions for anyone not having a worker…"

"And you want an exception for her," interrupted the Captain

"Yes, that is what I'm asking."

"We leave her alone, and you provide the whiskey, is that it?"

"Yes sir, except that the cost will be discounted. Can't go free all the way. Half price I think is a good deal."

"Accepted, but you deal on selling only to Sarge or me, no one else. I don't want my men drinking without our knowledge. Another concern, Mr. Baritone. We are new here and may need information from time to time. I'm sure we can count on you to provide help when necessary. For example, let's say I want to ask you who you think is the best, say, the best leader of men in the patch?"

"That's an easy one. Everybody knows its Patty Driscall and second is the Negro fella, Willie Towns."

"Thank you Mr. Baritone. I believe we can work together in the future. We'll talk again about your lady friend. Right now I have other matters to attend to." He got up from his chair as did Tony who slipped on his gloves, buttoned his coat, said his goodbyes and left. Once Tony was gone the Captain asked to see Bull to confirm what Tony said about Patty and Willie. Satisfied, he walked immediately to house number one to convey the information to the superintendent. Patty and Willie would be assigned as temporary bosses the next day. They were instructed to complete the Bottom in three weeks.

CHAPTER XXIII

PATTY ACCEPTED THE assistant pit boss position and the challenge to construct the Bottom. He took the job seriously by recruiting the best and pushed them hard. He reminded the men often that the Bottom was the heart and soul of the mine, thus he needed their total effort.

Willie Towns was also assigned as the pit boss and led the second shift. His knowledge of this type of construction was extensive. He was responsible for starting a number of small mines in Alabama and was instrumental in installing the Bottom for the Hawkes. He knew his stuff and gained the respect of the men through his work and direction. Oftentimes his ten-hour shift outworked Patty's. Doing so cemented his stature in the mind of his crew as a man and a leader.

The Bottom was completed in the two month time period. The underground facilities were ready. The Ridge Valley men could now begin to mine coal.

Winegartner was impressed, very impressed, when George Boyle told him of progress made with Patty and Willie in charge. "They saved us a lot of time. Did outstanding work and the men followed their lead. We have to take advantage of those two; after all they put the place back together."

"Patty, I want to thank you and Willie here for all you did in getting the mine ready and constructing the Bottom. I want to get straight to the point. I want you and Willie to continue to work in the assistant pit boss positions. George Boyle will be the general foreman.

We feel you know the men and the mine better than anyone."

Patty lowered his head and rubbed his forehead with thumb and forefinger. His mind swirled, he was not prepared so quickly for the offer.

"We can't delay any longer, plan on getting started tomorrow, what do you say?" said Winegartner.

"I need to know how much say I have in running things. I say mining can't start until a full and thorough inspection of the entire mine by a Fire Boss is completed. Once mining is started I say the inspection will be carried out before every shift. Willie or I must be given the authority to close down any section that does not pass the basic checks for methane gasses. For now the airflow needs final checking and brattices placed where needed. The roof must be sounded throughout and checked for any weakness."

"How long will all this take?"

"Reckon a full day."

Winegartner thought for a minute. "If I agree, we have a day's delay. If I opt for someone else, we may face longer delays." He decided to offer Patty and Willie the jobs.

"The job is yours Patty, and Willie. Take the day to get the mine ready.

The ghosts were aroused on the morning of May 1st nineteen-twenty in the Ridge Valley Mine shaft. Drilling and blasting at the face in sections off the main haulage awakened the souls of every man who gave his life digging in the shaft. You could feel their presence, for their spirits remained, lingering in the passages and hollowed corners of every section

Declaring the mine ready, Patty announced that the mine was safe and secure so, "Let's go to work, but first let us ask the Lord to bless and protect us in our work and remember those who are no longer with us."

Patty took on the pit boss job with zeal. He was everywhere, visiting sections, constantly checking the airflow, observing crews at the face and giving advice during lunch. He usually exited the mine late in the shift and gave a thorough report to Willie. He marked the progress made on the mine layout map on the wall. He colored in the progress made by each crew, and using his own time-tested formula, calculated the amount of coal extracted that day. He also used various colorings to mark the water leakage, roof concerns and areas that presented the potential for methane buildup. This was his way to keep track of everything happening in the mine.

Production exceeded all expectations as crews charged into the backbreaking work. They faced clean coal, nine feet of it, which produced clean wagons. Slate was non-existent, so wagons loaded were pure coal. The chechweighman had no choice but to mark each wagon as a twenty, which was perfect. The men labored without complaint at "dead time," work like timbering, laying track, drilling and blasting. The dreaded "Grant hump" previously added to each wagon, "for the Company" was eliminated at Patty's insistence. The men cheered the change.

"Give it time," said Winegartner at his daily morning meeting. "Things are going well. The Pittsburgh office is happy and we are getting top production with the number of workers available. We'll introduce changes and take control slowly.

The operation ran smoothly during the honeymoon period. Winegarter was smart enough to let things roll and permit Patty and Willie to have complete say in running the mine. They obliged, working diligently as long as the men got a fair shake.

The Coal and Iron Police settled into a routine of patrolling the mine complex, and the patch. They rode horses throughout the area, initially making friends with the children who loved petting the animals. The populace of the patch generally accepted their presence. Things were good and all was well throughout 1920 in Ridge Valley.

CHAPTER XXIV

THE NORTHERN WINDS finally lost their grip, allowing breezes from the south to penetrate the valley. Twisting and turning around the bowl, the warm winds melted the ice and snow. Crocuses, accepting the warmth, thrust their green shoots from the ground. Patch people began the initial survey of the backyard where the garden would soon be planted. They decided another week of warm weather would be needed before they could spade the ground. After all, the onions and peas needed an early planting and mid March is that time. Water generated from melting snow in the hills formed small streamlets and prepared for a downhill run. Joining the streams would be the sooty coal dust deposited everywhere from chimneys. No areas were immune from the black specks. They collected in fields, hillsides and glens. Larger and larger runlets collected the resting cinders in its path and provided them with the ride of their life down the hill. The water and cinder runoff gained momentum and size on the journey to the valley floor and wetlands. The combination of water and soggy black dust formed gray gooey syrup that seemed to be everywhere. Unable to penetrate the ground, the sticky concoction collected in puddles and sat on top of walkways and paths. It attached itself to shoes like glue. Only the rains of April would provide a good washing of the territory and relieve the locals of the gooey mess.

In Carbon Hill, Alabama, spring brought renewal to the fields already planted with crops. Greenery sprung from trees with new growth seen on pines and flowers. The warmth of the sun brought smiles to the returnees. Many resumed their old jobs in sawmills, mines and farms where planting of cotton and peanuts were in season. They had to accept employment at a lower wage than received before going north. The owners showed no mercy. The blacks in order to survive had no choice.

Bella continued her recovery, gaining strength slowly but measurably every day. She added weight to her thin frame, gaining about half the amount lost due to her injuries. However, what she gained physically she lost mentally. Visits to her home left her depressed at the sight. She became more and more despondent with each visit, realizing that repair of her home was beyond her means. She had no money to purchase supplies, let alone to hire someone to fix up the place. She talked to momma at the grave but talking turned to convulsive crying adding to her gloom.

Her trips out of the house were dictated by the weather. The sun was her enemy. The hot rays agonized the nerves of the burned skin kept her inside all summer. Only cloudy rainy days were acceptable for travel. Therefore she spent most of her time close to the Towns' house seeking contact from men who returned from up north. Those she talked to had nothing to offer concerning Rufus and Leroy. The men who knew them and lived in the boxcar in Ridge Valley found work as porters on railroads in Chicago. All those who had acquaintance with Rufus found jobs in the north and never returned.

Frustrated and forlorn, Bella had no contact with Reverend Washington. His failure to contact her since the Christmas holiday remained a mystery to her. It had been over a year since she last saw him.

"He won't come to me so I'll go to him," she announced to Isabella.

Ash Wednesday in 1921 dawned cloudy and cool with a breeze from the North.

"There is a feel of rain in the air, I'm thinking rain by evening. Best I be going and the sooner the better," Bella said to Mrs. Towns.

"Be careful and take time to rest, don't push yourself too hard. You sure you don't want me to go with you?" asked Isabella.

"No, you done enough already. I'll be fine."

"Tell the reverend I send my best."

Bella covered her head and shoulders with a black shawl that hung loosely to the ground. Walking cautiously, she moved like she had leaden feet. She shuffled up the road. People she met avoided her by passing quickly at a distance.

"Why am I treated like a leper?" she wondered. "Is it because my burns have turned my skin white, or because I don't have my man about or is the Klan warning my own to stay away from me?"

Tiny beads of perspiration gathered on her forehead and back. The wetness under the clothing irritated skin and nerves. A stinging rash resulted. She stopped often to rest. She walked, rested, walked and rested, finally reaching the spur. The pace she set placed her arrival at the church early in the afternoon. She wanted to know why the pastor failed to see her and why no letters for months from Rufus pushed her forward. Turning a corner, Bella smiled as the church came into view. She saw a person in the distance, just for an instant near the back entrance. "Must be the reverend," she thought.

"Why is he peeking around that corner?"

The reverend saw someone with loose flowing clothes advancing up the road.

"I'm not expecting callers, who is that, why covered up like that? Not one of those please!" The ghosts came at night from out of the pines, he heard and saw them, none came during the day. "Who or what is this coming here?"

Reverend Washington had stayed at the church every day for the past year. His only departure from the building and grounds came on short trips to Carbon Hill. He was called to the Hawkes' mine recently to administer to accident victims. While there, both whites and blacks avoided him. The blacks that dared talk to him became the "pit dogs" and were assigned to the worst section in the mine. The message was clear, associate with that man and suffer the consequences. Attending services at the Holy Gospel Church resulted in being assigned to work the three-foot coal seam section. The womenfolk became frightened for their men and ceased attending the services for fear of reprisal. The Hawke's had spies watching every move the reverend made. They kept their distance, but would let him see them briefly, and then disappear. The harassment continued on and on day and night.

Working independently the Possum Man roamed the church grounds. He scraped a twig on the side of the church at night every week for the past year. He continued scratching until the Pastor investigated. He retreated into the scrub avoiding the man when he came out to check the noise. Finding nothing the reverend returned to his room, only to hear the racket again. Over and over, at different times, in different places every week for a year the Possum Man made his calls. Once the Pastor reentered the church, the Possum Man collected pine tar from tree drippings and rubbed it onto the stilts supporting the church. The preacher heard the rubbing but remained in bed, afraid to check the outside again. He at first thought it was an animal, but soon became convinced it was a ghost.

Black squirrels dashed about searching for buried nuts. Bella interrupted the search, scattering them up trees with her appearance. Once she was near the church the animals returned to search once again. They ignored the Possum Man, who observed Bella climb the back steps.

"It's Bella, Bella Johnson," she shouted while knocking on the door.

"You alone?"

"Yes, I'm alone."

"What you want?"

"I want to talk to you, Pastor, about Rufus and ask if you got any letters?"

"You alone?"

"Yes"

The minister flipped the latch; slowly opening the door just wide enough to peek through the slit, then swiftly slammed it shut. After closing the latch he stepped back into the room. Sweat oozed from his forehead. He did not see Bella but a ghost in a flowing black shawl and hanging, loose fitting, clothes. Ghosts at night are one thing, but should be avoided at all cost during the day. The reverend pulled a white cloth from his front pants pocket and wiped his forehead.

Bella, shocked at the move, stepped back from the door. She quickly recovered and approached the door again. She knocked as loud as she could.

"Reverend Washington, this is Bella Johnson, wife of Rufus. I must see you. I don't understand please open the door. I'm Bella Johnson."

"If you are Bella Johnson, why you dressed like that? Bella never looks like you, tell me, if you be Bella then why you dressed like that?"

She paused in answering, thinking about what was just said. "Do I look silly? Is that why all those folks stayed away from me?"

"The loose clothes and head cover are best for my burned skin, need baggy clothes to wear, regular dresses causes a burning pain, hurts real bad."

"Tell me your son's name?"

"Leroy

"And your dog, what's his name?"

"Brownie"

"Answer's right, but a ghost knows all the answers, you look like a ghost."

"Listen, I answered all your questions, and you know I'm right. I am Bella Johnson, and why are you fretting like this? You ailing or something?"

"How you guarantee you're not a ghost?'

"Simple. If I'm a ghost I'd be in there already. A ghost goes through doors. I'm no ghost so open up." Bella stated in a firm voice.

Hearing the latch slide open, Bella removed the shawl from her head. The door hinges squeaked as it slowly opened and the reverend appeared wide-eyed in the widening chasm. He stepped back, Bella entered in a rush and the preacher quickly shut the door and secured the latch.

"I've been ailing a long time. I healed enough to walk here. Now, I got to know fin's you got any letters from my Rufus?" she asked.

"I got letters, never opened em."

"Why, why not?"

"Didn't have the signal."

"Signal, what signal?"

"Middle initial, all letters to make certain they were from Rufus or Willie are to have a middle initial in the address. Without the initial the agreement was that I destroy the envelope immediately. I burned them, they did not have the initial."

"Why, why didn't you look inside?"

"No initial that's why. That was our agreement. They, the Klan, can trace things you know, someone watching all the time, did you hear that? I can feel them, you know."

"You got mail all this time, from Rufus and they are gone, you burned them?"

"Didn't have the signal."

Bella slumped in her chair. She buried her face in both hands. Suddenly tired and despondent from the news she realized that her only hope was to talk to momma. Momma will know what to do.

The Possum Man followed Bella to the back entrance to the church. After seeing her enter the closet office he quietly entered the back door. He was now ready to carry out his plan. He secured a long pole with a V shape at the top. He placed the V end under the doorknob and secured the opposite end in the corner where the floor meets the wall, locking the inhabitants inside. He left the church; looked about, satisfied he crept under the building. What he planned to do took only a few seconds.

Bella smelled it first; burned the eyes next, then a cough from the fumes. Burning pine tar smoke lifted through the cracks in the floor, ever thickening. The preacher tried desperately to force the door open. Smoke entering his lungs accelerated weakness in the body. He collapsed to the floor. Mrs. Washington seeing the smoke ran into the back entrance. She tried to open the door but was overcome by the smoke and fell to the floor. Bella sat in the chair, singing a prayer to momma and God. The flames followed the smoke and broke through the floor, engulfing the closet office, then the entire building, sending thick black smoke into the sky.

CHAPTER XXV

THE RIDGE VALLEY mining complex ran smoothly during the entire year of 1920 for workers and owners alike. Patty's selection as foreman was a major reason for the success of the operation. The miners trusted the Man to place them in the best environment possible, and they responded. Production started strong and improved each month. All was well in the Valley as spring flowers blossomed, tree buds expanded into leaves and green onion shoots emerged from the ground in back yard gardens.

Just as spring replaced winter, speakeasies replaced established saloons. Moonshine, rotgut and bathtub gin became common names for homemade booze. Children welcomed the spring weather as boys gathered at the meadows to play mush ball. Others fished in mine reservoirs or Redstone Creek. The girls played hopscotch or jacks on front porches. Neighbors chatted across fences and gardens were planted with onions, lettuce and beans dotted the ground of every homestead.

The Coal and Iron Police patrolled the community without incident. They were accepted as a necessary evil. Necessary to oversee the curfews, for example, yet except for the boys who occasionally harassed them, the people kept their distance. Most remembered the Old Country and the total jurisdiction of Cossacks over their lives. And so for now the police kept a watchful eye on activities and reported their observances to the sergeant and in turn the captain at the end of each day.

"No sign of problems, all the men seem content at work they even accepted that Negro, Towns, as a boss. He was assigned the Fire Boss position by Patty, a demotion from his assistant pit boss position, but retains the same pay. He is responsible for inspecting the entire mine, and gives the okay before the men are allowed to enter the shaft. They place a lot of trust in that man, and he's awfully cautious. He could really slow things down. Maybe we should have someone, one of our best, go along with this Towns fellow, just think about it, fin's he can shut down a section, he could shut down the mine. Has a lot of power, this man.?" said the captain to Winegartner.

The summer of nineteen-twenty brought mass production with everything made in America. The increase in the output of goods required the same increase in raw materials. The United States grew to become the wealthiest country in the world after the war. Work for the masses was plentiful and steady. Everyone in Ridge Valley benefited from the need for coal. Men worked extra hours that brought more production that equaled higher profitability. However, the additional hours worked did not add up to an equal addition to wages. First, the subtle changes in the checkweighman calculations, leaning toward the Company, were unnoticed by the workers. Nevertheless, the times were good, the men working; the wives happy, good whiskey at Dolly's, or moonshine at Chubb's. The gardens grew in abundance. Peddlers like the knife and scissors sharpener, a button salesman and the medicine man that sold medicinal syrups, which according to him cured every ailment in existence, were seen frequently roaming the patch to sell their wares.

Evenings found girls playing Ring around the Rosie. Here we go round the Mulberry Bush and London Bridge is falling down were other favorites heard in front yards. A gathering at homes with ethnic friends where men imbibed in-home brews and women talked about the family was the custom. Accordion music usually completed a Sunday with songs and dancing, depending on how much drink was consumed. The summer ended with the canning of garden vegetables. Piccalilli was processed in quart and pint jars to John's delight. The mine worked every day since the mine reopened.

Ridge Valley

Not one day was lost to accidents. The miners accepted the wages for now since work was steady. The Grant Company profited handsomely and Mr. Moses happily counted his bonus money. Although cautious, he accepted Patty as the foreman for the remainder of the year. He allowed him to continue but the winds of change began blowing from two opposite directions.

The colder weather in late fall brought frost and with it hog butchering and meat smoking parties. Since money was available, families purchased a piglet in the spring from Mr. Glover, who raised them with other pigs on the farm. The fattened pig was butchered. Sausage and head cheese made; bacon, hams and pork shoulder prepared for smoking. Pig's feet were placed in jars for pickling and fat rendered into lard on kitchen stoves completed the process. All will have a Merry Christmas. The slow methodical approach resulting in good working conditions continued through the end of 1920 and into 21. Patty's diligent work as foreman and Willie's efforts to insure a safe environment slowed production. However, the approach used by Patty and Willie was wearing thin with the Pittsburgh office. Pressure to increase production from the top echelon offices at Fifth and Carnegie intensified over the summer. The streak of good working days and cooperation between labor and management was nearing an end in Ridge Valley. Winegartner understood that a change was necessary and planned on the move for some time. He will move when a reason for replacing Patty was presented. The reason arrived in the fall of 1921.

Patty was precise to a fault in checking and rechecking each section and the progress made by each crew. He marked the weekly progress made in each section using coded colors on the wall map of the mine, located in his office. From this he calculated the tonnage mined and compared his totals with those reported by the weight master. His totals agreed with the Company's calculation early on, after the mine reopened, but began to show a marked difference in favor of the company in late spring of '21. The difference widened during the summer. He double-checked his map and found that John and Leroy moved farther than any other two man crew, yet felt by his numbers did not get full credit for loaded cars. Patty expressed his concern to the checkweighman often but was assured that all was correct. He checked his map in other sections closely and found more disparity in honest car weight calculations throughout.

" Seems the greed for profit has finally arrived. If I go to Boyle he'll deny any wrongdoing and pass on what was said to Winegartner. The Superintendent will back Boyle. He'll call me in and demand to know why I'm causing a problem when in his eyes none exists. If I do nothing, the men will not get their fair share and it will get worse," Patty thought as he downed a shot and sipped a beer at the end of the bar at Chubb's.

The next day Patty will check the map carefully with Willie. He reviewed with him how he ciphered the tonnage allowing for error on the side of the company. Together they double-checked the weekly records Patty kept. The result was as expected. The workers were being shorted, and it got progressively worse.

" I have no choice. This has gone on too long. I must take this matter to Boyle and Winegartner," said Patty.

" Are you sure? You know they will replace you for challenging them. It's either for or against. That's how they operate. You know that."

" I can't let this go on any longer Willie."

"Then I'm with you, when do we go?"

The winds of change clashed on a rainy fall day in Ridge Valley in 1921. Winegartner refused to accept Patty's weight master's accusation. A stormy heated argument ensued. Patty was fired from his Foreman's job and Willie stepped down from his Bossing job. The two will be employed as laborers. In better days they would be blackballed but the need for men outweighs any thought of complete dismissal. The word was passed that George Boyle was in complete charge along with new assistant foreman and fire bosses. All had no choice but to accept the change and move on.

The boys, Leroy and John teamed up soon after the mine reopened. They worked well together and succeeded in being among the best diggers and loaders in the mine. They also became the breadwinners in their families. Leroy took over the letter writing to the Reverend Washington after Rufus, due to the high fever, suffered a mental collapse. Hoping against hope, Leroy waited for his father to come around but it never happened. Rufus couldn't remember things. All he did was sleep, eat and rock in the rocking chair in his room. Rufus neglected to tell Leroy about the signal that consisted of the middle initial used to verify the authenticity of the letters. When writing Leroy did not tell of his father's condition, but made up a story about Rufus injuring his hand and therefore unable to make his mark. This information did not matter since the letters were destroyed before being read because of the lack of middle initial. Leroy was the main provider for the family now and he would continue working extra hours if available, and save enough money for Bella to travel to Ridge Valley. Although he wanted to receive letters from his mom he understood the non-communication from her. He just assumed that she was getting the letters and the money. He understood her not wanting to leave momma.

Willie and Billie moved to a vacant house, a move they thought would allow Isabella to join them. They debated on a time with Leroy for her and Bella to come and decided that the spring of 1922 would be the best choice. By then enough money would be available for transportation and the house would be furnished, and maybe Rufus would "come around " by then. Isabella continually balked at their efforts and stayed in Carbon Hill. She always had an excuse to stay and one was that she would not leave without Bella, and Bella needed more time to talk to momma. She never informed them about Bella's and the Washington's fate. She used all the excuses she could until another summer was long gone, and fall fast approaching. Her men knew she had never faced cold weather so a spring move would allow her time to adjust to the area and the seasons. Their efforts would be in vain. Isabella balked at moving from her home in Carbon Hill. She would never leave and stated in her letter that Bella would not leave either but never stated why.

The move by the Towns added to Leroy's burden. He was now on his own caring for Rufus and doing all the cooking, washing clothes and cleaning. His father simply rocked and stared only leaving the rocker for a drink or a trip to the outhouse. Early on a neighbor lady looked in on Rufus but that ceased because he chased her away, hammer in hand, thinking she was an intruder.

Back to work on a December Monday the two young men returned to two left and the excellent seam they were mining.

"Looks like our luck is continuing. The nine-foot seam is holding but it's turning. We've gone as far as we dare without support, so we better do the timbering and laying track to the face.

Going to be a lot of dead time today, may take most of the morning, best we get started," said John.

The two put their backs to shoring the ribs and timbering the roof. Laying track came next. It took all morning to get the face ready to load coal.

"What say we eat some lunch and then push up a car, get to loading and making some money?" stated Leroy.

Hungry and thirsty, they ate quickly, rested but a few minutes, and then pushed a car up the tracks to two left. They drilled the face and placed charges for blasting. The blast loosened large clusters of coal. Once the dust thinned a sledgehammer and pick were used to break up huge chunks into sizable lumps for shoveling. All the time flecks of black dust danced in the air, persistent in their presence until sucked into lungs or left clinging to sweaty faces, necks and eyes. Carbide lamps lighted the way. The burning lamps emitted smoke that lingered with the coal dust, patiently waiting to rest in the workers' lungs. Without hesitation the car was pushed into position. The place was free of water leakage, thus providing a solid floor to load. The two worked in unison, one on each side of the car. Thrust into the pile, the number four shovel was filled, retrieved, lifted, a turn, a quick jerk of the hip, arms thrust forward sent a twenty pound load of coal into the car. Thrust, pull, lift, turn and release, a forever-endless motion of arms, legs and backs. Over and over, without letup, stopping only to reverse sides. Finally the car was full. A small circular metal tag, placed on a hook on the side of the car, identified the loader who would get credit from the weight master. The first tag belonged to Leroy; John's tag will go on the next car. A push out to the haulage for pickup, then an empty is placed at the face for filling.

They worked without letup through the afternoon and changed shoveling sides often in order to equalize the load on tiring muscles. They cleared the pile, blasted the face again, broke up the large chunks and began loading again.

"I'd like to finish this pile, clean up the area and do some timbering. Get her ready for tomorrow. I'll finish up if you fetch the timber," said Leroy.

John left as Leroy assaulted the pile. His shoveling intensity heightened as twenty-pound shovels of coal found the wagon. The pace slowed only slightly as the pile dwindled. Speckles of black dust and carbide smoke were suspended in the air, dancing in place. Perspiring profusely and breathing hard, Leroy slowed his pace yet persisted in shoveling. He began to quiver, breathing in gulps; he lost his balance, falling to the floor. The hardhat fell from his head, the carbide lamp, sizzling spewing smoke, rolled away to a corner. Using the shovel as a crutch, his head pounding, legs spread for balance, he moved along the wall toward the haulage.

"Bad air," he mumbled, "Get out!" his brain told him, Get out!"… Now!"

Dizzy, nauseous he staggered forward; tripping, he stumbled to the floor. Gulping air, he scratched and crawled his way to the haulage. John returning with the timber saw Leroy crawling from the section. He rushed to his side.

"Leroy, what are you doing? What's the matter?" He shouted as he grabbed Leroy's shoulder and turned him on his back. His eyes were rolled back in his head, his breathing labored. John checked his head for an injury. Finding none, he dragged Leroy across the haulage. The improved flow of air revived Leroy. He tried to get up.

"Just sit still, take in a good breath, good, now talk to me, talk, tell me what happened."

"Couldn't breath, no air, my head is pounding bad, and I done seen the dazzling light, I know I saw flashes."

"How did this happen? We did the same as we had always done. We know the ventilation was a bit thin because we went further into the section but what caused the airflow to cease? Let things as they are and we'll bring Willie or Patty down here to get an answer."

"All I know is that the "skunk gas" hits you quick like and you begin fighting yourself and don't know why. You can't think straight, John. I swear I don't know how I got out. I don't remember," said Leroy.

"I know of men who got caught and couldn't get out, stayed too long in the skunk gas and it killed their brain. Once that happens, and your brain is lost, you never get it back. Take Chicago John, the man who brought your Dad home from the woods. He got caught in a gaseous section, fainted and wasn't found until the next shift. They dragged him out, and he came around, but left the mine confused and went to the wrong house. He finally made it home, with help of course. He never recovered his senses and been absent minded ever since."

"And he's the one who found my Dad?"

"Yes, he lives in a shack back in the woods beyond Glover's farm. His father died in an accident, and his mom took care of him, thinking he would come around. His mom passed away and that left him to fend for himself. He was eventually forced out of his house. He lives by picking coal and selling it cheap, and working for Mr. Glover. He's as strong as an ox. Story goes that one-day he was walking to the slate dump and saw ole man Glover putting bales of hay in a wagon. Apparently the load was lopsided, because the wagon tipped over, trapping the farmer under the wagon. Chicago runs over and lifts that wagon enough to allow Mr. Glover to get out. That's the reason the Glovers looks out after him to this day."

"Why is he called Chicago John?'

"Well, he roams around the patch and when asked where he's from he says, "Chicago." So he's called Chicago John. Folks accept him as he is. He's a kind soul by nature, strong as a horse but won't hurt anyone and some say he looks out after the kids. He's an icon in the patch, an example of what could happen if you suck in too much bad air. Anyway, looks like you're better, what say we get out of here?"

"Head still thumping bad but stomach feels better, let's give it a try."

They stopped to pick up their lunch pails then John and Leroy arm in arm slowly ambled up the haulage.

"John, one thing?"

"Sure what."

"You got to help me find that Chicago John fellow."

"Consider it done."

Ridge Valley

John and Leroy exited the mine in daylight, a rarity since they began working steadily in Ridge Valley. They immediately ran into Jerry who was posting a notice on the message board. Jerry greeted them exuberantly like they were long lost friends.

"John, when are we going for walnuts again? I know we been working a lot, so how about next Sunday? Looks like the only day in the week available."

"I don't know, Jer, haven't even thought about going back for nut picking. It's late December, don't expect much be available this late."

"Aw, c'mon John, Leroy, how about you?"

"Well, all right, Sunday at noon, meet you at the store."

"Good, I best be going before ole Shaun comes a looking for me."

John and Leroy reported the airflow problem to George Boyle.

"Sounds to me like you hit a gas pocket. Have to check it out, in the meantime report to the north section until we clear up the problem on two left. Water leakage in the north section; so be prepared to work in ankle deep water.

"Hey John, nice day for picking walnuts. Is Leroy coming? You got your sack? We going to the same spot as before?" spouted Jerry.

"Leroy is coming, and I have my sack. No use changing where we pick the nuts. Always been good to us. Only thing is that I want to stop at Glover's on the way back."

Leroy arrived and the three began the trek up the road, across railroad tracks, through the junk graveyard finally reaching the creek. Then walking along the rill, up the hill past the ventilation shaft, then through the cornfield with the woods and walnut trees beyond.

"Back in there," Leroy said pointing to the woods, " kind of reminds me of home. I had my own secret hideout in a wooded area in the back of my house."

"Do you miss Alabama Leroy?" asked Jerry

"Sure, especially now that winter is coming on. But I really miss my mom. Can't talk much to my dad since he had the fever. We did a powerful lot of talking to convince my mom to let my dad and me come up north. She was against our coming but I guess we finally

Bob Menarcheck

wore her down. I remember her saying that, "once a person takes a path to follow it's hard to turn 'em around. So here I am."

They found the trees, collected the walnuts, filled their sacks and decided to walk to the spring for a drink. They rested there; observing the meadow, hoping the deer would appear.

"Say, are these the woods where that Chicago fellow lives?"

"Yeah, he lives in here somewhere and his place has never been found, bunch of us tried looking for a whole day and finally gave up. Figure a man wants his privacy that bad we should let it rest and never looked again."

"How about looking one more time? What do you say?" asked Jerry.

"No, Jer, I'm here for walnuts, then Glover's, and best we get going."

Both Jerry and Leroy decided to join John. Jerry was hoping the farmer would have some fresh milk cooling in the springhouse. The day was wearing on to evening as the three left the woods and headed to the farm.

"I've been trying to figure out why a man I never seen before offers me good money to use my barn for a meeting, Mr. Glover mentioned to the boys. "I say, who's going to be at this 'ere meeting? He says it's for the miners. I say in that case anything for the miners is free. He says he will pay so I won't get into any trouble with the law. Maybe you boys can tell me what he's going to use it for?"

"I'm not sure but it sounds to me like he's a union organizer. Been a lot of talk between the Big Shots in the mine office lately about men coming in to try and get a union started. They will do anything to keep a union from forming in the mines. One reason for the Coal and Iron Police is to keep those people out of the patch." Said Jerry.

"They can't do anything if these union agents hold organizational meetings on private property. Only thing they can do then is to get the names of men attending the meeting. Then they can make big trouble for them," said John

"What kind of trouble?" asked Leroy?

"Lose your job and get blackballed and evicted from the patch. Your name is sent to all coal companies as a troublemaker. No one will hire you. So if there is a meeting planned they better not let the likes of Winegartner or that Captain Ross find out.

"Well, let me say that if someone is helping the miners and wants to use my barn, they're welcome to it. Right now it's time to eat and we've got plenty. The Mrs. wants me to invite you'all for supper. Hope you can join us 'cause she has plenty. She still cooks like George is here so join us if you will."

The boys didn't hesitate in accepting the invitation. Besides it wouldn't be neighborly to refuse. Anyway, Mr. Glover was right. A hearty stew greeted the hungry boys along with homemade bread, fresh churned butter and fruit preserves. Mr. Glover offered grace, his wife ladled out a large dipper of stew and to the delight of Jerry she poured large glasses of fresh cold milk from the springhouse.

Leroy ate heartily and ignored the conversation between John, Jerry and Mr. Glover.

"Thanks for asking, John. We hear from George at least once a week. He is doing very well, earning good money and he sends a fair amount home on a regular basis. He will take over the farm in a few years. He plans to expand the planted acreage and that will require a tractor, tiller and such. Wants to increase the cattle herd and swine. He certainly misses the farm; mom's good cooking and a good ride on his horse Spike. Figures another year or so and he'll be back."

"That's great news," said John who added, " Next time you write tell George that Bull, the fellow who went with him, is back in the patch as a Company policeman."

The day moved on from late afternoon to dusk. A warm piece of freshly baked apple pie and another glass of fresh milk concluded the meal. The boys lingered to let their full stomachs settle a bit. Dusk moved to dark as the North Star appeared and sparkled in the sky. Struggling to move, the boys thanked the Glovers, shouldered their walnuts and began the walk home. The air was cool with a slight breeze making it feel colder. Clouds dotted the sky, occasionally blotting out the moon. Reaching the airshaft, the path turned down the hill toward the creek. The trail followed the stream, until it finally crossed the Republic-New Salem Road. Leroy said his goodbyes, and then walked up the road toward his house on the number two side of the patch. John and Jerry climbed the fence surrounding the horse pasture and entered the Grant property. They began to walk across the field.

"Hold it right there, don't move, and drop those sacks."

The boys froze, surprised at the command.

"I said drop the sacks, you're in trouble for sure being on Company property after curfew and if that is Company property in those sacks, you're in deep trouble."

The boys dropped the sacks to the ground. They turned in the direction of the voices. A cloud blocked the moon's brightness. Unable to see the person behind the voice they assumed it was a member of the Company police. Bull and two other policemen had the duty to feed and brush down the horses and clean the stalls. They were proceeding to the far end of the field with a wheelbarrow load of waste when they ran into John and Jerry. They challenged the two for being on Company property. Not knowing what to do with them, the low ranking pair hesitated, then decided a ranking officer should be contacted to render a decision.

"Stay put, don't move, going to summon an officer to deal with you," said Bull.

"Why, what for? We been crossing this field for forever and never had a problem."

The men said nothing in return. The three simply held their ground, facing each other, waiting in silence. The moon peeked from the back of a cloud revealing two men, dressed in police uniforms approaching the field from the patch. One was Bull, the other known as "Hoss" a huge man the equal of Bull in size. Sassy, cocky and mean spirited he is known as "the enforcer." His own considered him to be a bit crazy with a cold-hearted personality. His furrowed forehead smoothed out at the top of a baldhead. Small ears, a wide flat nose and beady green eyes were attached to a round head. A gap in his front teeth caused a whistling sound with S words when speaking. The Hoss man ambled along after clearing the fence. After all, this was his first assignment as officer of the day and he was going to prove himself here and now.

Patchy clouds dispersed enough to allow the moon to appear in its bright autumn glow, lighting up the area. Leroy, well up on the number two-side hill, looked down to see his two friends with their

Ridge Valley

sacks on the ground and two police officers close by. He noticed another one about fifteen yards away standing beside a wheelbarrow. Looking back to the barn, he spotted a man move into the building shadows. A passing cloud swallowed the moon, darkening the field below. Leroy dropped his sack, looking, but it was to dark to see. The cloud passed now allowing the moon to light the field once again.

"What do those "Dogs" want?" he thought. Instinctively he began to walk back toward the field, thinking his presence would even the numbers. Rivulets of sweat dripped down his forehead as he skipped down an embankment. The moon ducked behind a cloud as Leroy hurried up the side of the creek looking for a way to cross the swift running water. A rock, a big one in the middle of the creek, caught his attention. "Jump to the rock and then the other side," He thought. He misjudged the distance and slipped into the water, hitting his head on the intended target. Blood flowed from a deep gash above the right eye. Trying to stand he fell again, dizzy, fighting the swift stream. Stumbling, again he fell into the creek. Swallowing water he struggled to catch his breath; choking he went under. A hand grabbed Leroy's wrist and pulled him to the bank. The man quickly retreated, unseen, back into the shadows of the barn. Leroy lay in a stupor, unable to move, coughing up creek water, the gash on his forehead bleeding.

Hoss and Bull ambled up to their prey. Acting cocky, Hoss circled the boys while eying the sacks. Bull stood watching, and then followed the grunting Corporal.

"What's this?" asked Hoss, pointing to the sacks.

"Walnuts," said Jerry sarcastically.

"You say that, I say its stuff from the mine. I say you can hide anything in those sacks and we're going to take a look. Have to confiscate these sacks, take this evidence back with us to have the sarge look it over," said Hoss.

"Look," said John, " There is nothing but walnuts in those sacks. We were out picking, now going home, like I said before, we took a shortcut across the pasture like we always do…and there is nothing but walnuts in those sacks."

"Yeah, we'll see. You do all this in the dark. It looks suspicious."

"Are you calling us liars?" interrupted Jerry. "Well we ain't liars and, I think you're just using your so-called badge to lord it over us. You're stealing from us is all? You always were that way Bull, acting against your own. You're asking for big trouble taking our stuff," sputtered Jerry.

"You just shut your mouth, you little pipsqueak. All you do is talk and I'm tired of your talk Jerry, you could use some shutting up, boy," said Bull

John anticipated his friend's charge toward Bull. He grabbed Jerry by the arm. Jerry fought to get loose, finally relenting to John's request to stop his charge. Panting in short quick gulps, Jerry slowly calmed down enough to permit John to release his hold. John, with poise and sincerity, explained their routine. "Noon start, picked nuts, stopped and ate at Glover's, you remember, Bull, you been there. We got a late start home, cut across the field like before, never had any trouble, and not looking for any."

"Yeah, he's right, done it before."

"Well, that was then, this is now. You're on Company property after dark so we have to confiscate those sacks, take them to headquarters for inspection.

Jerry seethed, grunting, "I need my sack, keep the damn things but I want my sack, and I hope they choke on em, the bastards."

"What you say, corporal?" said John, "Once they dry you'll be a hero bringing back black walnuts, you keep em but we need our sacks."

"It isn't fair, we picked and carried those nuts all the way here. You owe us for that, we want some kind of token or something saying you took stuff from us...

"Tell your loud mouth friend to shut up and I'll give it a good thinking."

"How good?" questioned John.

"Tell you what, let's shake on it, that's how good," spitted Hoss, who wanted to squeeze the feeling out of John's hand and make him yell "uncle." John held back eying the big man.

"Well, corporal, around here a person's word is his bond. A handshake seals that bond; however we take a man's word as truth and honor, you say we get em back, that's good by me."

"C'mon, shake on it," said Hoss, advancing with an outstretched hand and a sneer on his face. This was followed by a chuckle that changed to an arrogant smile. John accepted by clutching Hoss's hand and driving his own deep into the space between the forefinger and thumb. Hoss, caught off guard by the move, immediately tried to squeeze and clutch John's hand. He could not do it. The corporal faced a pressure that pinched nerves and numbed fingers. John held on until he saw the big man draw sweat to his brow. Jerry smiled to himself.

The man at the barn watched intently. Satisfied, he returned a pick handle to the corner and left to check on Leroy. Nothing more was said between John, Bull and Hoss. The handshake ended with John's release. The two officers picked up the sacks and began walking. John and Jerry stood watching.

The man at the barn walked to the creek and found Leroy where he left him earlier. He saw blood oozing from the gash in the forehead. The man walked back to the mine machine shop. Locating a clean supply he secured a handful of axle grease. Returning to Leroy, he tore a piece of cloth from his undershirt, spread grease on the cloth and tied it around Leroy's head. The procedure stopped the bleeding. He then helped him up the hill. Although groggy from the hit on the head, Leroy staggered along the path to his home. The man watched John and Jerry start their walk across the field; he then turned and began walking toward the woods.

"They're going to get theirs someday, mark my words, John."

"Jerry, you got to stay away from those guys and don't let them get to you," said John while crossing the junk graveyard.

"It's not fair, John, taking our stuff, how can you stand em?"

"I believe some men are born to be what they are, just like being born with the color of one's eyes. Some people are born to be nasty and I'm afraid that we have a lot of nasty guys in uniform in Ridge Valley. The bad part is that they have the law on their side. They are big physically, yet small minded. They got to build up their ego at the expense of others. They can't think for themselves and they are like puppets on a string, dancing at the whim of their bosses. They are good at instigating trouble and blaming it on someone else. They think they are important and are big shots and that itself is a very dangerous situation. The yellow dogs enjoy controlling folks and know how to antagonize to get your goat. This gives them an excuse to use force so promise me, Jer, that you won't let them get to you."

Jerry grunted and grumbled. He did not give John a straight answer but half-heartedly promised he would try to hold his temper. After crossing the bridge they separated, with Jerry walking up the hill and John continuing up the road. He thought about all that was happening, particularly about the talk of organizing. "Surely the Company will not stand by and let it happen. They want to keep all the money and we want a bit more just to survive. Sooner or later things will certainly come to a head."

"Hold it right there," came a shout from a gruff sounding voice, "What you doing here at the Company store after dark?"

"Heading home that's all, just heading home."

"Where you coming from?"

"I've been up yonder picking nuts. Got a late start…"

"Well, where are they?"

"Your fellow officers took them."

The policeman laughed. "So that's the story. What's your name?"

"John Ignatius"

"Well, John, I'll check out your story, and if it doesn't mesh I'll be seeing you again."

John started walking again, thinking the conversation was over.

"Hey you, before you go, I do know you, yes, you're the one that pals around with that honky boss of yours. That Patty guy, has been sounding off lately, particularly at Chubb's place where he's been drinking. He stops off at Dolly's cellar too. We've been a' watching him. We know what he's doing and what he's saying, so he better watch his step."

John was aware of Patty's drinking after work every day. Instead of leaving after a couple of shots and a few beers he languished on at the bar. The problem was that it took more and more alcohol to ease his mental pain. The pain began when the new superintendent started installing his own men in prominent bossing positions. That would have been acceptable to Patty had the replacements been knowledgeable miners, but that simply was not the case. He saw it before when greed ruled. Take all the coal you can get, at the cheapest way possible. Use the men like another piece of timber that holds up the roof. If it breaks just get another to replace the destroyed one. If a worker is hurt or killed, replace him with another. Patty understood the mine and listened to its call. He knew that when the outside air is warmer than air inside the mine, the roof sweats. The moisture is absorbed and the roof begins to expand and eventually breaks apart. The roof talks and workers must listen to what it says. Tapping the ceiling with a wooden handle tells a story. A hollow sound means there is a pocket that can cause a fracture leading to a fall. Since slate falls kill or maim more men than any other accident, Patty insisted the men take time to tap the roof often. He worked to teach, especially the new workers, all he knew about digging coal. He thought he was fair to the Company and the workers. He saw things improve in working conditions and happy workers who trusted Patty totally. What he did not see was the fear the Company saw in Patty gaining too much power and trust with the men.

"This man could close the shaft with just one word, or for that matter organize the men to join a union," said Winegartner.

They needed to discredit Patty. Somehow, some way, the Company must take control of operations with their own personnel. The morale of the miners will be tested. Friends will question the loyalty of friends; false rumors will be started to create divisiveness between ethnic groups.

"Patty performed a miracle to reopen the mine and develop trust and cooperation with the workers. He is still our leader, regardless of the circumstances. We need him. I will talk to him. He must realize his importance to us," thought John.

In house number three, on Bosses Row, at this very moment a discussion was being held with the superintendent and the chief of the Company police. They were talking about rumors they heard that a union organizer was in the area. They needed more facts to be certain if any of the miners were contacted.

"This Bull fellow, he lived here and should know the people and the territory. He should be able to get some news from the patch folks. Chief, lean on him if you have to. We got to know what is coming down, and the quicker the better," said the superintendent.

CHAPTER XXVI

JOHN LAY IN bed unable to sleep. His mind wandered, recalling the many times he talked with Patty about work down under. He talked incessantly about safe digging and ways to avoid danger zones. Patty not only gave his best, he assigned the best, like Willie as the Fire Boss to check the mine carefully before he allowed the shift to start. Patty insisted he was right on running things his way. The Company wanted changes made. Patty argued for his way but the Company had the power and might, the weight master and a short memory of where they were without Patty only months ago.

A wondering and concerned mind caused John to toss and turn, sleep continuing to fail him. He worried about Patty since he was dismissed from the assistant foreman position. Patty did not accept the change well. He drank heavily, turned mean and threatening and it happened more and more frequently. He got the attention of the "Yellow Dogs" one day with his rhetoric following a long evening drinking at Chubb's. Leaving the bar he stopped at house number three shouting and cursing "the puppet bastards," over and over. Another evening he stood in front of the superintendent's house for over an hour, just standing and looking. Many nights he preached at the bar to anyone who would listen. After a time the men simply drifted away from his drunken utterances. They had their own problems to contend with.

John was glad when morning came and he got up eager to go to work. He had lost sleep thinking about Patty's recent behavior and wanted to talk to him. He left the house early, planning on meeting Patty before entering the shaft. For all his drinking, sick or not, Patty never missed a day of work. He knew his mentor always arrived early and sat outside the lamp house, smoking one cigarette after another. He didn't chew tobacco anymore like most of the other miners while working, so prior to entering the shaft he smoked profusely to load his body with enough nicotine to last the shift.

"What you doing here so early, John?" asked Jerry talking as he walked a short distance to hang a metal check on the board to signify John's presence in the mine. He returned to add, "Been thinking about a way to get those walnuts back. Listen, I got some information I just learned about to tell ya," Jerry whispered.

"Can't right now, got to see Mr. Driscall. Did he come through here yet?"

"Sure, a couple minutes ago."

"Talk to you later, Jer, I have to go."

John left the window and walked along the hallway to the outside when Leroy came in the door.

"What happened to you?"

"I tripped and fell down, slipped on a rock crossing the creek and hit my head. I remember a man helping me. He put a bandage on my cut and helped me home."

"The creek, why are you crossing the creek?"

A Company assigned foreman entered the building and seeing Leroy's bandaged head asked, "You working today, boy?"

"Yes, sir, I'm a' working."

"Report your injury to the boss before going down so we know you didn't get that gash in the mine."

"I've got to talk to you tonight, see you at the store later," said Leroy as he left with the foreman watching. John eyed Leroy until he turned into the washhouse and disappeared. Open-mouthed, John wondered what Leroy was talking about because he clearly had seen him take the bridge over the creek home. "Who is this fellow he's talking about?"

Ridge Valley

He finally exited the door to the outside and walked over to where Patty was sitting.

"Good morning, sir."

"Morning, John, what brings you here?"

"I'm needing to talk to you, I need to get some things straight in my head about happenings here at Ridge Valley. Also, I'm, well I'm truthfully worried about you Patty, sir. I mean I'm real uneasy about you not being the foreman anymore and I know the men feel the same as me. I'm worried about you."

"Listen, John, we can't change the past, what's done is done and we have to live with it. Don't worry about me; I'll be okay. Takes time to adjust but I too worry about the future of this place. I worry about young guys like you. Men my age are few in mining. Look around; do you see many my age? No, John, you don't, because they are either injured or dead. The unlucky ones live without an arm or leg. Others can't breathe because of too much coal dust in their lungs. Some are silly- like from sucking in too much skunk gas. Yep those, and me die a slow death from working in the pits. Best you get out and the sooner the better."

"I ain't got no place to go, my family is here and here I'll stay. Not much of a choice."

"Yeah, I know John. I thought things would change after the explosion. They let people like Willie and me and a few other locals have a say in running the mine, but it looks like the blue bloods can't stand the least little bit of directing. They have all the say and we do the following. I hate to admit it but the only way to change things for the better is to unionize. The problem is that the Company will fight it all the way and they hold all the power. Believe me, John; they will use every mean spirited way to stop any organizing."

"There are more of us than them, that has to help."

"Look over at the shaft John, the last shift is coming off the cage. Those men represent the melting pot of the world. They work well together, however when the workday is ended they return to their roots and their customs. The Company knows this and will try to exploit one group against another should union talk comes. Let me warn you to be prepared because the need for coal is lessening and I think a large stockpile exists. My calculations tell me there is more coal mined than recorded. Production will slow down and fewer days worked during the week. Things could happen at any time."

John listened intently, trying to absorb all that was said. He at least had a better understanding of why Patty was drinking so much. Patty had a lot on his mind and like most workers in Ridge Valley alcohol was the way to alleviate the pain. He sat in silence, not knowing what to say to Patty in reply. The bell at the cage awakened John from his stupor. It was time to go to work and gather at the cage entrance for a ride to the bottom.

"Clear your mind boy. There is a lot of concern on that face of yours. Best you shake whatever is bothering you. One needs clear thinking in the pits."

John smiled, stood with Patty and began walking with him to the cage. The crowd of miners that just emerged from the pit remained in place at the cage. Three of the men began talking loudly, waving their arms.

"What's going on?" asked John.

"Sounds like one of the Irish boys claims he was shorted on his wagons. Claims he had clean coal and a full load but didn't get full credit. Others joined in agreeing with the Irishman."

"Funny, there are four people I don't recognize over there," said John.

Another man John did not know echoed his resentment in Slovak to having been shorted. A Croat who shouted about his being cheated followed him. Shouting quickly turned to bedlam as fists filled the air, angry voices clamoring for fair treatment. A load of miners exiting the cage added to the numbers gathering near the entrance to the mine. More workers leaving the lamp house were stopped short near the center of the compound by the onrushing mob emerging from the cage. Patty stayed behind.

"Don't look like we be going down today," Patty said to the operator.

"Been brewing for some time. All they needed is for someone to start the move. You know the one that started the commotion is new to me. Don't recall seeing him before," said the cage operator.

"Because he's a union organizer that's why. He brought a few more along with him to help. I believe everyone knows that the man that checks the cars goes to the side of the Company, but now that they heard it from others it sure got 'em roused. I never thought it would happen so soon, but now the time is right. The men are tired and you don't think straight when you're dirty, thirsty and hungry. Those leaving the shaft are yearning for a shot and a beer. Those ready to go down won't challenge those that just came up, yep' the timing is right," stated Patty.

The men crowded into the center of the compound with what the men thought was a worker who just exited the pit in the middle. He commanded their attention with rhetoric of various languages finally ending with, "I say we show them." He pried open the top of a lunch bucket then lifted it high above his head and poured the water to the ground.

"Who is with me?" he shouted to the top of his lungs.

A roar from the cluster of men resounded as water poured from buckets signifying the willingness to walk away from work. Those with empty lunch buckets lifted them high while vociferously answering, "We are with you! We are with you!"

John ambled back to where Patty and the cage operator stood watching. A bell sounded indicating that workers who finished their shift were ready to be hoisted topside. The operator answered their call just as John arrived.

"What's this all mean, Mr. Driscall?" asked John.

"It means trouble. I'm thinking the Yellow Dogs have been notified by now and I expect to see them here soon. I don't know why they're not here now."

"Can you talk any sense into them? I think they'll listen to you."

"No, I don't think so. The men are at a stage where they will listen to what they want to hear, and those union organizers will give them that. It's beyond me, John. My time is over, soon it will be up to you."

Leroy walked out of the lamp house door as the gathering of miners rushed to the center of the compound. He quickly moved to the edge of the throng, watching wide-eyed at the shouting, fist waving and water pouring from lunch buckets. He also saw something else, bottles of liquor being passed around by four miners he did not know. The unknown encouraged the workers to "have a snort, drink up, have another," and they obliged. Bottles were passed from one to another. There was more drinking, more shouting and more men, who just exited the cage, swelling the number in the compound and joining in on the party. Without warning an empty bottle smashed against the side of the lamp house. Empty liquor bottles found the message board and the one light bulb above the building entrance.

"Honest pay for honest work," one union organizer shouted and others quickly joined in. A chorus of voices screaming the phrase in unison as the bottles made their way around and, once empty, smashed against buildings.

Leroy spotted John, Patty and Willie standing near the pit entrance. Willie just finished the shift, exited the cage, and stood with Patty talking and watching.

"Shaun, what's that ruckus going on outside?" asked Winegartner.

"Don't know, sir."

"Well then, send Jerry out there and have him report back as to what is going on."

Jerry left the lamp house and entered the mob scene at the height of their exuberance. He knew every man who worked in the pit except a couple he did not recognize in the crowd. He was shocked at the stage of inebriation that existed. The men, who exited the cage, and those reporting for the next shift, converged in the space between the lamp house and the pit mouth. Over a hundred men crowded the grounds that Jerry entered. Soon he found himself in the middle of the mob, not knowing how he got there. A strapping miner searching for a drink jostled him.

"Over here, give me that, this way, this way, dammit." A nudge became a push, then a shove. A request became a demand. What started as a demonstration against short wagon counts was now working toward a drinking spectacle? The last of the bottles were drained, "just enough to get em riled, and I think we did," said an organizer to a cohort. "Start passing out the notices and let's get out of here."

> Don't let the Company short you
> Fight for decent wages

Ridge Valley

Give your family a better life
All for one and one for all
Join us at the Glover Barn
Tuesday, December 21st 1921 -7:00 PM
Come one come all
KEEP THIS NOTICE SECRET

CHAPTER XXVII

JOHN NOTICED THE commotion in the middle of the mob first. He saw Jerry in the center and challenged the crowd by inching his way toward his friend. The crowded conditions and close quarters made it difficult for John to move forward. He did not understand why the men were pressing in on Jerry so he pushed and shoved his way through.

"This man is not one of us," John heard.

"He is one of us, he works in the lamp house," shouted John.

"Why is he out here if he's supposed to be in there?"

"Mr. Shaun asked me to come out and see what all the commotion was out," shouted Jerry.

"Don't let him go back, he can give names, and if they want to know what's going on why don't they come and find out for themselves?" said a miner.

"We don't need you to talk for us, we do our own talking," said another.

"He's more them than us, I say he don't go back."

"I got to go back, I could get fired if I don't,"

"Make way, leave this man through," yelled John as he tried to push his way out.

The circle tightened at the instruction of a self-proclaimed leader of those clustered around John and Jerry. The boys tried escaping in one direction without success, then another. The circle of men refused to budge.

Patty seeing the commotion at first ignored the fracas. He thought that the men aroused by drink were feeling their oats and arguing about their next move.

"Leave me outta here," shouted Jerry.

"Move, MOVE!" grunted John.

The men in the circle responded by tightening the ring around the boys. Jerry began to shove and kick at the person in front of him, and then turned to the next. His shoving became a thrashing melee of arms and legs.

"Goddamn it, let me out," Jerry yelled. Tears of frustration appeared and one rolled down his cheek. The taunting from the crowd infuriated Jerry, who grabbed a lunch bucket from the ground and began flailing it at anyone in his range, hitting shoulders and backs as men ducked his blows, Jerry slowly made a pathway for himself and John. Progress stopped when one of the miners grabbed Jerry from behind. John reacted by challenging the man and wrestling him to the ground. Those who saw what happened pulled John away. They succeeded in separating John and Jerry as the two continued to fight back.

"Shaun, Shaun, did that boy of yours come back?" asked Winegartner.

"No, sir."

"What the hell is he doing? It's been a good while that he's been gone."

"You want me to go and find out, sir."

"No, I'll go and see for myself."

"Hey, are those two in the middle of that crowd John and his friend? Look's like a couple of guys are scuffling with them. You see that?" said Willie to Patty.

Patty did not have to see the action to react. He heard that John was having a problem and that was all he needed. Without hesitation he charged across the compound and into the mob. Jerking one, shoving another, he pierced the outer edges of the circle. Willie and Leroy were right behind.

"Let me through," he shouted, "get out of my way, NOW!" he commanded speaking in Croatian, then in Slovak. Those that understood stepped aside; those that didn't were pushed away. He reached the inner circle as one of the men held John down on the ground while another kicked a blow to John's side. Jerry was also on the ground, arms over his head trying to protect himself from fists and shoes.

"Goddamn you," grunted Patty as he grabbed the kicker from behind and flung him to the ground. He delivered a swift right shoe to the man's side.

"How do you like that?" snorted Patty, standing over the man. Leroy helped John to his feet as Willie yanked a man away from Jerry. Patty pushed the culprit forcibly into the crowd.

"Take him," pointing to the man on the ground, "and the rest of you back off, and I mean now. Back off, I said. I don't know why you want to harm these boys, I'll have none of it"

"He's been spying on us, for the boss," came a loud voice from the back.

"I was ordered to come out and see what all the noise was is all. Anyway, I was here the whole time. Never had a chance to go back to my job. You' all are accusing me of doing something I would never do."

"No harm has been done by this boy, he was asked to do a job and this boy did just that. He did his job," said Patty.

"Is the lad with us or with them," questioned an agitator from the crowd who continued, "What say, Patty, is he for us?" A couple hundred eyes centered on Patty waiting for an answer.

His name was Porky Podorzski. He looked every bit a miner. Short and squat, a potbelly hanging over his belt, he had a pudgy face, thick lips and a wide nose. He was admired for his strength and tireless work. He drank beer by the quart, two cach night after work at the bar and then home to the boarding house. He was a loner and because of a severe stuttering problem did not talk. Fact was all accepted him as being dumb, until this moment.

" TTTTThey bbbeen sssscrapping on me MMMr. PPlaty?" TTThey nnnot gggiving mme mine tthat I wwworked ffor, cccompany tttaking ffrom me aaare tthey...MMMR. Pplaty?" shouted Porky.

"My God," mumbled Patty, "Porky is only asking for fairness and without help he doesn't stand a chance." He motioned for Porky to come forward. The crowd separated providing a path, but Porky was too frightened to move from his spot. He hesitated. Those around him encouraged him but he stood his ground.

" I dddon't wwant tto cccause aaany ttrouble fffor yyou Mr. Pplaty. I sstay rright hhhere pplease?" stuttered Porky.

All eyes now turned to Patty. Willie, John, Leroy and now Billie stood at his side. Patty turned slowly looking beyond the mass of workers gathered in the dark on the grounds of the Ridge Valley mine. He saw that fog began to settle in the area creating a halo effect above the group. Breaths of air from the men, gathered above the heads, hanging in the mist. An organizer dressed as a miner who spoke in German broke the silence. "What do you say, Mr. Driscall. Are we gonna help people like Porky here and get a union in here?"

"I must warn you that there will be a lot of heartache, hurt and suffering. Once you decide to go against them," he said pointing in the direction of the office. "You will be faced with an onslaught of troubles that will challenge you, and your family, to the depths of your soul."

The superintendent left his office and exited through the back door and walked around the building. He turned the corner as Patty began talking to the crowd.

"Figured it would be him. He's the only one they'd listen to," he thought.

The men packed into the center, surrounding Patty, like a preacher at a tent meeting. They waited in anticipation for their Messiah to speak. Their leader was gone but now he is back. What does he have to say about-facing the absolute power of their employer?

"The fact is," he began in a slow drawl, " the coal operators own the politicians, the sheriff and just about every local and state official. Remember, they also own Ridge Valley. They own your house, they run the company store and for that matter they own you. They own the policemen and I don't know why the yellow dogs haven't arrived to confront us and break up this meeting."

"All the policemen went to some kind of police school for training at the Washington Run Mine, in Star Junction. They have some kind of training school there. They're all gone said an organizer from back of the crowd

"So that's why them union boys picked this time to start things. They knew the thugs would be gone," said Willie.

The superintendent saw Patty and Willie in the center holding court. He did not see Jerry in the group. He looked around for him but could not locate him in the crowd. Just then he noticed the crowd of men separate, forming a path.

"I better get back. Been gone a long time. Ole Shaun be a' wondering what happened to me," said Jerry. The men separated to allow Jerry to pass. He turned to give a goodbye wave to John when he saw something from the corner of his eye. What he noticed was a shadow on the side of the machine shop moving away in a hurried walk, now disappearing entirely. He hesitated, looked again, then moved to the lamp house and opened the door. Inside the opposite entrance stood Mr. Winegartner, panting, staring him down.

"What took you so long boy?"

"Mr. Shaun asked me to go outside and see what was happening. I've been watching and talking to some of the men is all. Didn't think about the time."

Mr. Shaun, upon hearing voices in the hallway, shuffled to the hall window. He saw Jerry and shouted, "Where have you been? The super is asking for a report, so lets have it."

"Well, the men are kind of mad because they said they were shorted. They done spilled the water from their buckets. Some Czech started it, and then all the others joined in and refused to get in the cage and go down. Some bottles were passed around. I don't know where they came from but they were there. A few had too much to drink, things got out of hand. You know Mr. Shaun, they called me a spy for the company and they come after me and they wouldn't let me go until Mr. Driscall held them off. They would have pummeled me for sure."

"You telling the truth?" Asked the Superintendent.

"Yes, sir. Mr. Driscall helped me out a lot," said Jerry to the superintendent. Taking a couple of steps toward him Jerry continued, "Someone out there thought I was a company spy. They came after me but Willie and Patty called them on it and they left me alone."

"What else was said? What are they clamoring for?" asked the superintendent.

"Like I said they feel they been shorted, cheated by not counting the full load. There are other things but this seems to be the main one. They done spilled the water so I'm sure they're not going in today."

"If they don't, we'll get somebody, sooner or later, I guarantee that. You'll never see a union in this or any other Grant mine; your man Patty is treading on dangerous ground. He's right about the law being on our side."

"He was outside, it was him in the shadows; that's why he knows what Patty said, 'cause he was there, listening," thought Jerry.

"The Company police will be back tomorrow. You tell your man Patty he better have the men at work by the time they return, or else. Now go out there and tell him that and come right back and give me the answer."

"Sir, you want me to tell Mr. Driscall that he is in charge again? Is that what you are saying? He had nothing to do with the stoppage so I don't know what he can do to talk the men into working. Besides, you fired him from the pit-bossing job some time back. You put Mr. Boyle in charge; maybe he should talk to them. I'm not sure that Patty is the one to help."

"You listen to me boy, and listen good. You do as I say and I will not tolerate any more back talk. Now get going."

Jerry walked toward the door and as he reached for the knob a shout from the superintendent stopped him. "Wait, you tell Mr. Driscall to come in here and see me. I want to tell him myself about the dangerous course they're on by walking out. Now go."

Outside, a misty rain began to fall. The men dispersed into small groups and were talking about what to do next. The union men walked around urging all to attend the union meeting tomorrow at Glover's. "We'll win an honest contract for you, so come and hear the good news," they told the men.

"All these boys will be wanting different things. Some want higher wages, or fewer hours or pay for dead time. They all want an honest and uniform pay scale but different ways to judge the scale. Add this to the different ethnic groups and you have a challenge to weld all these differences into a strong organized group willing to sacrifice for each other," stated Patty

"They work together down under in dangerous jobs. If someone gets into trouble and needs help, they all volunteer to come to the rescue. They do it down there, why not up here?" asked Willie.

"We'll see," said Patty, "We'll see."

CHAPTER XXVIII

PATTY ACCEPTED THE Superintendent's invitation. He entered the office and greeted Mr. Winegartner by saying.

"You sent for me, here I am."

"Yes I did. I want to talk to you about the demonstration in the yard. Got the word that the men will not report to work. You've got to talk some sense into these men before a disaster happens. You know that the security forces are away in training and not available, otherwise things like this stoppage would not have happened. I'm telling you to get the men back to work tomorrow."

"You released me of that responsibility a time back. I'm one of them now, just a worker. Once a fellow miner becomes a boss, feelings change with the men. They're for you at first; trust you, then slowly for some reason start thinking that same person is now a Company man. No matter what I did, that never changed. You drift apart from friends you've known for years just because you're a boss and not a worker. Soon you drink alone. Now, you and the big shots from Pittsburgh forget who and what got you here. Big Shots think they can run things better. The Company decides that since everything is going well they can take over. You decide you don't need people like me anymore and bring in what I call the "pushers." You get greedy and want more and more. Get the coal out and forget about the men and basic mining rules. More and more is demanded. The men work harder, do more, but get less pay. Another thing, sir, many of the workers have been in a war. They faced tough times, even faced death, so I don't see them backing off from you...."

"They'll be in another war," interrupted Winegartner who continued, " one they cannot win. Don't they understand we govern Ridge Valley and we own everything and you own nothing? We have the God given right to do as we see fit."

"Then they have nothing to lose even if I try to intervene. They believe they have already won by taking the big step by not going down the shaft. It takes courage for them to walk out and face an uncertain future. They are as one now and ripe for unionism, I'd say."

"That will never happen. Under no circumstances will anyone in the Grant Company allow a union to occur. There will be hell to pay," said Winegartner. With an icy look he raised his index finger and pointing it at Patty uttered loudly with a slight stutter," You have until tomorrow morning to get the men back or pay the consequences."

Patty sat looking at the man across the desk in disbelief. "This man is in deep trouble with his superiors if a walkout occurs," he thought. "Maybe he'll listen to reason."

"Listen, sir, for once help the miners get a fair wage, and a fair shake with the checkweightman, that's all they want. A bit of a raise and the men will be grateful and go back to work. They will be grateful enough to work hard in return. The extra effort will do more than make up for what you will pay out in extra wages. Don't you see the value in this? They will forget about a union and a lot of suffering and trouble will be avoided," said Patty.

"Mr. Moses will never, never accept men walking out, so do you think for one second he will offer a wage increase? You make me laugh," said the Superintendent with a chuckle. "Hell, he'll just get himself more diggers somewhere else."

"Yeah, Where?"

"Same place as before."

"Tried that, remember."

"This time it will be different. Plans are being made to bring in those workers families with them and provide housing. We've been considering this move since the last time. Only thing though, we never expected bringing em back so soon."

Patty got up from the chair, slowly walking to the door, now knowing the real reason for the Coal and Iron Police. They want to control the patch and stop any type of union organization and will lord over the people with the threat of evictions. The weather is getting on to winter; the earliest they would get replacements from the south would be the spring. "Surely," he thought, "after the last venture they would not bring blacks up north in the cold weather. Would they delay operations for up to three months to prove a point? Do they have other plans in the works? What happens now?"

Patty slowly walked out of the office without uttering another word. Through long years of working at the mine, by habit he returned his lamp. The Super followed Patty and walked him to the outer door to make certain he was leaving and to see what was happening in the compound. He did not notice four friends waiting for him around the corner. Although they sought shelter under the machine shop overhang, the cold misty rain found them anyway. Ignoring the conditions, Willie, John, Leroy and Billie waited for Patty to emerge from the super's office. The miners left the area a while ago to continue their exuberant celebration with drinks at Chubb's. The Negroes will retreat to the "Blue Jay's Club," a speakeasy located in an abandoned shack on the number two side. Some will seek out Tony for a loan to purchase a pint of Dolly's sipping whiskey.

"The Grant company people are cunning, and smart. They knew about the possibility of union activity, and already did some planning to replace us if a walkout happened. The organizers had to be watching. Those union men are smart also and waited to take advantage of a time when the security forces were away."

"Bet the Super got a big surprise." Said John.

"Yeah, and those yellow dogs will get a bigger one when they find out what happened," echoed Leroy.

" I'm getting a bad feeling from all this, Patty. You say the company knew of possible union activity and the union men were watching to make a move, and we are the ones caught in the middle. Looks like we may be caught in a no-win situation. Anyway, where do they plan on getting workers if we go on strike?" asked Willie

"From your part of the country again, Willie. Only this time they plan on bringing in whole families."

"That has been tried before, that's why I'm here. I might not come again, knowing what I know now, but surely not in the winter, no sir. Word has to be out about the cold. On the other hand I know Hawke is giving the ones who came back a hard time so some may try it again. If they come, it'll have to be in the spring."

They began to walk away from the mine.

"What are we going to do now, Mr. Driscall?" asked John.

"Well, I'd like to go to Chubb's for a drink, but I'm sure the place is full and most of the men there are probably drunk by now anyway. I think I'll go to Dolly's for a pint and then home. Got a powerful lot of thinking to do."

"Why not join me at the Blue Jay Club?" asked Willie.

Patty sent the young men on their way home and accepted Willie's invitation. All eyes centered on the two as they entered the door. Soon drinks were downed as Patty drank with the best at the bar. He was presented with a key and welcomed as a full-fledged member of the club. Today at this time Patty drank, ate and made new friends. Tomorrow would be another day, with unforeseen happenings. He understood miners, all of them. They work hard, drink hard, play hard and once challenged, fight hard. What he doesn't know is how much they, and the families, are willing to sacrifice to join in organizing a union.

"What the hell are they thinking about over there in Ridge Valley? Only a stupid jerk sends the entire force away for training at the same time. That's like sending out an invitation to union organizers and they jumped at the chance. They'll be hell to pay for this and we got to jump on this situation and jump hard. Hood, I want you to get to Ridge Valley as soon as possible and take over security operations there. Get on this. Look, if they are brazen enough to challenge us, and we back down, then why not all the other mines in the district? I want this movement squelched," loudly proclaimed J. G. Chambers, the head of security for the Grant Company from his office in Pittsburgh. "And get more forces. Get all you need to handle this."

Ridge Valley

"Things were quiet here, I tell you, there was nothing going on to give us any indication a walkout was imminent," said Lloyd Barnes.

"Answer me this, Mr. Barnes. How did the union organizers pull this off? These Hunkies could not do it themselves they had to have help. There had to be insiders who knew that the police force were away."

"Again, I'm not aware of any strangers around. Therefore it has to be someone the men can trust. I have a good idea who that person may be. We have the men out looking for any strangers who may be lurking about. We're also talking to the locals. Perhaps if we get enough booze in a few, they may talk. We'll come up with the answer, I assure you," said Mr. Barnes.

The force arrived back from a shortened training session with an attitude. Sixteen angry thugs were determined to find the culprits and "make them pay the price." Additional forces were shipped in from the Pittsburgh Industrial Company program, swelling the complement of company police to thirty-six. A number were immediately dispatched to the mine complex. They secured the area by setting up roadblocks and patrols. Others under the guise of sanitary inspectors entered houses at will, with or without permission of the inhabitants. The police had access to every inch of Ridge Valley. They also had a listing of every inhabitant living in the houses of the patch. Should they find a person not on their list, they would be dealt with severely. The force scoured the territory.

"Tell me, Mr. Winegartner, had you seen anything to give you any indication of the action taken by the miners?" asked Hood.

"No, nothing from my standpoint. Fact is, we were making a good transition in changing personnel at the mine. I thought it was going well. Apparently the union organizers were close by monitoring our every move. They saw the police leaving in mass and took advantage of their absence."

"I have a number of questions, gentlemen," said Hood. "Was this work stoppage as instantaneous as it appeared? How many organizers were involved? Are they still around the area? How did they communicate? Did they have help?"

"Like I said, we're checking the patch as you speak. We'll get an answer," said Barnes.

Determined to find those answers, the police descended on the patch like a horde of locusts. Their goal was to canvas all patch homes and the patch outskirts. Two of the thugs were assigned to enter the top row of houses on the number two side. They, along with all members of the police force, had a list of inhabitants living in every house. They were to assume that any person not on the list should be treated as a conspirator. That person was to be brought directly to the police station with no exceptions. Finding nothing to report in the first four houses, the two entered the fifth, the Johnson's. Leroy went to the Towns' to have Willie check and change his bandage. He left his father home alone. Rufus, since his encounter with the fever, rarely left the house. Early on, while recuperating he ventured to the Post Office in Fairbanks. Having forgotten his route home he soon quit going out of the house. He remained in his bedroom, leaving only to eat in the kitchen and using the thunder jug to relieve himself. He was not on the list in the tablet carried by policeman. The door was unlocked, allowing easy access for the two officers. One checked the downstairs and the basement, the other, going upstairs, discovered Rufus. His name was not on the list. Rufus wide-eyed retreated to a corner

"What's your name?" asked the officer.

Rufus, cowering in a corner, did not answer. He called for Leroy. The second officer heard the call and ran upstairs.

"You're going with us, get your shoes on, move."

Rufus refused to move, actually he was too scared to move, so the bigger of the two grabbed the front of his shirt and jerked him to a standing position. Rufus struggled to get away. A quick backhand knocked him to the floor. He began crawling trying to get to another corner. A kick to the side stopped his movement

"That's enough," said the big one. He held Rufus up while the other handcuffed him. They forcefully put on his shoes, and then guided him out of the door.

Leroy returned, surprised to find his father gone from the house. He double-checked each floor, then outside, looking, searching.

"Bull, do you know this man?" asked the lieutenant.

"Yes, sir, name is Rufus Johnson. Been around since his kind came to Ridge Valley from Alabama a while back. He lived in the boxcars,

Ridge Valley

worked a bit but then caught the fever. He was never the same since. He lives with his boy, Leroy, who works with John Ignatius on Patty Driscall's crew," said Bull, who began to talk freely about life in Ridge Valley. He told about others getting choice assignments but not him. How fortunate he was to be recruited into the Police Department and assigned to his hometown. Mr. Hood entered the room as Bull was speaking. He listened for a short while. He finally interrupted asking, "Bull, tell me how the men working the mine communicated with each other, and second, were there any union men here when you were working?"

"No union people around that I was aware of, never any talk about that when I was working. The men get together at places like Chubb's, maybe they talk there. I'm not sure if union people were there, I doubt it though."

"There seems to be a lot going on and we have no clue who is involved. For example, how did this guy, Rufus escape detection from our lists of inhabitants? If there is one, are there more we don't know about? Anyway it's obvious that Rufus is of no value to us so let him go. We need to concentrate on union organizers and leaders among the miners, not people like him"

Mr. Hood informed the Pittsburgh office that he would remain in Ridge Valley indefinitely. He would take charge of security operations. He was determined to take care of those responsible for the work stoppage. Furthermore, he would help get the mine operating with whomever is willing to work.

Rufus exited the police headquarters in a confused state and walked toward Fairbanks. The post office became his destination. In a brief moment he recalled the route and his post office number. He got the mail and met Leroy, who was looking for him, at the creek bridge. Anxious to show what he did, Rufus produced the mail and handed it to Leroy. Happily he took the items and then led Rufus home.

A habit of being early risers found most of the miners in Ridge Valley awake before dawn. Many awakened in an alcoholic stupor from imbibing heavily the day before. Not having a job, they loitered near home until the urge for a drink called. They then ventured to various watering holes. Men congregated at Chubb's, the Blue Jay Club and at Dolly's. Tony set up a lean-to type of canvas covering over a wooden table. He added a bench and some chairs so the men could linger, talk and purchase Dolly's brew. Tony was readily available for anyone who wanted to add his name to the book.

The company police were nearby observing who went where and with whom. Others were at the shaft overseeing the construction of the nine-foot tall fence around the mine complex. Placed on top of the tipple were powerful searchlights. They would illuminate the compound throughout the night. Only authorized personnel would be permitted to enter the fenced area. A list of men working inside the fence showed that Jerrold, Jerry Burdock and Shaun O'Rooney were in the lamp house. They would remain, under threat of their families being evicted, to prepare lamps for new workers. They were not permitted to leave. Food and sleeping arrangements on a cot in the lamp house would be their home until released by the Superintendent. The Coal and Iron Police had complete control of the Ridge Valley mine.

Rumors began spreading between policeman, and residents in the patch that work stoppages were planned for neighboring mines like Orient and Fairbanks. Although untrue, word spread to Mr. Hood and Captain Ross that Patty Driscall and Willie Towns were seen in these mining patches with known union organizers. Believing these reports to be true, Mr. Hood announced that, "I want these two shadowed by our best deputies day and night. I want to know who they meet and talk to. I'm convinced that they are the key to happenings at Ridge Valley. Somewhere, I tell you, yes, sometime they will slip, and we will be waiting."

Throughout the morning, despite the heavy drinking, no mention of the time and place for the miners meeting with union officials at Glover's barn was mentioned. Two rules never to be broken in the patch were to never take another man's job and never reveal the intentions of the mining brotherhood. Failure to learn of the miners' intentions frustrated company leaders.

"Things are too quiet, and I don't like it," stated Hood. "The police force is useless…bunch of goons and not a brain among them. It's too late to plant a spy in the group; they'd spot it right off. They have to meet sometime soon to get organized, but where or when? That Driscall fellow is sure to be a part of any meeting. Make certain he is watched at all times."

"Well," mumbled Winegartner, "how about that Willie fellow, or this young man, John?"

"We know about this Willie. But who is this John you're talking about?"

"He's a young one who is looked after by Patty and seems to always be where things are happening. He spends a lot of time with the Negro boy, Leroy. I think it would be worth your effort to tail that one also."

"Get someone on this John right away," Hood ordered the captain.

The day after the walkout became a standoff with the company police and the miners. Both parties eyed each other from a distance. The locals drank the morning away and by afternoon began to leave their watering holes. Individually or in small groups they meandered home, or to the post office and some went down to watch the policemen struggle to put up the fence. John stayed at home most of the morning helping his mom with chores. Around noon he decided to visit Jerry who always had something new to say.

"He's not been home since yesterday," said Jerry's mom. "I've been told he has to stay at the mine and work. He is not allowed to leave or he'll be fired and that means we will lose our house. That's what this deputy man told me. I'm deeply worried about him, Listen if you hear anything please let me know. All the stories one hear…I don't know what to think anymore. I wish my husband was here, but." Jerry's mom stopped talking. She wiped her eyes with the bottom of her apron and left the doorway.

John walked away and, for a second, thought of going over to see Leroy, but decided against it and started walking home. He saw some deputies he had never seen before standing around. He wondered how many new police were added to the force.

"They seem to be everywhere," he thought.

" Sarge, I heard something I thought I should report. I think the miners are planning some kind of meeting soon. I listened through the front door of my mom's house and heard the neighbors talking.

I don't know the exact time or place but it could happen in the next day or two."

"Thanks, Bull. Appreciate your report. Good job. I'm sure the captain will be pleased. In fact you did such a good job that we need you for another assignment. We want you to keep an eye on this old friend of yours, his name is John, John Ignatius."

"Yes, I know him, what do you mean watch? And for what?"

"Where he goes, what he does and who he sees. Anything out of the ordinary you report to us immediately."

John changed his mind. When he reached home he informed his mom that he was going over to the other side. He told her not to hold supper for him since he would be late coming back. No mention was made of his going to the proposed meeting at Glover's barn.

"Please be careful, and stay away from that Blue Jay Club," his mom said worried about him picking up the drinking.

"Don't worry, mom. Going over to see Leroy."

"Just be careful, saw a lot of deputies milling around the store. Stay away from them."

Just then Bull exited house number three, down the path from John's house. He spotted John walking toward him. To avoid being seen by John, he hurried out of sight, around the corner of the house and watched as John walked towards the store. Instead of going in, he continued walking past the store and headed toward the number two side of the patch. Bull followed a short distance behind. He asked a fellow deputy to join him in shadowing John, a move he learned at the training school. They could trade off watching him, particularly in the open. John stopped at the bridge and took a moment to look over at the fence-building project going on at the mine complex. He then continued up the road. For the moment he was oblivious to the fact that he was being followed. John now approached the first row of houses on the lower section of the hill.

"Hey, John, whatcha doing over here?' yelled a friend, Tom Gregory, that he knew from school days. Tom walked over to chat, causing Bull and the deputy to stop short of the bridge. They pretended to check the bridge and began pointing into the creek. John and Tom continued talking on the road for about ten minutes.

"Funny," said Tom, "those two have been at that spot since we met. John, if I didn't know any better I think those two are following you. Are they after you for some reason?" asked Tom, giggling.

"I don't know why they would spy on me, maybe it's you they're watching," replied John laughing.

"Listen, we're kidding, but you may have something. Let's find out what they're up to…you head down to your house and I'll walk up the hill to Leroy Johnson's. We'll find out if they're following me or you," said John.

They shook hands and parted company. Bull and the deputy departed from the bridge and followed John. He walked down a path away from Leroy's home, now across the alley circling back to Tom's house and back up the hill. Bull and the deputy followed his every move.

Frederick Moses, head of the Grant Empire, left for his vacation in his resort above Johnstown. Word about the work stoppage and possible union organizing reached him as he arrived at his estate in the mountains. He tossed the message aside, thinking it was just a blimp, a small problem in his coal region soon to be settled by the Superintendent. Spreading word of other stoppages in the region concerned Mr. Moses but he would remain at his vacation resort. Later, more announcements about additional shutdowns came in quick order. Infuriated, Mr. Moses decided he had no choice but to return to his office immediately at Fifth and Carnegie in Pittsburgh. Before leaving he ordered his secretary to send notices to Andrew P. Anderson, District Superintendent, M. L. Blanchard, South Regional Supervisor, Winegartner, Harold Hood, Alexander E King, Director of the Pinkerton's and John D. Felts, the CEO of Felts Security, to meet in his office that same afternoon.

"We will deliver a quick direct response to the workers at Ridge Valley. They started it and they will suffer the consequences. I want replacement workers there within weeks. I want the leaders identified and I want heads to roll. I want those people to know and understand that the H. C. Grant Company will not tolerate a union. I want Ridge Valley to be a lesson to all other patches that we run the mines, and any who do not follow our direction will be dealt with severely." Mr. Moses paused to sip a drink of water then continued, "Hood, I want you to return and reestablish the security with additional men from Felts and Pinkerton. M. L., don't we have plans to handle this? I realize the move happened faster than we expected."

"They caught us off guard, but not for long, sir. We will get Scottdale humming for accepting new recruits and have the mine operational within weeks," interrupted Mr. Anderson.

Since daylight saving time was not yet in effect, darkness arrived early in the Valley. Once the sun disappeared behind the high ridge in the west, the area darkened quickly. The patch would be engulfed by midnight blackness early in the evening and remain that way until morning. The dark conditions were perfect. Movement of men throughout the Valley would be difficult to detect. After darkness fell, patch men, individually, and in small groups, avoiding company police, meandered from homes, speakeasies and boardinghouses toward the woods and beyond the hill behind the third and last row of houses. To avoid detection, some walked far beyond the patch to enter the farm property. Others walked to Fairbanks that was the opposite direction from the barn. Once there they doubled back to the Glover farm. Beyond the fence they were on private property that was out of bounds to company agents. John and Leroy proceeded from the back of the Johnson house over a hill undetected to the barn. Bull and his partner walked the path in front of Leroy's residence, waiting for John to end his visit. Once John exits the Johnson house, Bull will again follow him wherever he goes.

It is difficult to picture the collection of humanity gathered inside the Glover barn this night. A most perplexing question facing organizers was how to gain cooperation among the gathering of various ethnic groups. Many different nationalities including Polish, Magyar, Lithuanian, Italian, German, and a number of other ethnic groups were part of the scene. Each specific group gathered together in various parts of the barn speaking in their own tongue, waiting for the proceedings to start. It will be difficult for one to communicate with the gathering because of the many different languages represented.

Ridge Valley

John, Leroy and Billie sat up front on hay bales waiting with other younger workers for the meeting to begin. Patty arrived with Willie and a few other old timers. They sat in a far corner, waiting.

A man from the Bohemian contingent broke the murmurings among the groups when he got up and began to speak. He talked loudly in broken English, his roar reverberating off the walls of the barn. Those understanding his meaning nodded in agreement, others sat looking at him trying to find meaning in his speech. Individuals in various ethnic sections who understood the language got in front of their contingencies interpreting what the Bohemian said. Once the Bohemian finished his speech, a person from a different nationality would arise and speak to the crowd. Interpretations once more rendered by spokesman in their native tongue filled the room. The men not knowing the language listened intently, leaning forward with blank expressions, attempting to understand what was being said. The speakers to this point were all stoutly built, slow in speaking and making gestures with each word. Then came the Italian speaker, who jumped to the center of the room. Seeing him, a dozen fellow countrymen arose to their feet. They cheered him on as he physically emphasized every word. With gyrations and stamping of feet, waving arms and a fast utterance of words his own cheered him on as all other non-Italians watched in amazement. Just as fast as he started his harangue he quickly stopped, waved to the crowd and retreated to his seat.

The barn was filled with men from the patch, waiting in anticipation as the union man entered and walked to the middle of the floor. Raising his hand for silence he strolled about, eying the throng. A man thirty-five years old, he wore the jeans of a worker and the shirt of a gentleman. A greatcoat, opening in the front hung down to his knees. This tall, clean-shaven Irishman, who claimed attention with his good looks and ease of movement, walked in a circle, eying the crowd. The hat he carried he now tossed to the middle of the floor.

"I respectfully ask for each and every one of you to carry the torch for those that came before you." He continued, "I pray that you honor your fathers and grandfathers who paved the way for us to be here tonight. I admire you for your willingness to fight for your rights, fight for your family, fight for your fellow workers." The men moved to the edge of their seats as the orator continued with his presentation. He urged them to join together for the benefit of all. He appealed for solidarity. Words flowed continuously like water rushing over a waterfall. Those that understood jumped to their feet gesturing approval. After a period of time talking, the Irishman brought all to a standing frenzy by stomping on his hat. "This is the way we will stomp out injustice, and bring honest pay and fair working conditions for all."

At the conclusion of the talk the interpreters in front again voiced their understanding of the speech to the respective groups. Obviously some misunderstanding was evident for after a vote was requested, most agreed with a positive vote, but a small number held back.

"On one side in my head rings the fine words of the labor man, but the other side rings with worry because without work, the family has no food on the table," stated a voice from the German group.

"I'm one to agree with you, Irishman, and I like what you have to say, you are here now when things go good, so tell me, where will you be when things get rough?" questioned a younger worker.

"They're probably looking for us right now, trying to find out who's at this meeting," said another miner.

The Irishman answered," I'll be here with you all the way, don't back away now, we need all of you to stay together."

"Those who ain't got family to feed can make it, only got themselves to worry about. I have a big family, ten to feed, where do we get flour, lard and such till things are settled?"

"We already owe the Company Store more'n we can pay back in a couple month's work. Tony doesn't have enough money to loan all of us to pay em back," brought a chuckle from the Polish group along with more moans from others.

Trying to quiet the guffaws moans and murmurs of the small but loud group the Irishman countered with, "The Company needs you. Who's going to do for them if not you? Yes, many of you are deep in hock at the store but remember, they will allow you to charge as much as you like. They need you and they also know you will pay all you owe. Remember, I say again, they need you and the higher wages we will get for you will make up for any losses."

Back and forth they went, statements and counter statements for the better part of an hour. The words of the labor leader began to lose their luster, doubt crept into the room as the liquor drunk earlier wore off and reality crept in.

"What was once a certainty is now all messed up? They all were sure when they walked out, but a lot are not sure now. All have to be as one because a split in the ranks will only divide the loyalties of the men and then the company will divide and conquer. Pit one against the other, and we will lose. Someone they know and trust has to talk some sense into them and turn this around, fast. It will take years for another to light the torch for a union if the flame is distinguished now. The power of a company to hold a man hostage because he is dependent on the company for work, and the company store for food, the company house to live in, the company preacher, the company doctor…the company everything is against the Lord's teaching. I wish I knew how to explain the need to stand up and be counted as a man should," said Patty to Willie.

"You can do it, you just said some of what needs to be said and you are someone they all trust. How about you doing some talking to this group?"

"I can talk mining, not good at this."

"Just tell it your own way, that will do, and they will listen."

"Let me think on it a second."

CHAPTER XXIX

HAL BORSCH DID his job. He followed Patty as ordered by Mr. Hood. Built short and rotund, he looked like a miner and, to perform his duty, dressed like one. He shadowed Patty until he lost him in the woods, and then found him again crossing a fence entering Glover property. Ignoring the law he set foot on the farm and followed a few of the patch men to the barn. He took a position just inside the door where he watched the proceedings. He listened to the Irishman struggle to convince the crowd to accept a union. Hal became sure that the speaker lost the initiative and was ready to leave thinking the case for the miner's organizing was lost.

"I'll stay a few more minutes just to be sure," he thought.

"I may need your help," Patty said to John.

"You going to talk, Mr. Patty?"

Patty did not answer but moved to the center of the barn floor. He picked up the flattened hat. He turned to the Irishman saying, "You did fine, but the men are a bit unsettled. They need to hear from one of their kind, let me try." Patty walked around in a circle, twirling the hat, looking at the crowd. He waited for the mutterings to die down. It was clear to him that a number of the workers wanted to follow the Irishman, but on the other hand a large number were not ready to cross the line. Nothing would happen unless all were in the fold. Patty twirled the hat, walked, watched and waited.

John watched and waited, now concerned for Patty because the murmuring never subsided. He decided to act.

"Look," he shouted to a surprised Leroy, "there's Patty, Patty Driscall. How about saying something, Patty?"

John walked to the center of the room and shouted again, "Want to hear Patty, men? How about it, Patty?" John slowly lowered his raised hands, the crowd calmed down enough for Patty to be heard.

"Hear me as I tell you that I have been in this coal region all my life. I began working down below when I turned fourteen. Been there ever since. I'm now fifty-five. That means a lot of years to survive underground. I have been fortunate. My father and grandfather were miners. Both died before their time from miner's asthma. My brother died in a slate fall, and not to long ago an explosion took most of my buddies."

He paused and took a deep breath. A rattle in the lungs came with a cough. He gathered himself and started talking again.

"You don't last as long as I have without your Lord watching over you." He tossed the hat to John, then slowly removed his coat and placed it on the floor. Rolling up his shirtsleeves exposing his arms, he held them up and said, "Take a look, you will see the purple marks of healed cuts left from falling slate. I also have them on my back and legs and I know all of you have the same. My hands are as brutalized as yours, my arms hardened muscle from years of using a number four shovel. Like yours, my body aches when I arise in the morning. We live with the black spit we cough up from our lungs everyday. We see the troubled look of our women who suffer inwardly without complaint. The only relief they feel is when we arrive home safe from our day in the mine."

The barn air increased in its warmth and stagnation from the many bodies in the room. Patty gasped for air, coughed, took a breath and began talking again.

"You and me are like any worker, we need a fair wage, an honest wage, and not only the money one brings home, but what the money will buy. Even with steady work we end up owing the company store. Are we better off now than when we started?" A number of whispered "No's" came from the crowd.

Hal was impressed by the way Patty held the interest of the group. He watched and listened as Patty's words were interpreted to the various groups. They all listened intently. "I can feel it. They heard the Irishman, but listen to this man," thought Hal Borsch.

"Let us consider our fate, say compared to the horses and mules at the stable. The stable boy is told to never cut feed to the animals. If the horses or mules need food they get it, if they need oats, get it. If they need hay, get it, special feed, get it. Now take us, powder, buy it, shovel, pick, buy it. They give us nothing and we earn our keep, and pay the price."

Patty wheezed as the warm stagnant air along with the hay dust began to affect his breathing. Gasping for air he labored to catch his breath. He coughed hard bringing up blackish spittle he deposited on the barn floor.

"Patty, sir, are you all right?" asked a concerned John, who walked to his side. At a wave of Patty's hand, he stepped back as Patty began to speak again,

"I have been there, through it all and so have you. Every day, morning to night, we are down there," pointing to the floor, "working in water, breathing bad air and coal dust. We do this because this is our living. We ask only for a tiny bit of recognition and fairness. We are not greedy. Let the owners have theirs. We don't want any of what belongs to them, only what we work for and deserve. Just give us ours and we will continue to do our best. Just give us ours is all we ask."

The throng hooted and hollered in unison, "Just give us ours! Just give us ours!" Patty looked exhausted, coughing, wheezing and gasping for breath; he bent over fighting for air. The atmosphere in the barn was close.

"This talking is worse than loading coal for a ten hour shift," thought Patty. Leaders in front of each ethnic group held up their hands to quiet the men. The crowd quieted down, wanting to hear more but Patty was spent, his worsening asthmatic lungs let him know it was time to stop.

"I am old," Patty started in a low raspy voice. The crowd leaned forward. He paused, clearing his throat, then said, "I have had my say, I am done," Patty paused as "No's" murmured in the crowd. Holding his hands above his head, "Please listen as I tell you that it now will be up to the new boys, the young ones, to carry the load. You can hear and see that I have sucked up too much damp and coal dust over the years. We had our day and I had my say it's time now to hear from others, and make a choice."

John walked away with Patty.

"Are you okay? Are you feeling all right, Patty, sir? I've not seen you like this before. I didn't know you had the asthma sickness."

"Every miner my age has it, John. I think the hay dust activated the spell. It's kinda heavy in here, hard to breathe. I need to get some fresh air."

"C'mon, let me help you out the door."

"No, John, you stay and do some talking. It's time someone like you had a say and I know you talk well. Your dad always said you had what it takes." Patty slowly walked away, leaving John standing in the center. Leroy edged himself up next to John. The circle of men parted, letting Patty pass toward the door. Hal Borsch not wanting Patty to see him left his position and mingled into the crowd.

"Say something to the crowd, John."

"Me?"

"Yes, you. Patty told me if I need advice to lean on you. Heard stories from others about your dad and he said you are a spitting image of him. The men respected him and in turn will respect you. C'mon they will listen, go talk to 'em."

Mostly a listener in life, John felt uncomfortable with his friend's request. "Why would anyone listen to me?" he questioned silently.

The delay caused restlessness among the crowd. The Irishman tried but had no effect in stopping the grumbling of the discontents in the gathering.

Shouts of dissention erupted from one side of the Italian contingent while voices of agreement arose in the other section. Gestures from those for and those against drew the attention of other ethnic groups. The Czechs and Poles joined in their own discussions for and against. Heavy accents in slow deliberate speech resonated in sharp contrast to the Italians. Other tongues from English to German to Austrian showed the diversity and separateness of the crowd. The direction for unionization within the gathering was unraveling.

Ridge Valley

John ran to find Patty. He found him outside the barn, under an eave that provided protection from a steady rain. He was coughing and heaving deeply trying to catch his breath.

"The meeting's not going well. It's breaking up. You got to do something to get 'em back. That Irish fella is trying but he can't hold on to 'em like you. We're going to lose the men fin's you can't talk to 'em. Sir."

Patty, bent at the waist, struggled to breathe, wheezing, coughing up blackish phlegm from deep in his lungs. He tried but could not speak. The rumble of dialects from inside the barn became more pronounced. Patty righted himself, grabbed a surprised John by the arm and led him into the barn. Breathing sporadically, he stopped, regurgitated a glob from his lungs as he splattered a mouthful of spittle on the floor. A drivel of pink appeared in the small puddle.

Patty righted himself and pulled John through the crowd to the middle of the floor.

"Listen to me," the union man shouted, but the multitude ignored his plea. He yelled again,

"Hear me, hear me, quiet please. Patty Driscall is back and has something to say. Listen, look who's back, Patty is here." A member of the Italian group saw Patty and shouted to the crowd, "BE QUIET!" and pointed to Patty.

Hal Borsch walked out of the barn. Smiling as he thought, "They will never get together on a strike action, there is nothing to worry about." He adjusted his collar against the rain, donned his hat and began to walk toward the fence. A short distance away he stopped. He then cocked his ear and listened. He looked in astonishment toward the barn. The loud bickering talk was gone, now a bit of a murmur, then quiet. The rain pelted down as Hal quickly made his way back to the barn.

He didn't hear Patty in a raspy voice calm the crowd. He didn't hear him ask for forgiveness for his "asthma attack." He didn't hear him in a grating voice introduce John.

"He is talking for me and he is the new and young. I talked about the young workers taking a leaders role. Here is one of them, please listen with your heart and soul." Tired and drawn, Patty slowly drifted to the side, leaving John standing in the middle of the room. Hal Borsch walked through the open barn door.

John began speaking in Polish, switching to Slovak, then some English. Each ethnic group listened intently when he talked in their tongue. Others interpreted. They listened when John said, "We are all one, we are men, we all work hard, we believe in God, we all value our families, we are one, and we are family." The crowd listened, spellbound at the words of the young orator.

"H. C. Grant Coal and Coke Company owns all you can see from one hill to the other. They own everything in the valley in between those hills. You and me, we live on those hills and work in a deep hole in the valley. In essence the company owned and ruled us, body and soul…until now." John hesitated, letting the interpreters speak to their respective groups.

"Beginning now, this very moment, we take back our lives, our hearts, our self-respect and our soul. Together with determination, will power and grit we will triumph. We will walk with pride…we will walk like a man." The men nodded to each other in agreement. John held up his hand for silence, the crowd obeyed.

"One last thing, they will try to take away our togetherness, our manhood, our friendship, never … NEVER will we relent."

Hal Borsch once again started for the door, intent on leaving. He heard enough.

"The company is in for a long slog, this young buck got them back together again," thought Hal as he stepped out into the rain.

John went on to eloquently cast a spell of acceptance for the cause. The group ignored his youth as the message John presented inspired beyond his expectations.

"We want four items to be considered for approval by the company before we return," John emphasized then added forcefully, "those four are: better wages, a person to represent us at the weight station, final elimination of the Grant hump and finally a God-granted right to join together in a mine workers' union. I now urge you to register here and now for union membership." The union agent quickly distributed registration cards for the men to sign. Most of the crowd either signed or made their mark.

Ridge Valley

As the men left, Leroy, Willie, Billie and Patty joined John in a corner of the barn. John and Leroy decided to try and make contact with Jerry at the mine. The others would accompany Patty on the walk home. He needed assistance because of his breathing problem.

"Jerry's mom hadn't seen or heard from him when I talked to her. I promised her I would try to sneak down and see him. Now seems a good time to try. I don't think the "Yellow Dogs" will be looking for us to be coming, plus the rain will help to keep them inside," said John.

The route taken led from the barn through the woods to the tree line where they exited and crossed the Republic- New Salem Road. Well above the heights they advanced toward the slate dump. Mine waste deposited from the mine formed a lengthy hill behind the tipple. The man-made hilly slope provided clear passage down the slope that ended at the fan house. Ahead sat the machine shop and the lamp house where Jerry worked. Rain pelted down as the boys made their way to the rear of the lamp house. A back window had been left open and the door left ajar.

"Corporal checking doors, who's in charge in there?" a deep voice announced through the window then added, "why is this door open?"

"Jerry Burdock, sir, sorry but we never lock that door."

"I want you to come out here, NOW!"

Leroy, wide-eyed and open mouthed in a semi shock, stared at John whose deep voiced Corporal-pretending routine brought Jerry in a rush to the door.

"John, Leroy, my God, how did you get here?" asked a shocked Jerry.

"Jerry," John whispered, "is there any one else in there? What about Mr. Shaun?"

Jerry remained speechless for a few seconds then said, "No, no one else is in here, I'm it. They sent Mr. Shaun home, said he couldn't take it without a drink. They made me stay since I'm the only one who can charge lamps. How did you guys get here?"

"Won't say, Jeer, your not knowing is for the best. Anyway, your Mom is worried about you and asked us to check on you, so here we are. Are you okay?"

"I'm doing fine, so tell her not to worry. I get decent food but I still wish I was with you guys."

"No, we need you here where things are happening. Need all the information you can get. What can you tell us?"

"They went south again, talk about busting this up by using Negroes again. That's all I know now. One of the cops keeps an eye on me; threaten to evict my family if I leave. They think I'm the only one who can do this job but anyone can do it. You know me John, I'll keep em going. Hold on a minute, time for them to make their rounds. Be right back."

"They got a new bunch of goons that makes Bull look like a baby, so watch yourselves with them, they're a nasty and a suspicious bunch, and they snoop around to watch what I do. I act like they need ole Jer and let them believe they can't do without me. Hold it, there he is again."

Jerry was gone this time about ten minutes while Leroy and John huddled against the wall. They tried but failed to protect themselves against the drenching rain.

"He's a lazy one, that big bohunk. I think he keeps coming back in to get out of the rain. Get this; he wants a lamp to wear on his cap so he did not have to carry a light. I told him it would blow up if it gets wet, and he believed me."

"Jerry, please don't fool around with these guys. We need you here. Keep your eyes and ears open. We'll be back to check with you from time to time."

"How will I know when you are coming?"

"Yes, well, next Monday night about ten o'clock turn the lights off in the back room. That will signal if the coast is clear. We'll contact you only if the light is off you got it Jer?"

"Got it, and remember to watch yourselves, those goons are mean."

"You be careful yourself, be real careful and keep your head, keep your head."

The two retreated back up the slate dump and climbed the slope about half way to the top. Sliding down the side they retraced their steps, ending up at the back of Leroy's house. They entered the back door unseen. John exited the front door a short time later and said his goodbyes loud and clear so anyone near could hear him departing. Bull never strayed from in front of the Johnson house the entire evening. He heard and watched John leave. He followed John home, convinced that he was at Leroy's the entire evening. Bull decided to spend the night with his family. He would report to the Captain the next morning that John spent the entire afternoon and evening at the Johnson's.

CHAPTER XXX

COMPANY POLICE MAINTAINED their distance from the patch people, guarding the fence around the mine on horseback, and keeping a watchful eye for any strangers in the territory. They patrolled all roads into and out of the patch.

"Anyone not known or familiar is to be regarded as a union organizer. Anyone you don't recognize must be brought to the headquarters immediately for questioning" was the order of the day. "For now, keep away from the workers, let them simmer, get restless, and get in debt at the company store. Pittsburgh office says to let them charge all they want to their account. They will owe so much that they'll have to come back to work it off. They'll be back sooner or later, mark my words," announced Captain Ross to the morning roll call meeting of police.

"The new members of the force not familiar with the area will be teamed up with the regulars," continued the Captain. "I understand that we'll be getting more manpower from as far away as New York and Chicago. Fact is, they may be on their way now as I speak, so get these new guys acquainted with the patch area quickly. We'll work with the new ones when they arrive. If you have no further questions, except for Hal and Bull all others report directly to your post."

Once the room was cleared Mr. Hood came straight to the point. He began with a direct finger-pointing question to Hal Borsch.

"Did you follow Patty Driscall and have knowledge of his whereabouts the entire evening yesterday?"

"Yes, sir, I did."

"And?"

"I think he had an idea that I was following him because he tried and succeeded in giving me the slip, but I found him, at Glover's barn with most of the miners from the patch."

"They had a meeting at this farmer's barn?" asked Hood.

"Sure did, and it was a big one."

"How in the hell did all those men congregate at one place and we not know?"

"It was pitch black last night, heavy rain at times, and they had the advantage of knowing where they were going and how to get there unseen. Most all took the long way around but I figured it out. I was at the meeting the entire time."

"Well?"

"Well what?"

"Goddamn it, Mr. Borsch, quit playing with me. WHAT happened at that meeting?

"First of all the place was full of the most diverse group of men ever assembled in one place. Groups of people not fully understanding each other's language all gathered together to decide whether to go for union membership or not. Sometimes it seemed they all talked at once, gibber jabbering one time and verbally fighting the next. The scene was almost laughable except for the seriousness of it all," said Hal Borsch, who rose from a seated position and began to stroll about the room.

"Gentlemen, believe me when I tell you that getting these men to continue this walkout is, well, a miracle. First a union organizer spoke and did little to convince the mob to agree to anything. I was convinced that they could never get a consensus. There were too many splinter groups in the crowd to combine into one. Then this fellow Patty Driscall arrived on the scene and he rallied the men. He was doing well but lost his voice. He was choking and gagging so much he had to leave. I also left thinking it was over."

"How the hell did they get together then? Someone had to convince that "motley crowd" as you call them to continue the walkout,"questioned Mr. Winegartner, who entered while Hal was talking.

"You'll not believe this, I left and got a short distance away then heard this cheer. I went back of course and heard this young man give the most elegant talk. He rallied the crowd to stay the course."

"Who was that man?"

"A John Ignatius."

"NO WAY, you are dead wrong," retorted Bull walking toward Hal, pointing his finger and sputtering." You are wrong. I followed him the whole night. He went to Leroy Johnson's house and stayed there the entire time. He never left that house until after ten o'clock. Then I followed him home."

"Sorry, Bull, he gave you the slip."

"He was at the Johnson house. He never left. I watched the place all evening."

"Bull this Leroy fellow, is he a Negro man, uuumm, say about eighteen? A scar on his forehead?"

"Sumbitches, they going to pay for this," mumbled Bull as he sulked back to a corner.

The next day Superintendent Winegartner joined a delegation from the Southern district in a meeting at Fifth and Carnegie in Pittsburgh. Isaac Baldwin led the Northern District. Frederick C. Moses himself ran the meeting. After a discussion on past happenings leading to the work stoppage, the assemblage then concentrated on their next move with the men and union organizers.

"The company has no intent whatsoever of accepting the workers' demands. We will break this effort to unionize with all the strength we can muster. First, by paying the nineteen twenty scale, we will employ anyone that wants to work. We will maintain an "open shop" in our mines. Each one will be treated independently. That way you can pit one against the other to fill employment needs. Each mine has the authority to hire as many armed guards as they deem fit. Remember…we have the law on our side, all the way up to the Governor. I have already sent a telegram to the Federal Secretary of Labor to seek an injunction to compel the men to return to work. Lastly, you know we planned for some time for a contingency like this. Presently recruiters are combing the South for replacement workers. I expect them to arrive in a couple of weeks. This time they will have their families with them, and houses to live in. I tell you we will break the backs of these hunkies that started this mess. They won't think of striking again for a long time," stated Moses. He answered questions, and then closed the meeting. He asked those from Ridge Valley to stay.

"Gentlemen, I am not going to mince my words. From all indications this stoppage began in Ridge Valley. Seems to me that you were not attentive, not aware of happenings in your mine district. You let your guard down. The men in your mine are heroes to miners all over the territory. What we do now, and in the immediate future at Ridge Valley mine and in the patch there will be followed closely by other miners. Now listen to me. You will find out who are responsible and get rid of them. Hell, get rid of all of 'em if you have to. I want that mine in operation. Do you understand gentleman? No excuses. I want a message sent out that we will not tolerate a union and any person joining one will be dealt with severely. Get what company police personnel you need and do the job or get out of the way and I'll get someone else. Good day," said Moses.

The meeting adjourned. The Ridge Valley leaders left in silence.

Reality began to set in as the Uniontown Evening Standard newspaper trumpeted the news that "The Grant Coal and Coke Company will not meet or take part in any meetings with union personnel regarding the work stoppage at Ridge Valley, or any other mine that followed their lead. This occurrence is an illegal action; therefore, we consider those jobs open. We are hiring anyone available for employment," said L.R. Houseman who added, "These will be permanent non-union jobs and if needed, housing will be available." Across Fayette County, Pennsylvania, thousands of concerned miners began to buttress themselves against a long hard fight.

"According to the newspaper the company intends to blackball us, Leroy," said John.

"What do you mean, blackball?"

"Means no one will hire you and you'll never have a job in the Grant district. Paper also says that they are going to hire new people to take our place and what we are doing is illegal."

"Sounds like we'll be sitting on your porch for a long time. I've been thinking about home, John. You know I've had no word from my mom for months. I been sending letters to the pastor like my dad told me but I got no answer back. Got me to thinking when we saw Jerry and he said they are recruiting down south again."

"Yeah, that's what he said,"

"Like I said, John, I've been thinking, and since there'll be no work I thought of getting on that train that delivers those southern workers and taking it back home. Billie is thinking about going with me to see his mom too."

"What about your dad? Someone's got to look after him."

"Mr. Towns said he would look after him."

"Listen, Leroy, I'll help looking after your dad. Just tell Willie to let me know what help he needs and consider it done."

"Thanks. I really appreciate the offer, but I need to ask you for another favor."

"Sure, Leroy, just name it."

"I want to go with you the next time you visit Jerry. I want to find out when that train will arrive so I can make plans."

"No problem, next Monday we'll head down to see him."

John went back to reading the paper and passing on the news to Leroy. None of the news was good, especially the stories about the work stoppage and the threatening remarks by company leaders. Finally turning to the last page the boys got a laugh from the Gashouse Gang comic strip.

"John," called his mom from inside the house. "I need some flour from the store, can't find your brother, would you mind going? I'm in the middle of baking and ran out."

Leroy walked with John to the company store. He would continue to his house on the other side of the patch. John bid his "So long," and entered the store. A Union Supply Company Store contained separate and specific areas for particular items. The left section contained soft goods and sewing supplies. The back left contained an elevated office manned by the ever-watchful Mr. Joshua. Large tables in the center section were stacked with work clothes. The butcher shop was located in the right back. The confectionary department was located in an alcove off the front door. John headed to the packaged goods counter that occupied the entire right side of the store. He ordered a twenty-five pound bag of flour. The attendant, an elderly lady, took the order to the back storage section. She returned and told John "The clerk needs help getting the flour from an upper shelf. I couldn't help him. Could you go back and give him a hand?"

John went around the counter then to a doorway opening to the back.

"Hi, Corky, so this is where you work, nice to see you. You know it's been a while."

"Sure has, things have changed a lot since I last saw you."

"You can say that again. Jerry working in the mine office, me in the pits, you here and Bull a Company Policeman."

"Aren't you worried John? I mean things don't look good, strike and all. Mr. Joshua ordered me to stock up on worker's needs. Bunch of new men a' coming soon, I guess."

"I appreciate your concern but I have to stand up for fairness. Can't go on living hand to mouth. Got to stand up and be counted. Anyway, since I'm here I'll help you get the rest of those flour sacks down".

Bull, determined to make amends for his failure to follow John earlier, now watched him with keen eyes. He promised Captain Ross vehemently that if given a second chance, he would shadow John totally and completely. With a severe warning, the Captain gave him the chance.

"Mess up, and you are done," stayed with Bull as he observed John enter the store. He stationed himself directly across from the entrance and never took his eyes off the front door. He waited and watched, and waited and watched.

"John went in there a good while ago, should be done shopping by now. Damn, did he know that I was tailing him and lit out the back door? No, maybe he's getting a big order. Hey, a lot of people went in after John and came back out. I got to go in, even if he sees me I have to risk it, I have to know where he is," Bull told himself.

Bull began running toward the store. He cleared a small-sloped terrace leaped across the streetcar tracks and bounded through the door. He surveyed the inside of the store, now going from one department to another. No John. Quickly he moved to the alcoves on the right, then to the left side, no John. He checked the entire first floor, no John. Panic began to set in as he made his way up the stairs to the second floor where furniture is sold. Looking around, behind and under furniture his effort was futile, no John. Beads of perspiration dotted Bull's face as he bounded downstairs, two steps at a time. He looked again, retracing his steps. His actions aroused the curiosity of the clerks and Mr. Joshua in the office. Fear now etched Bull's face. Wait, one last place to look; jogging he moved around the counter, and entered the back room. He stopped short, gazing at John, who had a sack of flour on his shoulder.

"Why are you in here? You're not allowed back in this area. Who's in charge? Where's Corky, what's going on here?"

"Hi, Bull," said John.

"What's going on, Cork? Why is he back here?"

"He's helping me out. You okay Bull?"

Leaving his office Mr. Joshua followed Bull into the back room; perplexed he approached Bull and said, "What's the trouble officer?"

"This man said he is helping to get flour sacks down, helping or not, he should not be in the back of the store, ever," said Bull.

"I needed help. I asked him, that's all, sir."

"You," pointing to John, "take your sack, go and finish your order," said Mr. Joshua. John honored the request. While waiting at the counter for the clerk to process his charge, he heard a heated argument coming from the back room. Finally completing the transaction he shouldered the sack and left the store. Heading home, he chuckled at the recent happenings, yet became concerned that Bull was following his every move. "I wonder who else they're following? I may have to talk to mom and let her know that police folks may be watching the house, and I better talk to Patty about this," thought John.

Darkness came early on this cold winter Monday. Jerry, expecting a visit, made every effort to get information to pass on to John. However, John had grave concerns whether he should take a chance on going to see Jerry. He had promised Leroy, but things had changed. He was being followed and did not want to take a chance of going. His friend would have to go alone. John remained at the Johnson's as Leroy took the same route as before to the lamp house. Since Bull was outside, John walked by the window often so that he was easily seen. Leroy made the trip and returned.

"Jerry said that some men, don't know how many, are coming in from Southern Ohio or perhaps Kentucky. They may arrive before the recruits from the South. The labor agents are having a difficult time getting men to come; none are from Carbon Hill. He heard them say that a couple of the agents got beat up pretty bad there, so they left the area. Mine owners are fighting to keep their workers, causing recruiters to go as far away as Mississippi for farmhands, sharecroppers and general laborers, Jerry said. The company leaders from top to bottom are mad as hornets and swear to get those responsible for starting the walkout. He heard they're getting more goons to add to the force. That's about it. I didn't want to stay longer than necessary so I said my goodbye and left. Oh yes, he asked about you, and I told him why you didn't come. Of course he had a few choice words for Bull."

"Leroy, did he say the recruiters by passed Carbon Hill?"

"Yep, that's what he said."

"Whatcha going to do, then? I mean, how you going to get back home?"

"I'm thinking my best bet is to catch a streetcar to Brownsville, catch a train to Pittsburgh, then I'll jump one to Alabama. May take a little longer but no other choice left as I see it. I'm actually thinking of leaving as soon as tomorrow or the next day."

"Sounds like you may not be able to leave later, so the sooner the better. I may not see you before you leave. Since I'm being followed I better stay away so you can leave without being noticed. Be careful, and good luck. And Leroy, give my best to your mom."

They shook hands, embraced, and John left. He felt alone for the first time in his life. For certain he would talk to Patty about the news from Jerry.

A few days later, two freight cars rumbled into the spur behind the company store. The cars caught the eye of some of the men lounging in Chubb's bar. The men watched as a curious bunch exited the cars and began relieving themselves beside the track. They were dressed in baggy coveralls that hung on their large frames. Floppy full brimmed hats sat on longhaired, fully bearded faces, causing all to look like they came from the same family. Some wore high top clodhopper shoes while others had no shoes at all. They ignored the cold as they gathered around a deputy who was pointing toward the Company Store. All began moving slowly in that direction. The men inside Chubb's left the bar and started toward the store. The assemblage of the two groups happened outside the back entrance.

"Where you SCABS come from?" shouted a Chubb man. "Go back where you came from. You're taking another man's job, Taking food from his children's mouth. Only scabs do that. We got nothing against you unless you go to work, and then watch out. Remember these Company people are using you against us and we have to protect what is ours. God knows you would do the same for your family. Go home where you came from. Don't let them rule you. Be a man," shouted a man from the Chubb group.

"We're here to work. We were told they needed help and promised good jobs. We're here to work, not take your jobs, nothing was said about that," came a reply from a freight car person.

"That's what you're doing, taking our jobs. So it be best if you head back."

The deputy stepped in front of the group along with six other officers. Bellowing above the chatter the deputy said. "You're not taking any jobs, these boys laid down their tools and quit. And if they don't stop harassing you boys and get out of the way, we'll do it, SO MOVE, and I mean now."

The Chubb group closed ranks and held their ground. Someone in the group shouted a question.

"Where you all from?

"Kentucky."

"We would NEVER go to your town in Kentucky and take work away from you. All we ask is for you to do the same for us."

The remark apparently hit home. The Kentucky men talked in a muffled tone amongst themselves. The deputy urged them to follow him through the strikers and get the supplies they need at the store. Other policemen moved about the group saying things like, "You came for a job, they quit, get good pay, stay and work, don't let them tell you what to do."

The prodding was ignored as the Kentucky men continued to discuss the situation. Finally a spokesman for the group calmly said to the deputy that they did not come to cause trouble and they did not come here to take another man's job. Without another word said, the Kentucky men ambled back to the train, climbed into the railroad cars and closed the doors. Talk was over, a decision made.

The Chubb men, expecting a fight, stood quietly and watched the men leave. Happy and relieved that they stopped the intruders from taking their jobs, they retreated to Chubb's to celebrate.

"We showed em," said one miner. "Sure did," said another, hoisting a drink at the bar. Back at a corner table, Patty sat alone watching the festivities. He raised his drink and thought, "Yes, you showed 'em all right, did well. Next time you better be prepared because these company boys will not forget what happened today."

After downing the shot and beer he left the bar and was seen by the deputy in charge of getting the Kentucky group to the store.

"That's it, there is my excuse, Patty Driscall. I'll blame him for those Kentucky boys not staying." The deputy quickstepped then jogged to tell the Captain his lie.

CHAPTER XXXI

LEROY MADE ARRANGEMENTS with Mr. Towns to care for his father. He agreed to take Billie with him to Carbon Hill to see his mom. As planned, they left in the afternoon via streetcar to Brownsville, and then caught a freight train to Pittsburgh. Leaving the car at the freight station, they roamed the yard trying to figure out the next move. Day turned to night, then to early morning. Finally taking a chance, they jumped a freight car with the Norfolk and Southern logo on the side. They were on their way. They made a bed from straw left in the car. Tired from the long trip the boys lay down and promptly went to sleep as the train ambled along.

New members of the Coal and Iron Police arrived in Ridge Valley. Two trucks unloaded twenty-four of the most menacing looking policeman the company could find.

"Review records from Felts and Pinkerton and hire the biggest and most intimidating people you can find. Hire and deliver them to Ridge Valley as soon as possible," said Hood to the recruiters.

In the late eighteen hundreds tension and turmoil reigned in the coalfields and steel mills in Western Pennsylvania. Trouble was so rampart that local sheriff's departments were unable to provide basic security. To solve the problem, around nineteen hundred the Pennsylvania State Legislature, through constant persuasion from

Bob Menarcheck

coal and mill owners, authorized the creation of what became the private Coal and Iron Police. For one dollar, the state sold commissions conferring police power to mine and steel mill operators. This decision gave police power to whoever was hired by the companies. Furthermore, enforcement of the police power was conducted at the will of the operators.

They succeeded in following Mr. Hood's request. The Pinkertons and Felts found the hoodlums and thugs requested and sent them to Ridge Valley.

"We now have the numbers to control all the territory within the patch. Those men who have been here the longest and know the area will be assigned patrol duty around the mine and store. They will also check the railroads and streetcar stops for intruders. The second wave will guard the roads leading in and out of the patch and occasionally check the woods. Under no circumstances will labor organizers or newspaper reporters be permitted to enter Ridge Valley territory," announced Mr. Hood to the captain.

"What about my men?" asked the leader of the new arrivals?

" We'll need them to check houses and for eviction duty. Have them settle in and double up at the boarding house. We'll get going and assign their work areas in a couple of days."

The couple of days arrived and eviction notices were presented. The twelve chosen were given ten days to leave or the company will move them out. Included among the twelve were the Driscall and Ignatius families. One notice was rescinded. A Magyar woman was expecting a baby soon. The family was permitted to stay until the birth, plus two days.

"John what are we to do. We have no place to go, and what about the girls and of course your brother. He can't handle much as it is, let alone this. My God what we going to do?" said John's mother while wringing her hands.

"It came quicker than I expected, move out of our house in ten days, not much time. I've got to think we got no truck or any way to move our furniture or our stove, even if we did, where to go?" replied John.

Panic set in across both sides of the patch as news spread about the eviction notices. Who was served, when, how long before they have to leave? Over fences, in local bars, in homes and at the Company Store, all talked about what to do if an eviction notice was served to them. Rocco Saracina, a feisty Italian, minced no words when he announced to the Chubb's bar patrons,

"I'll fight them, by God, they're asking for trouble for sure if they come after me." Those present shook their heads up and down in agreement.

"That's telling 'em, Rock, I'm with you on this one," echoed others at the bar.

Some had relatives to call on in other patches to take them in, but what about the furniture and belongings? Most had large families; friends and relatives didn't have room even if they wanted to take them in. What about food? The eviction notice said, "Once you leave, neither you or any member of your family, under penalty of the law, will be permitted to enter Company property."

"This means we will not be able to go to the store." Fear and trepidation struck mothers' hearts with the thought of not being able to feed the family.

"My man gave his life in that mine, my first son hurt bad under a fall and my next son is working there to keep the family going. What else do they want from me?" a neighbor sobbed to another across the fence.

"I don't care where we go, I can do anything, and face anything but my family deserves a decent meal." The neighbor answered. "I get the bones free from the butcher at the store and make my own noodles. Using vegetables from the garden, I make soup; we eat soup all the time… What else can I do?"

Dolly, hearing about the evictions from Tony, immediately headed for the Ignatius house. On the way she pretended not to see three of the latest police recruits eye her move down the alley. They liked what they saw and once she returned, one of them would follow her to find out where she lived.

"I heard the news and came as soon as I could. I am so sorry for you, you must be worried sick, and I will help. I'll take the girls to live with me, at least until you get settled," Dolly blurted out excitedly then added, "Why are they doing this? Why, John? Why?"

"They're planning on bringing in new workers and their families. They need houses for them, and by doing this they're trying to break our will, scare us into breaking ranks."

"What are you going to do, Mrs. Ignatius, John? Do you have any plans, a place to go? Like I said, I can take the girls."

"No. We got no plans. Dolly, may I talk to you outside? Mom's pretty upset, fretting, crying, let's go outside."

The two girls, seeing their mother crying and shaking, tried to comfort her. The brother sat silently in the corner. John followed Dolly out the back door. They walked around the corner of the house where no one could hear their conversation. They both saw the three company policemen move a few steps from an open view to behind the outhouse. They were now out of sight.

"I saw em when I came, acting peculiar. I know most of those boys by selling my whiskey to 'em but I didn't recognize these three. They must be new," said Dolly.

"I like your offer regarding the girls and may have to accept, but I got to know about Tony? I have to know because of the girls." John hesitated as he covered his mouth with his hand, now grabbing his jaw with thumb and forefinger…

"Yes, Tony is at my house a lot. He is all I have, and God knows I needed somebody when the explosion happened, and he comforted me then and, well, we are close John, that's all I'll say. I know all the talk about us, and it's true, maybe some day we'll make it permanent," said a blurry-eyed Dolly, who added, "Well there it is, John, yet my offer stands. I will take the girls and will never disclose anything to them between Tony and me. John, the girls have been at my house when Tony was present. They got along and I think he likes them being around. Don't let his looks fool you. Down deep he's a nice person. I can attest to that because he has been nice to me for a long time now."

John listened as he looked in the direction of the outhouse where the three policemen were last seen. Occasionally one of the men peeked around the corner and then quickly moved back. He thanked Dolly for offering to take the girls and said he would let her know soon. He told her the three men were still in the alley and was concerned for her safety on the walk home.

"Don't worry about me, John," she shrugged her shoulders, then said, "Like I said, I've been selling those kind liquor for a long time. I handled the others, I can handle them," she answered in a cocky voice.

Dolly left and John watched one of the three follow her home. Once there, she flicked a porch light to signal John that she arrived safely. He returned to the kitchen. He needed time to ponder his situation. He had a lot to think about, been through a lot in life already and survived. John wished he had someone to confide in now…he needed answers to unanswerable questions. He could take care of himself, but he had his family to consider. There were so many things weighing in on his mind. He never felt so confused as thoughts rushed through his mind in rapid succession but nothing seemed to connect. He was mentally exhausted. He needed rest. First thing tomorrow morning he would call on Patty. He would know what to do.

"You want us to break through the line of company guards, on foot, at Ridge Valley and reach the miners?" questioned Richard "Dickey" Gilford a union organizer.

"Yes, that's exactly what I am saying," stated John "Jack" Brady, Union President of the Southern District, who added, "Now, when you get through turn over the paper contracts to a trusting miner to distribute and collect. We have plans to go tonight with as many as we can get in the field. That Irishman who held the first meeting at the Glover barn got some signed up but was intercepted by company police and they confiscated the lot. Worked him over a bit. He's still out of commission but did mention one man, a Patty, as one to contact. Problem is, he can't remember his last name. Listen, if caught simply give up and they will probably arrest you. We will bail you out of jail as soon as possible. Okay we go in one hour."

The organizers departed the Brownsville office and drove an old Model T Ford to the outskirts of Ridge Valley. Under the protection of darkness only one man made it through the company guards' line. He avoided company policeman that seemed to be everywhere. He dodged them for over an hour, remaining under cover. Eventually he found himself near Chubb's, and saw a miner exiting the bar. He approached the man and thrust a package into his arms. "Give these to Patty," he said, and disappeared into the darkness. The miner a non-reader took the items with the intention of giving them to Patty Driscall first thing in the morning.

John got up early the next day. He immediately tended to the kitchen stove. His head was pounding from lack of sleep. He tossed and turned, thinking, most of the night. Shaking the grate, he loosened the ashes used to bank the stove the night before. Some hot coals remained. John added coal; a fire resulted, heating the surface. He placed a pot of water on top and exited to visit the outhouse. Returning, he sprinkled a container of ground coffee into the boiling water. He removed the pot from the stove to allow the brew to steep. He buttered a slice of homemade bread, poured himself a steaming cup of coffee, sat at the table and ate.

"This good bread, good coffee, good home and good family is all I need. I think that feeling is the same for everyone else in Ridge Valley. The only thing missing is to earn enough money to afford this. Why can't it be that way?" John thought.

He sat, finishing his coffee thinking, still trying to find answers.

A kick to the bottom of his shoe awakened Leroy with a jolt He sat straight up, and for an instant forgot his whereabouts.

"Better get ready to leave the car when the train slows. You don't want to ride all the way into the yard. Railroad dicks beat hell out of you if they catch you," said a hobo who entered the car up the track while the boys were sleeping. "Never seen you all before, you must be beginners. Anyway, there is a stew pot at this stop. Do you boys have anything to add to the pot?"

"All we got is hard tack," answered Leroy.

"Is that meat?"

"Well, sort of, I guess, yes, it's meat, dried meat."

"That'll add flavor to the stew. If you're willing, then follow me to the travelers' rendezvous spot across the tracks. You add to the pot, you get from the pot."

Arousing Billie, they exited the car before it entered the yard. They followed the new friend to a hideout in the woods away from the tracks. A large pot over a fire hung from a wire tied to a limb. Crude benches, mostly tree trunks, surrounded the fire.

"Add what you got, and you can share," said a hobo. The boys deposited about half of the hard tack into the pot.

"Tin plate, cup and fork over yonder. Clean and put back when you're done."

"Where are we?" asked Billie.

"Outside Chicago," came the answer.

"Isn't that north? Did we go north? We want to go south, to Carbon Hill, Alabama," said a startled Leroy, who added, "We're going the wrong way."

The new friend came closer to the fire where the boys sat. Because the stew disagreed with them, the boys ate very little of the concoction. That and worry about going north instead of south left them hungry and confused.

"We don't see many of your kind running the rails. Fact of the matter is you're the first I've ever seen. Most of 'em don't have to ride the rails; they work on passenger trains. You two should check the depot downtown; maybe pick-up a job there."

Without delay, they got directions and began walking. It took all morning to get to the passenger train depot. They were in awe when they saw the huge expanse in the building. Roaming around, they saw people everywhere. Negroes in skycap and conductor uniforms crisscrossed the premises, seemingly moving in every direction. Heading for the restroom, Leroy found more Negro's operating a shoeshine stand outside the facility. His kind was working everywhere. They found a custodial washroom where one washed while the other stood guard. The best decision made this day was to go down another flight to the track area. Maybe, just maybe, they would locate a train heading south. Not certain what trains to look for the boys roamed around the platform all afternoon hoping to find a train south.

"Well LORDY BE, I know you, and you," said a middle-aged Negro dressed to the nines in a conductor's uniform. "Let me think a second, Ridge Valley it was, and you are a Johnson and you a Towns," said a man wearing the nametag of Vernon Jefferson. They talked about old times and how each arrived at this time, in this place.

"So you want to go back to Carbon Hill," said Mr. Jefferson. "The Lord looked after you this day, so how you boys at washing dishes?"

John was followed as he left his house and walked to Patty's. The initial shock of the eviction notice wore off. Where to go and live had to be planned. John needed direction from the best man he knew. Apparently, so thought others. Four men were sitting on Patty's porch talking with him when John arrived. John joined in on the discussion.

"Found these on my doorstep this morning," said Patty, showing the union registration forms. "Don't know how they got here; too late to do much with them anyway." He placed the forms on the porch floor. They were forgotten about as each man discussed his move because of the eviction notice. Some would move in with relatives, a number of others, like John were still unsure what to do.

Unseen, Hal Borsch observed the meeting on Patty's porch through a spyglass. Besides taking names he was intrigued with the bundle of papers Patty showed the men. He waited until all left, then walked up to the porch. He reached through the barrier and snatched a sheet from the bundle. Glancing at the form, he stuffed it into his pocket and walked away.

"One of the helpers from Glover's farm came by after getting the mail from the post office and asked for your brother. Mr. Glover needs some help and wanted to offer Mike some work. Said he would keep him overnight. He also said for you to come up and see him. Maybe he could use you if available," said John's mom.

"Mr. Glover probably doesn't know about all the happenings down here. Think I'll go up to see him. I'm thinking that if he can take brother and Dolly the girls, that leaves you and me," said John.

"I'm not for breaking up the family John, go see Mr. Glover, see what he wants, then we can talk about what to do next."

John took Mike and as Bull followed, they walked to the Glover farm.

"Sorry to hear about your ouster, John. Like I said, I'd take your brother in, he can share George's room with my hired worker. Only other thought is to offer you the barn, at least until fall. Be full of hay and straw then. Maybe all the problems will be over by that time.

Can't put a stove in there, too dangerous. Build a shed out back for that. The barn is fairly tight, not a house but it'll keep you out of the weather."

John didn't hesitate in answering. "We'll take your offer. You win the Ignatius family lock, stock and one last jar of piccalilli."

John smiled as he shook the farmer's hand. Before departing he made arrangements to borrow the horse and wagon to move the furniture to the barn. He let his brother stay and hurried home to tell his mom the news.

"Thank God," she said, "at least we have a roof over our heads."

Like a flock of crows sizing up a cornfield, so too the new police recruits from New York and Chicago sized up the people of Ridge Valley. Roaming at will, the vermin disregarded the law they were supposed to uphold. Initially they bided their time, exploring opportunities to take advantage of their position. Now the time came to exploit their position. It started with two of "New York's finest" entering a house; pushing aside the mother and children, they confiscated loaves of bread to take back to their quarters. Now entering another house, they took more food for supper. Other new officers began to follow suit by entering any house without warning. They took what they wanted, slapping down any that challenged their authority. Those preyed upon, fearing retribution, said nothing about the intrusions to neighbors or friends. They had no recourse but to suffer in silence or face the wrath a second time. Besides, where could they go for help? The Company had local police and government officials under their control.

Even their own used the miners as fodder. The lack of solidarity from officers in the National Union took away help from miners when they needed it most. The struggle for power in the highest offices of the union organization caused wide dissention. Questions abounded about the type of representation and leadership within the union. Should there be one huge union or various groups of independent unions? There were pros and cons argued on both sides of this issue. In addition, efforts to get elected to top echelon positions took precedence over all else. The election process caused arguments within the ranks and took away efforts to challenge the coal operators. The union contained members whose demeanor stretched from conservative to radical and everything in between. Seeking positions of power created an ego so big it caused a rift among top administrators. They ignored the patch people and failed to help in securing political and financial assistance for the miners.

The coal company public relations firms took advantage of the dissension in the union's leadership ranks. They succeeded in turning the public against the miners. Issuing claims that wages should be reduced rather than raised appealed to the public, who had no understanding of the civil war raging in the coalfields. They depicted the miners as fanatics who brought their radical attitude with them from Europe to America. The coal baron propaganda machine succeeded in depicting the miner as a troublemaker. "We offer a job, place to live, and a place to purchase food and still they want more money. Our only recourse is to offer jobs to another who wants to work". With the union leadership in turmoil there was no way for the miners to tell their side of the story. The workers in the patch fought the battle to survive in a degree of isolation.

Once again an impromptu meeting took place on Patty's front porch. More men were present than could be accommodated, so the group decided to move to Chubb's. Walking past the Coal and Iron Police headquarters on the way, they aroused the curiosity of the officers and men inside. They saw Bull and Hal Borsch, with what appeared like notebooks probably charting names.

"I tried to find a place, but it is hard with six kids and a wife," said one attendee.

"Same here, me too," said another and on it went.

John told of his luck in finding a place in Glover's barn and his willingness to share.

"We need places for a lot of people. I suspect this is only the beginning; certainly more evictions will follow. The barn is a start but it won't do for the number of people we need to house," stated Patty.

Then out of the blue John blurted, "Too bad we don't have a disaster of some kind, and then we'd have all kinds of help. The Salvation Army would bring food, and the Red Cross would bring in tents.

Hey wait, that's it, don't you see? What we need are big tents. I'm certain Mr. Glover will allow us to put them up on his farm."

"We don't have much time, so we got to act as quickly as possible. John, you and a couple of others should go to see the Glovers and ask for permission to install tents on his property. If he gives permission, look around for a good spot to erect them. Some others and me will find a way to contact the union office in Brownsville to see if they can get us some tents. Pass the word to meet here tonight, say about six o'clock to see where we stand," instructed Patty.

The group exited Chubb's under the watchful eyes of Hal and Bull. They also drew the attention of the company leaders, who viewed the exodus from their quarters.

"Something has to be going on with those boys. They don't look like folks about to be kicked out of their house in a couple of days. That Patty guy, always in the middle of things, and there he is again," said Winegartner to Mr. Hood, Captain Ross and a Sergeant Polson.

"Mr. Hood, let's get Hal and Bull in here and do some talking."

For the first time miners visited Chubb's and did not sip one drop of liquor or down a beer.

"Mr. Glover said it was okay to place the tents on his land. He suggested a good spot on the south pasture where the parcel is flat and Redstone Creek runs close by. Good mountain water flows from springs nearby. Looks like a good setup," said John to open the meeting.

"Union office in Brownsville jumped on our request right away. They got word back from the Pittsburgh office of the Red Cross that World War I surplus tents are available. The only problem is that they are stored in a warehouse in Indiantown Gap, an Army training station in the middle of the state. It'll take three, maybe four days to get them here it could even be a week," announced Patty.

"But we only have two days left, will the company let us stay a couple more days?" said one of the miners at the meeting

"Do you think you can talk to that Winegartner fellow, Patty, and ask for a couple of extra days?" said another.

"I'll try, but don't get your hopes up. They get set in what they do and won't listen to nobody. But I'll try. Fact is the sooner the better. I'll go over right after the meeting and see what I can do.

"I want to talk to Winegartner," said Patty to a new policeman he did not recognize. It was Sergeant Polson who answered the door. He was new to Ridge Valley, the man in charge of the New York contingent. He did not answer but stood inside the door looking Patty over, finally saying, "Wait here."

Patty didn't wait. He noticed the superintendent sitting at his desk with others crowded around, all looking in his direction. He walked up to the desk and began speaking. He asked for a few days grace with the evictions and explained why. He concluded his talk with, "because of the children mainly, they didn't hurt anyone. You've got to allow time for the tents to arrive if for no other reason than the kids."

"You got a lot of nerve coming in here like that. We gave ten days notice; I would think that's enough time. It's hard for us to allow more time 'cause folks will think we don't mean what we say. Listen I have a better idea. You get the miners to go back to work and guess what, they won't have to move at all," countered Winegartner.

"Sure, I'll tell em what you said. Hell, I'll go back to work myself," Patty paused as those in the room gasped in unison. They smiled but the mood quickly changed when Patty added, "the terms are an eight hour day, an upgrade in wages, and pay by the true weight of loaded cars."

"You son of a bitch, you come in here asking for us to give you more time," angrily replied Winegartner, now pointing a finger at Patty and shouting, "Goddamn you! What else do you want?"

"We ask for nothing but a fair shake, if nothing else, give us a few days until the tents arrive."

"You get nothing, Take that back to your buddies," Winegartner said as he approached Patty; now standing face to face with him. "Soon we'll have all the workers we need. We'll get all the coal we need. Then I'll blackball you," he said punching a finger into Patty's chest.

"You greedy, filthy bastard. You'll do anything for money and make women and kids suffer for your own benefit." Seething, Patty grabbed the superintendent's shirt and shoved him away. Hood, Ross and Polson stepped in between the two.

"Get him out of here. You don't come in here and talk to me like that. Get him out, now."

"You're having your day, but ours will come, count on it," said Patty. He then turned and left the room.

"You going to take that from him? He's nothing," said Polson. "I told you we know how to handle his kind. All you have to do is give me the word."

"You got it, teach him a lesson, and Captain Ross, I want twenty five more eviction notices served first thing tomorrow. This time we'll give them a whole three days. See how Patty Driscall likes that one."

CHAPTER XXXII

"MY GRANDMA USED to tell Bible stories every Sunday afternoon at our house. She always finished by telling us what she thought heaven was like. Billie, let me tell you we're not in heaven, but we got to be awful close," said Leroy with a big smile.

Vernon Jefferson took the boys to the Chicago and Western conductor's combination dining room and worker's dressing room. The barber came and gave them a gratis haircut and they took a hot shower. Shoes were taken to the shoeshine stand for cleaning and a shine. The final touch was a dining room worker's uniform. The Georgia and Southern train would arrive in Chicago from its southern weekly run on Thursday. Arrangements would be made for the boys to work in the dining car as dishwashers for the trip south. Until then the boys would be provided meals taken from dining cars and they would sleep in the off track Pullman sleepers.

The train arrived and they worked as dishwashers on the return trip south. They would depart the train in Jasper, Alabama. Changing into regular clothes, they carried the uniforms in knapsacks. Now a fast walk up State Route Seventy-Eight on to Carbon Hill, then up Sandy Road and home. It was late morning when the boys reached the Y. Leroy began running and as he approached the front of the house he slowed, then stopped. Stunned at the sight, he stood in his tracks looking at the house, thinking he was in the wrong place.

Billie arrived at his side and they slowly began walking around the house. It became immediately obvious that no one was living there. The front screen door was gone, outhouse overturned, hole in the roof and the back door broken.

"Who is that there, is that you? Yes, you is Leroy," said a stunned Mrs. Jones. "My Lord, you have grown."

"My mom, the house, where is she, what happened here?" he asked, "What happened?"

"Come over to my house, rest a spell, eat, you must be exhausted." She put her arm around his shoulder and led him like a small child to her home. Billie followed.

"Your mom visited the church often and was there when it caught fire. Yes, she was with the Lord when she passed, is how we see it. We buried her next to her momma. She went there a lot to visit and talk you know. Now she can visit and talk all the time."

"The house, what about the house?"

"Big storm hit and did most of the damage. Some folks breaking into the place and doing damage," she quickly answered.

"My mom?" asked Billie.

"She's fine, just fine."

Leroy sat in stunned silence, unable to accept the happenings to his home, and that his mom died in a fire at the church.

Billie broke the spell. "You're going to my house with me. We can come back later if you wish. C'mon, lets go."

"God Bless you both, God bless you both," said Mrs. Jones as the boys left.

They walked up the road in silence.

"May I please speak, sir?" asked Bull.

"What do you want, big boy? Speak up."

"I heard about your meeting with Patty. He's just trying to talk for the men, that's all. I know he may have been out of line but he was the man who did most to put the mine back Sir, one more thing, throwing all those families out can cause some big problems. Some I've known all my life. Most have small children and they have no place to go. I know they are barely getting by. You have to take their plight into consideration, you have to."

"Does anyone consider my situation? I have more problems than those you talk about. My job is on the line. I've been ordered to get this mine operational or else. I offered Patty an out and he wanted less hours and more pay. He wants to tell me what to do. So who considers my plight?" sputtered Winegartner. Walking back and forth as he talked, he stopped in front of Bull.

"What about you? We brought you here, gave you a job. We thought you would help. Come to think of it you have not helped one bit have you? Now Bull, I want to know, from the way you're talking, whose side are you on, theirs or ours?"

Bull, shocked into silence, stepped back. He did not know how to answer, thus remained silent. Winegartner stepped forward, now face to face with Bull.

" I say again, FAT BOY, whose side are you on?" Bull's silence angered and frustrated the superintendent.

"Get out, you are done here. Not answering my question leaves me believing that you are not with us, or you would have said so. Now get this useless jerk out of here…now." Polson opened the door and pointed. Bull hesitated. Polson moved forward and grabbed Bull by the arm and shoved him out, slamming the door behind him.

"What you want me to do about him?" asked Polson.

"I'm not concerned about him, it's the other one that worries me."

"Well, don't worry any more, Mr. Winegartner, sir," smiled Sergeant Polson as he exited the house.

Bull walked up the path, both scared and confused. Like a man without a country, so too was he without friends in the patch, or on the police force. Even Corky turned against him since he almost lost his job over the incident in the company store. He wandered about with no destination in mind. Dusk settled in as he found himself in front of John's house. He stopped, hoping to see John outside. He bided his time, hesitating, watching, he could wait no longer. He approached the Ignatius back door and knocked. John answered the door.

"I'd like to talk to you, out here if you don't mind."

John put on a jacket and walked around the corner of the house so that they would not be seen.

"We been at odds most of our life, and although I disagreed with you at times, you always gave it to me straight and honest," Bull stated. He continued talking about his time in Detroit, and all the demands people made on him because of his size. How he tried and never succeeded in the mines. He now believes the company police wanted to use him only as a stoolie because he lived here. Bull talked on and on, John listened.

"My mom misses the old country and wants to go back. I guess that time is now. She wants to get away from all the things happening here. I made good money working with the police folks so we got enough to get to Europe and start a new life there. We'll be leaving soon. Before I go I wanted to tell you to be careful of that new bunch they brought in from New York. They are goons, John, the whole lot. They are bad and don't give a damn about nothing. Watch out for em, and tell Patty to watch himself."

They reminisced about old times and chuckled remembering the tussle they had and John losing his pop money. The evening wore on, time passed. They said goodbyes with a heartfelt hug. John wondered as Bull passed out of sight, how difficult it must have been for him to live up to all the expectations others placed on him because of his size.

"I hope you find what you're looking for, wherever you go," he mumbled to himself as Bull slowly walked up the path.

CHAPTER XXXIII

SERGEANT POLSON WAS also on the prowl this night. He wasted no time in rounding up three of his meanest and biggest bruisers. Huge men who intimidated others simply by their size and mean disposition, they knew the routine well. Pound the midsection, crack a few ribs, then kidney punches hard and deep enough to cause blood in stools and urine. Leave a man incapacitated but without marks that can be seen. Two others, standing by and hearing Polson give the orders, decided to keep close to the three to watch the show.

Patty left the meeting with Winegartner and walked directly to Chubb's. He told the men waiting there what took place with the company leaders and apologized for not getting additional time for the men to move their families. He was disappointed but could not give in to the cocky attitude displayed by Winegartner. Since tents wouldn't arrive in time, the only choice left was to construct some type of shelter over at Glover's. They had only two days so an early morning start was vital. Those in attendance would pass the word to meet early at Glover's barn with tools ready to work. Patty informed the group that he would go over to the Blue Jay Club and tell Willie and his buddies there about building the shelter and to be prepared for more evictions. Darkness was at hand when Patty left the bar and decided to walk up to Dolly's for a pint. He enjoyed having a drink at the Blue Jay place, but enjoyed it more if it was one he brought from Dolly's. He'd surprise Willie, who also likes Dolly's brew. He could handle any drink in his time except the rotgut they served at the Club. He was watched by the three assigned to "take care of him," as he approached Dolly's basement window. He found another person already there at Dolly's basement window waiting to be served. The man wanted a full pint but was short of money. Recognizing who it was, he told Dolly to give the man his full pint and charge it to "my account." Patty then got his pint and walked down the back yard around the outhouse and into the alley. He saw the man he helped buy the whiskey from Dolly walking ahead.

"Probably on his way to the woods above Glover's." he thought.

Patty stopped to take a swig, replaced the cap and returned the bottle to his pocket. Suddenly he saw a man, a big man in a police uniform, coming in a fast walk toward him. Then he noticed two others in the shadows on his right and left. The first man approached Patty. Without warning he grabbed Patty by the front of his jacket and swiftly raised a knee to the midsection. Patty took the blow, emitting a grunt, but sustained no damage to a hardened stomach, made that way from years of heaving a number four shovel. Patty reacted. He reached out and placed a chokehold around the attacker's neck. Patty squeezed hard, pushing the Adam's apple back into the throat so far that he cut off the man's air to the lungs. The Adam's apple lodged in the man's throat. The man weakened fast allowing Patty to move behind him. A quick jerk and the man slumped to the ground, dead with a broken neck.

The two waiting close by, thinking one would be enough to handle this man, saw what happened and closed in on Patty. They began beating him with their fists. Surprised at his strength, they reverted to nightsticks. Patty warded off the blows, taking most with his arms. He managed to grab an arm of one of the gorillas, placed it over his shoulder, lifted the man and flung him to the ground. The third continued swinging and caught Patty with a hard solid hit above the eye. Blood gushed from a huge deep cut caused by the blow. Patty responded by blocking the next blow, garnered an arm hold around the head, a quick and decisive twist, a cracking sound, neck bones shattered, and then the breathing stopped. Patty dropped him and immediately snatched the one still lying dazed on the ground. He lifted him to a standing position and delivered a sledgehammer blow that shattered the jaw. The policeman fell backwards hitting his head hard fracturing his skull.

Blood squirted from the gash on Patty's forehead. With every heartbeat blood oozed in alarming amounts from the wound. Patty was loosing blood fast, a lot of it flowing into his eyes.

The two who stood by to enjoy the show were shocked to see this man, Patty, dispose of their fellow lawmen. They recovered and moved in to join the fray. Patty, weakening from the severe loss of blood, was no match for the intruders. He blocked the blows he could see, but many found their mark. Blindly, he managed to grab one and with all the strength he could muster wrestled him to the ground. The other continued to deliver blows with the nightstick to the head.

Chicago John, after leaving Dolly's began walking back to his shack and was just a short distance ahead of Patty. He heard a ruckus behind and retraced his steps to investigate. Seeing his friend in trouble he grabbed a shovel and joined in the fray. The crash of solid flat metal against a hard surface reverberated in the alley between the outhouses. The one beating Patty stumbled to the ground from the bash to the head. Because the thick furry cap helped soften the blow the officer was not out but dazed. Recovering quickly, the grounded one stumbled to his feet and charged the unknown man. His right hand high above the head, nightstick in hand, he attacked. Patty's helper pulled back and with all the strength he could muster thrust the sharp end of the shovel like a spear at the charging man. The number four shovel, razor sharp at the business end from months of use, was rammed vertically into the front of the immense body. The thrust cut through clothing deep into the midsection imbedding the shovel from groin to chest. The man fell dead instantly in a pool of blood and oozing intestines.

Patty in his blinded state found the throat of the one he knocked to the ground but was weakening fast from the severe loss of blood. His last ounce of energy was used to place a death grip around the neck of this last opponent. Later, it would take two strong men a good while to pry Patty's hands from the dead man's throat.

After the struggle ended, Chicago John checked Patty but got no response. Scared, he left the scene.

Early the next morning Dolly took her usual stroll to the outhouse. She saw a ghastly scene of dead bodies in the alley. She ran back to the house to tell Tony. He in turn checked the men. Finding all dead he ran back to inform Dolly that Patty was one of the men and all the others wore the uniforms of Coal and Iron Policemen. He reported the information to a Sergeant Polson while Dolly ran down to inform the Ignatius family. John ran up the alley, viewed the scene then proceeded immediately to Patty's home to inform and comfort the family. Tony spread the news to neighbors, which spread like wildfire throughout the patch; many disbelieving what they heard. Those that could stop what they were doing and rushed to the alley. Soon a large crowd gathered at the sight; women were crying and the men cursing the "bastard yellow dogs."

"You're telling me that five of your policemen are dead?" asked an unbelieving Captain Ross.

"Yes, along with Patty Driscall."

"Patty, and five of your men. Where, how did it happen?"

"Up the alley a ways. A Tony fella said it must have been one hell of a fight."

"It wasn't supposed to be this way," mumbled the captain.

Winegartner was awakened and given the news. Shocked and angry he issued names of men to contact for a meeting, now, especially Polson.

A large crowd became a boisterous mob, angered and scared at what they saw. Shocked, women screamed, some wept, others prayed in their native tongue while patting their breast with the palm of their hand. The men angered at the site, shouted obscenities first directed toward the "yellow dogs" then to the "bastards" that ordered the attack. " We'll get even with the sum bitches," threatened a miner. More patch people arrived at the site shoving those in front aside in order to view the bodies. The small alley way was crammed with humanity. Someone continually checked Patty to no avail. Two strong miners finally succeeded in prying Patty's hands from

Ridge Valley

the neck of the dead policeman. John along with Patty's wife who insisted on seeing her husband came scurrying down the alley.

" Make way for Patty's wife," John shouted at the top of his lungs. "MAKE WAY, MAKE WAY," he clamored as he nudged people aside. The folks on the fringe of the crowd, hearing John's command parted to let them pass. Those that saw Patty's wife joined in yelling with John, "Mrs.Driscall's here, " MAKE WAY, LET HER THROUGH." All parted to let her pass. The throng went from a shout to a murmur then quieted down to an eerie silence. She approached the body and knelt down, as one of the men closed Patty's eyes and placed the dead man's hands on his chest.

At this precise moment, a small contingent of Coal and Iron Police sent by Hood, and led by a Corporal, approached the crowd on foot from far down the alleyway. The men in the crowd, seeing the police immediately moved to the outside of the throng. Coal patch kids that traveled in "gangs" divided along ethnic lines, roamed about, beyond the crowd. The gang members mirrored their father's feelings, despising the hated "pussy foots." The boys fought against what they felt was an unfair ten o'clock lights out curfew rule imposed by the company police. To show their anger and frustration the boys sneaking out at night threw rocks at the horses, causing them to buck and throw the mounted policeman. The kids were chased but never caught. To retaliate the mounted police irritated the youngsters by running horses over marble games or charging and knocking them down.

The gangs seeing the "yellow dogs " quickly scattered, to take positions on both sides of the road behind coal sheds and outhouses. The police force marched slowly up the narrow alleyway. Soon the marchers came into range and were showered with chunks of flying coal thrown by gang members. A good number of the raining projectiles found their marks, hitting heads, causing cuts, and drawing blood. The force had no place to hide. The force scattered, some chasing the boys while most of the others retreated back down the alley. The Corporal would report the attack to Polson who in turn informed Hood. He ordered the mounted troops to get ready to move to the alley, disperse the mob, and recover the dead policemen's bodies.

The crowd did not wait for further intrusions from the police. They wrapped Patty's body in a blanket and carried it to his house with the patch people following. The five other bodies were later recovered and taken, also in blankets, to house number three.

Both sides went their way, shaken, unbelieving, and unprepared as to what to do next. The shock would wear off eventually and anger would surface, but for now things like a wake and a burial for Patty would take precedence. A truce was needed, but none was offered or asked for. Patty was dead and he took five of their best with him.

"He went down fighting, he never surrendered," was the talk of men in the patch. A carpenter volunteered to make a casket, while others prepared Patty's living room for viewing the body. Later that evening a wake would honor Mr. Patty, and because of the continual flow of mourners, the wake continued throughout the night. Food and drink from friends and neighbors arrived in abundance. John spoke at the wake first and broke down when he referred to Mr. Driscall as his second father. He recovered and among other remembrances got a chuckle from the group when he told the story about the "extra bucket of food" for a first day worker. Willie Towns stood and expressed his deep sorrow for losing a dear and trusted friend. Many more followed talking about Patty.

With eviction facing families in two days, the church service and burial would take place as soon as tomorrow. John, who was to use the outfit from Glover's to move furnishings, offered the horses and wagon for transporting Patty's body to the church in New Salem. Quickly, almost everyone in the patch made preparations to view Patty's body. Many of the miners would stay the night and attend the church service the next day.

"What the hell happened, Mr. Polson?" asked Winegartner.

"I know that man was strong, real strong, 'cause I felt his hard body when I ushered him out. Solid like a rock he was. But I find it hard to believe he handled those five himself."

"Well he did, now what do we do?"

" Right now I say we stay put and don't do anything. We got to bury our men and then try to settle the force down after that. Men will be furious, don't know what they'll do to avenge our guys. I'll try to control them the best I can."

"You have to control them; we have new workers and their families moving in soon. We can't have a bunch of crazed policeman roaming the patch scaring the new men and their families. Get those new eviction notices out, move the patch people and get on with business as quick as possible. Stick to the schedule. We got to get the miners out of the houses and get past this stupid blunder," said Mr. Hood, who walked toward Polson and added. "Give them a day to mourn, then we move and be sure you keep your boys under control."

"I tell you that Patty had to have help…"

"Did you hear me? Polson?" interrupted Hood.

"Yes, I heard you," shouted Polson, "I'll try but," his voice trailed off for he knew that the thugs were already venting to "make 'em pay."

At dawn the next day, John and a hired hand from Glover's farm pulled up in a horse drawn wagon in front of Patty Driscall's house. A crowd, including many that stayed up all night to grieve, was waiting. They loaded the wooden casket onto the wagon and immediately began the long trip to the New Salem church about three miles away. The procession started with a contingent of men dressed in miner's clothes to honor a fellow worker walking behind the wagon. As it ambled on its way, more joined in on the march. Company police on horseback simply stood by and let the people pass. The procession gathered more mourners as it moved through Fairbanks then on to New Boro. Word spread beyond Ridge Valley about Patty taking on the thugs and they all wanted to pay their respects. He was viewed as a hero. As the wagon entered Buffington, more miners joined in on the march, swelling the numbers following the casket. Two company spies dressed in miner's clothes became concerned about the growing numbers following the wagon. The horses lumbered up New Salem Hill where at the top a right turn led them to the church. The big crowd filled the house of worship to capacity. The overflow milled around outside.

The company spies left as the followers entered the church and would report to Winegartner all was calm and orderly and saw no need for concern. The church service was completed. All attendees and the throng outside filed past the casket paying their last respects. A quiet seething engulfed the crowd, especially those that knew Patty from working with him in the mine. A last gesture of respect was shown when miners took turns carrying the casket to the gravesite. With the final blessing in the cemetery completed, the huge throng started to trek back to Ridge Valley. The men sent the women and children ahead as they paused to give a final salute to Patty. A man in the front shouted, "I KNOW YOU GOT A PINT ON YA, I SAY WE HAVE A FINAL DRINK TO THE MAN. HERE'S TO YA PATTY, MAY GOD REST YOUR SOUL."

Those who had a pint raised it in the air as a tribute to Patty, took a mighty slug, then shared it with those who were without. The toasts continued as the throng walked slowly back to Ridge Valley. The liquor changed the men from a quiet seething to a mumbling disgruntled group. They held their composure, at least to this point, but one could feel it all unraveling. Tension built more and more with every sip of booze. Alcohol that can loosen tongues can also turn a tense group of men from a silent fury into an out of control mob. The parade moved through Buffington where the first talk of revenge was heard and it continued into Fairbanks. The talk turned into intense shouts at the outskirts of Ridge Valley. The mass of men instinctively increased its stride and hurried directly to the mine. They charged en masse toward the entrance gate near the railroad bridge.

"Open the gate or we'll tear it down!" came the demand.

The guards responded with a counter demand for them to leave.

The mob pushed forward as company-mounted police arrived at the gate. One of the riders charged and knocked two men to the ground. The policeman was pulled down from the horse. A guard at the gate panicked, drew his pistol, and shot. Others guards followed some shooting into the air and a few shot into the crowd. Four miners were hit, none of the wounds serious.

That's all it took to put the mob into action. Without hesitation they blindly charged and overwhelmed all the sentries on duty. Their objective was now the mine complex. Guards who tried to stop the onslaught were pushed aside and warned not to interfere.

Out manned, they fled to police headquarters and reported the happenings to Mr. Hood in house number three. They left the mine unguarded.

The miners unleashed their rage on the fan house, machine shop and lamp house. Damage was quick and decisive, windows broken, fan damaged beyond use, cables cut and wires pulled off walls. Jerry heard the commotion and opened the door to investigate. The intruders charged by him to destroy a number of lamps in the room. Jerry, talking to some of the men he knew, learned about Patty and the eviction notices. Worried about his home he left to check on his mom and family. Assuring her that he was fine and perhaps home to stay, he went to see John and get updated about happenings in the patch. He found John at home, resting the horses. Upset at John's eviction, and Patty's death, surprised at Bull's leaving, Jerry pledged to "fight the bastards." He was brought to his senses by John who talked him into returning to the lamp house for two main reasons: "to allow his family to remain in the house, and to be where he could provide information."

The mob of men overran the mine and, once there, refused to leave. They encamped on the premises, vowing to remain until their demands were met. They were determined to stay and fight if necessary with rifles confiscated from the guards.

Hood, fearing the worst, ordered members of the Coal and Iron Police to stay away from the mine. Polson's New York police were to continue serving eviction notices and keep things under control in the patch. They would do just that, only under their conditions. Almost all of the men in the patch attended the funeral and now occupied the mine complex, only women and children remained in the houses. Chaos, uncertainty, confusion and fear permeated the women now being served the eviction notice. Intimidation by the thugs went from simple thievery to downright savagery. Having no protection, the women were defenseless against the vermin roaming Ridge Valley.

An Austrian miner who was holed up at the mine left a wife and children home alone. He had finally saved enough money to recently bring his family to America. The newly arrived mother and children did not speak nor understand English. Without warning the door of the home was forced open and four goons entered. Terrified, the woman retreated to a far corner of the kitchen. "Cossacks, Cossacks" she shouted.

"My children, I'll do anything you want but do no harm to my children," she begged speaking in her native tongue with hands folded as in prayer. A former felon turned policeman stayed with the women in the kitchen as two checked upstairs and one the basement.

"Please," she begged, "leave my children alone tell me what do you want? I'll do anything but do not harm my children." The thug did not understand her nor did he care.

Once the others were gone, the goon grabbed the women and dragged her to the parlor next to the kitchen. He forcibly threw her to the floor. She became dazed when her head hit hard. Once he had her down the man straddled the victim, tore open the top part of the dress and undergarment exposing breasts. He ripped off the apron then quickly grabbed and tore open the bottom section of the long dress. She started to recover and cried out trying to resist. A hard and swift backhand silenced her. The thug then grabbed the throat and squeezed to cut off enough air to subdue and scare the women. She was unable to fight off the huge thug who now had his way and forced the women to yield to his desires. Fearing for her children and struggling for air she muttered, "Cossacks, Cossacks, they are here in this country too. Please don't hurt my children." Now came the penetration along with the burning pain from tearing dry inner flesh. She suffered in silence, tears sliding down her cheek praying for her children and for " this Cossack to finish with her." The one who checked the basement returned and found his fellow cop completing the attack.

"Go ahead said the first," and the one from the basement quickly advanced toward the victim. The woman was hurting. She was torn inside, had severe burning from torn tissue, choking, fighting for breath she would have to endure the second attack and the excruciating pain it brought.

"We'll be back to check to see if you are out of this house. If not, we do it for you." The woman, still not understanding what was said, sat stunned and frightened, trying to cover up cowering in a corner.

Once the thug's left she dressed as best she could and crawled up the stairs to her children.

Walking to the next house the two who checked the upstairs were angry when they heard about the fun the others had.

"Goddamn you two, the next one is ours while you check the upstairs." They laughed aloud, now looking forward to serving the next eviction notice. Throughout the Ridge Valley patch the vermin roamed preying on the women. Resist and they would drag her out of the house and beat her in view of her neighbors. Forcing her back inside she would be raped. Many women were terrorized in this manner at the will of the Coal and Iron goons.

"They came on us all of a sudden like, and they kept coming. We ordered them to stop but they overwhelmed us, we tried but."

"But what? You had a rifle and a pistol, why didn't you use one?" asked Hood.

"We got a couple shots off, but like I said, they rushed in and crowded us against the fence… we couldn't move."

"What about the men on mounts? A horse could stomp em easy."

"Horses spooked when the shots were fired. With all the shouting they panicked. Mine threw me right off and then ran. Most of the others did the same. It seemed to me that the miners were determined to take the place and nothing was going to stop them. Funny thing, once they got our guns they passed us by and let us alone. I guess they were more interested in taking over the mine. Once most passed we came here."

"How many guns did they get?

"Don't know for sure, but the fact is, they could fortify themselves in that mine complex for a long time. Hell, a couple of em could climb the tipple and shoot anyone comes near the place."

"Captain Ross, I want you to instruct the entire force to stay away from the mine area. I don't want to cause any casualties by challenging them with guns, and I don't want to give them an excuse to cause more damage. I'll give the Pinkerton office a call and sort out our options."

CHAPTER XXXIV

LEROY STAYED WITH the Towns and spent time helping Billie with needed repairs to the roof, siding and porch. It took a week but he finally found the courage to visit his mom's grave. He had a difficult time accepting her death. Finding the cemetery in disarray he pledged to make the grave as nice as possible. The swamp had begun to reclaim the former church grounds so Leroy went to the Holy Gospel Church gravesite everyday, working to restore the cemetery. He often walked past his house to and from the burial site but refused to go inside. Time passed as he talked away evening hours with the Towns. The problems Bella and Mrs. Towns endured were never mentioned in conversations by Billie's mom. "Why cause more heartache and pain about something that can't be changed?" is the motto of all mothers. Isabella was a mother.

"I'm thinking about staying," said Billie. "Mom refuses to leave here so I feel I must stay and help her. I thought of looking for work at the sawmill, and doing some sharecropping. Grow peanuts and cotton. Maybe do corn, get a cow and some porkers. We'll always have food, even if I don't make a lot of money."

"Sounds good, but you know I have to go back. Dad is the only one I have now, and he needs care. I have to go back."

"You'll talk to my father about my plans to stay?" asked Billie.

"And tell him I miss him and hope he'll consider returning. Tell him his place is here and about Billie's plans. Tell him Billie could use an extra hand," said Isabella.

Leroy was gone more than a month and continually worried about Rufus. He did not want to delay his stay much longer. He would have to leave soon. The next morning Leroy walked to his old home, looked about, and then journeyed to the hideaway beyond the cornfield. The place was exactly the same as he remembered. He sat in his favorite spot, thinking of the good times in his home, now a broken down shack across the way. After about an hour he walked back to the house. He gathered some dry grass, and placed it under the back of the dwelling. He took one last look, and then lit the grass. The back wall caught quickly. He walked away never looking back.

Leroy would stay one more day, and then catch the train to Chicago. There would be only one dishwasher instead of two working in the diner.

Eviction notices continued to be dispersed throughout the patch. The deputies continued their intimidation of women and children in the process. The dregs that roamed Ridge Valley forcibly ravaged countless numbers of women and those that resisted were beaten into submission. The brutality continued unabated, as the ladies of the patch endured in silence. Their husbands holed up at the mine complex would never know about the attacks and suffering the women of the patch endured at the hands of the Coal and Iron Police.

With Leroy gone and Willie holed up at the mine, Rufus remained in his house alone. Willie, knowing he would be at Patty's funeral, left enough food, along with canned goods, to keep Rufus supplied for a good while. Rufus's routine was to stay upstairs, rocking in the old rocking chair most of the day, leaving only to eat and drink in the kitchen. To relieve himself he used the chamber pot at the top of the stairs. He was careful to always close the door to his room quietly after returning. Two deputies, who entered the house to serve an eviction notice on the Johnsons, forced open the kitchen door, shattering the silence. The noise from the back door being forced open caused Rufus to stop rocking. He listened; the quiet in the house returned as the deputies, finding no one home, placed the notice on the table and turned to leave. Rufus began rocking again alerted the cops that someone was at home, and hiding upstairs. They climbed the steps; the rocking stopped. The first deputy opened and walked through the door. Rufus stood hammer in hand, swung and missed. The surprised cop reacted quickly and easily pushed Rufus to the floor. Recovering, Rufus jumped up and thrust at the cop a second time. The deputy snatched Rufus's arm and twisted it behind his back, forcing him to drop the hammer. A swift move and Rufus broke the hold. The deputy, using his nightstick, rammed the end into the midsection. Rufus doubled over in pain holding his stomach, choking, now trying to catch his breath. The cop's mighty uppercut punch knocked Rufus through the open door. Rufus lost his balance and tripped over the chamber pot resting at the top of the stairs. Tumbling down the stairs he went, hard and fast tumbling head over heels. He landed on his head and neck at the bottom so hard he fractured his skull and broke his neck. He died instantly. The chamber pot tipped over by Rufus slowly bumped its way down step by step, spilling the smelly stinking contents all the way. The deputies walked down the steps, checked Rufus and found him dead. One policeman looked to make certain the notice was on the table.

"Let them clean up that mess," said one of the cops on the way to the next house. The next day the processing of eviction notices was called off until a settlement with the miners occupying the mine was finalized.

The head of the Pinkertons, Alexander E. King, was contacted and he stated that the best way to dissolve the situation in Ridge Valley was to use the State Militia. Property was seized illegally, and now it was up to the state to get it back into company hands. With all the financial support provided by the Grant Company, the governor surely would act without hesitation. He did so by issuing an order to assemble a military force that would immediately proceed to Ridge Valley and remove the intruders from the mine property.

The militia was backed with armored vehicles.

"We can't fight the government," the men agreed. "Our fight is not with them. Let it be known we will surrender to the militia only, not the company."

The final agreement negotiated by the commander was to have the trespassers give up their weapons and leave without punishment rendered. The Company would permit the wives and children to remain in the houses and not face eviction until after the miners left the mine. Before he left, the commander got a written agreement from both sides that there would be no retribution or he would return and settle the problem in the court of law. "I was put in charge. I had no intention of firing on our own people and the situation was settled peacefully," reported the commander to his superiors. "They handed in the guns and left the mine complex peacefully."

Company guards, along with Jerry, returned to the mine. Jerry would be busy cleaning up the lamp house and repairing broken lamps. Other company workers would have to inspect the premises and begin emergency repairs. Trudging home, the men faced a devastating scene. Furniture, including tables and chairs sat outside on streets and in front yards. Only the beds, mattresses and stoves were left in the houses until the men returned. The women, happy to see their husbands, hugged, kissed and cried at the sight of their husbands. Technically, the company felt that they honored their pledge, and now it was time to act.

The time from the first walkout to the present took all of two months. The initial waiting by the company for the strikers to come to their senses took time. The additional hiring of new police took time. The recruiting of workers in Kentucky that failed took time. The decision to fence in the mine took time. The recruiting down south took longer than expected. The negotiations between the militia commander, the miners and company took time. The calendar was well into March 1922 when the inhabitants of Ridge Valley would be forced to leave their houses. Fortunately, those about to be ousted welcomed the news that the tents had arrived. The company understood that replacements were on the way. The separation of management and employer was at hand.

John's family, along with the other original families ticketed for removal, were included in the negotiations between the militia and

Ridge Valley

the company. John, already having moved some items to the barn, escaped the onslaught of deputies removing furniture from the house. The men accepted the welcome home from their wives, but at the same time were devastated at what they saw. Now angry at abandoning the mine and surrendering the guns, the only recourse left was to relocate the families. The only option available was the south pasture on Glover's farm.

Accepting their fate for now, the men wasted no time and headed for Glover's to erect tents on the south pasture. The next day a steady flow of men, women and children, carrying household items, walked from the patch to "Tent City." The one item the women would not do without was the coal stove. It took four men over two hours to carry the heavy iron stove from the house to the tent. Later, stoves and "Hoosier" cabinets were taken apart making their trip easier. Pots, pans and the few dishes the families owned were packed in barrels and carried to the south pasture. John assisted where he could and helped move the heavy items on the horse-drawn wagon.

The children tried as best they could to lug clothes, or blankets to there new home. The Coal and Iron Police stood by and watched every move. The large rectangular tents housed two families per tent. Both would have their own accommodations, with blankets hanging in the center to provide some privacy. A common public outhouse was built for all to use just beyond the cornfield. An always-running spring, a short distance away on a ridge provided all the fresh water. A large flat area near a waterway called Redstone Creek was selected as the site for a communal garden. There were sixty-two family and seventeen one family tents making up the compound. Mr. Glover would have all the help he needed and more to work the farm. Before that however, the stoves would be reassembled, beds arranged and furniture arranged in the best way possible. One item of significance was the crucifix that was carefully carried from home to tent and placed in a prominent place. The other was a calendar turned to the month of April 1922

Within a few days, Negroes from the south arrived to work the Ridge Valley shaft. They would fail to see the no trespassing signs on trees and fences posted around the edge of the patch. Once evicted, anyone from the tent colony seen in Ridge Valley would be arrested on sight.

The new arrivals were ushered to the company store to set up an account and make purchases. The men would be outfitted with work clothes and tools. Many that occupied the houses recently evacuated by the tent people wondered why broken household items were strewn about in front yards. This would be the first of many questions the new arrivals would have during their life in Ridge Valley. Believing they were recruited to add to a workforce, they had agreed to come. Little did the new workers know that they were brought here to take the place of former patch men now living in tents.

Leroy worked on the Georgia & Southern now heading to Chicago. He immediately reported to Vernon Jefferson in his office. He apologized for his lengthy stay and for Billie's choice to remain with his mother. Mr. Jefferson understood. Leroy then told about his father's problems and the need to go to Ridge Valley to check on him as soon as possible. Once done and with accommodations arranged, he would return and definitely work on the railroad should Mr. Jefferson want him.

"You are welcome to return and you may want to consider the boarding house where we are staying. Your father is welcome. Some of the older fellows remember him and I'm sure will help when you're away. Take your time deciding, we'll be here."

"I done checked the schedules Mr. Jefferson," said a ticket agent assigned to the task. " The Baltimore and Ohio train takes a route through a town called Connellsville, fairly close to Ridge Valley. He'll have to take a streetcar and find his way from there. Leroy should get ready because that train will pass through Chicago in two days," said Colin, a ticket agent.

Arriving in Ridge Valley via streetcar Leroy went to his house and found another family living there. Told that since the man who lived there had died, the company had given them the house. Leroy dashed to Willie's house. Again strangers who were occupying that house directed him to Tent City. He ran to the south pasture where he found Willie living in a tent with three other men.

Ridge Valley

"He fell down the stairs and hit his head hard. Died instantly they say with a bad laceration and a broken neck. We buried him on the hill behind the patch," said Willie.

Leroy was devastated, he lost both his mom and dad and was now the only one left in his family. He informed Willie of Billie's decision to stay in Carbon Hill and the request from his wife for Willie to return there also. Leroy told Willie about his Mom's death in a fire at the church along with the Reverend Washington and his wife. " They found Mrs. Washington along side the Reverend and figured she ran inside the church when the fire started, and got caught in the smoke and flames." He told about meeting Vernon Jefferson, and named many others now working on the railroads in Chicago. " I was offered a job there and by the look of things here I may return and work in Chicago." They talked further about all the things that happened since Leroy left. Finally, Willie joined Leroy in a walk to Rufus's grave. He stayed and prayed for a time. Leaving, Leroy went to seek out John as Willie headed back to his tent. He had a lot to talk about, and needed some direction. John was easy to discuss things with and usually gave good advice.

For both the occupiers of the tents and the houses in Ridge Valley, things remained at status quo throughout the spring. Those that lived in the tents made the best of a sad situation. The children adjusted by enjoying the new freedom to roam and explore the woods or play games most of the day. The mothers were the backbone of survival and carried the burden of feeding the family from meager supplies of food. Cabbage and potatoes became the staple of some tables while bean soup, pasta and sauce in others.

The workers in Ridge Valley tried hard to perform their mining jobs, but the challenge was overwhelming for most. Their lack of experience in working the mine left them vulnerable to accidents and many happened.

Meanwhile, the national union in 1922 continued to squabble over how to settle the work stoppage. Some officers wanted a national settlement, while others favored individual agreements. The owners wanted to run the operations without interference from either. With the union leadership in disarray, the coal operators decided to consolidate by appointing a manager to handle all of their concerns.

This individual would speak as one, thus eliminating any confusion that can arise from various points of view. Without stable union representation, and the owners standing strong, a long stoppage seemed in store for the tent dwellers. A difficult period of adjustment continued for the Negroes. Many were not miners and once enough money was made some returned south to a friendlier atmosphere.

The Red Cross made their presence known during the summer in Tent City. They became concerned about the children living in tents and notified the office in Pittsburgh. The officers decided to recruit families in the city to house the youngsters for the summer. John's brother, along with Hanna and Joanna, joined others who would stay and work in the homes of prominent families in the city. Since they now had plenty of room, Leroy accepted the invitation to stay with the Ignatius family, at least for the immediate future.

Across the south pasture stood tents with a discord of cultures. All of Eastern Europe was represented, and they contained a maze of dialects and customs. John and Leroy spent summer days roaming around Tent City. They helped those without a man in the tent with chores like cutting firewood and making trips to the spring for buckets of water. They conversed with the old timers, actually listening most of the time. The old miners enjoyed the company and talked for hours about the past, both good and bad. They always ended the conversation thanking John for "standing up to em" and pledged to "stay out for as long as it takes."

When the Irish organizer visited, it was John who took him around and introduced him to the families. The man preached trust and total support from the union to all he met.

The first of May arrived, along with a new arrival in a Bohemian tent. The child must be baptized and the grandmother would perform the ceremony. The family planned a celebration of life. Word spread, the people responded with food and drink. The party was on and worries about living on the edge of life were forgotten, at least for one day, in the birth of a child. The celebration was enjoyed so much by a Polish family that the father announced, "It is a tradition that must be honored regardless of the times. Jesus saw fit to invite all to His Supper. I now invite all of you to my daughter's wedding next month."

The weeks passed, preparations made and the day arrived. A Slovak man played the accordion, an Italian a banjo, a Magyar the violin, and they danced the evening away. Dandelion wine and potato vodka provided the impetus to break down any differences in the crowd. Mr. Glover butchered a hog for the spit. They danced, laughed, ate and drank. It was a wedding, and that's what everyone did at weddings. For the newlywed's to have a honeymoon suite the hired hand would give up his bedroom in the Glover's home for a week. All was well on the south pasture.

The days moved along and the tent residents adjusted to life with a positive attitude, along with cooperative efforts by all. With the children away, the adults concentrated on working the garden, hunting and fishing. The food not consumed would be smoked, salted or dried and stored. The newly constructed vegetable cellar would be packed full. Summer was coming to an end and all waited for some sign of progress in settling the stoppage.

"They're closing down furnaces in Pittsburgh," was printed in the Evening Standard. "Maybe it's because they are short of coke and will be needing us soon."

A few weeks later the news came that only rogue mines were working and paying nineteen-twenty wages. Some of those mines planned on signing an individual contract with their workers. That news was a deep disappointment for the tent families. They vowed however to continue to endure.

John and Leroy were constant companions throughout the summer encampment. They helped Mr. Glover with a second cutting of hay and stacked bales in the loft. This lessened the amount of room in the barn for the Ignatius family. The next cutting would mean that they would be forced to move into a tent. Picking elderberries, wild cherries and apples became a game of seeking and finding the cherished fruit in the woods. The evenings were saved for visiting and talking about the past and plans for the future. Leroy talked often about his life growing up in Alabama and most recently his train adventures.

"Would you believe they eat off white table cloths in a train car? They sleep in a bed on the train and ride in seats during the day."

John talked about school and growing up in Ridge Valley, "'cause I haven't been any where else," he said.

Arrangements were made in advance to visit Jerry every Monday after dark. These visits became routine and often lasted for hours. Company guards never caught on about the visits and never checked the slate mine waste dump for possible entry into the mine complex. Jerry, always upbeat and happy to see his friends, was somewhat subdued during a late August visit.

"I heard news from the superintendent's meeting yesterday that they have larger stocks of coal on hand than previously thought. That, along with what is mined by replacements, will supply needs for months," said Jerry.

"We heard the mills are closing down furnaces and we thought it was because of the lack of coke. If that isn't the case, then why are they closing those furnaces?" asked Leroy.

"I'm guessing that demand has lessened for iron and steel," replied Jerry, who added; "I'd say they are using the new Negro workers as pawns. They work as best they can but one thing is certain to me and that is, even though they work hard, they are not miners…"

"You have to start young and grow up with mining in the blood. Even then it's tough. Believe me, I know," interrupted Leroy.

"I hate to think that a guy like Patty died for nothing fighting the goons the company brought in. We can't go back under their terms. We have to stay out and fight for justice. I remember when I was small and it was during the War. My dad came home after working long hours, he was so tired he just washed, ate supper and went to bed. The ache in his bones never left. "Get the coal out," said the President of the United States. "Do this for the war effort," he said, and they froze the wages. He worked beyond what was asked, without complaint. Seems they all forgot about us when the war was over," said John.

"It seems to me like we're working for the same money now as back then," said Jerry.

"Boy, all of this doesn't sound good for me. I guess I have some hard thinking to do," said Leroy.

"I guess we all have a lot of thinking to do," added John.

Hearing a noise the boys froze. A deputy walked into the hallway, looked around, satisfied he then left. Feeling uneasy they decided it was time to leave. A pat on the back, whispering goodbyes, Leroy and John departed.

With fall approaching and the barn filling up with hay, John his mom and family are forced to move into a tent. The girls and their brother would be coming back from Pittsburgh in a couple of days. Realizing that there was barely enough room for him with the Ignatius family, Leroy decided to crowd into the tent with Willie. The mention by Jerry of coal being available for a long time, because a large stockpile existed, could create a long delay in returning to work concerned John. Willie hearing about the surplus of coal told Leroy that he too was concerned, and even worse; he hated to think about spending the winter in a tent. He stated that if things were not settled by late fall he would seriously consider going back to Carbon Hill. Leroy decided that he too would leave before winter and planned on going to Chicago to become a dining car worker on the railroad. The thought of leaving his friend was difficult and emotional. The thought of not seeing each other again seemed likely, although they would try.

"Listen, every second Saturday in October me and Jerry have a standing date to pick walnuts. This is one day each year we promised to save for that purpose. If you're near Ridge Valley and can make a detour, we'll meet at the company store at seven o'clock. I'll always have an extra sack for you."

A last visit on the following Monday night to say goodbye to Jerry with John was the final get together for all three friends. Early the next morning Mrs. Ignatius filled a knapsack with food. John and Leroy walked to Fairbanks in order to avoid the company police. Willie was there waiting. Before entering the streetcar John shook hands with Willie, then he and his friend embraced. Leroy began to enter the car.

"Hey, Johnson!" Leroy turned. " God bless and good luck."

Leroy waved as John watched the car move down the track.

Persistent rains came to the valley in October and saturated the ground. Redstone Creek held the water within its banks until the third consecutive day of heavy downpours sent waves of water cascading over the side. A quagmire developed in and around the tents, creating a sloppy mess. The dampness penetrated the old canvas tents. The moisture was retained in the mattresses, cots and blankets. The humidity was tolerated well at first but soon gave way to coughing, colds and recurring low-grade fevers, suffered mostly by small children and the elderly. The old folks suffered from the cooler temperatures and damp conditions. Weakness from high fevers and flu-like symptoms bedded a number of them. The fragile and infirmed grew weak from the damp conditions. Cool frosty nights further deteriorated the health of three aged women, who were the first to die from the conditions. Four children, ill with a high fever, succumbed and added to the gravesite at the top of the hill. It was only October. The dreaded winter weather is just around the corner.

The men living in Tent City occupied their time by playing cards, talking and drinking homemade booze. Some worked on farms as far away as the next county. They stayed on site and slept in the haylofts, working during the week and coming home to tent city on weekends. They were paid with eggs, vegetables and an occasional chicken. "Better than nothing," was their attitude. Meanwhile news about the people ousted from their homes and living in tents waned. The south pasture inhabitants were unable to tell their story to the outside world and that world basically ignored their plight.

Bright orange and red along with brilliant yellows faded from leaves as frost hit with a vengeance. The weather turned cool and crisp. Surplus tents failed to hold out the currents of air that traveled down the ridge. Worry filled the mind of mothers for the winds of winter have yet to come.

Fortune temporarily changed for the better with the arrival of Indian summer. It warmed the tent inhabitants and dried the fields. Tent flaps were raised to allow the warm breeze to enter and clear the moistness from damp tents. The warm breezy weather lasted until late October.

Leaden skies with low hanging clouds returned. November of '22 arrived with lowering temperatures and snow flurries. The tent dwellers buttoned the flaps and stacked logs for the stove. The numbers in Tent City stayed the same as a child was born to a Slovak family and an old man died, adding another grave on the hill.

Down the row a mother sat on the edge of a mattress, rocking a sick child. This was just one of many mothers caring for sick children. The cold replaced the dampness in the tents.

"We're not getting much information, John. Things have settled down. The police placed more NO TRESPASSING signs about and increased their patrols. They are intent on keeping everyone out of the patch, especially the newspaper writers. The company is determined to keep our story quiet," said Jerry. "People on the outside heard about our plight early on, housed the kids over the summer, now nothing. Makes one wonder. I guess people tend to forget about us after eight months."

Offices for the National United Mine Workers Union were being contested for the upcoming elections in late November. Splits developed among the candidates running for office nationally, regionally and in local districts. The war of words led to disarray among the leaders who were concerned more about winning an election than about the rank and file. Morale sagged among miners as rumors persisted that some regions were told to go back to work, then others told to stay out. Confusion reigned. Campaigns became bitter and deceitful. Wild stories were rampart about candidate's promises the workers knew would never be kept. None of those running for office addressed the conditions of residents in Tent City. The candidates for office spent time arguing amongst themselves instead of addressing major issues. Feeling forgotten, some of the staunchest men found it hard to endure the suffering of their families in tents. A few with the largest families decided to migrate elsewhere, anywhere.

"I'll work for less money if I have to, just work more hours. I can't stay and watch my children starve and do nothing to help," said a disheartened miner.

A few left, while others pledged to hang on for a while longer.

The snows of early December fell in flurries, dusting the ground with a white blanket. Additional snow would accumulate as the week wore on to the glee of children and despair of the adults. The bowl, once accepting storm clouds, now captured them and swirled the system around and around the valley. The tent dwellers hunkered down. Christmas would not be celebrated this year. The end of December would mark a ten-month anniversary of living in Tent City.

"We lasted this long, we can last a year if necessary" became the battle cry. The enthusiasm for continuing the fight became heightened when a district meeting was called. The meeting would be held in New Salem on January nineteenth, 1923. John was selected to represent Ridge Valley. He would take with him the old miners he heard talk about inequities in working conditions they faced over the years. Their stories would no doubt explain why a win for the tent dwellers was a must.

Unknown to the attendees from the Valley, the real purpose for calling the district meeting by the union was to present reasons for calling off the work stoppage. The four with John were determined to tell the reasons for continuing.

"Let the men talk, and talk some more. Don't hit them right off with what you have to say, but give them all the leeway they need to vent before presenting the facts. Let them ramble on if they wish and take time to let them go on for as long as they want. After a while they will become tired and the news you present will not be as devastating as bad news presented immediately," said the district President.

There was a stark contrast between the gentlemen in front on a small stage, handling the meeting, and the miners in the audience. Those facing the miners were clean and well dressed in shirts and ties. This was in sharp contrast to the miners in their worn and tattered work clothes and boots. The labor officers introduced themselves and welcomed all who came. They expressed thanks for the support and sacrifice of the men present and their families.

"Before making any announcements we want to hear from you."

"I be first," said an excited Austrian who worked at Ridge Valley.

"Please go ahead, sir."

"This is the first time I have chance to tell you how bosses, and weight man swindle me. First, boss says we buy only at company store or they make it mean for me if I don't. Next, boss says where you work. You have no say. May be bad air, high water or dig more slate than coal. No get paid for digging slate for sure. Another time, boss ordered me to unload car and lay track, do timbering and you know I work full ten hours to finish. The next morning I check time worked with timekeeper, he say I work nine hours. I see boss who says he will change time, he never did. There is more I tell you because the company man do a lot of sneaky stuff."

"That's true," interrupted another miner. "This weight man says he always gives exact tonnage credit on each car of coal. We know he no do that, but no can put up fight. If we do we be called troublemaker and lose job. How I know that I am shorted? Well let me tell you. Now he, this weight man fella get leg banged up by coal car and he be off work one week. New man gives honest weight. Much better pay. Old one comes back and we go to old stuff again. We no can say nothing and need you to help us. They get enough. All we ask is our due."

"There are owners who have increased the wages per car. We know that because we bargained for that. So there is improvement," said the Irish organizer.

"They sneaky, them boys. Who here checks if that is true? No one. You end up with the same pay. They say take it or leave it. I no can leave I have big family to feed. Man got to have bread with his soup. That's why I stay out," said another to cheers of agreement from the men in the audience.

"Gentlemen," John said, "You've heard these men and we can provide you with more of the same, like loading two ton and getting paid for seventeen hundredweight. This is not right to a worker's manhood. The man is denied the pay he honestly earned. We cannot be dishonored any longer. Take this message back with you. If they pay us fair weight then we go back to work tomorrow."

Those in attendance gave a resounding cheer. When the bellowing died down John held up his hands for quiet. The men honored his request.

"Now, gentlemen, you tell us where we stand, how you gonna help us and what you know."

"Please understand that the Union Executive Board studied all parts of the economy and concluded that at the present time, there is no hope of gaining a new contract." Many in the audience became restless, staring at the speaker in silence with a questioning. They did not fully comprehend what the speaker meant by his remarks.

"After much thought and following lengthy discussions, and in order to protect you against further losses, the board voted to call off the strike in the coke region in your district."

"What did he say? Coke, not coal. He did say coke, right?" said a man in the audience.

"You mean that you are backing down? We no back down. Why you say this?

"To protect you."

"How do coke men going back protect us, or are you talking about us but not saying so? Did you sell us out? You sold us out, you quit us and left us dry." shouted a shocked miner who started to charge the front table who was held back by fellow miners.

"Goddamn you," shouted another disgruntled man.

"You quit on us, now we go it alone without you."

"You say you protect us. I know how you do that, you surrender to 'em, that's how."

"The mills are getting coke elsewhere, you have no choice."

"We have choice, we no quit, tell your board that, WE NO QUIT!"

The men were devastated, hopes so high and now dashed. "We have come too far to quit now," said a voice from the back. "You go back and you tell your union men that we no surrender." The men in the audience stood, pointing fingers at those in front. They began to shout obscenities and some started to move toward the stage. The growing resentment prompted the union men to leave. The miners shouted them out of the room.

The men trudged back to shacks and tents with more questions than answers. Winter was at hand with the cold of February ahead. The food supplies were dwindling, family members sick, many suffering the effects of the cold.

"My wife is sick and can't take care of the children. I have no choice. I need a house for my family," a dejected man announced to a group of men in Tent City. "Let me tell you my heart is sad. My little girl must walk to the toilet at night in freezing cold and snow. Top of shoes are good, the bottom part is worn out. She no tells us about that. She walks across the cut cornfield and the short frozen stalks under snow she no see go through foot. She cut up feet more walking out. I no can do it anymore," he cried. The trickle of families leaving tent city began in earnest.

John was feeling bad, real bad then dejected at the turn of events. He did feel that most of the men wanted to continue the holdout at least until April. "If only we could achieve one issue like having an overseer work with the weight man," he thought. "Other issues we can get along with, but getting what is earned is a must. We must continue the fight for those that suffered, and for those who died for the cause."

February arrived, along with sub zero temperatures. Potatoes, bread and cabbage became the food of subsistence. Kids existed on starvation diets. A neighbor counted their losses of people, both in families leaving and additions to the cemetery on the hill. About half of those who were there at the beginning are gone. They were stuck in a morass, feeling helpless and forgotten. Time crept along slowly and at times seemingly stopped. Men used to working hard and drinking hard were just sitting doing nothing. Watching the family wither away in the cold is the most heart sickening feeling they could endure. The tent colony was in need of a miracle.

The closest happening to a miracle came in the change of the weather in early March. Warm winds from the south swirled in the basin and erased the snow from the landscape. Children emerged from the tent cocoons. They played outside for the first time in weeks. A carpet of daffodils dotted hillsides. Robins chirped and squirrels scampered about. Hunters surprisingly cornered a flock of wild turkeys and bagged enough for all the families in Tent City to enjoy.

The first of April 1923 fell on a Sunday. Both sides in the dispute considered this date as the anniversary of the work stoppage and planned rallies for the cause. Women from the tents walked outside the patch limits with small replicas of scales, indicating the desire for fair weight of coal cars. The owners countered with a bonus offer for anyone willing to return to work immediately. While the tent residents ate cabbage and beans, the company provided families with picnics, and the children enjoyed movie shows.

On Monday, with nothing accomplished, a few more families planned to move on and accept the Company's offer. Although the majority of the families hung on in tents, the first thought of their losing the battle entered their consciousness. This was not the case for extremists. Scare tactics started with retaliation coming from strikers. Sneaking into the patch at night houses were stoned, windows broken and outhouses burned. Guards wanting to keep their jobs turned their backs thinking they would be needed because of the destruction. Only a token effort was given to catch the culprits. Explosives destroyed coal cars and fences around the mine. The destruction was short lived for nothing changed. The status quo remained.

Summer arrived and with it a despondent, demoralized contingent of people in the tents who felt forgotten and deserted. The union movement was disorganized and the Red Cross, along with the people of Pittsburgh, failed to offer the children in the tent colony an opportunity to stay in the city again. Things were desperate on the south pasture but those that remained, endured.

John's mother remained quietly in the background and was loyal in support of her son throughout the stoppage. Never one to complain or speak out, she prayed often and continually encouraged her son to fight for the families. From John's early years his mom considered him to be very smart beyond his years. She never lost hope for him until the dog days of August. She felt for John, but the time came to face defeat. Keeping her feelings in check she never discussed the effects of the work stoppage with anyone, even with John until now. She recognized that her son was suffering with anguish and pain and felt his depressed state of mind over recent developments. The time has come for her to speak.

"You have tried so hard to help your fellow miners and their families. I pray that God will reward you someday for what you did. Now we must face the fact that neither we nor other families can survive another winter in tents. You are young and will have many more chances. I know you did your very best. Now we must face the facts that the time for getting help is over. She reached out and embraced her son and held him lovingly to her breast, with tears running down her cheeks.

It was mid August of 1923 when after months of anguish, pain and suffering the tent colony was abandoned and the people reluctantly returned defeated to the patch. There was nothing to show for the long stay on the south pasture. Bitterness and resentment would show its ugly face toward the workers and families who failed to persevere. Grudges would last a lifetime. Trust in the National and District union organizations was never regained. Years passed before miners would consider walking out again. They returned to the pit, beaten and battered. Years passed before miners would consider dumping water from their dinner buckets.

THE CONDUCTOR PUSHED the lever to the maximum. You could hear the electrical currents humming in response as the streetcar joggled from side to side, speeding down the track. The run from Connellsville must hurry to reach its destination on time. A schedule had to be kept if passengers were to transfer to an outbound car from the Central Station in Uniontown. Once he arrived at the station Leroy scrambled to find the streetcar traveling to his next destination. Leroy located then entered the streetcar traveling west ending the route in Brownsville. Reaching Ridge Valley, Leroy exited the car in front of the company store. Walking toward the store alcove he approached the back of a person looking up the path.

"I came to pick up my sack."

John turned quickly. He couldn't believe his eyes. "You, my God you remembered."

They hugged, happy to be together again.

"Hey, lets go, c'mon," said Jerry, who had just arrived.

They became boys again, all speaking at once as they jostled down the road. Renewing old stories, telling jokes, talking about the present happenings; merrily enjoying each other's company. Over the bridge, across the junk graveyard, along the creek they laughed and talked as the morning brightened. Up the hill and now beyond the airshaft they walked as the sun peeked over the ridge. As usual they stopped at the cornfield for Jerry. They spent the remainder of the morning filling sacks with walnuts and then retreated to the spring for a refreshing drink. They just sat, resting. John finally broke the silence.

"To this day I think of that lassie."

"You been thinking on her for a long time, John, when you gonna do something?" said Jerry.

John did not answer but continued to sit silently pondering the future, as did both Jerry and Leroy.

Finally Leroy broke the spell. "Time is a' getting on, we'd better move if we're going to stop at Glovers," he said.

They accepted lunch at the farm. Leroy gave his sack of walnuts to the Glovers in appreciation for the many meals he had in their kitchen. John and Jerry ordered a ham for Thanksgiving and they started walking toward the patch.

"We better hurry and go straight to the streetcar stop. I have to be in the Connellsville station on time to catch the train to Chicago. I need to make a clear connection in Uniontown to make it.

The wait was short. Jerry shook hands with Leroy, and then turned away; head down, he pawed at the dirt. The streetcar approached from around the bend. The two friends, speechless, looked at each other. John then reached down, opened his sack and tossed Leroy a walnut.

"Something to remember me by."

Leroy came close, embraced John, and John responded in kind. The streetcar stopped and before he entered he whispered to his friend,

"I will always remember you, I will never forget you." Leroy started up the steps to enter the car. He stopped and turned to John and with a big smile said, " John, I hope you find your Annie some day, I really do."

Leroy entered the car and ran to the back window. He waved as John and Jerry waved back until the streetcar disappeared around the bend.

EPILOGUE

IT WAS DIFFICULT to convince the miners to strike again after 1923 since many said they had nothing to show for their fight. It was in the late 1930's when the United Mine Workers of America started organizing again. It was December 1941 when the UMWA and the coal companies finally reached an agreement.

Building a standard beehive coke oven required thousands of bricks, tiles and stone. In the beehive oven, the bituminous coal was baked for two or three days at about 2000 degrees. This produced a yield of 2/3 ton of coke from one ton of coal. The coke was nearly pure carbon and in great demand in the steel making process. At the height of their existence a total of 44, 252 coke ovens were located in the Connellsville Coke District.

Since 1870, Pennsylvania's Annual report on mining Activities has recorded 51,483 deaths from mining accidents---31, 113 deaths in anthracite mines and 20, 370 deaths in bituminous mines--- Taken from the Pennsylvania Department of Environmental Protection report dated January 27, 2000